"When I assume Yuri's identity, will Raisa know I'm me?"

"That will be your supreme test, Yossef. You have to fool her," Yabin said.

"Suppose—suppose by that time that they're sexually involved? I mean, damn it, men have different ways of screwing, even twin brothers."

Yabin's raucous laughter filled the small trailer.

"And—and what about penis size and length. I mean, are we equal in *all* areas?" Yossef's eyes were wide with innocent inquiry.

The placid demeanor of the South African broke down. Tears of laughter filled his eyes as he fumbled for an appropriate response.

"There are some areas where you're going to have to be extremely creative and innovative, Yossef. We can't do *everything* for you."

"How much time do I have, Yabin?" asked Yossef.

"Until you know Lenin's Tomb backwards and forwards."

THE COUNTERFEIT HOSTAGE

Soldier of Fortune books from Tor

SOLDIER of FORTUNE
MAGAZINE PRESENTS:

THE COUNTERFEIT HOSTAGE

CARL H. YAEGER

A TOM DOHERTY ASSOCIATES BOOK

THE COUNTERFEIT HOSTAGE

First printing: July 1987

A TOR Book

Published by Tom Doherty Associates, Inc.
49 West 24 Street
New York, N.Y. 10010

ISBN: 0-812-51208-1
CAN. ED.: 0-812-51209-X

Printed in the United States of America

0 9 8 7 6 5 4 3 2 1

I hold it a noble task to rescue from oblivion those who deserve to be eternally remembered.

Pliny the Younger

I.

Yossef Ayalon was used to sirens. Berne was a city of sirens, especially in his neighborhood in the Bohemian section of Old Berne. The siren that was now piercing his semi-sleep was different somehow. He had slept through all of the others. Why not this one?

He swung his stocky, muscular body off the bed and toward the wall, and padded quickly to the window, peering down the slippery whiteness of Stassenstrasse. It was still snowing lightly. He could see the flakes by the glare of the streetlights lining the snowbanks. The flashing light of the ambulance was almost out of sight as it turned the corner to the right, speeding toward the direction of Beth Sholom, one of the city's oldest synagogues.

Yossef looked at the clock. Two-thirty. He reached for a cigarette, the single one that was out of the pack.

The flare of the match revealed a ruggedly attractive but not a classically handsome face. His sandy-colored hair was curly and, if styled differently, could have been developed into a short Afro. His large blue eyes gave him the look of one who is in a constant state of surprise.

He slipped into his bathrobe and put on a pair of heavy woolen socks. He pulled a pair of tan cords over his shorts. In spite of the cold Swiss winters, he slept with only a pair of undershorts on.

Yossef settled into the warm softness of the easy chair and inhaled deeply on his cigarette. He was wrestling with the decision to either make a cup of coffee or try to go back to sleep. Perhaps he could squeeze in a few more hours before he had to report for work at the embassy.

The ringing of the phone jarred the stillness—and Yossef's nerves. It was three in the morning straight up. Nobody called at this hour unless it was an emergency.

"Yossef? This is Eli Sharon. I'm sorry to awaken you at this hour, but something terrible has happened. You're the first one I've called."

Yossef could hear Rabbi Sharon choking on his tears.

"Yes, Rabbi. I'm fully awake. What is it?"

"I'm at the municipal hospital, Emergency Room . . ."

The siren! Yossef thought: *This is related to that siren I heard thirty minutes ago!*

"Ariel Makleff was just brought in. He's—he's dead. He's been murdered, Yossef. He's been—been brutally tortured. It's hideous, Yossef," the Rabbi sobbed. "Who would want to kill a harmless old man in that manner?"

"I'll be right down, Rabbi," Yossef murmured, his mind trying to process the grisly information. "I suppose that the authorities want me to identify him?"

"Yes, Yossef. I told the police that you and he were friends. I also told them that you were the primary embassy official processing Ariel's immigration papers for Israel."

Yossef dropped the phone in the cradle with a plastic crunch, doused his face with cold water, and swirled a blob of toothpaste around in his mouth. He ran a brush briskly over his sandy hair as he was punching the other arm through the sleeve of his heavy parka.

Five minutes later he was nosing the Volvo station wagon, an Israeli embassy staff car, out of the alley to the side of his apartment and onto the snowy stillness of Stassenstrasse.

The Emergency Room of Berne's sprawling municipal hospital could have done nothing for Ariel Makleff. Taking him there was an administrative procedure: All patients living or dead were taken to Emergency when brought by ambulance.

Yossef was met in the sterile, light green corridor by Rabbi Sharon, a short, portly little man with a pointed white goatee. His large, dark eyes seemed to float in liquid when he talked.

"He was such an old man—such a gentle old man, Yossef. Who would want to kill him like that? What manner of men could do such a thing to a man like Ariel?" The rabbi panted as they walked rapidly through the corridors toward the morgue.

They were stopped by a policeman and a white-coated intern outside the closed door to the hospital morgue. Yossef shivered slightly as he felt the cool air seep from under the door into the heated corridor.

"I'm Yossef Ayalon. I'm a friend of—of the murdered man, Dr. Ariel Makleff."

He showed his embassy identification card to the policeman and followed the intern into the cool, white-tiled room. Along the wall were rows of stainless-steel doors, each covering a slab on rollers that intruded seven feet into the wall. Any corpse over seven feet, and there were few of those in Berne, would have to be processed differently.

An older man, tall, with bushy eyebrows and a hawklike nose, approached them.

"Mr. Ayalon? I'm Chief Inspector Schumann, Berne Police."

Yossef absently shook the inspector's hand.

"I've been assigned to this case. I'm afraid that I'm going to have to ask you to identify the body."

Yossef nodded, his eyes glazed with tears. The intern walked to one of the gleaming doors, yanked it open, and pulled the slab out to its full seven feet. He removed the sheet, revealing the naked old man, his ivory-white flesh contrasting sharply with the stainless steel.

Yossef felt a mixture of nausea and anger as he observed the circular red marks all over the old doctor's body. He was not a physician, but he could tell from the misshapen fingers and arms that they had been broken. The naked body was not battered in a spontaneous or casual manner. Makleff was the victim of planned and sustained torture.

"Yes. It's Ariel Makleff. The red circular spots," asked Yossef. "What are they?"

"My guess is that they are from the terminals of an

electrical shocking device of some sort. His assailants must have brought a portable generator with them. They came prepared and were thoroughly professional. They knew what they were doing," replied Schumann.

"But why? Why?" cried Yossef, tears of rage streaming down his cheeks.

The inspector wiped his sleeve across his large nose, scratching it.

"They were definitely looking for something. The apartment was systematically torn apart; couch cushions ripped open, the walls torn apart. When they couldn't find whatever they were looking for, they turned to Makleff with a very professional vengeance."

"The bastards!" exclaimed Yossef, his tears turning to anger.

"What could Ariel have had that anybody would want badly enough to—to do this?" asked the rabbi, his moist, dark eyes darting to the tortured body. "He lived so simply. He'd sold most of his possessions and moved to a modest little apartment here in Berne to be close to the synagogue. He walked there every day to meditate or attend services. He had nothing that was of any value. If he had anything, it was kept elsewhere. His home was so sparse."

"How old was Dr. Makleff?" asked Schumann.

"He would have been ninety-one next month. He was born February 15, 1900."

The inspector shot the rabbi a suspicious glance.

"I make it a point to remember the birthdays of everybody in my congregation. I could give you the exact birthdates of all of my people, all two hundred and sixty-three. If I'm to be an effective shepherd of my little flock, I must know my sheep." Sharon smiled nervously.

"Poor Ariel," Yossef murmured. "The next thing he wanted to do was emigrate to Israel. He would have left in less than two weeks. He told me only yesterday that his greatest desire was to kiss the Wailing Wall in Jerusalem and fondle the stones. He said he wanted to merge with the wall and become part of it: then he could die in peace."

"Yes," added the rabbi, "Ariel Makleff approached his

religion like a man possessed. It was almost as if—as if he were trying to be a 'super-Jew.' I would often comment, positively of course, on his devotion and piety. He said little about that, but he did make a statement which has baffled me ever since. He said, 'Rabbi, a man with my experiences—with my past—must do double duty. Yes, Rabbi. To find my God I must be a double-duty Jew. I must make up for a wasted life.'"

Yossef and the rabbi left the morgue to the sound of the rolling slab and the metallic slam of the stainless-steel door.

The snow was descending in heavy, wet flakes—falling rapidly like little white missiles. A gray, murky dawn was spreading over the city.

"Grab a bit of breakfast, Eli?" asked Yossef.

The portly little rabbi shook his head.

"Normally I'd be famished after being up for so long, but after this!"

"Yes, I agree; I think I'll just leave from here and go to the embassy. I can shower and shave there."

"Yossef. If you learn of any new developments, please let me know. Ah! I have poor Ariel's funeral to prepare."

He shook Eli's hand softly.

"I will, Eli. God be with you."

"God be with you also, Yossef."

Yossef barely heard the knock over the clatter of type-writers in the outer office.

"Come in!" he bellowed over the noise without looking up from his papers.

A well-groomed man entered. He was dressed in a gray pinstriped suit with a flamboyant red-and-black striped tie which was adorned with a diamond stick-pin.

"Mr. Ayalon? Yossef Ayalon?"

Yossef stood, extending his hand. "I am Yossef Ayalon. What can I do for you?"

"Perhaps it's what I can do for you," smiled the dapper stranger. "I'm René Altmann, an attorney with the firm of Altmann and Charboix in Zurich. I represent the estate of the late Dr. Ariel Makleff, the old gentleman who died two weeks ago?"

"Oh, yes," exclaimed Yossef, his interest piqued. "What a coincidence. I was closing out his request-for-immigration file just now. Please, please be seated, Herr Altmann." Yossef gestured to a chair as he walked around his desk and joined the attorney.

"An immigration file? Was Dr. Makleff planning to leave Switzerland?"

"Yes. He wanted to leave while there was still an Israel to emigrate to." Yossef's voice trailed off thoughtfully.

"Dr. Makleff left a tidy little estate, Mr. Ayalon. He wasn't wealthy by any stretch of the imagination, but he was a man of some means. He left the bulk of his liquid assets to the Jewish Refugee Organization in Vienna."

"Yes. That is what Ariel would do," Yossef replied gently.

"He left you something, Mr. Ayalon."

"Oh?" Yossef wrinkled his forehead in surprise.

Altmann reached into his coat pocket and pulled out a large manila envelope. The outline of a key was clearly impressed upon the paper from the inside.

"He left this with me almost two months ago. He told me that if he should pass away, this was to go to you. I'm sorry that I can't hold out the promise of a monetary gift, but . . ."

"That's all right." Yossef smiled. "I have more than enough for my needs. Ariel Makleff owes me nothing."

"Well, my passing this on to you"—he pressed the envelope in Yossef's hand—"concludes my involvement with the Makleff estate. I wish that all estates could be terminated so tidily."

"Thank you, Herr Altmann."

The attorney shook hands and left, disappearing into the clatter of typewriters in the outer office of the Immigration Section of the Israeli Embassy.

Yossef toyed with the envelope for several minutes before he decided to open it. Finally, he slit it open and pulled out the papers. A dull silver key fell to the desktop. There were three pages, written in a tight Germanic script.

He flipped to the last page. It was Makleff's signature all

right. He'd had to get enough of the old doctor's signatures for his immigration application. He started to read.

Nov. 21, 1991

My Dear Yossef:

My death will come as a surprise to many. Not that a ninety-one-year-old man should not die, but the manner of my death will not be consistent with the image which people have of me, those who know me as a quiet, pious little Jew, always sitting in the third row of the synagogue, a man of steady habits.

I will get directly to the point, Yossef. What I am leaving you can be vital for the survival of your beloved homeland, a land which I will never see. The key is for a safety-deposit locker. The number is #144390 at the Diskonto Gesellschaft in Old Berne, facing the plaza. You will find papers and documents there—many of them. I have rented a large locker, so you should bring a fairly large and secure box with you when you come and remove the contents. Central in importance is a thick, brown journal. It is leatherbound and held by two straps with brass buckles. You cannot miss it. I have written very small, and very carefully, in three languages depending on the mood I was in at the time. I have written in German, Hebrew, and Russian.

Does the Russian surprise you, Yossef? It is a language I speak and write with authority, as do you. Whereas you were raised in a Russian-Jewish household in Israel, I have lived a great deal of my life in the Soviet Union. This is a part of my life that I have not shared with very many people and, I'm afraid, I withheld this information from you on my application papers. I am sure that it will not matter.

I am considered to be, by those who will kill me, a Soviet citizen. Nobody ever loses their citizenship in the USSR. This means that I have always been under the jurisdiction of the KGB. They are the ones who will ultimately release me from the "obligations" of citizenship in their customary, brutal manner.

My journal, dear Yossef, covers a period of time from the late 1890's to 1956, the year I escaped the Eastern Bloc during the Hungarian Revolution. You see, Yossef, I am a man who has a great deal to account for to my God. I must also carry the burden for my father, who was the personal physician to the devil—the midwife to the evils that have been set loose upon the world and now threaten to engulf Israel. I am referring to Vladimir Ilyich Ulyanov, Lenin, a man at whose feet I sat and worshiped as a teenage boy and young adult. I have much to say about Lenin in my journal. It should be read carefully. There is information which can prove harmful to the Soviet state.

We Jews are a clever people, Yossef. If anyone can turn this information to their advantage, we can. Right now, with the loss of American support and sponsorship, with the Camp David Accords shattered and rejected by the new Fundamentalist Islamic Republic of Egypt, and the loss of Israel's friends in Europe, it is only a matter of time before a new Soviet-armed Arab "golem" will smash into your homeland and try to submerge it forever.

Yossef flipped to the third page, squinting to read the tight Germanic writing.

You will find notes in the margins, Yossef. These were made recently, within the past two years since I have come to know you. They refer to your real family, the one in Russia.

Yossef's heart started to pound. Beads of sweat were forming on his forehead. The gaps in his early life, the vacant spots in his existence, were about to be filled. He felt it, and feared it as he read on.

I was an intimate of your grandfather in those heady years of the Bolshevik movement, and I knew your father and mother. You were born, along with your identical twin brother Yuri, four years after I fled Budapest in November of 1956.

A father, mother, and brother in the Soviet Union? No! He was a *sabra,* born and raised in Israel. His real mother and father were killed by *fedayeen* terrorists in the Gaza in 1961.

He was raised by their sister, Aunt Sophie, and Uncle Viktor in Shareem, in the Negev. This is insane! The ramblings of a senile old man.

I tell you these things, Yossef, because I believe that one's identity and heritage are precious things. I have seen thousands—yes, entire nations and classes of peoples—stripped of both, packed into boxcars and shipped to the Gulag. It is an evil practice. The only commodity which we can take with us to meet our God is our identity. This thing which we Jews call the soul is nothing more than our identity, the collection of experiences and attributes which we call our personality; our character. I will be who I am when I stand before the Great One, and that frightens me. It was the realization of this which caused me to question my Marxism. It led to my subsequent disaffection and escape from Russia.

Naturally, you will give my papers and journal to your MOSSAD. I did not leave them directly to them because I wanted you to know who you are, and to become acquainted with your roots, your glorious roots in the history of resistance to the tyranny of Lenin. You will come to know and love your parents and grandfather as I did, because of it.

Adieu, my fine young friend. You epitomize everything that is fine and noble in Israel and I love you for it.

Your brother in God,
Ariel Makleff

Yossef stepped into the brightness of the late morning. The sky was almost cloudless, unusual for Berne in January. The newly fallen snow sparkled like a million tiny crystals in the sunlight. The traffic had not yet turned the street snow into a gray sludge.

He thrust his hands into the pockets of his heavy parka and walked briskly from the embassy, which was in New Berne, toward the collection of old, gray stone buildings with their red-tiled roofs—the medieval portion of the city called Old Berne.

Yossef reached the river Aare, the meandering waterway that divided the city, giving it its schizophrenic character. He loved this route and often walked this way while meditating. Berne was a city of bridges and parks, of the old and the new, dramatically contrasted by the two sections of the city.

He trotted across the old Theresastrasse stone bridge and turned into the narrow streets.

A box! Ariel wrote that I must have a fairly large box! But how large is large? Certainly a frail old man like Ariel couldn't have lugged a large box down here. Besides, the largest safety-deposit boxes are no larger than a hatbox, pondered Yossef.

A glass merchant, a fat little man in a blue turtleneck, waddled from his shop and dumped a sturdy cardboard box on top of a galvanized trash can. It was perfect. Yossef emptied the shredded newspapers, took out the cardboard dividers, tucked the flaps back in, and continued toward the bank.

As he reached the plaza, the ancient clock tower struck the hour: eleven o'clock. He stopped and peered up. A wooden rooster appeared from an aperture under the clock face. It disappeared, and a man in armor, followed by dancing bears, then a man on a throne, all made their appearances, disappearing just as quickly back into the tower.

Yossef would walk by the clock whenever the opportunity arose, especially when the clock struck the hour. It held a special fascination for him.

The Diskonto Gesellschaft looked like many of the older financial institutions of Switzerland. It was unadorned; no flashing marquees advertised its function. In staid dignity, it blended with the old buildings flanking it. One of the oldest and most venerable of Berne's banks, it was located in the center of the old city, facing a small plaza.

Yossef walked through the large hammered-copper doors and into the rich, mahogany-paneled interior. After some initial questions by a bank clerk, he was led into a large vault in the basement.

"Ah, yes. Here is Dr. Makleff's box," smiled the bald little clerk, his pince-nez slipping down the bridge of his nose.

"If you need me, please press the buzzer on the table," he added as he slipped out the door and locked it.

It was a big locker, larger than Yossef had expected. If it was full, perhaps the cardboard box wouldn't be large enough. He turned both keys—the one the clerk gave him and Makleff's—simultaneously. The mechanism clicked. Eagerly, he yanked the locker door open. Inside, there were several bundles of paper and the large leather-covered journal. It was about four inches thick and held together by two frayed leather straps, secured by tarnished brass buckles.

Everything fit in Yossef's container with room to spare. He tucked in the box flaps and pressed the buzzer.

Yossef shuffled absently through the piles of documents. It was all he could do to concentrate on the mounds of paperwork on his desk. As Chief Immigration Officer of the Embassy, it was his job to screen and process the hundreds of immigration applications from Jews all over Switzerland. His load was backlogged for three weeks.

At five-thirty, he bounded down the stairs, the box under his arm, to the underground parking lot. He threw the box onto the seat, started the Volvo, and headed for his apartment.

Yossef could smell the pungent aroma of Rum-and-Maple pipe tobacco from under the door as he fumbled for his key.

"Come in, Yossef," boomed a familiar voice. "It's open." He entered slowly, trying to balance the box under his arm. The two middle-aged men, both Israelis, lifted their glasses to Yossef in a mock salute.

"Your taste in brandy is excellent, Yossef," said the tall one in the checkered sport jacket.

"We anticipated your hospitality and helped ourselves. We hope you don't mind."

"Help yourself, gentlemen. Whenever the MOSSAD comes to call, my hospitality knows no bounds," said Yossef, sarcastically.

Colonel Moshe Yabin, a bear of a man, stood swirling the plum brandy in his glass in slow, circular motions. He emptied the ashes from his pipe in a flowerpot and smiled knowingly at Yossef. "You have Makleff's journal, I presume?"

Yossef stammered in surprise. "Why—why yes. I—I picked it up this morning. That's why you're here, isn't it!"

The tall major in the checkered jacket walked casually to the door and slipped the dead bolt.

"Yes. That's why we're here, Yossef. We've been waiting for the journal ever since Makleff's death. Lucky for us that it was left to you. Very considerate of the old doctor."

"Are—are you going to confiscate it? There are personal references that I'd like to read before you take it."

The huge colonel relit his pipe after plunging a new wad of tobacco into the bowl and clapped a hand on Yossef's shoulder.

"Sit down, my friend. We'll read it together. This journal is going to become a very important part of your life from now on. Soon, very soon, you'll know it backwards and forwards and have entire sections of it committed to memory."

"I—I don't understand," said Yossef.

"You will, you will," smiled the major. "You'll be thoroughly briefed on the courier plane tomorrow."

Yossef gasped in surprise.

"Pack your belongings, Yossef. You're going back to Tel Aviv in the morning," commanded Moshe Yabin.

II.

"Vasyl Ruban, Izrail Ruston, Alexander Rybakov, Vicktor Solaty, Eduard Samoilov . . ."

The loudspeaker continued to blare the names across the desolate hill country of North China's Shansi Province. The billowing flames of Taiyiian, the recently bombarded provincial capital, lit up the night sky behind the huddled figures of soldiers in their foxholes, remnants of the 142nd Motorized Rifle Battalion, Soviet Expeditionary Force to North China.

"Pyotr Starchik, Algis Statkervicus, Alexander Stepanov, Mindaugas Tamonis . . ."

The loudspeaker continued the litany of names. Finally, the cadence was broken by an announcement.

"Solidarity Comrades! The list goes on and on! The names read are just a few of those who have been selected by your executioners in Moscow. The operational orders of your unit have a death list attached: a list of known or suspected Solidarity members who are to be sent into the jaws of death.

"We know who you are and we, your brothers in Solidarity, welcome and salute you! We do not seek your death. We seek your alliance. When you have the opportunity, turn your weapons on your officers and the noncommissioned ranks. They, not we, are your enemy. It is they who will order you into suicidal battle knowing full well that you will be slaughtered.

"If you should find yourself in hostile contact with the People's Liberation Army, raise your hand and shout

13

'Solidarity' and surrender. You will be treated as a comrade."

"Pissers of slime!" hissed the political officer, a morose-appearing, bulky man with beetling brows. "Every name is correct; they're *always* correct. How and where do they get their information?" He checked off the last of the names on his personal list of Solidarity suspects.

The battalion commander, a seedy-looking major with scraggly, dirty-blond hair and a bloodied combat tunic, thumped his back wearily against the blackened hulk of a Soviet T-82 Main Battle Tank—one of the hundreds which littered the Shansi battlefields.

"Perhaps the Tartars call Number Two Dzerzhinsky Square. Don't you fellows have an information office there?"

"Don't get cute with me, Kozov! My job is difficult enough without your obstructionist remarks. I'm going to run an attitude survey on you and your staff when there's a lull in the fighting," snarled the commissar.

The major chuckled acidly. "Ha! The ultimate weapon. How many attitude surveys have you conducted since the beginning of this asinine war—ten? twenty? Attitude surveys and Solidarity death lists: that's what this war is all about, isn't it, Shimanov?"

A young private, an Armenian-looking lad with dark, sad eyes—one of those whose name was announced over the Chinese Army's psychological-warfare loudspeaker —swallowed down the lump in his throat as he fumbled nervously with the fragmentation grenade. He was only forty feet from the two officers when he made his decision. He pulled the pin.

The lethal missile of death sailed in a graceful arc and landed with a soft thud in the sandy soil. The intended victims didn't notice it. Their argument had escalated to the shouting stage.

The explosion and flash of orange red ended the discussion. The young conscript bolted, then snaked through the nearby gully—his prearranged escape route—toward the Chinese lines.

The conscript-soldiers of the 142nd huddled a little deeper in their foxholes when they heard the blast. They all knew what it was. Fraggings were a common occurrence in the Soviet Expeditionary Force to North China.

The BMP armored personnel carrier bumped awkwardly over the two stony ruts that served as a road. Mladshiy Serzhant Yuri Spinnenko braced himself by holding on to the circular weapons-mount surrounding the open turret. As a junior sergeant, Troops of the Border Guards, KGB, Yuri often led the reconnaissance probes into the battle zones.

Officially, the China War was classified still as a "border incursion," although the numbers of Soviet troops in North China now numbered a million and a half men.

Yuri Spinnenko was more than a soldier of the Border Guards; he was an example. A product of the multifaceted shaping influences of the Soviet system, Yuri Spinnenko was as close to being the "New Soviet Man" as the system could produce.

Born in the town of Kuybyshev in the Volga region in 1960, he had lost his parents shortly after his second birthday—or was it his third? Uncle Pavel, his mother's brother, mentioned two different ages when pressed for details.

His father, as Uncle Pavel had often explained with pride, was a military man: a Hero of the Soviet Union and a recipient of the Order of Lenin, and a major in the newly created elite Rocket Forces. Major Anatoli Kiktev and his wife Natalya, Yuri's mother, were killed in a commercial plane crash on a routine flight from Moscow to Omsk.

Two-year-old Yuri—or was he three—was assigned to the Kiev State Orphanage for the Children of Deceased Military Heroes. The KSO was more than an orphanage; it was a totally controlled environment—a model Communist mini-world where the "New Soviet Man" could be molded without the corrupting influences of the outside world. The Soviet system spared no effort or expense at

KSO to shape and pamper these, the future leaders of the Soviet Union. When Yuri was fourteen, he left the KSO and went to live with Pavel Spinnenko—the man known to him as his mother's brother.

The rutted road narrowed to an end, and a foot-trail —really no larger than a rabbit-track—snaked into the ravine.

"Sergeant Spinnenko!" called the point-man. "We're going to have to continue on foot. The BMPs can't go any farther."

Yuri lifted his stocky, muscular body out of the turret and stepped gingerly on the only flat surface of the sloping armor plate. His wide blue eyes darted from side to side, scanning the ravine. The beetling crags overhead could provide excellent cover for an ambush party. He was fearful that this could be a trap.

He took off his steel helmet and wiped the perspiration from his neck, then brushed the sand and grit from his sandy-colored curly hair. How he yearned for a hot bath!

He hopped down, yanked a map out of his broad tunic pocket, and spread it on the forward armor plating. His eyes probed the sector where his unit was deployed.

"Right here, Alex." He pointed to a series of tiered oblong circles that represented the terrain they were in. "The ravine is short—no more than eight kilometers: then it breaks out into the Plain of Taiyiian, outside the city. We link up with the 142nd MRB right there." He jabbed a grimy fingertip at a spot just outside the provincial capital.

"Sergeant Spinnenko, helicopter recon has made three passes over the ravine in the past twenty-four hours. No sign of activity."

"Sensors?"

"Yes," responded the point-man. "Electronic impulses are negative. Just to make absolutely certain, they did a gas recon."

Yuri recoiled slightly at the mention of gas. It was becoming a standard Soviet practice in this war to saturate an area suspected of enemy activity with toxic gases. It was a violation of the Geneva Convention, but his government had conducted chemical warfare for years: in Yemen, Afghanistan, Cambodia, Laos, and Ethiopia. The Tartars were everywhere. It was the only way to equalize the struggle. Besides, they started the war with their attack on Khabarovsk on the Amur River in the fall of 1984. Anybody who would dare attack the sacred Motherland is deserving of the full fury of the Soviet people.

"On foot then, men," shouted Yuri. "Alex, post a guard with the vehicles. When the regiment catches up they'll provide drivers and crews and take the southern route flanking the hills."

Halfway into the ravine, little mounds of earth started to appear along the hillsides, soon taking the shape of green-caped soldiers breaking through the clods of dirt. They had been buried for several hours—motionless, their gas masks worn tightly over their faces. The ambush party gathered up the tiny, Japanese-made electronic "scramblers"—sensor-foiling neutralizing devices which deceived the electronic sensing probes of the Soviet helicopters.

The People's Liberation Army platoon leader motioned with a variety of hand signals. Each soldier took up his prearranged position. The leader adjusted his field glasses —focusing on the stocky Russian sergeant leading his detachment through the rocky ravine. He slid behind an outcropping of rock and aligned his sights on the single file of Soviet border troops heading for the Plain of Taiyiian.

The wind whipped through the Dzerzhinsky complex in short, violent gusts, driving the hard pellets of snow before it.

The Complex—headquarters of the Komitet Gosuparstvennoi Bezopasnosti, Committee of State Security of the Soviet Union—was housed in the huge stone block of offices taking up the entire northeastern facade of Dzerzhinsky Square at the end of Karl Marx Prospekt, one of Moscow's most important streets.

The Complex was actually a hollow square, the front and both wings being devoted to the KGB, the rear block being the infamous Lubyanka interrogation center and prison.

General Pavel Spinnenko puffed nervously on a long cardboard-filtered *papirosa* and stirred his glass of iced mineral water. He stared wistfully through the tall, draped, bulletproof window overlooking the square, his eyes fixed on the twenty-foot bronze statue of Feliks Dzerzhinsky, the founder of the CHEKA—the forerunner of the KGB. Dzerzhinsky's sightless eyes stared from the center of the Square down Karl Marx Prospekt to Revolution Square.

"Ah, if only old Feliks were alive, we wouldn't have these problems, Raisa. He didn't have to go through a dozen committees to initiate an action. Everybody in the system today is afraid to take any action by themselves. If anything goes wrong they want to make sure the blame is shared. Old Feliks didn't care, though. He had a direct line to Lenin himself. Ah, yes. They were iron men back in those days. They didn't have to claw their way through layers of bureaucracy to get things done."

Raisa Karezev, Personal Secretary and Chief Computer Technician to the Director, Border Guards Directorate, KGB, looked up from her filing and arched her pencil-slim eyebrows. Her large green eyes narrowed purposefully as she sauntered toward the squat, bullet-headed general. She placed her strong slim hands on his shoulders, at the juncture where his thick neck seemed to countersink into his torso.

"Pavel, such frustrations will only increase your blood pressure. Think happy thoughts. Your nephew is coming home today, a survivor."

"Yes, yes, a survivor," he mumbled thoughtfully.

"Is the door locked, Raisa?" asked Spinnenko, turning toward his attractive secretary-technician.

"I lock it as a matter of routine, Pavel, in case the urge for a massage overwhelms you. I know how quickly your headaches develop."

"And you know all of my pressure points. I swear, Raisa, that you have little spies within my body reporting to you daily. You know my body better than I do."

Raisa laughed softly as she unbuttoned his tunic.

"That's only because you're too busy protecting the Motherland. If you don't take care of your body, then I must. Do you want to be arrested for sabotaging State property?"

The general snorted a laugh.

"I, dear Raisa, am one of the chief arresting officers in the country. Who can arrest me—but me?"

"Come, come, Pavel. On the couch. Take off your undershirt and lie down. Let me get started. I still have to put the Kazan Solidarity file together."

Spinnenko sighed and lay on his stomach, his hairy, beefy torso spread lengthwise, his head drooped over the edge of the cushion.

Raisa's skilled hands started from the base of the spine and worked upward in short, probing jabs. They manipulated the spinal column and crept to the shoulderblades, fingers probing gently but firmly for nerve junctures.

"Ah! Oh! Ahhh! Right there, Raisa! Right there! If you could grab that nerve and yank it out by the roots! I feel the pain from my right eyeball to the sole of my foot when you touch it."

"I'll do nothing of the sort, Pavel. I'll coax it gently to behave. I want to leave your nervous system intact. Just relax. Talk if you wish. It helps."

Raisa probed and massaged rhythmically, synchronizing her movements with the rhythm of her voice, which she modulated with each probe of her fingers. The general sighed, his stocky peasant's body relaxing like a limp kitten's. He stared at the little, intricate patterns in the Oriental rug in a near-hypnotic stupor.

"I don't know if I could function in this job, Raisa dear, if it weren't for you," he slurred. "Hiring my brother-in-law's niece, in spite of the regulations against nepotism, was the most intelligent thing I've done all year. Ahhh! Right there! Now, a little lower."

Raisa worked the flanks of his spine with the heels of her hands. Small drops of perspiration dampened the dark, brown curls on her forehead and formed on the end of her pert nose.

"When do you need the Kazan printout, Pavel?"

"By—by late afternoon," Spinnenko murmured sleepily. "We need the names and addresses of all Solidarity members of Kazan and where they work."

"By late afternoon, Pavel? I'll be lucky if I can get the programming completed by tomorrow morning." Raisa worked her fingers into his thick neck.

"Oh! Oh, ecstasy, Raisa! If we Communists ever find out that there really is a heaven, I hope that it's one eternal massage. Yes, Raisa, it must be completed by five. We have infiltrated a special tactical force into the city to pounce on these traitors. We expect a large roundup, in the high hundreds. We must get the completed program to central processing so they can create the data link and send it to KGB, Kazan. The special force will strike during noon, late tomorrow when most of them are at work. Oh! Oh—to the sides, by my rib cage!"

"When does Yuri arrive, Pavel?" asked Raisa, digging into the general's sides.

"Nine. He's coming in at Sheremetyevo."

"State airline?" Raisa frowned.

"Military flights are backlogged for weeks. We've been relying on Aeroflot for Border Guard wounded. Many of their planes have been converted to medical evacuation transports."

"How serious are Yuri's wounds?"

The Chief of the Border Guards grinned slyly.

"The Americans called wounds like his 'million-dollar wounds' during the Great Patriotic War. They were not bad enough to disable, but they were serious enough to get him out of the war. The best kinds of wounds. Yes, Raisa, if I were to plan his wounds myself it would be exactly as it had happened: a bullet wound to the fleshy part of the shoulder and shrapnel to the thigh from a grenade. I wish I could thank the Chinese soldiers who inflicted such convenient wounds. After a short period of convalescence, a series of prestige assignments, Yuri's future is assured. I predict that one day he'll be an officer—a good officer."

"Pavel." Raisa dug her fingertips between his ribs and worked them toward the spine. "What will Yuri's attitude be toward the war? The discontent is reaching critical proportions among the veterans, and especially among the two-year conscripts and—"

· "And Solidarity's behind the agitation!" snarled Spinnenko, raising his chest slightly. "Solidarity and the Jews!"

"The Jews?" Raisa arched her eyebrows, and firmly probed the general's spinal column.

"Irrefutable proof, Raisa. Israeli agents, MOSSAD, have infiltrated Solidarity and are now setting policy. Solidarity is funded by Jewish gold. You know the Golden Rule: he who has the gold—rules."

"But Gregierenko isn't Jewish, Pavel. None of the Russian Solidarity leaders are Jewish."

"Of course not, dear Raisa. Israel would be stupid to use Jews. They work through proxies—native malcontents. That's why Solidarity has jumped national boundaries since it went underground in Poland in 1982. It has spread like an insidious cancer, calling itself different names, but Solidarity is the umbrella organization. It's a tangled web with international links. We destroy one cell and five others spring up. It has infected the armed forces like a virus."

"Do our people know where Vasily Gregierenko is right now?" Raisa smoothed on a cooling lotion.

"Ah! The dessert after the main course! That feels so good, Raisa dear. Oh! That's cold!" Spinnenko shivered as she dribbled the lotion the length of his spine.

"Ever since Gregierenko escaped from our detention center at Yaroslavl, he went west, beyond the Bloc—we're sure. We had word that he was in Switzerland, then Yugoslavia. He moves like a gray shadow, that one."

Raisa Karezev breathed a silent sigh of relief, her ample chest heaving slightly as she patted the general's shoulder.

"There, Pavel. Put your tunic on. If I'm going to get the Kazan file ready for central processing, I had better be on it."

Three hours later, the Solidarity membership file was complete and on its way to the data-processing center of the complex. Raisa smiled a secret smile and braced herself against the blast of cold wind which assaulted her as she left. She steadied herself and headed for the Kremlin metro subway stop, the details of the Kazan file indelibly impressed upon her photographic memory.

The Tupolev 134 banked sharply, dipping its wing in order to give the wounded soldiers a better view of Moscow. The city was ablaze with lights, the spires of the Kremlin lit up like Christmas trees.

Yuri Spinnenko felt a slight twinge of pain in his bandaged shoulder as he tensed his muscles to compensate for the banking aircraft. His wide blue eyes scanned the city, looking for landmarks. It had been nearly three years since he had last been in the capital, but he could make out the major landmarks, thanks to the peculiar Soviet penchant for lacing the outlines of their important buildings with strings of multicolored lights.

Almost directly under him were the brightly lit onion domes of the Cathedral of the Annunciation and the dark hollowness of Dzerzhinsky Square. The KGB complex was one of the few public buildings in the city not lighted.

A dumpy stewardess with a flat Slavic face prowled the aisle, checking seat belts.

"Time of landing is approximately ten minutes from now. Seats will be in an upright position. Extinguish all smoking materials," the stewardess intoned. Another stewardess checked the rows of wounded soldiers strapped to stretchers in the forward compartment.

"Well, Yuri. That's it. Down there. The real world!" chattered the dark-haired corporal sitting next to him on the aisle seat. "After wading up to my ass in Tartars for the past year and a half I'm going to enjoy the delights of Caucasian women. I've got two glorious weeks in Moscow before I report for duty in Kiev. I'm going to make up for lost time. What are your plans?"

Yuri closed his eyes as the plane made its final approach to Sheremtyevo International Airport, thirty-two kilometers from Moscow in the flat, snowy countryside.

"No more fighting Chinese for awhile. I've paid my

dues," said Yuri softly, almost sadly, referring to the Soviet Union's unpopular no-win war with the People's Republic of China. "If things fall into place, my next assignment will be to the Kremlin Guards. It's been a dream of mine since I was a boy to guard Comrade Lenin's Tomb. I can't think of a greater honor for a Soviet citizen. If my uncle has done his part, I'll be reassigned within a month."

"Ah, Yuri," sighed the corporal. "Always the model comrade. I predict that someday you'll be an officer, a field marshal perhaps. I don't understand why you haven't applied for officer cadet school already. All you'd have to do is show an interest and they'd jump for you, a fellow with your connections."

"All in good time, Mishka, all in good time. There are certain goals which I must reach—certain assignments which must be fulfilled. I must be a serving citizen, not a special citizen. It must be one step at a time for me."

"Like being a Tomb Guard for a few years?"

Yuri Spinnenko adjusted his tunic collar and put on his gray-green garrison hat as the wheels of the Tupolev smoked on the tarmac of Sheremetyevo.

"Yes, my good Mishka. Like being a Tomb Guard for Comrade Lenin," said Yuri reverently.

"It will take more, much more!" Vasily Gregierenko persisted. "To purchase equipment on the black market in my country is to pay triple the price. Presses, newsprint, paper, and copiers are all commodities controlled by Eastern Bloc governments. My suppliers have to pay premium prices for Swedish and West German equipment."

Gregierenko flopped on the couch in resignation. He was extremely tired. He was a man constantly on the run, keeping at times only hours ahead of KGB assassination squads.

The slightly balding Solidarity leader, usually a mild scholarly man, was clearly agitated. He refused a cigarette from the MOSSAD colonel.

"No, thank you, Yabin. My stomach revolts at nicotine

or alcohol. Nerves, you know. Do you have any tea? Weak tea if you have it."

The pockmarked colonel put a kettle on the stove and dropped a teabag into a china mug. The kettle whistled and he poured the hot water over the bag.

"Cream and sugar?"

"Yes, both," said Gregierenko.

Vasily pressed the mug to his lips and sipped the soothing liquid.

"Ah, that's good! That's good."

He leaned back in his chair and looked out the large third-story window, out over the low, flat suburbs of Tel Aviv.

"Tel Aviv is one of the few cities I feel completely safe in," Gregierenko murmured thoughtfully.

"Well, don't become too secure or you'll lose caution, my friend. The KGB might not have any hit teams in Tel Aviv, but they probably have proxies."

"Like the Palestinians?"

"Them, among others. They have no trouble finding people to work through."

The Solidarity leader squeezed the teabag between his thumb and forefinger, trying to get a few more drops of flavor from it. The sunlight flooded the room and warmed him all over. The pains in his legs from beatings inflicted by brutal guards at Naryan Mar in the Gulag two years before were responding to the sun rays playing over his body. He sighed deeply, stretching his full length on the couch. He hadn't felt this relaxed for months. In spite of the dangers and constant anxiety, he felt that his role as Solidarity leader of the Soviet organization was a sacred cause.

It hadn't always been so. Vasily Gregierenko's introduction into the clandestine world of International Solidarity had started some five years ago, November 1986 to be exact, with a great deal of self-doubt. As a prosecuting attorney for an Oblast, a governmental administrative unit outside of the Soviet city of Kazan—a job which he initially embarked upon with a great deal of enthusiasm —he came into contact with the first of the Solidarity writings to enter the Soviet Union from Poland. They were *samizdat,* clandestine underground papers which had long circulated in the USSR and the Eastern Bloc. But these were different. The usual samizdat format followed the standard appeal of the Charter 77 message, the manifesto of the Czechoslovakian human rights group demanding basic freedoms: to create a form of communism with a "human face." The Communist Party well knew that if you "humanized" communism, it would cease to be communism—and that could never be allowed.

The Solidarity samizdats called for a new political power alignment—of workers, students, intellectuals, and enlisted men of the armed forces—to be an alternative political force to the Communist Party. In Poland, Solidarity tried to work within the system and was crushed for its efforts. The New Solidarity demanded not only basic freedoms, as did the Charter 77 movement, but economic and political freedom as well.

The Polish Communist government tried to deal with Solidarity, but failed. The imposition of martial law in 1981–82 only drove the movement underground. The workers retaliated, first with passive resistance and then with massive industrial sabotage. The Polish army was called out to fire upon demonstrating workers in late 1984. They refused, and were replaced by troops of the UBT, Poland's "little nephew" to the KGB. It was Prague, 1968, all over again. The Polish conscripts, infected with the Solidarity virus, turned their weapons on the internal security troops. The inevitable happened: the Soviet, East German, Czechoslovakian, and Hungarian armies roared into Poland to "save the victory of socialism" at the request of Poland's Communist leaders.

Vasily moved his legs to catch the warmth of the shifting rays of the sun. He was feeling twinges of guilt, basking in the balmy subtropical weather of Tel Aviv while his revolutionary comrades were working under the noses of the secret-police forces of half a dozen countries in the Eastern Bloc. But Israel was the only nation willing to support International Solidarity, and he must milk that relationship for all it was worth. If it weren't for the organizational support of Israel's secret intelligence service, MOSSAD, and the generous influx of South African gold, Solidarity would soon collapse.

As the occupation troops were rotated back to the Soviet Union and other Warsaw Pact nations, the Solidarity virus was brought back with them. The ideology was too powerful, too appealing to be kept in isolation. It was an idea whose time had come. The conquering armies, in the course of their repressive duties, had to mingle intimately with the Polish population. Polish dissidents were rounded up by the tens of thousands and sent to internment camps in the satellite nations. These were hastily constructed, crude affairs, temporary holding facilities, until new and more secure prisons could be built in the Soviet Gulag Archipelago. Thousands escaped and found refuge among sympathetic populations in the Warsaw Pact nations. The virus spread anew.

Gregierenko could vividly remember his first encounter with Solidarity dissidents. They were young students from the University of Kazan, his own alma mater, and, ironically, the same school where Vladimir Ulyanov, Lenin, studied law. They were so young, so idealistic. Three of them were ex-conscripts, veterans of the Polish occupation. Four of them were young women.

Vasily had never witnessed a KGB interrogation before. His duties as provincial prosecutor involved him primarily with the metropolitan and provincial police. Subversion against the state was a crime with which he rarely, if ever, dealt. Some of the methods used by the local authorities were crude, even brutal, but he was totally unprepared for the sustained and systematic torture inflicted on the youthful dissidents of Kazan by the professionals of the KGB.

Subsequent duties in connection with the Solidarity menace took him to some of the internment centers throughout the republic. The dissidents held there were mostly workers, students, and enlisted members of the army, the very segments of the Soviet population who were supposed to be the most faithful supporters of the Communist system.

* * *

International Solidarity obtained an unexpected and welcome ally in the mid-1980s. The World Peace Council, a KGB front organization, conducted mammoth demonstrations throughout Western Europe in protest against the placement of American medium-range missiles carrying enhanced-radiation warheads—neutron bombs. The peace movement shook governments and toppled cabinets. Sympathetic terrorist groups attacked American bases and military personnel. The inevitable happened. The United States withdrew its military presence from Europe after forty years. NATO had its guts torn out and ceased to exist as a credible deterrent to the Warsaw Pact.

The jubilant mobs of demonstrators who were responsible for America's withdrawal naively assumed that the Soviet Union would follow suit and reduce its military presence and military forces in Eastern Europe. Nothing of the sort happened. The Soviets increased their strength and their pressure on Western Europe. An invasion seemed imminent. Europe would fall into Russian hands like an overripe plum.

A hasty alliance between Britain, France, and West Germany—more like a suicide pact—caught the Soviet Union by surprise. A united policy statement warned Russia that if Soviet troops crossed the West German border the nuclear arsenals of all three nations would be launched against Soviet cities.

It was a desperate gamble, but it worked. The overage, senile leaders of the Soviet Union were not willing to lose Moscow, Kiev, and Leningrad.

The mobs which had once rampaged through the streets screaming for American withdrawal now screamed for Soviet withdrawal from Eastern Europe. Russia had always claimed that her military presence in Eastern Europe was necessary because of the American threat. The threat was now gone. Why didn't she leave?

Those who manipulated the policies of the World Peace Council would offer no valid reason. When pressed by the rank and file of the peace organizations in Western Europe, the KGB ordered its puppets to disband its national organizations. It didn't happen. Through a series of surprise lightning moves, the national leaderships were voted out of office and new leaders appeared, seemingly from nowhere. In a tightly orchestrated maneuver, the Western European peace movement lost its KGB sponsorship and came under the control of the Israeli Secret Intelligence Service—MOSSAD.

"It will take more than Solidarity to bring about changes at the top, Yabin," Gregierenko said, slowly sipping his tea as he looked out at the setting sun, now a dull red orb sinking into the eastern Mediterranean. "They are scared old men in the Politburo. They have become physically and psychologically isolated from their own people. They are out of touch with the feelings and yearnings of the young of Russia. They could care less! They are more concerned with clinging to power and perpetrating an obsolete, discredited ideology."

"Marxism?" inquired Yabin.

"Marxism-Leninism; their own version of history. The government has increased the number of compulsory hours of study and instruction in Marxism in the educational system from nursery schools through graduate schools at the universities, but nobody, not even the little ones, takes it seriously."

Yabin walked to the window, his huge frame temporarily blocking Vasily's view of the sunset. Suddenly he turned, his face wearing a strange half-smile.

"Vasily, I want you to think seriously about this next question." The MOSSAD colonel paused dramatically, his expression turning grim.

"If—if there was an incident in the Soviet Union—an incident showing the entire population that the government and Party had been systematically deceiving the people on a single but important issue or subject, a subject which the population believed in with a near-religious fervor—and if it was demonstrated, beyond all doubt, that this falsehood had been consciously and cynically perpetrated for decades by the Party and the government, what would that do to the system?"

Gregierenko knit his brow into a frown and scratched the patchy baldness on his head.

"I'm not sure I follow you, Yabin. As I mentioned before, communism, as a pseudo-religion, is no longer the opiate of the masses. Indeed, according to reports from the China War, opium is now the religion of the masses —the masses of Soviet soldiers fighting there. Just what are you getting at?"

The colonel smiled his half-smile again and abruptly changed the subject.

"The China War, Vasily. Your analysis, please. I never did ask you."

"I'm sure that your MOSSAD people can give you much more information than I can. Why ask me?"

"I get dry reports: order of battle, casualties, weapons performance, and so forth. You have your finger on the pulse of your people. You have direct access to their collective soul. This is a factor that we professional intelligence people often overlook."

Vasily sighed wearily.

"More tea, please, before I launch into this distasteful subject." Yabin plopped a fresh tea bag into the mug and poured in the hot water.

"The Politburo decreed at the last National Party Congress in 1989 that the Soviet Union faced two grave threats to its very survival: corrupting, foreign ideologies—"

"Solidarity, right?" interrupted Yabin.

"Yes, especially as adopted and revised by the Soviet members. The second threat was the arming of China by the United States and Japan. The pragmatic leaders of the People's Republic of China have 'humanized' the Party to the point where it has ceased to be Communist, except in name. The Solidarity movement has leap-frogged a continent and found fertile ground in China. It has been accepted as an unofficial form of Party ideology, and it has worked."

There was a slight pause while Gregierenko marshaled his thoughts.

"The Chinese experience has shown that Solidarity can

humanize a totalitarian regime without creating chaos if the leadership is willing to take the risk of trusting the natural wisdom of the people. The Chinese masses did not run amok burning, tearing down, and destroying."

"Like the Red Guards did in the late 1960s?" offered Yabin.

"*That* was an artificially designed crisis, designed to create the hardships of the revolutionary period all over again in order to chasten and harden the young to recapture the flavor of Yenan—the revolutionary center of Mao's armies. The Cultural Revolution almost wrecked the nation. The Chinese will never turn the clock back to that period. The Solidarity virus has infected them for good. Those comrades who have visited China have said, upon returning to the Soviet Union, 'I have seen the future, and it works.'"

Yabin scratched his ear thoughtfully.

"That's what one American Communist, a journalist, I believe, said about Lenin's Russia when he visited it in the early 1920s," he added sarcastically.

"And now, very little works in my country except the military: that *always* works," noted Vasily, acidly.

Yabin tamped a wad of tobacco into his huge meerschaum pipe. "Continue, please." He touched a match to the bowl.

"As you know, Yabin, one of the burdens my country carries is its aging senile leadership. The average age of the Politburo is now seventy-seven. It's a year older in the Central Committee. Premier Igor Krylenko is seventy-six. The average age of the Council of Ministers is seventy-four. The leadership structure all the way down to the level of republic and local government has aged and calcified. My country is ruled by a gerontocracy."

Yabin knitted his brows. "A what?"

"A gerontocracy, rule by the aged: scared old men clinging to power and the privileges such power brings. The aging party leaders can be seen being driven to their magnificent villas in the cities or dachas in the country in their magnificent Zil limousines. They drive quickly to their destinations, those *nachalstvos*—"

"Nachalstvos?"

"A 'fat cat,' a privileged Party person." Vasily almost spat the words at him. "They drive quickly to their destination in order to avoid the resentful stares of the people—especially of the young."

Gregierenko stood, and started to pace the room. He waved a cloud of tobacco smoke away from his nose.

"May I open the window, Colonel? The smoke bothers me. Allergies, I'm afraid."

"To be sure, Vasily. I'll put out my pipe." Yabin spoke apologetically. The MOSSAD colonel emptied his pipe in the sink and washed the ashes down the drain. The pungent sea breeze wafted into the room, dispersing the smoke.

"At the time the Solidarity movement entered the Soviet Union, the Afghan scandals were made known, primarily through the samizdat underground. Do you remember that, Yabin?"

Yabin smirked, then laughed knowingly. "Of course, my dear Vasily. MOSSAD people were in Afghanistan spreading the word among your soldiers."

"As you were arming the Afghan guerrillas with sophisticated weapons, including toxic gases which could be fired from man-portable weapons into Soviet troop compounds."

Yabin shrugged his massive shoulders.

"And why not? Your people had been gassing the Afghans, not to mention others, for several years. Our weapons only equalized the struggle."

"The reprisals taken against the Afghans were fearsome, Yabin," Gregierenko interjected. "The population of that country has been cut almost in half."

"And what did these reprisals do to your soldiers?" Yabin arched a bushy eyebrow.

"First it brutalized, then disillusioned them. When the word was spread that the Afghan War was simply a ploy to train troops and test tactics and equipment on a continuing basis—"

"A dress rehearsal for the coming war with China, right?" interrupted the colonel.

Gregierenko ignored Yabin's comment, immersed in his own thoughts.

"How cynical can a government get! We rotated hundreds of thousands of our young men through the Afghan campaign, hailing it as a 'Socialist Internationalist duty' to help our Afghan comrades, while the Party and that aging group of nachalstvos planned it as nothing more than a gigantic and continuing military exercise. They never intended to win that war."

"And from the reports we received, Vasily," added Yabin, "they would have kept it going indefinitely as a training ground for the China conflict and future wars. The fact that the Afghans are natural and fanatical warriors actually aided and abetted Soviet planners. And let's face it, my friend: casualties and equipment losses were tolerable until we started to arm the Afghans secretly."

Gregierenko took a slow, meditative sip of his tea and added, "Krylenko saw the China campaign as a way to reinstitute the spirit of self-sacrifice and duty into the young; a glorious patriotic war to save the Motherland, like World War Two. That was the way to handle the young, especially those infected by Solidarity. Known or suspected members were placed in high-risk units where casualties would be the greatest. It's an old Russian trick. Get them killed off. Unit commanders were ordered, through attached political officers, to ensure the battle deaths of thousands of selected young men. Death lists are attached to operational orders. The gerontocracy could kill off its radicalized young men, and have its glorious patriotic war too. Now that America was out of Western Europe, they had no fear of a two-front war."

Yabin loaded his pipe again and lit it.

"Sorry, Vasily. I'm an addict to Rum-and-Maple—an American pipe tobacco. Sit near the window—not in front of it. I don't want you to become a target. Continue, please."

Gregierenko cleared his throat.

"Premier Krylenko miscalculated. He didn't count on the massive infusion of conventional weapons into China, especially anti-air and anti-tank weapons from Japan.

These are small but potent portable weapons, perfect for guerrilla warfare. Our massive armored thrusts and helicopter assaults have been decimated by them. When the Japanese switched from televisions to missiles and from Hondas to helicopters, they changed the whole nature of the war."

"And that's when Krylenko threatened to use nuclear weapons?" the colonel queried.

"Again, typical of the gerontocracy. It overreacted when the war did not go as predicted. They didn't mind losing men, but when equipment losses exceeded replacement capabilities, they threatened to use nuclear weapons," replied Gregierenko, grimacing slightly.

"The American policy of sending in volunteer pilots and technicians was a stroke of genius." Yabin chuckled, a wreath of blue smoke circling his head. "It's the Flying Tigers of the early nineteen-forties all over again. The people of China think of the Americans as self-sacrificing saviors. And the American decision to arm the Chinese with long-range missiles has added a whole new dimension to the war. The Chinese put their own warheads on them so the Americans are clean as far as contributing nuclear weapons are concerned."

"Yes," replied the Solidarity leader, settling back in his chair and staring absently out the window. "Now the gerontocracy is faced with losing Vladivostok, Leningrad, or even Moscow, if they go beyond conventional war. As the Americans used to say about Vietnam, 'We've got them right where they want us.' They have no alternative but to throw millions more into the bottomless pit of China or quit."

The MOSSAD colonel walked over to Gregierenko and put his hands on the Russian's shoulders from behind. A faint smile twisted at one side of his mouth.

"I asked you before, dear Vasily, what would happen if there was an incident of some sort showing the people of your country that the government had been perpetrating a gigantic deception—a lie unimaginable even by Communist standards since the very founding of the Soviet state. If such a thing were known, would it destabilize the system to the point where Krylenko and company could be deposed?"

Gregierenko bestowed an ironic smile on him. "My people are beyond caring anymore. They accept deception and lies as the normal course of events. All truths are blurred with falsehoods. The KGB would, of course, protect the governmental infrastructure of the gerontocracy. Do you know that the number of KGB troops and personnel exceeds that of the total armed forces of the United States? That includes the Border Guards, of course."

"What if the regular military forces of your country sided with millions of your countrymen, demonstrating against the government of Krylenko?"

"Such a thing is not imaginable, not even in my wildest fantasies. Russia is not Poland." Gregierenko sighed sullenly.

That strange smile still tugged at the corners of Yabin's lips.

"But what if? Just what if? . . ." insisted Yabin.

"I cannot conceive of such a thing happening. The catalyst for such a scenario as the one you have described would have to be a severe trauma—to the very soul of the Soviet system itself."

III.

The kibbutz of Shareem in the Negev desert was not typical of the cooperative and collective communities sprinkled around Israel. Shareem was a *N'HALLAL* kibbutz—a quasi-military cooperative settlement established along the frontiers of the country. Shareem was carved out of the forbidding desert landscape by troops of the Israeli army.

In early 1957, only a few months after Israel's November 1956 war against Egypt, Israeli soldiers, male and female, pitched their tents in the barren wastelands of the central Negev at the foothills of Mount Ramon on the border facing the Sinai. Here they planted the Negev's first orange groves.

Viktor Ayalon and Sophie Elyashar were pioneers: hardy Russian Jews who were two of the lucky ones evacuated from the Ukraine during the Nazi invasion of Russia. A clandestine Zionist organization spirited the children, orphaned by the war, out of the Soviet Union through Iran, and to British-controlled Palestine in 1942.

Both were in their early teens when they first took up arms to secure Israel's freedom in 1948. Since then, Viktor and Sophie had been fighting and building for their new nation, a gun in one hand and a tool of some sort in the other.

In the early 1950s, they became part of the GADNA, (shorthand for the Hebrew "G'dudei Noar,") the Youth Battalions. It was a paramilitary youth movement which was part of a larger organization: the NAHAL, from the

Hebrew "Noar HaLutzi LoHem," the Fighting Pioneer Youth.

In the spring of 1958, Sophie, a sergeant in the CHEN, the Israeli Women's Army Corps, and teacher of backward Yemeni Jews, married Viktor, an agricultural technician-soldier responsible for the establishment of a citrus industry in the valley of Shareem.

The marriage was rooted in hard pioneering skills and devotion to their kibbutz. The efforts of Viktor and Sophie were fruitful. Four years after its establishment, Shareem, to use the words of the Prophet Isaiah, "blossomed as a rose." By 1961, the rows of orange, grapefruit, and lemon groves marched in orderly ranks from the valley community, up into the terraced foothills of Mount Ramon itself.

Deep wells provided the life-giving water for the NAHAL project but, as everybody knew, they would not last forever. A huge, state-of-the-art desalting plant was built at the port city of Eilat. Soon, millions of gallons were pumped the eighty miles overland to the fertile valley floor of Shareem.

While the desert was fruitful, Sophie's womb was not. War-induced trauma and disease—and Sophie had had an abundance of both in her short, violent life—had left her barren.

Fortunately for the Ayalons, the kibbutz of Shareem had another function. Younger orphans and parentless adolescents, especially the children of deceased military personnel, were sent to Shareem and assigned to soldier families. The pioneering hardships of the kibbutz were ideal for creating the GADNA—the tough, dedicated youth who would assume positions of responsibility and ensure the survival of Israel.

Sophie and Viktor applied for adoption; they asked for an infant boy. Their request was granted within a year —and the source of the child was not the Defense Force Adoption and Welfare Agency, but the MOSSAD, the Israeli secret intelligence service.

It was a chilly, dry winter day in 1961 when the tan Land Rover station wagon drove up to the Ayalon's concrete-block house. Viktor was in the front yard pouring kerosene into the smudge pots in anticipation of a citrus-killing frost that night.

A large bear of a man with a pockmarked face and a flowing handlebar mustache slipped out of the Land Rover. A young woman sat by his side, rocking a flannel-covered bundle and cooing tenderly. Viktor's heart leaped as he heard an infant's high-pitched chortle and saw a tiny hand grab at the woman's nose. The MOSSAD agent was blunt and to the point.

"Viktor Ayalon?" inquired the flowing mustache.

Viktor stood and wiped the black smudge from his palms.

"Yes, I'm Viktor Ayalon." He held out a callused hand. The MOSSAD agent's huge, meaty grip engulfed his.

"Captain Moshe Yabin, Security Service. May we talk inside?"

"Certainly," replied Viktor, trying to contain his anxiety.

Sophie stepped out of the kitchen and greeted the captain, wiping her hands on her apron.

"I'll get directly to the point, Mr. and Mrs. Ayalon. You have applied for adoption. Right?"

"Yes, yes!" answered Sophie anxiously. "Are you—you from the agency?"

Yabin broke into a broad smile, the tips of his mustache touching his cheeks.

"Not from *the* agency, but from *an* agency —Intelligence and Security Service."

Viktor and Sophie looked at each other, bewildered, trying to control their excitement.

"MOSSAD?" they chorused in unison.

The MOSSAD captain threw back his head and laughed.

"You don't exactly consider the MOSSAD an adoption agency, do you?"

Viktor's craggy features clouded in suspicion. Yabin sensed that it was time for less humor and more explanation.

"Mr. and Mrs. Ayalon. At times, we at MOSSAD are charged with placing special children in special homes. We have such a child, a boy of eight months, that we would like to place with you."

The Ayalons broke into smiles, their anxiety dissipating.

"The child in the car, he's—he's . . ."

"Yes," grinned Yabin, his mustache twitching.

"Oh, may we see him?" inquired Sophie, her hands nervously wringing her apron.

"In a few moments, Sophie. Oh, may I call you both by your first names?"

"Yes, please do," answered Viktor, his excitement mounting.

"Before we get into the formalities of giving you the child, I—"

"Oh dear." Sophie emitted a low soft groan. "Red tape and delays?"

"All you have to do is take the child after signing the forms," Yabin informed them.

"You—you mean take him today?" gasped Viktor. "We don't have a crib, diapers, baby food, formula, anything! We're completely unprepared."

"We anticipated that." Yabin glanced coyly at them. "We brought a crib and a three-months' supply of everything you need."

The Ayalons shook their heads in disbelief.

"Before you decide to take this child, you must agree to abide by certain conditions," warned the captain.

"What?" Viktor's countenance clouded.

"Anything! Anything!" Sophie insisted, casting a sharp glance at her husband.

"First and foremost, you must teach the boy Russian. You must speak Russian in the home exclusively if you take him."

"What?" Viktor rose, his face reddening. "We had to knock our heads against the wall to learn Hebrew and English, and now you want us to speak only Russian around this child?"

"You speak it, I assume?" Yabin cocked a bushy eyebrow.

"Of course. It was our childhood language. We lived in a Russian-Jewish settlement after arriving here in 1942. There are many Russian Jews here in Shareem. We hear enough of the language to keep it alive in our memory, but why—why this child? I don't understand."

"You will speak Russian, northern dialect exclusively, and teach him the Cyrillic alphabet and writing. By the time he is fourteen, we want him to speak and write like a native.

"There will be other skills and subjects which we want you to teach him. We'll contact you from time to time with information on—er, 'revising' his curriculum," counseled Yabin.

Viktor scowled, his hard, callused hands clenching and unclenching.

"What you want us to do, Captain Yabin, is to raise a spy. Raise him, love him as our own, and then have him whisked away and sent into Russia. It's insane! We can't make that kind of an emotional investment in this child, knowing he's being groomed for an assignment which may end in his death!"

"Viktor, dear"—Sophie was begging for understanding —"You—you may be overreacting. I don't think they would . . ."

"Oh yes they would, Sophie." He scowled in disgust. "MOSSAD can be just as ruthless as the Russians. I've seen them at work when I was in the army. People only exist to be used and discarded. That's their mentality."

Yabin stifled a yawn. He had heard it all before.

"As you well know, Viktor, the diplomatic corps has chosen an unusually high percentage of its young men and women from Shareem. Similar arrangements have been made with other families here in the past."

Sophie clutched at her husband's sleeve.

"Oh, Viktor, perhaps it's all right. Couldn't we . . ."

Viktor folded his arms in finality and stared toward the kitchen, his expression set in grim disappointment.

While Sophie was pleading with her husband, the MOSSAD captain padded to the door and motioned to the woman in the Land Rover.

Viktor was startled by the hearty squeal of the infant. He turned and stared at the wriggling flannel bundle in the nurse's arms.

His eyes connected with the wide, sky-blue eyes of the infant. The baby's head darted from side to side, scanning the four faces above him. His chubby pink cheeks puffed out, and he blew through pursed lips, sounding like a backfiring motorcycle.

Viktor bent over, touching his nose to the child's, staring into his eyes.

"And where did you come from, little fellow?" he whispered gently, continuing to stare as if trying to discern the child's origins.

"That can never be revealed, Viktor," replied Yabin.

The baby frowned, his little head reddening through the sparse, sandy-colored hair. He verged on tears.

"Don't cry, little man," cooed Viktor, rubbing his nose against the infant's.

The baby squealed with delight and grabbed Viktor's nose and tried to nurse on it.

"Does the child have a name?" asked Sophie, her voice choking with emotion.

"Yossef," answered Yabin, a victorious smile twitching the ends of his mustache.

Viktor took the baby from the nurse and stuck his face into the blanket, kissing Yossef on the cheek.

"Yossef it is," he agreed, beaming. "Yossef Elyashar Ayalon."

"Are you going to let me read Ariel Makleff's journal or not?" Yossef's voice was tremulous with controlled anger.

"Parts of it, Yossef. Much of it is sensitive material. We are translating the information into classified and nonclassified sections. You know how that works."

"But the part that pertains to me, Yabin!" Yossef lurched to his feet, pointing a shaking finger at the MOSSAD colonel. "I have a right to know about—about this family of mine in the Soviet Union. You—you and your people confirmed that what Makleff wrote was true. I've got a twin brother in that country." He slammed his fist on the coffee table. "Damn you, Yabin! I want to know!"

The colonel stood by the window, his huge frame blocking the skyline of Tel Aviv. Casually, he lit his huge meerschaum pipe and turned toward Yossef.

"I think, my hotheaded young friend, that we owe you

that much." Yabin drawled deliberately, rotating the flaming match around the bowl of his pipe.

"I was raised on lies, Yabin. My so-called aunt and uncle were all part of an elaborate conspiracy to rob me of my identity. If it weren't for Makleff, I'd never know about this."

Yabin glanced at Yossef, a sly smile flickering across his pockmarked face.

"Do you think that your meeting and knowing Makleff was an accident, Yossef?"

"What do you mean?"

"I mean that we—MOSSAD—arranged your assignment to Berne. We arranged for Rabbi Sharon to get you involved in Ariel's life. . . ."

"Then Rabbi Sharon is one of you?" Yossef gasped incredulously.

Yabin relit his pipe.

"Not directly. We just set things in motion and he did what was predictable. Rabbis are very predictable people." Yabin bestowed an ironic smile on him.

The expression on the colonel's face suddenly became serious.

"Sit down, Yossef. I think it's time for me to be as honest as I can be under the circumstances. . . ."

"Are you capable of being honest, Yabin?" snarled Yossef disdainfully.

"I'll ignore that, Yossef. Let's get on with your life story."

The colonel paused dramatically.

"Sit down!" Yabin commanded, "and listen without interruption."

The Volkswagen bus bounced stiffly over the undulating dirt-and-gravel road to Shareem. It was mid-January, a beautiful time of year in the Negev. The gray-browns of the desert were consistently broken by splashes of green laced by threads of blue irrigation ditches that nourished the flourishing citrus groves flanking the road.

Yossef wasn't sure if Uncle Viktor and Aunt Sophie could add to what Yabin had told him, but it was a good time to visit and try to glean some additional facts about his childhood. It was a holiday season, Rosh Hashanah La'Elanoth—"New Year of the Trees," a sort of Jewish Arbor Day—a very important and practical holiday in this part of the country, where the planting of trees symbolized the literal building of Zion.

Yossef's old VW strained to reach the crest of the hill. He almost stopped, slipped into first gear, and crawled up the steep incline.

He always enjoyed creeping over the crest of the hill, watching the valley of Shareem spill into the horizon before him. To Yossef, this was his Israel: new, raw, carved out of the wilderness. The urban sprawl of Tel Aviv and Jerusalem, almost a continuous blob of a city by now, linked by industries and suburbs, was almost indistinguishable from Rome, Madrid, or Zurich: a smaller version, perhaps, but the loss of identity was similar.

"Yossef! Dear Yossef!" cried Aunt Sophie excitedly. A plump, little woman in her mid-fifties now, with apple-red cheeks, she hardly looked like the rugged pioneer warrior who had helped carve a thriving community out of the Negev.

"Hello, auntie," smiled Yossef sheepishly, remembering the harsh things he had said to Yabin about Viktor and Sophie. He touched the *mezuzah* at the doorway and kissed her hand before entering and hugging her. This was a common greeting during the Rosh Hashanah season. He had arrived just in time for the evening's Tu B'Shvat party.

The Tu B'Shvat festivities were held in the kibbutz's community center. It was an intimate, informal affair. Yossef noted, with some sadness, that most of those in attendance were older. Most of the youth of Shareem had lost the commitment of their elders and had left the isolated kibbutz for the glitter of the cities. Some had left Israel altogether for greener fields in America or Canada.

A variety of familiar aromas assaulted Yossef from the communal kitchen. Soon, mounds of food were brought out and served. There were several types of knishes, *kishke* cooked in *cholent, lokshen kugel*, stuffed cabbage and *pitcha*, followed by several desserts—honeycakes, strudel, apple *pirushkes,* and figs—in turn followed by a lengthy speech on the founding and building of Shareem and a toast of *"l'chaim."*

At 11:00 P.M. the festivities were over and Viktor, Sophie, and Yossef walked slowly along the gravel path from the community center to the house. The night sky was clear and cold, ablaze with a million stars.

"I've almost forgotten how clear the air is down here," observed Yossef as they crunched along the gravel. "The smog in Tel Aviv is getting as bad as Europe's. This is one of the few places left on earth that is so clear and unpolluted."

"Speaking of—of clearing the air, isn't that why you're here, Yossef?" inquired Viktor, his voice calm and controlled.

The tightness in Yossef's throat almost prevented him from speaking.

"I had a lengthy discussion with a Colonel Moshe Yabin about my debut into the Ayalon family back in 1962. I always thought that—that the stork, not secret-police captains, delivered babies."

There was an awkward silence.

"You have to understand the times, Yossef, and—and the—the . . ." Sophie started to sniffle, the sniffles becoming sobs.

"Let's get into the house," murmured Viktor, trying to control his irritation.

"Yossef." Viktor started slowly, pacing the living room of their house like a caged lion. "We've always considered you our son, and raised you like one. In order to adopt you, we had to abide by certain agreements dictated by MOSSAD. Part of the agreement was to keep your identity from you—not that we knew that much to tell you."

"That was the easy part, dear Yossef," added Sophie quickly, drying her tears. "We didn't know anything about your origins. They never told us until last week."

"Last week!" exclaimed Yossef, his blue eyes flashing. "You mean you know something now?"

"Enough to satisfy you. Yabin called us last Saturday and told us that you knew about your adoption. He said it was time for you to know about your parents, your real parents." Sophie choked on the words.

"We—we received a lengthy statement by courier yesterday. It was taken from that old doctor's journal and edited especially for us. It will tell you everything you want to know about the Dubrov family from western Russia—your family, Yossef."

EXCERPT FROM THE
MAKLEFF JOURNAL

Compiled from the Journal and Marginal
Notes

1884 New York City U.S.A.	In 1884, Ivan Dubrov, a metalworker and radical Social Democratic political organizer, was exiled from Russia for his political activities. He emigrated to the United States, settling in the New York City area, where he worked in a foundry. He was never satisfied with his new life in America and maintained contact with revolutionary groups in Russia; in fact, his home was the American "headquarters" for SD activities and he acted as a fundraiser and organizer for various Russian Marxist groups on the east coast of the U.S. It was known that Leon Trotsky, later Lenin's confidant and Red Army organizer, stayed with Dubrov when he visited New York.
1892	In 1892 Ivan married an American woman, an Irish Catholic named Mary Flannery from Union City, New Jersey. She was a second-generation American born in New York. It was a strained and unnatural marriage, with Mary's piety and Ivan's revolutionary activity often colliding. The marriage did produce a son, however, Aleksei, who was born in 1895.
1895	

Aleksei Dubrov was Yossef's grandfather and grew up as a streetwise, typical American boy. He was greatly influenced by his father's political views and absorbed many of the radical Marxist ideas expressed in his home.

1916   In 1916, when Aleksei was twenty-one, he joined the American navy, which was in a period of buildup in preparation for World War I. He served as a gunner aboard an American cruiser and was involved in convoying supplies to Murmansk in Russia. **1918**   In 1918 he became alienated from the policies of his country when they sent interventionist forces to the Russian city of Archangel to support the revolutionary provisional government of Alexander Kerensky. The sailors from Aleksei's ship became part of the garrison of that city.

1919   In 1919 Aleksei made contact with local Bolsheviks in the city and engaged in sabotage, setting fire to a warehouse in a part of the city where Tsarist war supplies were kept. It was a huge fire and destroyed much of the docking and loading facilities in the city, thus hampering the Allied cause. From then on, many supplies bound for Archangel had to be rerouted to Murmansk.

Petrograd 1919   Aleksei deserted the American navy and made his way to Petrograd, formerly called St. Petersburg, where he fell in with the American Communist journalist John Reed and his mistress. Reed took the young deserter under his wing and introduced Aleksei to Lenin. Leon Trotsky remembered the young man and his family from New York City. Vladimir introduced him to me and we became fast friends. My parents often had young Aleksei over to supper or for tea and cakes. We were about the same age and shared many of the same thoughts and feelings.

In no time, Aleksei Dubrov was a celebrity and a genuine hero of the Revolution. With Lenin's and Trotsky's personal endorsement, and John Reed's journalistic propaganda, Yossef's grandfather became the toast of the Petrograd Bolsheviks. Lenin commissioned him an ensign in the new Soviet navy and assigned him to the Kronstadt Naval Base in Petrograd where he was favored and given privileges and responsibilities far beyond his rank. Lenin took a great personal interest in young Aleksei and treated him like the son he never had; the son that Krupskya could never, or would never, give him.

Kronstadt 1920

The sailors at Kronstadt held a special place in Lenin's heart. It was the Kronstadt garrison which first rebelled against the Tsar and organized the first Bolshevik cells in Russia. Members of the Kronstadt garrison provided the honor guard which met Lenin at St. Petersburg's Finland Station in 1918 when he returned via the sealed train from Germany.

It was the Kronstadt-based cruiser *Aurora* which fired the first shots of the final assault in November against the Fortress of St. Peter and St. Paul. The Kronstadt sailors were the vanguard of the shock troops who invaded the Winter Palace in Petrograd.

1920

Aleksei married Krupskya's niece, Natalya, who was living with the Lenins. A vivacious, attractive girl, she was immediately drawn to the young American celebrity. The marriage took place in the Tsar's Winter Palace. It was as close to a "royal Wedding" as the Bolsheviks could stage. Lenin served as Natalya's father and gave the bride away. I can still remember the good spirits of Vladimir that day. John Reed served as best man. Papa and I served as ushers. It was a wedding which seemed ordained by the Communist heaven and sanctified by the Party.

I could see it coming before it happened: Aleksei's moodiness and his fault-finding; but I never doubted his love for Natalya or hers for him. I loved Natalya also, but could never express it. Her aunt Krupskya never said it openly, but she would never let her niece marry a Jew.

It is difficult to understand why Aleksei Dubrov forfeited everything by his involvment with the Kronstadt revolutionaries of 1921. It can only be discerned, by those who knew him and testified at his trial, that he was more democratic than Socialist. His American sense of social justice and democratic idealism was too well ingrained, perhaps. He quickly perceived the betrayal of the Revolution. As a confidant of Lenin's, he gained insight into his deceitful and cynical mentality and the treacherous operational style of the Bolsheviks. He was aghast at the early excesses of the CHEKA, Lenin's secret police, the forerunner of the KGB. He spoke out against these excesses and stated several times in public that the Revolution had been betrayed by the very people who had created it. He was only saying openly what all of us, including myself at this time, felt but were terrified to admit.

January 1921

Only his association with Lenin's wife through marriage to Natalya saved him from the firing squad. When Lenin was informed of Aleksei's statement, he refused to deal with it. As an American, Aleksei was used to speaking his mind.

When Aleksei saw injustice, he spoke out against it and mobilized others to combat it, a typical American reaction. He pleaded with John Reed to report on the mass executions and the newly developed slave-labor and execution camps of the CHEKA. Reed, by this time, was more Communist than American and used dialectics to justify the excesses. He cautioned young Aleksei to "keep his mouth shut if he knew what was good for him." Aleksei was crushed at Reed's attitude and came to my apartment one evening and got roaring drunk. He became very loud and abusive, cursing Lenin, the Communist system, and himself for supporting the revolution. Just before he staggered out the door, he warned me that he was going to do something which would stand the damned Bolsheviks on their ears.

March 1921

The rebellion of the Kronstadt garrison against the tyranny of Lenin started when the sailors declared their support of striking workers in Petrograd. They were protesting the harsh economic regulations and the mass arrests by the CHEKA. The Kronstadt sailors quickly took up arms when the CHEKA attempted to move into the naval base. A prolonged and bloody battle ensued and thousands were killed, many executed after capture by the CHEKA. Among those captured was Aleksei Dubrov.

Lenin was personally outraged that his favored sailors would rebel, and he vowed that he would destroy them and the navy, altogether. This explains, perhaps, why the Soviet navy was always the "poor relative" of the Soviet military until the late 1960s. Stalin, and even Khrushchev, still harbored a distrust of the Soviet fleet because of the Kronstadt affair. Lenin's true nature was shown to Papa at this time. His vindictiveness and brutality knew no bounds. He personally witnessed the torture and execution of many, forcing Papa to watch and certify death. It was at this moment, I believe, that my father decided to become an anti-Leninist whenever the opportunity presented itself. He did not have to wait very long.

As for Aleksei, he was severely wounded in the fighting. Lenin had to somehow explain the defection of a favored foreign comrade. The story was fabricated by the CHEKA that Aleksei was an American agent and that his defection to the Bolsheviks, and even his marriage to Natalya, was nothing more than a clever ruse. His real mission was to destroy the fledgling Bolshevik movement whenever the chance arose.

Summer 1921

There was a short but spectacular "show trial." Aleksei was dragged, half-dead, from the newly created torture chambers of the Lubyanka prison. The prison was the rear wing of the now-defunct All-Russian Insurance Company, taken over by Feliks Dzerzhinsky, founder of the CHEKA. Yossef's grandfather had the dubious honor of being one of the Lubyanka's first victims, the first of hundreds of thousands.

In one spectacular session of the trial —and I shall never forget the majesty of human spirit that my young American friend displayed—Aleksei was confronted by Lenin himself and was offered amnesty if he would confess his misdeeds and renounce the Kronstadt rebellion. This was unheard of! The great Lenin himself offering mercy to an accused counter-revolutionary. Certainly even an idealistic young hothead like Aleksei Dubrov would jump at the chance to save his skin.

Aleksei electrified the audience, many of whom were foreign journalists, with his response. The journalists were invited to this particular session of the trial since it was a foregone conclusion by the CHEKA torturers that Aleksei was so far gone that he would accept the magnanimous offer of Lenin. Indeed, Aleksei even indicated that he would.

He did nothing of the sort. He denounced the Revolution as a sham. He denounced Lenin personally as being worse than the Tsar. I'll never forget, and I hope that young Yossef will burn this scene into his consciousness as I have, the terrible majesty of his grandfather as he stood, his hands chained, as he quoted foreign revolutionaries of long ago in another country—America's Tom Paine and Patrick Henry.

A bit dramatic perhaps, but the impact was electric. There were demonstrations in the streets of Moscow demanding Aleksei's release.

A week after the trial, Aleksei Dubrov was taken to the cellars of the Lubyanka where he was tortured beyond endurance. Lenin and Feliks Dzerzhinsky witnessed —and savored—every phase of the torture. Poor Papa had to stand by with injections to revive Aleksei in case he passed out from the pain.

Aleksei Dubrov was barely recognizable as a human being by the time of his execution. Papa, not a religious man by any means, prayed silently for Aleksei's death during this time. He was converted into a human vegetable by his torturers, unable to speak, hear, or see. He was paralyzed from the waist down. When he could no longer respond to the pain, his entertainment value was gone. He was shot in the nape of the neck, according to witnesses in an adjacent cell (who later escaped while being transferred to the Gulag), by Lenin himself.

Aleksei's body was buried in the dirt floor of the Lubyanka and cemented over. The strange and twisted logic of Vladimir Lenin demanded that the presence of the traitor, Aleksei Dubrov, the trusted American whom Lenin had accepted as a son, permeate the center of the prison. Even today, the molded and rotted remains of this early anti-Communist revolutionary lie buried under the concrete floors of Lubyanka.

April 1922 Lubyanka

Aleksei was executed on April 20, 1922, and his name was purged from all public records and newspaper references. He officially became a "nonperson."

His identity, however, would continue partly, in another form. At the time of the Kronstadt uprising, Natalya was four months pregnant with Georgi, Yossef's father.

Yossef stared numbly at the floor, fumbling to speak, the excerpt from the journal dangling from his fingertips.

"My grandfather must have been an iron man. He was so young to die. He was only twenty-seven." Yossef swallowed, the lump in his throat becoming an ache.

"In any other country, he would have become a martyr, perhaps even a great historical figure." Sophie spoke thoughtfully.

"You might say that he was the first Solidarity spokesman and activist in the Soviet Union," added Viktor. "The problem was that he was sixty-nine years ahead of his time."

Yossef turned the page of the single-spaced, officially typed MOSSAD report and continued reading.

1922
Gulag
Archi-
pelago

Georgi Dubrov, the father of Yossef Ayalon, was born August 12, 1921, on a prison train en route from Petrograd to a camp in the Gulag. Aleksei was told nothing of Natalya's pregnancy or the birth of his son. Natalya was in Moscow the months preceding her husband's revolutionary adventures. She was sent to the Gulag even before Aleksei's trial. She was automatically considered guilty by her aunt and uncle; such was Lenin's and Krupskya's wrath.

Natalya almost died in childbirth, but fellow prisoners tended to her and pulled her through.

The first ten years of young Georgi's life were years of incredible hardships and sufferings. Witnesses who knew Natalya told of her working in the forests in sub-zero temperatures, twelve hours a day, with little Georgi strapped to her back, wrapped in strips of old flannel. She was imprisoned in the Kolyma region, the largest and most terrible of the Stalin era's concentration-camp complexes, stretching a thousand miles from the Arctic Ocean to the Sea of Okhotsk. It was a place of horrible massacre, where three million died alongside of husky, well-fed guards.

1930s
Volga-Don
Canal

In the 1930s, when Georgi was only ten, he slaved beside his mother. By this time her beauty and vivaciousness had been torn from her by cruelty, disease, and overwork. She had turned into an old woman—digging the Volga Canal complex from the Dnieper to the Don. Millions

worked on the project as entire families
were conscripted to slave labor. Lenin, and
later Stalin, committed an entire genera-
tion to slavery in those days.

1935   Natalya died in 1935 when Georgi was
fourteen. She collapsed on the bank of a
ditch—one of the tributary canals. A
guard kicked her for at least two minutes,
cursing and trying to wake her. Young
Georgi attacked the guard with a shovel
and was beaten severely. He was sentenced to a penal battalion in Siberia—a
fourteen-year-old, working on one of the
Trans-Siberian Railroad's maintenance
crews, which were under the control of the
Red Army.

1941   In 1941, the Soviet Union was attacked
by the Hitlerite forces of Nazi Germany.
All available manpower was needed. Georgi volunteered for regular military service,
but was refused. Instead, he was assigned
to a special regiment of prisoners who
were given especially hazardous duty. Very
few soldiers survived units of this type.

Georgi distinguished himself in several
engagements and was cited several times
for bravery. His exploits were brought to
the attention of his corps commander, a
general who recognized the name of Dubrov, and had been in attendance at his
father's trial. He took pity on Georgi and
had him transferred to the regular army as
a medical aide. At the time, I was serving
as a combat physician with the Fourth
Guards Field Army and knew of Georgi, as
he worked at the regimental aide station. I
did not speak to him, or of him, since I was
fearful that it might endanger me. The
Communist system makes cowards of us
all!

1946   Georgi finished the war in that capacity

with honor and was pardoned by a general amnesty for political prisoners serving in the army in 1946.

The postwar years were years of growth for Georgi, and years of catching up. He had never lived as a free man before, as free as one can be in the Soviet Union, and compared to his previous existence, he was indeed—free.

1948
Tashkent

Under a government rehabilitation program, Georgi attended a school for former convicts and antisocials in Tashkent. He had never had a day of formal schooling in his life, for twenty-four years, but his mother had taught him everything she could. Those who knew them on the Don project told of an emaciated Natalya teaching Georgi how to write with a piece of broken glass on birchbark. How she loved the little fellow! How she must have grieved knowing that he would grow into, and die, a slave.

By the time Natalya died, he was reading at grade level (had he been in school) and knew mathematics and could recite entire sections of Pushkin and Tolstoy. Natalya had taught him well.

1950–
1954
Tashkent

By 1950, Georgi was eligible to take his examination for entrance into a teacher's college at Tashkent and, in 1954, was graduated. He was thirty-three at the time, the oldest member of his graduating class.

Samara
1955

Under the apparent thaw of Stalinism in the Khrushchev era, Georgi was making progress. By 1955 he had obtained a job teaching science and math in a secondary school in Samara.

In Russia, you cannot escape your name and your past completely. The name of Dubrov was remembered by some, especially in the KGB. Many petty harassments were inflicted on Georgi and made his life unpredictable and miserable. He knew that his life in the Soviet Union would forever be circumscribed, and there was enough of his father in him to fire a flame of rebellion.

1956   The watershed in Georgi's life came in 1956 when he was thirty-four. He married a fellow schoolteacher from Samara, a pretty blond-haired girl eight years his junior named Tanya Kaido. He and his wife were outspoken against the Soviet Union's crushing of the brief but gallant uprising of the Hungarian nation. Their activities after that were in the literary underground which was just forming in the Soviet Union during the early Khrushchev era.

Vorturka   Despite repeated warnings and arrest,
1961   the Dubrovs continued their activities and, in 1960, they were both sentenced to the slave-labor camp of Vorturka in the Gulag Archipelago. It was a sort of homecoming for Georgi. He and his mother had been there before.

Tanya was pregnant in 1960 and gave birth to twins in the . . .

Yossef stopped reading. He stared vacantly at his aunt and uncle.

"Good Lord! What kind of people were these Dubrovs? Didn't they know when to quit?" he exclaimed.

"I'm not sure I can read any more of this!" Tears of sympathy formed in Yossef's eyes and fell onto the paper.

"Read on, Yossef. It's your heritage," commanded Viktor.

    . . . in the middle of a howling blizzard in a woodcutter's shed outside the main camp. Even though pregnant, obviously with twins, Tanya was forced to work in fifty-below-zero weather until she collapsed. Yuri and Yossef, her twin boys, were wrapped in old newspapers and brought into the camp dispensary.

The Dubrovs had to make a painful decision. They arranged for Yossef to be smuggled out of the camp by a woman who was about to be released and allowed to emigrate to Israel. Her own baby had died but the death was not recorded. Yossef was brought to Israel in this manner.

"Just think: they could have chosen my brother to leave that camp. I wonder what strange twist of fate made them choose me to come to Israel," Yossef murmured absently.

Vorturka Rebellion '961   In 1961, a revolt of massive proportions broke out in Vorturka. It was well planned and coordinated, and the rebel prisoners broke into the guards' armory and turned their weapons against them. Many were killed, and the prisoners burned and dynamited the entire camp complex.

The Dubrovs, ringleaders in the uprising, were killed in the fighting. The captive prisoners were executed. The surviving children under five, however, were considered innocent, an enlightened attitude since Lenin's time and, in fact, the government sought to make "model" citizens of the survivors. Yuri was one of these, and at age fourteen months was sent to the Kiev State Orphanage for the Children of Deceased Military Heroes. His past was "destroyed," buried deep in the KGB archives, and a complete fabrication was created for his life story. He was given the name of Kiktev, the son of Major Anatoli Kiktev, an army officer killed in a commercial plane crash with his wife.

1975   It was well known that the children sent

to the KSO were programmed to be model Communists, and elite Party members were often the recipients of these children. In 1975, when Yuri was fourteen, he was adopted by Colonel Pavel Spinnenko, a chief of one of the major directorates of the KGB and considered a "rising star" by those who followed career paths of governmental officials.

It can be supposed that Yuri Spinnenko will someday assume a position of great responsibility and prestige in the Communist Party and Soviet government.

"Unless the name of Dubrov creeps out of the KGB files to haunt him," Yossef said thoughtfully.

IV.

The guided-missile cruiser *Liepaja* nosed its sharp gray hull out of the teeming water traffic of Haiphong Harbor. Little cargo lighters scampered like hyperactive waterbugs from the anchored warships and troop transports to the waterfront. The docks were crowded with other ships unloading the men and material of war—needed for the meatgrinder that was the second front of the Sino-Soviet conflict, the Vietnam-Yunnan theater of operations.

Captain Third Class Vaclav Suskov stood on the bridge watching the seagulls wheel and turn, looking for scraps of garbage in the green, oily waters.

Suskov was a third-generation naval officer. The men of the Suskov family had served in the naval branch for five generations. His grandfather was one of the original mutineers on the battleship *Potemkin* in 1905, one of the early Bolshevik organizers, and one of the few to escape the wrath of the Okhrana afterward. After the mutiny, his grandfather jumped ship and worked his way north to the Baltic fleet, where he re-enlisted under an assumed name and continued his subversive activities in the navy. The revolutionary credentials of Captain Suskov's family were impeccable.

The captain adjusted his visor, snugging his hat more securely as a slight, moisture-laden breeze whipped in from the seaward side of the harbor.

Suskov was a tall man, tall by Soviet standards: six feet two inches. His height gave him a commanding presence. Combined with his articulate Russian, slightly accented with a Latvian lilt (a gift from his Riga-born mother) it carried him far in the Soviet naval service. He often stood in sharp contrast to his shorter, more Slavic-looking colleagues in the staff meetings at Kaliningrad, headquarters of the Baltic fleet where the *Liepaja* was ported.

This had been Suskov's third voyage to Vietnam since the China War began. When Soviet troops became bogged down in North China the USSR began a second front in China's Yunnan province bordering North Vietnam. It was a stupid mistake, Suskov often thought: hundreds of thousands of young men thrashing around in the jungle, getting picked off by Chinese snipers or impaled on feces-smeared *punji* stakes. Hadn't Krylenko and company learned anything from America's involvement in this part of the world sixteen years before?

It was a logistical nightmare. The jungles of South China swallowed up men and equipment as fast as ships and planes could bring them in. All available transport was being commandeered for the war. His own vessel, a floating intercontinental ballistic missile, with a twenty-megaton warhead sequestered under its aft deck, was impressed into service carrying troops to Haiphong and wounded back to Leningrad. The dead were left to rot in the jungle.

* * *

The cruiser glided noiselessly past a rusting old transport, the *Osipenko,* a lend-lease American liberty ship lent to the Soviet Union in 1943. She was no stranger to these waters. She plied the gray, heavy seas between the Soviet Pacific port of Vladivostok and North Vietnam regularly, carrying troops from the eastern terminal of the Trans-Siberian Railroad to the South China front.

Vaclav Suskov felt a chill in his intestines and an angry tingling to his scalp as he passed the *Osipenko.* This was the transport which had carried his only son Boris to the jungles of Yunnan six months ago.

Somewhere—several hundred miles north of Hanoi —Boris Suskov, conscripted out of the security of his studies at the University of Leningrad, was hacking his way through the bamboo thickets of Yunnan with his patrol.

His name was #117 on the Solidarity-suspect death list attached to the operational orders of his commander.

Even though her eyes were closed, Raisa Karezev could feel the stares: the dozens of eyes probing her tawny, muscular body. The Crimean sun was hot in early March and the coarse sand of the Black Sea beach of Alupka could be felt beneath her thick towel, but this was the place to be, not in the wintry blasts of Moscow.

A young man, obviously a college student, jogged along the beach. His eyes scanned the sunning vacationers and fixed on the tanned body in the red-and-white-striped bikini. He whistled softly in appreciation and wheeled from the water's edge toward the attractive computer technician.

Raisa squinted at the jogger, an annoyed frown knitting her smooth brow. She fluffed her short brown hair unconsciously as she rehearsed a rejection of what she knew would be an offer of a date. She took her two-weeks vacation to relax—to decompress—not to get involved with men. She had all of that she wanted in Moscow.

The young man jogged past her, his eyes glancing briefly at her tanned slightly freckled cleavage. Raisa tugged self-consciously at her bikini bra.

"Well, he's gone," she thought. She pulled her sunglasses down on her nose, took the instruction manual for the new Swedish BESO 100 computer out of her straw carrying bag, and flipped through the pages.

"I see that you're into computers." The voice was boyish and unsure. Raisa felt his presence suddenly as he flopped onto the sand beside her.

"Do you always sneak up on people from the rear?" she scolded, annoyance wrinkling her pert nose.

He smiled broadly, almost bravely, trying to project a confident demeanor.

A slight smile flickered across Raisa's face. He was trying too hard. He couldn't have been more than twenty-one. She attracted younger men. Although twenty-six, she had the pixie face of a young girl. Her girlish looks were somewhat offset by her large, well-formed breasts and voluptuous body. She had her hair cut short and plucked her eyebrows to give her a more mature and a more professional look. It didn't work. She still looked like a college girl.

"I'm sorry." His broad smile changed to a sheepish grin. "I saw that circuit diagram of the BESO 100. It caught my eye."

"That's *all* that caught your eye?" Raisa smiled mischievously.

"Well, no. I could see your red and white bathing suit a half a mile away. There's not another like it on the beach."

"Are you into computers?" Raisa changed the subject, a slight smile tugging at the corners of her lips.

"Yes," the young man answered, his eyes locked into Raisa's large, green eyes. "I'm a third-year computer-science student at the Tiflis Technical Institute."

"Aha! That's why you're not in China," added Raisa sarcastically. "You're in a 'critical field'. Stay with it and keep your grades up."

The jogger glanced furtively around the beach, and then looked directly at Raisa.

"The red fox has re-entered the chicken coop." He whispered, his eyes pleading for confirmation.

Raisa drew in her breath involuntarily, her mind scrambling for the proper response to the coded message.

"And the chickens are now laying speckled eggs with double yolks," she whispered cautiously.

There was silence between them for a short interval, their eyes studying each other's faces. Finally, Raisa broke it. "Where is he?"

"In Feodosiya. Here is his address. He is expecting you tonight. Nine o'clock sharp." The young jogger handed her a folded piece of paper.

"How—how did he know I'd be here?" asked Raisa.

"Solidarity knows everything, Raisa Karezev." The young man's countenance changed—becoming more businesslike.

"Nine o'clock sharp. Be there, Raisa."

He stood abruptly, flashed her a quick smile, and jogged away, disappearing down the beach.

Raisa threaded her rented Muskvich through the narrow, cobblestoned streets of the seaside resort village of Feodosiya. There it was, number thirty-five Vilnoya Street. The second floor was dark.

She parked a block and a half away and walked briskly back to the apartment. It was an old half-timbered building with a pastel yellow stuccoed second story, typical of the nineteenth-century houses on the Black Sea coast.

Raisa entered the darkened stairway cautiously. It had a closed, musty-salty smell—an odor like a storage closet for fishing nets.

Slowly she climbed the stairs and, when reaching the landing, walked to the first door on her right. Her hand trembled slightly as it paused to knock once—then three knocks—a pause—and three more.

The door opened. A voice whispered from the darkened interior.

"Raisa?"

"Yes. It's Raisa Karezev." She whispered hoarsely, fear welling in her throat. She could barely hear her voice over her pounding heart.

She slipped in and grabbed the man in the apartment, encircling his waist with her strong, tan arms, kissing his cheek.

"Ah, little swallow. How I've missed you! Only thoughts of you have kept me going." He murmured gently against her neck.

Raisa slipped her hand behind his neck and pulled his face down to hers, kissing him fully, passionately, on the lips.

"Vasily, Vasily, how I've needed you. All of us have needed you. It's gotten so dangerous. The KGB has increased its surveillance and its raids. Nobody's safe anymore."

Vasily Gregierenko bolted the door and led Raisa to a small, floral-patterned couch near the living-room window overlooking the darkened street. Raisa sat against him, fitting her body to his. She studied his brooding face in the faint light of the half-moon. She noticed his saddened countenance. Vasily always looked sad, she reflected. He was a man of constant sorrow. He seldom smiled—even before he'd fled the Soviet Union and gone to Israel. The life of a Solidarity leader and the threat of sudden death constantly hanging over him had changed him. When Raisa had met him three years ago he was a quiet, meditative man—an optimistic man. He would laugh. Now, laughter and gaiety were foreign to Vasily Gregierenko. Solidarity was his life—his obsession. Everything and everybody occupied a lower priority.

"How long will you be in Russia, Vasily?" Raisa asked almost fearfully, her finger stroking his cheek.

"Until I've arranged for the details of our next operation," he answered slowly. His eyes, staring at her, were slightly out of focus.

"What is it?" Raisa asked.

"Ah!" A strange smile twisted across Gregierenko's sunken cheeks. "I can't tell you, little swallow, but it's big—very big. It's in the planning stage right now. At least, we're studying the feasibility of the operation. I can tell you that if what we are dreaming right now can be accomplished, it will give us everything we want."

"What *do* we want, Vasily? I talk to you, and you mention one set of goals. I talk to another section leader and he says something else. Solidarity means different things to different members. We have yet to come up with a unified set of goals."

Gregierenko nodded, agreeing. "All of that will change, dear Raisa. Operation Samson will create conditions in this country which will cause the gerontocracy to defecate in their trousers. Solidarity will unite behind Samson."

"Operation Samson?" Raisa's pug, slightly freckled nose wrinkled. "Wasn't Samson the Biblical character who pulled the Philistine temple down upon his enemies and himself?"

Gregierenko brightened. "Aha! You've caught the vision, little swallow. Yes. That's what Operation Samson is all about: pulling the temple of the gerontocracy down upon them. I hope we can escape before it comes crashing down upon ourselves."

Raisa studied him, her eyes narrowing in analysis.

"You went to a great deal of trouble to find out I was down here. I didn't exactly advertise my vacation plans." She sighed wearily, almost in resignation. "Vasily—What do you want of me?"

Gregierenko reached over and encircled her waist with his left hand as he nibbled on her earlobe, his mood becoming playful.

"What do I usually want of you, dear Raisa? I want your love and your warmth. I need you, Raisa. My thoughts of you have kept me going all these months."

Raisa responded less than enthusiastically. Vasily's voice had a hollow, mechanical ring to it. Her feelings toward the Solidarity leader, twelve years her senior, always swung from profound respect and awe for his mission to feelings bordering on what she thought was love. Certainly they had made love before, as they would do now, but Vasily made love like a man who expected the KGB to break down the door at any moment. During their lovemaking, Raisa would half expect him to check his wristwatch periodically.

"What I meant, Vasily, was—what do you want *me* to do in regards to this—this Operation Samson?" She pulled away and looked directly at him. "That's why I'm here, isn't it? Making love can wait until later. Let's discuss this operation *now*."

Gregierenko sighed and leaned back, releasing her.

"I'd be in a much better mood to discuss it after . . ."

"Now!" demanded Raisa, playfully poking her finger into his midsection. "If you want it—you have to sing for it."

Vasily threw back his head and laughed loudly. It warmed Raisa to hear him laugh so spontaneously.

"All right, little swallow. You win. Your job is simple. I want you to find out everything you can about the security system surrounding Lenin's Tomb."

Raisa stiffened as if jolted by an electric shock.

"Lenin's tomb? "You—you wouldn't *dare,* Vasily!" she gasped. "Not even Solidarity could get away with *that.* The Soviet people would—"

Gregierenko put his finger to her trembling lips.

"Ah, even you revere the Temple of the State, Raisa. You, like millions of our blind citizens, have been victimized by that monster in his hideous mausoleum on Red Square. We're all caught up in a form of idolatry that has been perpetrated by the gerontocracy."

Raisa breathed deeply, her breasts heaving, as she tried to compose herself. Shuddering slightly, she paused and marshaled her thoughts.

"Vasily, I am willing to do many things, you know that. I'm as committed to the Movement as the next person but—but an assault on Lenin's Tomb!" She stood, her heaving chest silhouetted against the pale moonlight.

"Who said anything about an assault?" Gregierenko gave her an appraising glance.

"Well, what then?" Raisa sat back down beside him, her voice now a conspiratorial whisper.

"I'm not at liberty to tell you just yet. Will you get the information for me?"

"I'll try." She exhaled a weary breath.

"That's better, little swallow. There's no great hurry. In about a month." He kissed her on the corner of the mouth as he unbuttoned her blouse.

Minutes later, Vasily Gregierenko was making love in the hurried, mechanical manner of a man possessed.

The Kremlin is a huge, triangular compound, the apex of which is dominated by the Sobakin Tower pointing due north. All of the ancient fortress's sides—and that's what the Kremlin is, the fortress of the old city of Moscow —are protected by a fifty-foot crenelated wall studded with eighteen towers and penetrated by four gates.

The southern two-thirds of the Kremlin triangle is the tourist area, separated from the northern section by a cleared area of tarmacadam that is constantly patrolled by security troops. The north apex is closed to tourists and ordinary Soviet citizens. Indeed, the Upper Arsenal Building is one of the most heavily guarded and most secure buildings in the world. It is in this building, on the third floor, that the Politburo, the real power group in the USSR, meets.

Yuri Spinnenko marched smartly between the two troopers of the Kremlin Guards. It had been a thirty-minute wait outside the guard shed on the Kuibyshev Street entrance opposite the Spasskaya Tower gate in the Kremlin wall while his appointment was being confirmed. It wasn't every day that a sergeant of the Border Guards had a meeting with Premier Krylenko.

Yuri's uncle, General Spinnenko, had arranged the meeting. It had a dual purpose: to interview Yuri as a candidate guard of Lenin's Tomb, and to give the Premier and selected members of the Politburo a "common soldier's" view of the China war. Yuri Spinnenko, the very epitome of the "New Communist Man," could not help but impress the Politburo.

The Upper Arsenal Building is a hollow rectangle. Inside is a narrow courtyard running north and south and dividing the complex into two even narrower blocks of apartments and offices. There are four stories, including the attics. Halfway up the inner, eastern office block on the third floor, overlooking the cobblestoned courtyard and screened from prying eyes, is the room where the Politburo meets every Thursday morning.

Yuri Spinnenko swallowed hard, desperately wishing for a drink of water to quench the dryness in his mouth that might prevent him from giving his presentation in his most articulate manner. He swore silently to himself as he felt a slight pressure on his bladder. Damn, he thought. I should have taken a piss before surrendering my appointment card to the guards. Perhaps I could talk them into letting me relieve myself. He cast sidelong glances at the stern-faced guards flanking him. There was no way.

Their footsteps thudded in a hobnailed chorus on the three flights of stairs in the Upper Arsenal Building. They were stopped by two other guards bearing assault rifles outside the Premier's office. Credentials were examined and Yuri underwent his second body search in an hour. A guard knocked on the door.

"What is it?" bellowed an annoyed voice, followed by the hoarse rasp of a cigarette cough.

"Comrade Premier," the guard said softly, almost apologetically, "your eleven o'clock appointment is here. Sergeant Yuri Spinnenko of the Border Guards."

The escort guard knew that Yuri would have to wait at least ten minutes: time for the Premier and his cronies to get fully clothed—and time for the young student nurses from the University of Moscow to make a quiet exit from the courtyard stairway.

Yuri continued to wait, nervously arching the soles of his feet in his glistening combat boots. The guards gave each other knowing looks.

"Bring the sergeant in," bellowed the rasp voice, finally.

A guard opened the door and ushered Yuri into a darkly paneled room smelling of medication and vodka. Seated behind a large, ornate desk was Igor Krylenko, a toad of a man with unruly, dirty-gray hair and bushy eyebrows which converged on a pug nose. Standing to his right, pouring a tumbler full of vodka, was Pyotr Blinov, Chief Director of the KGB. Blinov was a tall, angular, and evil-looking man with a mouth full of teeth capped in stainless steel and a bald patch on the crown of his head which was the same size and shape as an orthodox Jew's *yarmulke*. Yuri noticed that he was slightly inebriated and that his fly was only half-zippered.

"Comrade Premier. Comrade Director. Junior Sergeant Yuri Spinnenko reporting as ordered." Yuri clicked his heels and saluted sharply, his right hand vibrating slightly as he held it to his hat visor. Krylenko touched an age-spotted, blue-veined hand to his eyebrow in return. He gestured to a chair opposite the desk.

"So you're Pavel's nephew, eh, Sergeant?" slurred the Premier, belching slightly.

"Yes, Comrade Premier," replied Yuri pleasantly, sitting stiffly in the high-backed chair.

The KGB director walked around the desk and sat on its corner. He took out an aluminum cigarette case and offered a papirosa to Yuri.

"No, thank you, Comrade Director. I don't use them," replied Yuri to the gesture.

Blinov's pale blue eyes probed into Yuri's. They were cold and without expression.

"Sergeant Spinnenko. Why do you want to be a Tomb Guard? A soldier with your background and connections usually is interested in officer cadet school. How do you see a tour of duty with the Kremlin Guards as enhancing your career plans?"

Yuri swallowed hard. He'd anticipated this question and had rehearsed the answer several times. Now it seemed as if the words were frozen in his throat. He coughed gently.

"Comrade Premier. Comrade Director. I owe everything I have and everything I am to the State. To me, the symbol of the State is Comrade Lenin. He is the one person who has given our nation its life, its purpose and direction. I feel that the spirit of Comrade Lenin is the soul of the Motherland. I have partaken of the gifts of Comrade Lenin all of my life and have received personal meaning and guidance from his historical example. By serving, even briefly, as his personal guard, it would be my way of saying 'Thank you, Comrade Lenin.' "

Blinov's thin bloodless lips curled into a wry smile. He clapped his hands in mock applause, his inebriated eyes slightly out of focus as they stared at Yuri with amusement.

"Oh, well done, Sergeant Spinnenko. That's what we want—true believers, isn't it?" He turned to Krylenko with a sneer. He turned and leaned toward Yuri, his alcoholic breath assaulting Yuri's nostrils and his eyes now twinkling with an evil humor.

"Tell me, Comrade Spinnenko . . ." he slurred the words mockingly. "If you were on guard and somebody tried to assault the body of Lenin—let's say they tried to smash the protective glass with a sledgehammer—would you be willing to die protecting him? He's only a corpse, you know."

Yuri's mind reeled under the question. He couldn't believe what he was hearing! Not even the Director of the KGB had the right to make such irreverent remarks. Fear and anger welled up inside him. He was being mocked! Made fun of. They were toying with him. His mind fumbled for an answer.

This was a test: some kind of an absurd test. It had to be. People of the caliber of the Premier and the Director would never make such disparaging remarks about the sacred body of Lenin.

"I would assume, Comrade Director," replied Yuri cautiously, "that I would be expected to die, if necessary, in carrying out my mission." He looked directly into the Director's eyes and added, "Every Soviet citizen must be prepared to sacrifice his or her life in carrying out his duties on behalf of the Motherland."

Blinov blinked in surprise and stared into the wide blue innocence of Yuri's eyes. Was it possible that the system actually produced a few sincere true believers along with the usual opportunistic sycophants?

Blinov's cynicism abated. Yuri Spinnenko was as close to the new Soviet man as the system could produce. Suddenly, the Director felt ashamed of his cynical assault on his colleague's nephew.

"Comrade Spinnenko." Blinov's tone became respectful. "We are most anxious to hear of your views on the China War. Please join us in the conference room. The members of the Politburo will be joining us shortly."

Yuri felt hollow and drained as he marched across the Kremlin courtyard between the two guards. There was a metallic taste in his dry mouth; he fought the fatigue which assaulted him.

His presentation had gone well—he was sure of that. He'd been extremely precise, articulate, and he'd answered all questions without hesitation.

What he hadn't been prepared for—and Uncle Pavel

should have warned him—was the extreme age of the Politburo. They were so old—so feeble—so out of touch with the realities of the war and the feelings of the common soldier. Even Yuri, a junior sergeant, could see that. Many of the Politburo members had stumbled into the conference room with canes; two hobbled in using walkers. It appeared that old Spasinov, the Minister of Communications, was half-dead as they brought him in in his wheelchair. The vodka had flowed freely as the Politburo members asked their senile and asinine questions.

Yuri had expected this encounter in the sacrosanct Upper Arsenal Room to be akin to a spiritual experience: the ardent disciple reporting to the master. It wasn't. But it *was* a devastating revelation—that those who made policy at the highest level were far from infallible. The comments that Uncle Pavel had made from time to time—usually after half a bottle of vodka—were confirmed by Yuri's experience in the Politburo meeting room. Pavel Spinnenko had often used the pejorative "gerontocracy," followed by such adjectives as "self-serving" and "venal." Now Yuri knew what he meant. Only the presence of Comrade Lenin remained unsullied. If accepted as a Kremlin Tomb Guard, he would seek solace from the shining example of Vladimir Lenin.

As Yuri's hobnailed boots thudded across the courtyard toward the Kuibyshev Street exit, he felt an emotion which had been foreign to him—an emotion directed toward the very ruling body of the Soviet state—and it frightened him: alienation.

V.

Yossef tried to control his feelings, a mixture of numbing fear and anger, as he read the Order of Battle report.

"It's all there, Yossef," said the tall, blond major, who looked more like a Scandinavian tourist than an officer in the SHINBET, Israel's military intelligence agency. Yabin hovered in the background, shuffling through the latest batch of photographs taken by Israeli reconnaissance planes.

"If that report isn't enough to convince you, Yossef, take a look at these," offered Yabin. "They show the missile emplacements and the armor being moved up on three fronts: the Sinai, the Golan, and near the West Bank. The tanks are equipped to operate in a nuclear-chemical environment and the divisions facing us have all had intensive training in that sort of combat. There's no doubt, my friend. Our Arab neighbors are finally going to launch their *jihad,* their Holy War, and the Soviet Union has given them the tools."

Yossef stared out the window, through the forest of antennas that covered the headquarters building of SHINBET, toward the ageless hills of Judea, his beloved Judea, which would soon be lifeless heaps of sand if the SHINBET/MOSSAD estimates were correct.

"It's just a matter of time, Yossef," the major said softly, his face expressionless.

There was a watery glimmer in Yossef's wide, blue eyes as he glanced down at the paper in his trembling hands. He slipped it carefully back into its envelope with the broken red seal and the words *SODI BEYOTER*—"Ultra-

Confidential"—printed on it.

"The fate of *Eretz* Israel depends on you, Yossef. It's an unfair responsibility, but the fates have cast you for the part." Yabin spoke sympathetically.

Eretz Israel! The Biblical Land of Israel which God had promised the ancient Jews, not the truncated little nation Ben Gurion had accepted as a crumb from the world's table in 1946. All of this would be gone forever if Yossef refused.

Yossef continued to stare out the window, his shaking hands fumbling for a cigarette.

"Does Yuri smoke?" he asked.

"No," answered Yabin.

"Shit!" blurted Yossef. "That means *I* have to give it up, right?"

"Yes it does, and the sooner you start to taper off, the better," advised the major.

Yossef seemed to shrink under the impact of their words as he took a slow meditative drag from his Europa.

He knew that if he accepted the assignment, now being pushed upon him by his country, it would most likely end in his death. The chances of Operation Samson succeeding were miniscule. He would be sacrificing his life for the slim chance that Israel could buy time from destruction.

Eretz Israel! The Biblical Land of Israel which God had promised his forefathers. Whose forefathers? Certainly not his. He was pure Russian—Great European Russian at that—and American. What did he really owe Israel, the country which had deceived him since childhood and programmed and prepared him for a suicide mission? His *real* roots, his *real* heritage, were in the Soviet Union.

But his heart was in Shareem—in the sacred myths and traditions of his country. All of what he knew and loved would be smashed—gone forever if he refused. Yossef's breath was coming in shortening bursts. An oily slick of nervous sweat began to streak his temples.

"Yossef, are you all right?" Yabin clapped a concerned hand on his shoulder.

Yossef's lower jaw trembled slightly as he tried unsuccessfully to give voice to the words fear had trapped in his throat.

"I—I don't—know if I have the courage for this. I'll—I'll fail and simply give the Soviets an excuse to intervene directly instead of using their Arab proxies. Have you thought of that, Yabin?" Yossef turned in his chair and looked at the MOSSAD colonel with wild hope.

"You act as if we have a choice, my young friend." Yabin's answering voice was deep and controlled. "You've seen the evidence of the military phase of the Arab jihad. Let me show you the pacification phase."

"The—the what?"

"The pacification phase," the SHINBET major interrupted. "In other words, Arab-Soviet plans for the remainder of our people who are not annihilated in the nuclear-chemical onslaught."

Yossef scanned the MOSSAD translation of the pilfered Arab documents. He shuddered slightly as he read the words—the same kind of bureaucratic jargon used by Adolph Eichmann to describe the destruction of European Jews during the Nazi era: transport to final disposition, termination—a final solution for survivors.

Yossef could almost smell the fear and anger oozing from him like some putrid secretion.

"This is the Holocaust all over again!" Rage escaped Yossef like steam hissing from a ruptured pipe. "This must not be permitted to happen!" Tears of anger flowed down his cheeks.

"That depends entirely on you. We don't have the right to demand such a superhuman task of just *anybody,* but the fate of Israel is, or will be, completely in your hands. There isn't anybody else. That sounds terribly dramatic, I know, but the gods—or perhaps God, I don't know—has cast you in this role. I'm—I'm not a very religious man, Yossef, but I believe that you can be the literal savior of our country," said Yabin.

"I don't want to be a savior!" Yossef shot back. He rubbed his temples, now pounding with a migraine. "I need—I need a few days to think about this," he stammered.

The major and Yabin exchanged worried glances.

Yossef began to breathe deeply and methodically, and

twisted his cigarette stub almost ritualistically in the ashtray.

"Well goodbye, old friend. I'll have to get along without you until this is all over."

Yabin breathed a sigh of relief. "When can we get started on the—"

Angrily, Yossef lurched to his feet.

"I said—I need—a few days—and I will have them!" An understated sense of menace seeped into his voice.

Yabin swallowed, nodding his approval. "Very well, Yossef. Where will you be?"

"In the Negev—near Shareem."

Yossef had always loved the desert. Even as a boy the sands and hills of the Negev had offered him an escape into its solitude. It had always been a place he could retreat to and find a oneness with the universe. The emptiness of these expanses stripped life to its fundamentals. The desert was the incubator of the spiritual. Its unhuman solitude had often been the catalyst that drove men to extremes and caused them to seek answers to life's titanic questions.

Yossef sat on the rocky slopes of Mount Ramon just as the sun, now a blood-red orb, was sinking in the western Sinai. Somewhere beyond the sand dunes of the west, the armed might of the Fundamentalist Islamic Republic of Egypt was massing with awesome new weapons poised to destroy some three thousand years of his country's history and culture.

It was so damned unfair! Why should such a burden fall upon him? His country hadn't prepared him, emotionally or spiritually, for such a mission. He wasn't made of the stuff that saviors are made of, and yet that was exactly what he was expected to be.

If it wasn't for that damned Yuri! The MOSSAD was delighted, he had been told by Yabin, when they learned that they had the identical twin of a child assigned to the elite Kiev State Orphanage. Someday, they knew, Yuri Dubrov would assume a high position in his country's government. As he grew into manhood, the MOSSAD kept track of Yuri's education and training and tried, as far as practicable, to duplicate it in Yossef's upbringing. Someday, somehow, Yossef Ayalon would replace his twin brother in the Soviet government.

But Yuri was a disappointment to MOSSAD. He wasn't an opportunistic, self-serving nachalstvo. He was a "true-believer," a dedicated New Soviet Man. He could not be bribed with Jewish gold. He was a serving citizen, not a special citizen, and refused to take advantage of the many privileges offered him. It was unheard of for a product of the Kiev State Orphanage to serve in the enlisted ranks. But Yuri believed that if one were true to the pure teachings of Comrade Lenin, one must serve as a common soldier.

At age thirty-one, Yuri Spinnenko should have reached Yossef's position in his government—that of a middle-management executive. But Yuri would have none of that until certain obligations to the State were paid.

Yossef watched the rushing dusk from his rocky vantage point and silently cursed Yuri's single-minded dedication. Why in the hell did he have to choose to be a guard at Lenin's Tomb at this stage of his career?

Lenin's body: the holy of holies of the Communist empire; the Communist Ka'aba in a Marxist mosque; the mystical glue which kept the faltering Soviet system together. Lenin! The new religious icon for millions deprived of things spiritual. It was well known that as repression revived in the Soviet Union because of Solidarity, the lines of visitors to the Tomb grew apace. It was the one symbol of the Communist world which still had meaning and credibility for the average Soviet citizen. At the Tomb, at any hour of the day or night, one could see the long lines and the sad shuffling feet of the Russian people filing by the "Little Father" as he lay lifelike in his glass-enclosed coffin. The faithful would sometimes pause and communicate quietly with the corpse. He had been elevated to the status of a demigod in recent months. He had become a father-confessor; the faithful could pour out their feelings and frustrations to Vladimir Lenin. Many repeated the process weekly as a near-religious ritual.

At each end of the coffin a member of the Tomb Guard stood stiffly, his head bowed in a rigid position, staring reverently at Comrade Lenin.

A cold sweat broke out on Yossef's forehead as the faint suggestion of a breeze blew off the desert floor. Instinctively he reached for his pack of Europas in his left breast pocket. They were gone! The one little crutch that would help him endure the unendurable had been stripped from him. Right now, his Communist-pure, nonsmoking twin brother was probably standing reverently at the feet of the son of a bitch who'd murdered their grandfather and sent their infant father into the hell of exile.

Yossef leaned back on a large rock and stared into the diamond-studded night sky. The near-hypnotic effect of the sky's brilliance helped create the fantasy that Yossef was spinning.

Yossef was a guard, staring into the dead, arrogant face of Vladimir Lenin—the tormentor of the Dubrov family and the bastard responsible for the horrors that now awaited him as the main actor in Operation Samson.

In one deft movement in his fantasy, Yossef raised his automatic rifle and sprayed the shuffling lines of believers, spewing bullets into their stupid, reverent faces. He raised his rifle high above the glass case and smashed it downward, shattering it completely. The pungent, putrid odor of the dead Lenin escaped like gas from a bloated carcass. Yossef raised his bayonetted rifle and plunged it into Lenin's tunic-clad chest. A green gas hissed from the wound. In a frenzy, Yossef bayonetted the body again and again until it was lacerated beyond recognition, the green, malodorous gas now filling the tomb.

Suddenly, as if propelled by an unseen hand, Yossef lurched to his feet, almost losing his balance on the rocky slope. He raised his fists to the sky and shook them, screaming and sobbing uncontrollably.

"Damn you, Vladimir Lenin! Damn you, Yuri Dubrov! May your black souls rot in hell!"

While the subway system in Moscow was among the most modern in the world, the municipal sewer system was among the most ancient and decrepit. Some sections of the cavernous sewers built during the time of Peter the Great were still used.

Maintenance crews constantly prowled the miles of sewer tunnels like small packs of rats, plugging leaks, replacing the bricks that fell from the walls and arches, and welding pipes. Moscow desperately needed a new sewer system, but the municipal government refused to spend the money. After all, a sewer system can't be seen and admired the way a subway can. A new and shining subway had propaganda value, and so the old sewer system of Moscow remained run-down and unappreciated.

Unappreciated—except for the three-man Solidarity assassination team which sloshed along the main sewer tunnel under the sidewalks in front of the GUM department store.

Yevgeny Belov stopped at the tributary tunnel marked in chipped white paint.

"Here it is, lads. Number seven." He traced the faded number with the slim beam of his flashlight. "I can barely make it out, but this leads directly to the blind manhole."

Belov mounted a shallow set of slime-covered steps and shone his light down the stinking, dripping tunnel that ran directly under Red Square from GUM to the Kremlin.

"The tunnel's blocked off just before it enters the Kremlin," whispered Belov. "The two manholes which served this tributary are blind; sealed and tarred over. The gerontocracy didn't want any blemishes in the beauty of Red Square, so they erased all signs of them."

"They treat manholes just like they treat some of us." A short, balding member of the team spoke acidly. "They've obliterated them and redesignated them as non-manholes."

"Cut the chattering and wheel the explosives down here. Andrei, bring the ladder and keep it quiet. They can hear us up on the Square if we make a racket," cautioned Belov.

The assassination team probed the tributary tunnel until they came to a cylindrical concrete upright which reached the roof.

"There it is—up there." Belov swung his light in a

circular pattern, tracing the manhole cover. "Viktor. Andrei. Bring the charge over here."

"Piss up a rope! How much did we bring?" panted the balding Viktor.

"Two hundred and fifty pounds of Nippolite," answered the leader. "So handle it carefully or we'll be launched into orbit."

A grim chuckle escaped the throat of the lanky Andrei as he wheeled the explosives, packed in an oil drum, directly under the manhole cover. The edge of the drum was slightly larger than the lip of the sewer opening.

"Now the trick is, lads, to place the drum this side up"—he patted the yellow painted top—"flush with the cover. We'll use these two-by-fours and the ladder to support the drum. It should hold."

The team struggled with the drum until it was emplaced snugly against the manhole. Several two-by-fours were wedged between the drum's bottom and the tunnel floor. Suddenly, the street overhead rumbled slightly, vibrating the manhole cover. The supports held.

"Heavy truck—directly overhead. Good test," murmured the leader. "It'll hold until Tuesday."

"Two hundred and fifty pounds," exclaimed Viktor. "That'll take out half of Red Square."

"Not so," responded Belov. "This is a shaped charge. Nippolite's a new Swedish explosive—probably the most powerful non-nuclear stuff available. It has unusual properties. This stuff has been molded into a large cone. The force of the blast will be concentrated upward—through the manhole. Actually, very little of the surrounding square will be damaged."

"But why so much?" inquired Andrei.

"What we'll be blowing up is an eight-ton armored Chaika. Blinov's limousine is one of the heaviest in the country. It's built to withstand land mines. This fellow," Belov patted the ladder, "will put the bastard into orbit. What we'll see from the top of GUM will be similar to the launching of a cosmonaut. That's why we're going to call this 'Operation Soyuz 12' in our propaganda."

"If Kovhar loses his nerve on Tuesday, the whole damned project will be one big sweat for nothing." Viktor panted as he sloshed back toward the main tunnel behind the others.

"Anatoly Kovhar is the key. All we can do is go by what Gregierenko told us about him. If he does his part, we launch Blinov into orbit. If he freezes, we abort the mission."

Belov paused where the tributary entered the main tunnel and peered in both directions.

"Clear," he advised. "Let's go."

Anatoly Kovhar looked much older than his fifty-five years. The Comrade Chief Director of the KGB had commented, several times during the past month, at how poorly he looked and inquired after his health. Anatoly would politely brush aside Director Blinov's inquiries with humor.

"Too much nightlife, Comrade Director. Since Anna passed away I've been cavorting with the student nurses from the University. They can drain an old man like me of my energy." Kovhar would wink. That response never failed to send Blinov into spasms of wheezy laughter.

Kovhar was more than Blinov's trusted personal chauffeur. He knew all of the personal perversions of the gerontocracy and winked at them. Kovhar always had an appropriate joke at his tongue's tip. Blinov and the other Soviet leaders felt comfortable—and safe—around the jovial Kovhar. He was one of the family.

But Anatoly Kovhar was an extremely dangerous man. He was a man with nothing left to lose. Anybody with nothing left to lose in the Soviet Union was one who could not be controlled—and that made them dangerous.

In the incredibly short span of eight months, Anatoly's life had crumbled around him. His beloved Anna, his wife of thirty-five years, had died an excruciatingly slow death from cancer of the intestines. Seven months before, Anatoly Kovhar had received word that his only child, Sergei, had been killed in the China War—a Solidarity suspect sent to his death. The record of his involvement with Solidarity had been eliminated from the KGB computer tapes—thanks to Raisa Karezev.

Kovhar held open the door of the massive Chaika as Blinov and two heavily overcoated men emerged from the Dzerzhinsky Square complex. A sudden wave of pain and fatigue assaulted Anatoly as he slammed the door. It was a constant reminder of his own secret affliction—multiple myeloma, cancer of the marrow of the bone, which would take his life in three weeks to a month. Yes, Anatoly Kovhar was a man with nothing to lose.

He struggled to place the identities of the two strangers with Director Blinov. Yes, he knew who they were now. The names escaped him but one was the Chief of the AVH, Hungary's dreaded secret police, and the other was a Czech general in charge of training foreign terrorists.

"A trio of bastards!" Kovhar mused as he started the car. "Solidarity gets three for the price of one." He chuckled to himself.

"Where to, Comrade Director?" Kovhar asked pleasantly.

"Upper Arsenal Building," Blinov said absently, fumbling through the open briefcase on his lap.

A chill, early March wind swept across Red Square as the Chaika entered the Square's wide expanse from Karl Marx Prospekt.

"There it is, Yevgeny! Right on time! Yes—Yes! That's it. Right on time! He's heading for the drum!" exclaimed Viktor.

The three-man team was perched on the roof of the GUM department store and had a clear view of the Square. Belov held a small electronic transmitter in his hand, his thumb poised above the button. Inside the drum, several hundred meters away under the tarmacadam of Red Square, the receiving mechanism waited for the signal which would obliterate Blinov, the most feared and hated man in the Soviet Union.

"After this, the Soviet people will pay a terrible price, Yevgeny. The repression will be ferocious," his partner said.

"That's what we want." Belov responded grimly, his jaw set. "Repression—and lots of it—nationwide. Repression will be the refiner's fire which will prepare our people for Operation Samson. Be alert, lads! Here they come!"

"Anatoly. I said the Upper Arsenal Building. Why are you heading for the Nikolskaya Tower Gate?" asked Blinov.

"They're replacing the cobblestones in the street, Comrade Blinov. It's all torn up. I'll head down Red Square to the Oruzheina Palata entrance and turn in there."

Blinov frowned suspiciously. He hadn't heard of any such project in the Kremlin. Security would have reported such an activity directly to him.

Kovhar decreased the speed to under fifteen kilometers per hour as he nosed the heavy Chaika along the solid yellow line, straddling it. He squinted through eyes glazed by his pain medication and looked for a break in the line—that section painted black that marked the location of the blind manhole cover.

Blinov instinctively knew that something was terribly wrong. He could recognize the smell of fear as a male dog can smell a bitch in heat. He had smelled it a thousand times in the interrogation cellars of the Lubyanka. He looked at the back of his chauffeur's neck. It glistened with perspiration. His shirt and jacket collar were soaked with it.

The Chaika braked to a gentle stop, the center of the vehicle positioned directly over the manhole.

"Kovhar! Kovhar! Get moving! What's wrong with you, man?" shouted the Director.

Anatoly Kovhar breathed deeply and rested his head on the steering wheel and mumbled slightly, a peaceful smile curling his lips.

"Kovhar! Kovhar! Get going, damn you!" Blinov whipped out his automatic and jabbed it into his driver's neck. The two passengers were frantically yanking on the door handles, trying to get out. They were useless. Kovhar had seen to that.

The last words that Blinov heard were the death prayer of Anatoly Kovhar, who had been a secret member of

Russia's burgeoning Christian underground for over three years.

As thousands of workers from the stores and offices flanking Red Square poured onto the sidewalks for their ten-o'clock break, Yevgeny Belov pressed the signal button.

An unearthly roar shook the center of the city. The entire Square trembled. A few hundred meters away, the pallid figure of Vladimir Lenin shifted in his coffin as his guards fought to keep their footing.

A gigantic column of flame and debris shot skyward, lifting the heavy Chaika—still intact, but in flames. To the dumbfounded spectators it looked like a cosmonaut lifting off from its central Asian launching pad. The flaming vehicle sailed in a tight arc two hundred feet in the air and tumbled sideways like a flaming meteor, out of control, toward the Kremlin.

It crashed, tearing itself into shards of twisted metal and glass on the crenelated wall of the Kremlin. The occupants had been mercifully killed by the initial impact of the explosion. Their broken and charred remains, now smoldering hunks of flesh scattered inside the Kremlin wall, were unrecognizable as human beings.

The refiner's fire was soon to begin.

El Al Flight 247 touched down expertly at Johannesburg International Airport at exactly 9:35 A.M. It taxied slowly toward the terminal, but before it stopped at the ramp, three men dropped out of the bottom rear cargo door and disappeared quickly into a waiting van.

The nondescript vehicle drove slowly and inconspicuously past the corporate hangars and headed for the military annex that housed several units of the South African Air Force.

"Yossef, this is Major Van Leutow," said Yabin as the three alighted from the rear of the van. "He's flying us to the base camp. From there we take another vehicle."

The South African pilot saluted casually and motioned them into a waiting army helicopter, the rotors drooping —barely turning in the slight breeze which gusted across the expanses of concrete.

"What's the flying time, Major?" asked the blond SHINBET officer.

"About two hours until we reach base camp. Then another hour and a half into the canyon site."

The pilot busied himself with the preflight checklist as the three Israelis fumbled with their seat belts.

"All secure?" the South African asked over the whine of the rotors.

Yabin gave a thumbs up.

The helicopter lifted off, tilted sideways at five hundred feet, and chopped its way southwest—toward the stony tablelands of South Africa's Drakenberg Mountains.

"This country's like the landscape of the moon!" exclaimed Yossef as he stared out the back of the South African army truck.

"It gets worse, Mr. Ayalon," laughed the rangy sergeant, their escort on the arduous trip into the remote canyon. "This is one of the few areas of the world not covered by routine satellite photo-reconnaissance by any of the world's powers. Our little corner of the world, down here at least, gets the 'broad-brush' treatment from time to time, but that's all. This place is completely secure. It's perfect for your needs. You'll see."

The undulating, rock-strewn terrain gave way to an abrupt opening in the sloping face of a huge mesa. The gravel road penetrated the opening and continued for several more miles, the craggy overhang providing a nearly solid canopy of stone.

"This is where the Zulu nation held out against the Boers for years, Mr. Ayalon," the sergeant volunteered. "They had their entire governmental and military organization tucked up into this, and similar canyons, for decades. You'll see why it took so long to find them when we get to the site. The old kings held court up there, and administered the whole area from here to the Cape."

The truck crunched to a stop before a cyclone fence. Two South African army guards, FALN automatic rifles at the ready, examined their passes. They waved the truck through. Suddenly, the road roller-coastered and plunged between deep canyon walls. Slim shafts of light probed from above, creating a bizzare light-and-shadow effect on the smooth stone.

"I dare say that the early Zulus felt that this place had some sort of religious significance," observed Yabin, marveling at the shadows.

"Yes it did," responded the knowledgeable sergeant. "I can't remember the name of the old boy, but one of their major deities 'dwelt' here. The God of Light, naturally."

"Naturally," chuckled Yabin.

Suddenly, the road leveled out and broke into a clearing —the end of the blind canyon. The stone walls arched inward on all sides, almost touching at the top. A large single shaft of light plunged earthward, bathing the structure below in an eerie light.

"It's—it's like a cathedral!" Yossef's voice fell to a reverent whisper.

"You're missing the main attraction. Look—look, my young friend!" Yabin exclaimed excitedly, pointing to the middle of the clearing.

There—meticulously crafted out of lumber and plywood—was a perfect and exact replica of Lenin's Tomb.

VI.

Raisa felt his presence in the doorway and looked up from her filing.

"May I help you?" she said with a practiced smile.

"Ah, yes," replied Yuri. "I'm looking for my Uncle, General Spinnenko."

Raisa stood abruptly, revealing her shapely body, and slid around the desk, hand extended.

"So *you're* Yuri Spinnenko! The survivor," she quipped.

Yuri was taken aback by her boldness but pleased as he felt the warmth of her strong grip.

"Yes. I—I guess I can be thankful for that." He stammered slightly. "And you're Raisa Karezev, correct?"

"Yes." Raisa replied with a genuine smile. "Your uncle has told me so much about you, Yuri. All good. We're so proud of you here in the Directorate since you were selected as a guard for Lenin's Tomb. What an honor that is."

"Yes, it is." Yuri shifted nervously. "I feel the responsibility very keenly. Is Uncle Pavel in?"

"He's in conference right now. Why don't you wait here in the office? He should be back in an hour."

"An hour? What am I going to do with myself for an hour?" he moaned slightly.

"Let's see. It's almost ten. I'm on break for thirty minutes. Do you want to join me in the cafeteria for tea and rolls? My treat. Besides, I want to show you off." Raisa beamed as she glanced admiringly at his two rows of service ribbons.

Yuri felt a warm rush of enthusiasm as he agreed.

Normally he felt somewhat insecure around women, but Raisa's easy and familiar manner put him at ease.

The cafeteria on the first floor of the complex was noisy and crowded, but Yuri and Raisa were able to find a corner table with a window looking out at the Square.

"Uncle Pavel has told me that without you his job would be impossible, Miss Karezev."

"Call me Raisa, please." She smiled. "I feel like I've known you for so long. Pavel has kept me apprised of your exploits. With soldiers like you, the war should be concluded swiftly with victory."

Yuri's expression became strangely distant. Then he turned, his wide blue eyes locking into hers.

"China is a bottomless pit, Raisa. The Tartars breed faster than we can kill them."

"But the news reports constantly say that we're winning," exclaimed Raisa, a slight frown wrinkling her forehead.

Yuri breathed deeply and changed the subject abruptly.

"Tell me, Raisa, does your job give you satisfaction?"

"It's challenging. It taxes my technical abilities and satisfies my desire to serve the State." She answered mechanically and without enthusiasm.

Raisa looked down into her cup and swirled the little loose leaves of tea around in circular patterns. She could feel Yuri's eyes sweeping over her in approval. She looked up quickly. Embarrassed, he glanced at his watch.

"Well, perhaps I should get back to the office. I want to catch Uncle Pavel before he gets away again. Raisa, do you—do you go out or is there one special person?" Yuri asked awkwardly.

"Nobody in particular," she lied, "and yes, I do go out."

"Perhaps you would join me some evening for the theater?" Yuri stood and pulled out Raisa's chair.

"I'd like that. Is there anything good playing?"

Yuri frowned in thought. "I don't know. Do you know of any good movies?"

"I'll tell you what I'd rather do if it's all right with you."

"Anything," Yuri agreed, relieved.

"I'm a swimmer. I love to exercise and keep my body firm during these cold winter days. Working in a confining office can be depressing. I need to get out and work off my excess energies."

"You're a woman after my own heart, Raisa. Can I pick you up this evening for dinner and a swim about seven-thirty?"

"Sounds great," Raisa responded, her hips swaying slightly as she maneuvered deftly through the crowd. "Here's my address," she added as she hurriedly scribbled on a piece of memo paper.

"How did you *find* this place?" marveled Raisa as they entered the faded elegance of the Arbat restaurant in the Bely Gorod, the old White City, the Bohemian area of the city. "I didn't know that cafés like this existed in Moscow anymore."

"This place represents a side of my personality I don't allow too many people to see, Raisa. When I'm not guarding Comrade Lenin I come down here in my faded Levis and long-haired wig and listen to decadent Western boogie-woogie." Yuri winked, a smile tugging at the corners of his lips.

Raisa let out an audible gasp, which escalated into a throaty laugh. His comment seemed so out of character that she was momentarily stunned.

"That's a side of you I think I'd find *very* interesting," exclaimed Raisa. "One would have to be schizophrenic to live with those extremes."

Yuri's expression became thoughtful as he scanned the laughing, noisy patrons, most of whom were students. The Arbat was a known Solidarity hangout and the KGB was as thick as aphids in the crowds.

"This place has a kind of carefree atmosphere—a kind of mindless freedom that appeals to me in my weaker moments, Raisa. A friend of mine, an Armenian—you know how wild and absurd Armenians are . . ."

Raisa gave a ritualistic bob of her head.

". . . brought me here about three weeks ago over my protests. My first reaction was anger and disgust. These long-haired hooligans should be in China getting their rear ends shot at."

"Like you were, Yuri?" Raisa arched an eyebrow. "And

how do you feel about these people now?" She gestured toward the crowd of students.

"Oddly, I feel no resentment. Perhaps it's because I know that sooner or later they'll have to go. They might as well enjoy it while they can."

Yuri studied the carefree youngsters, a glimmer of envy in his eyes.

The Moskva Swimming Pool on the Kropotkin embankment of the Moskva River is huge, holding twenty-five hundred swimmers at a time. Its heated water gives the city dwellers a chance to escape the chilly confinement of Moscow's winters. Its crowds—and the pool was always crowded, day or night—offered one of the few places in the city where there was complete anonymity. Among the masses of humanity, one could conspire or exchange intimacies and not be noticed in the crowds of swimmers in or out of the water.

Yuri whistled to himself as Raisa stepped out of the women's dressing room. Her body, still tanned from her Black Sea vacation, stood out in marked contrast to the pasty whiteness of the other swimmers. Raisa flashed him a quick smile and dove into the chlorinated water without speaking. Yuri dove in after her, and soon they were swimming the length of the pool in strong, even strokes.

"I'm tired!" gasped Raisa as she grasped the edge of the tile. "Let's sit up by the wall."

"You *should* be tired, Raisa Karezev," panted Yuri. "I couldn't keep up with you. Do you realize that we swam twelve laps? I haven't done that since secondary school."

"You're out of shape, soldier." Raisa chuckled as she flopped down on the warm concrete by the yellow tiled wall. Overhead, the fluorescent lights bathed the area in a flickering blue.

Raisa scanned Yuri's muscular body. Medium build; muscles well defined. Aha! Tattoo on left forearm.

"Your body is full of interesting little items. Your tattoo: May I examine it?"

"Oh. That. A moment of indiscretion during a layover at Kharbovsk—and I was perfectly sober when I got it." He grinned.

Raisa held his forearm and squinted at the intricate blue and red patterns: crossed rifles with a red star atop the *X,* the words "Avenge the Motherland" underneath.

"Many of the young recruits get this particular design," explained Yuri. "It's supposed to show a commitment to the war and separate the Solidarity people from the patriots."

Raisa continued to scan Yuri's body. Gregierenko had told her to remember all of the details on Yuri's body, no matter how minute. What luck it was that he should almost drop into her lap. Now she wouldn't have to contrive a meeting through Pavel Spinnenko.

"Hmmm. Three small scars in a cluster approximately two inches below the lower right rib. Large scar, four and a half inches, in the fleshy part of the rear right shoulder." Her finger traced the faded line of flesh and scar tissue.

"You sound like a police report." Yuri laughed.

"Are all of these battle scars?" Her eyes were pools of sympathy and respect.

"Yes. Luckily all of the wounds were superficial —shrapnel and bullet wounds in noncritical areas. No organs were affected. Since you're counting my scars, I will count your freckles, Raisa. My, you have some sexy freckles on your back." Yuri's finger slid down the valley between her shoulders.

Raisa shuddered slightly. She enjoyed the slow, sensual movement of Yuri's finger as it swept down her back.

"I'm up to twenty-six now," said Yuri.

"That's no fair." Raisa pouted. "I've only counted four scars of yours. Do you have any more?"

"You've got to find them," Yuri responded, a slight smile playing at one side of his mouth.

Shrapnel from a grenade to the thigh. That's what Pavel said, thought Raisa. But which thigh? she wondered.

"Any scars, lower limbs?" she inquired, a suggestive tone in her voice.

"Aha! That's where the prize is. You've got to hunt for it." Yuri leered.

Suddenly Raisa sat up and nervously tried to fluff her wet hair.

"Well, I don't want to invade your privacy completely.

Examination over, Sergeant Spinnenko. I pronounce you whole and fit for further duty." Raisa pulled herself up. "Come on. One more swim."

As Yuri stood, Raisa glanced at his legs. There, below the hem of his bathing suit, right leg, about mid-thigh was a bluish-white line about three inches long.

"Race you to the pool, Yuri."

The Committee on Terminal Actions was a small group within the First Chief Directorate of the KGB and met bimonthly to discuss current projects underway. Because of its sensitive operations it met in the basement of the Dzerzhinsky Square complex in a wood-paneled cubicle which was once a cell of the Lubyanka. The prison was no more. It had recently been tastefully remodeled into small offices, conference rooms, and file rooms where the inactive KGB archives were kept. It was often referred to as "the morgue"; the oldest of the CHEKA, NKVD, and KGB records were kept in the filing cabinets lining the corridors.

Mikhail Kedrov, committee chairman, shuffled casually through the buff-colored folders on the table. His nicotine-stained fingers plucked one from the pile and held it up for the others to see. The four men around the table waited for the committee chairman to speak.

"While Comrade Blinov was alive the Makleff project was number five in priority actions. Subotin. Biryukov. You finished the old man and followed this case. What is its status now?"

Vadim Subotin ran his finger alongside of his porous nose and stared at the folder, trying to remember.

"Makleff—Makleff. Oh yes. The old Jew in Berne. *Ariel* Makleff. One of the old original Bolsheviks. A confidant of Lenin's. Comrade Blinov personally ordered us to take care of this one. The old man had a journal of some sort with incriminating information about Lenin."

"Did Blinov say what the information was?" slurred Kedrov as he poured himself a jigger of vodka.

"No. We worked on the old man in his apartment for only thirty minutes before he died. He was so old and frail we knew that he wouldn't last long. We had to get in and out in a hurry. His neighborhood was full of nosy old Jews who looked out for the old man and each other. Makleff would tell us nothing. He denied that he even kept a journal or even had information from those early years."

"Ah!" Kedrov sighed wearily. "The man-hours we have spent and wasted trying to tidy up the past. Blinov, for all of his progressive ideas, was a protegé of Stalin, and Stalin had a fixation about 'tidying' up the early years, especially when it concerned the events surrounding the death of Lenin. As far as I'm concerned, the Makleff case is closed. Who really cares anymore about those days except a few moth-eaten scholars? We have more important things to worry about than a few ghosts in our closets. We've got this Solidarity thing to sweat over. I'm sure that Solidarity and Vasily Gregierenko aren't dwelling on the past. I move that we cancel the Makleff project and consign the files to the morgue. Agreed?"

The others nodded their assent.

An hour later a file clerk switched on the single naked light bulb dangling from the arched corridor of the former cell-row. The adjoining cells, which once had held the tortured, howling prisoners of the CHEKA and its successors, now held the dull, gunmetal gray filing cabinets of the KGB. The clerk padded along the newly tiled floor that covered the concrete—concrete stained with the blood of thousands of prisoners who were beaten and executed in the corridors of the Lubyanka. The mellow, tan, textured-wood paneling that reached to the arched ceiling hid the gaping holes in the cement walls into which dozens of iron rings had been driven and from which the tortured wretches of the Lubyanka had hung and languished.

The clerk stopped by a cubicle, a former cell, and flicked on the switch. She sauntered up to the one marked "M–O" and slid the Makleff file into the third drawer. The Makleff project was now officially terminated by the KGB. Four cubicles down in a dust-covered cabinet was the D–F section of the archives. In the second drawer, the ninth folder from the front was marked:

ALEKSEI DUBROV AND POSTERITY
1919–1962

The winds sweeping off the South African veldt made a
cacophony of eerie sounds as they entered the canyons of
the Drakenbergs. Yossef lay in a bundle of rumpled sheets,
longing for an early-morning cigarette as the wind buf-
feted the small trailer, one of a half-a-dozen parked in the
blind canyon and arranged in a semicircle around the
replica of Lenin's Tomb.

"Come, come, m'boy," barked Moshe Yabin as he burst
in the door, his bulk seeming to fill the small trailer.
"Time for our early-morning briefing."

"What—what time is it, Yabin?" slurred Yossef, trying
to focus his eyes on the MOSSAD colonel.

"Six o'clock. We've got some very interesting details on
your brother. We've got his picture too. We want to share
this with you since it's going to result in a few changes of
your anatomy." Yabin twitched a grin.

"What? Just what in the hell are you talking about?"
frowned Yossef.

Yabin threw a pair of South African army fatigue pants
at Yossef.

"Put these on. Coffee's brewing in the headquarters
trailer."

"It's like I'm looking in the mirror." Yossef marveled as
he studied the image on the slide. The mixed aromas of
coffee and cigarette fumes jarred him to wakefulness. His
twin brother looked somber and purposeful in his uniform
of the KGB Border Guards.

"Spitting image. There's no doubt about it. You're
identical twins. We were able to steal his medical records
and compare his developmental patterns to yours. You
both achieved the same height and weight at approximately the same times in your lives. You learned to crawl, walk,
and even talk at the same time. Amazing! We also obtained pictures of Yuri at the various milestones of his life,
graduations and the like, and compared them to photographs of you during these times. Remarkable similari-

ties," intoned the South African army doctor who was conducting the briefing.

"How are we getting this information?" asked Yossef as he continued to stare at his brother through the steam of his coffee.

The image on the screen changed abruptly with the click of the slide projector, and the pixie good looks of Raisa Karezev appeared. Yossef whistled softly.

"This should prove to be the most interesting and pleasant part of your assignment," chortled Yabin.

"Who is *she*?" Yossef was now wide awake.

"Raisa Karezev, a Solidarity agent and very close to your brother. By this time she knows every scar, wart, and pimple on Yuri Spinnenko. She's the private secretary to General Pavel Spinnenko, Chief of the Border Guards. She's also the chief computer technician for her directorate. She's been dating your brother for over a month. Their little affair is getting rather thick. She's also a lover of Vasily Gregierenko."

"Do I get to duplicate my brother's activities in, ah, every area?" Yossef had a mischievous leer on his face.

"In every *area*, my dear Yossef," laughed Yabin. "When you take over his identity, you get Raisa."

"Spoils of war, m'lad," added the South African.

An image of crossed rifles with a red star, and the motto "Avenge the Motherland" flashed on the screen.

"This is a copy of Yuri's tattoo—on his left forearm. Thousands of Soviet soldiers get these in the tattoo parlors of Kharbovsk before departing for the North China front," explained the doctor.

The next slide was a pencil outline of a man in his shorts. A series of little lines had been superimposed on the drawing.

"These are your brother's scars. Some are the usual; an appendicitis scar, hernia, and so forth. The others are a series of battle scars. Yuri also has a vanadium bone plate in his right arm. His ulna and radius were broken when he was playing soccer," continued the South African.

"Do you have to go *that* far?" Yossef flashed an angry glance at the doctor.

"You've got to be an exact duplicate, Yossef." The

doctor's tone was grave. "In every way," he added.

Naturally, there are some things we can't alter, such as fingerprints or dental work," said Yabin.

"Has Raisa Karezev taken him to bed yet?" asked Yossef, hopefully.

"Evidently not." The doctor chortled. "We don't have any information on scars in the genital area."

"The hernia?" inquired Yossef.

"From his military medical records. Solidarity was able to send us his complete file. Raisa Karezev's observations just confirm what is already known—but that's important."

"When I assume Yuri's identity, will Raisa know I'm me?"

"That will be your supreme test, Yossef. You have to fool her," Yabin said.

"Suppose—suppose by that time that they're sexually involved? I mean, damn it, men have different ways of screwing, even twin brothers."

Yabin's raucous laughter filled the small trailer.

"And—and what about penis size and length. I mean, are we equal in *all* areas?" Yossef's eyes were wide with innocent inquiry.

The placid demeanor of the South African broke down. Tears of laughter filled his eyes as he fumbled for an appropriate response.

"There are some areas where you're going to have to be extremely creative and innovative, Yossef. We can't do *everything* for you."

"How much time do I have, Yabin?" asked Yossef.

"Until you know the Tomb backwards and forwards. You've got the detail of the guard mount down fairly well. Yesterday, however, you twitched your nose when a fly landed on it. You can't do that, Yossef. Your face has to be immobile as the corpse you're guarding. When you stand at the head or feet of Lenin you can't move a muscle—not even if you're attacked by a swarm of bees."

"We're going to truck you down to a mobile surgical unit at base camp tomorrow," added the doctor. "We'll give you the tattoo and the scars there. We'll screw a vanadium plate into your arm and fake the fracture so they'll both look authentic in an x-ray, should it ever come to that."

"You're not going to break my arm?"

"Not necessary," replied the South African. "Your wounds and tattoo should be healed in about six weeks."

"You'll be leaving for Moscow in June as a permanent member of the Swiss Trade Mission. Your German is perfect. Your years in Berne have given a nice Swiss lilt to your German."

"Why the Swiss?" Yossef asked.

"The Swiss have more accessibility to Moscow than any other group of foreigners. The Soviets are very lenient with Swiss trade delegates since they're the conduit for illegal or boycotted Western goods," Yabin answered.

"June. That's only three months away! What about the Swiss? Do I just appear at the trade mission and say 'Here I am'?"

"That's been taken care of." Yabin's tone of voice reflected annoyance. "The Swiss owe us a few favors. You'll be shipped in as a replacement. There will be no problems."

Yossef stepped out of the trailer and into the rocky clearing. The early morning sun was sending slivers of light into the canyon, stabbing its shafts into the Tomb. He had marched around and into the artificial edifice at least several hundred times as part of his training. He had stood for hours, stiffly at attention, staring at the lifelike dummy in the glass-encased coffin. He felt that he knew his mission, the Tomb, and the face of Lenin as well as the deserts around his home in Shareem.

Instinctively, he reached for his shirt pocket for a pack of cigarettes. His hand stopped in midair. He sighed resignedly and ambled back toward his trailer.

VII.

Steve McMurrin lay on the frozen clods of dirt and watched the fleecy white clouds scud overhead in the clear Siberian sky. He relished these ten-minute breaks. There were only two of them allowed a day and he used every second of them to plan his escape.

He turned his head, brushed a few strands of his blond scraggly hair away from his face and glanced at the thick, inviting forest half a mile away. A small group of reindeer were nibbling at the bark of one of the spruce trees.

What rank would he be now, he wondered, if he were back in the States? He'd be three-quarters through his thirty-year hitch as a naval aviator. He'd be retiring in three years—maybe as a four-striper. He'd be only fifty-three, and he and his wife would be young enough to start a new life, a new career.

Nancy was his little girl whom he'd never seen. She'd be twenty by now. A young lady. It had been nineteen years since he was shot down over Hanoi back in 1972. Since that time Lieutenant Junior Grade Steve McMurrin had been listed as one of the hundreds of MIAs—Missing in Actions—that the North Vietnamese government had held in scores of secret prisoner-of-war camps but had never admitted existed.

"Look at those reindeer over there, Nguyen. Man, what I'd give to sink my teeth into that critter. I'd eat the son of a bitch alive," McMurrin exclaimed in his New Mexico drawl.

"Don't show too much interest in those reindeer or the forest, my friend, or the guards will read your thoughts," whispered Nguyen Tranh, a former major in the South Vietnamese Marine Corps. "Our opportunity will come. Bide your time. You Americans are too impatient. Bide your time."

The whistles of the guards broke the stillness, blowing in a series of shrill blasts. Like wraiths rising from their graves, the thousands of Vietnamese and three hundred-odd American slave laborers lurched to their feet and stumbled toward their picks and shovels along the length of the Yakut section of the Trans-Siberian natural-gas pipeline.

Steve McMurrin picked absently at the frozen dirt, his sharp pilot's eyes darting from his work to the reindeer and the thick forest beyond.

"We have become as spineless as the petty bourgeoisie who ran the Provisional Government under Kerensky," thundered Premier Igor Krylenko. "We have lost our balls in the face of this damned Solidarity threat. We can't even beat those *chort*-eating Tartars. What have we become—a nation of weaklings?"

Andropov, the Minister of Transportation, raised the question that the Politburo had been avoiding during the entire meeting. "We've talked about a crackdown on Solidarity and yet it grows. We've talked about a replacement for Blinov and yet we've failed to make a move on that."

"Who can really replace Blinov?" offered Krotkov, the Party Secretary.

"What we're really saying . . ." slurred Krylenko, "is—who among us is willing to take the job of Director of the KGB? Be honest. We're afraid! For the first time since the Revolution, Party and government officials are afraid to assume their responsibilities because of fear of assassination."

Rakhmatov, Minister of the Interior, held up a computer printout—the indispensable crutch of the modern bureaucrat. "Here is the final list of KGB personnel murdered last quarter. Many of them are so-called 'secret' informants. Their names and addresses had become known to Solidarity."

"This means a serious leak within the Center itself. This virus has spread right into the vital organs of the State itself," muttered Krylenko.

"The pressures for internal reforms are mounting, comrades," piped Gorsky, the Minister of Communications. Sergei Gorsky was known as the liberal in the Politburo and in the Council of Ministers. His lone dissenting voice was often ignored. This time Krylenko turned on him in fury.

"We *must* maintain the integrity of the Party, Gorsky. We *cannot* abandon the basic tenets of Marxism-Leninism. If we start that process we'll wind up just like the Chinese: a watered-down form of communism with no guts left in it."

"I'm trying to be practical, damn it, Comrade Premier! We can either screw the lid on tighter or——"

"Which is exactly what we're going to do!" blurted Rakhmatov.

"Or we can initiate selective reforms to let off some of the pressure," continued Gorsky. "Let's be honest with ourselves and dispose of the self-deception that we often lull ourselves into. There is a huge credibility gap between the government and the people. There is even a larger gap between the Party and the people. Solidarity has exploited every contradiction which exists in our country . . . and the Politburo's policies have helped to create these contradictions. To put it bluntly, comrades, we are out of touch with the stark realities of our country."

The other Politburo members glared at Gorsky. They knew that what he said was true. Gorsky, in spite of his liberalism, was outspoken and often said what the others secretly thought but were afraid to admit.

Krylenko hung his massive head and stared absently at his half-empty tumbler of vodka.

"What *does* have credibility in our country anymore, comrades?" he said softly, thoughtfully. "Everything we have done has been botched. Gorsky's right, of course, but there are certain things we cannot do if we are to remain strong and in power." The crimson started at Krylenko's collar and spread rapidly to his cheeks.

"It seems as if everything we have done lately has failed.

Failure, failure, failure!" he raged. "Failure eats at us like maggots in a corpse!"

There was an embarrassed silence. The clock ticked monotonously in the Politburo meeting room in the Kremlin's Upper Arsenal Building. The members sat stiffly and pensively around the long T-shaped table topped with green baize.

"Lenin!" A sudden burst of inspiration registered on Gorsky's face like a tide of sunlight flooding out from behind a storm cloud.

"Lenin!" Gorsky repeated. "The one symbol of the State and Party which still has credibility. Have you noticed how attendance at the Tomb has increased since the troubles began? We've had to put a night shift on the guard mount."

"Ah, yes." The black arcs of Krylenko's eyebrows spurted upward, setting the wart in the middle of his forehead dancing on a ridge of flesh. "It *is* phenomenal. When our people are troubled or confused they turn to the Little Father in his glass sarcophagus. I suppose that he functions much the same as a priest does in his confessional booth. Ah! I wish we had a Lenin's Tomb in every city and village in the Soviet Union."

"Take Lenin to the people."

Gorsky's words produced a nervous rustle, then dead silence. The dead air in the Politburo meeting room seemed to quiver under the impact of his statement.

Gorsky stood and looked at the members seated at the table. Authority flowed from his voice like sound waves from a tuning fork as the Politburo turned to him.

"Create a special Tomb train. Use the same sealed car that Lenin first came to Russia in, in 1917. It's in the museum in Leningrad. Create elaborate security precautions. Include the guard mount and take Lenin to the people. We can cover the entire country in three months."

"Are you mad?" hissed Krotkov. "Are you absolutely mad? Do you have any idea what problems are involved just preparing for such a project?"

"Our American friends did something very similar back in 1947—or was it 1948?" Gorsky explained. "They created a special train, a so-called 'Freedom Train' that carried their most precious documents to the people. The Declaration of Independence, their Constitution, the Bill of Rights were put in special containers and filled with preserving gases. These are the credible symbols of the American political system. A Marine guard accompanied them and this train stopped in every village, city, and hamlet along the route. It was a huge success; a major propaganda victory for the government. It cemented the people to Washington."

"Do we have any credible documents that the people would go out of their way to look at?" asked Rakhmatov innocently. The other members chuckled sardonically.

Krylenko slouched uncomfortably in his chair, his forefinger picking at his lips, his head bowed as though in prayer.

"Lenin to the people—Lenin to the people. I—I don't know. The problems—the risks," he muttered.

"A massive assault on Solidarity could be launched just before the tour of Lenin's train," said Rakhmatov. "In fact, the publicity surrounding the tour would divert the public's attention from the crackdown."

"According to my estimates we need approximately a million and a half laborers to complete the Vladivostok-to-Sverdlosk section of the pipeline and the lateral and tributary pipes in the Yakut region," intoned Yaslov, the Minister of Energy.

"Haven't we given you enough Vietnamese and Chinese prisoners?" slurred Krylenko. "We even threw in some American prisoners from the Vietnamese War to sweeten the pie."

"Not enough, Comrade Premier. The winter weather has set us behind schedule. If we are going to finally crack down on Solidarity, I could use the bodies."

"Terror—the only way to handle these pricks of pigs," barked Andropov. "I've got enough spare rolling stock to take them all to Siberia. We'll simply attach coal cars to the troop trains going east."

"They'll freeze in the open cars," gasped Gorsky, horrified at the thought.

"So much the better. Enough will survive to complete the pipelines. We either go all out on this or we watch Solidarity erode our authority," countered Andropov.

"Andropov's right. If we're going to crush Solidarity it must be total. We must avoid weakness of any sort. Total terror! That's the only thing our people ultimately understand. Every so often we become soft as a people and terror, like a medicine, must be administered. Lenin and Stalin knew this. We were strong under these iron men. Terror can be therapeutic. Yes—Lenin to the people on one hand, terror to the people on the other. It will work, comrades!" said Rakhmatov.

"Comrade Premier." Gorsky's face was ashen. "Times have changed. The Soviet people will not put up with the terror of the 1930s again."

"The Russian people never change," thundered Krylenko. "Russia is Russia and will remain so. Our people cannot function under a liberalized system. They run amok! Look what happened to them under Kerensky's democratic government. We're getting to that point now —only *Solidarity* is the Bolshevik threat and *we're* the Russian government. No, Gorsky. The Russian people need terror. They want and expect terror from their government from time to time to show that we still have testicles. In the end, they'll appreciate it."

Gorsky shook his head in disbelief as the other members of the Politburo enthusiastically agreed with Krylenko.

"I—I thought we had evolved from those terrible primitive times. No, comrades," he said softly, "we can never go back to those times of total terror. The world has changed and Solidarity represents much of that change. We can't go back to the times of terror."

Gorsky's mutterings were drowned out by a toast offered by Andropov to crush Solidarity once and for all. The Politburo members stood, except for Gorsky, and drank their tumblers of vodka, head and drink thrown back. The vodka disappeared in one gulp to the accompaniment of a bellowed *"Na zdorovya!"*

* * *

"Captain Suskov. Admiral Vagorshnik would like to see you in his office just as soon as you complete your staff meeting."

Vaclav Suskov nodded to the admiral's aide-de-camp and concluded his meeting. He hurriedly stuffed his papers into his leather attaché case, adjusted his black uniform tie, and strode smartly down the ornate corridor of the old, baroque building that housed the headquarters of the Soviet Baltic Sea Fleet at Kaliningrad. He paused at the admiral's office door, gave another tug to his tie, and walked in.

"Ah, Captain Suskov, please sit down," the admiral said pleasantly, a tinge of sadness in his voice. Admiral Ivan Vagorshnik, a short fireplug of a man with kindly gray eyes, gestured for the captain to be seated. He pulled up a chair facing Suskov and, for a moment, there was an awkward silence. Finally, the admiral spoke.

"Vaclav . . ." the admiral began slowly, weighing his words carefully. "It is my sad duty to tell you that your—your son Boris was killed in combat in Yunnan two weeks ago. I received word this morning over the telex. I felt that it should come from me, personally, and not by official letter, not at first, anyway. You'll receive one of those eventually. I can't tell you how very sorry I am, Vaclav," concluded Vagorshnik, his sea-wizened face a mask of concern.

Suskov swallowed several times. The muscles in his jaws tightened and twitched as he tried to process his grief.

"Boris was a soldier. He died protecting the Motherland. Death is always a possibility in combat." Suskov's words were hollow and insincere.

"If there's anything I can do, Vaclav. Perhaps you'd like to be reassigned to shore duty to comfort your wife."

Suskov shook his head, his eyes glazed with tears.

"Life goes on, Admiral. Sea duty will help heal the pain. We have been taught to accept these things since childhood, have we not?" Suskov grimaced a thin smile.

"Would you like some personal leave time, Vaclav? We could get along without you for a short while."

"That's very kind of you, Admiral. Yes. I'll take a few

days to comfort my wife and—and I should go to Leningrad and tell Elena."

"Elena?"

"Boris's fiancée. They were to be married when his service was over."

"Oh, I *am* sorry. If there's anything I can do, don't hesitate to ask. If it were in my power, Vaclav, I'd stop this insane war, you know that."

"Thank you, Admiral. That means a lot to me. I appreciate the long talks we've had on this—and other subjects. But the China War isn't exactly a navy show, is it? We just ferry our young men to the meatgrinder and our duty is over."

The admiral threw up his gnarled hands in a sign of resignation and let them fall gently on Suskov's shoulders.

"May God be with you, Vaclav," he whispered in a conspiratorial manner. "May God ease your grief."

Suskov glanced nervously at the door. It was locked.

"Dangerous words, Brother Ivan. Are you sure your office isn't bugged?"

"It's not. I had it 'swept' two days ago. For what it's worth, Vaclav, I have some relevant scriptures dealing with grief. I had them photocopied for our study group. I'd like to give you a copy. It's the only source of real comfort available to our people who have lost loved ones. Here—take one."

Minutes later, Captain Third Class Vaclav Suskov, a member of the small but growing Christian underground study group among the officers and men of the Baltic Sea Fleet, left the Fleet Headquarters building and hailed a staff car to take him to the Kaliningrad railroad station.

The gusty April wind drove small pellets of hardened rain against Suskov's fine Harris tweed jacket, a souvenir of a visit to a Hong Kong tailor while his ship was on a goodwill visit.

He stepped down from the large red and green Leningrad city bus and trudged the two blocks to an ancient brownstone apartment building, one of the few structures that was not damaged in the Siege of Leningrad during the Great Patriotic War. The neighborhood had been designated by the city as a student housing area for the University of Leningrad and was known to be thick with Solidarity members and sympathizers. It was from this very neighborhood that Boris Suskov had been conscripted for the China War.

Suskov dreaded his meeting with Elena. She was an unpredictable girl with a mercurial disposition. He had often wondered what Boris saw in her. She would become completely hysterical when he told her of Boris's death. He was sure of that.

The door opened as soon as Suskov knocked. Elena met him, a strange expression on her round, Slavic face. Inside the small apartment were several other young people, among them a private of the Red Army.

"Captain Suskov. Please come in. Thank you for your phone call to make sure I was home. I skipped an examination to be here."

Suskov nodded grimly and entered the living room and took a chair vacated by one of the students. There was an awkward silence. Several of the youngsters shuffled their feet in embarrassment. Finally, Elena spoke.

"Have—have you been informed yet?" She knew the answer before she asked it.

Suskov frowned. "I came here—to tell you, Elena, that—that Boris was killed in combat two weeks ago. The immediate family is always the first to know."

No shock of surprise or grief registered on Elena's face. No hysterics. She knew! She had found out, somehow, before he did.

"Don't expect me to cry, Captain Suskov." Elena's voice was thin and icy. "I did all of my crying a month ago."

"What? A—a month ago? I don't understand, Elena. What do you mean?"

The young Red Army private spoke.

"Permit me to introduce myself, Captain. I'm Private Petr Svetanko. I served with Boris. We were conscripted together from the university. When Elena told me that you called, I wanted to be here when you arrived."

"You were with Boris in China?"

"Yes. Boris was killed a month ago, just three days

before he was to rotate out of the combat zone."

Suskov swallowed hard and let out a weary breath, trying to force the words to the next question. He rubbed his eyes with his thumb and forefinger. There was a wealth of agony in that simple gesture.

"Petr—how—was my son—killed?"

The dark-haired private shuffled uncomfortably, his eyes staring at the toes of his combat boots.

"Boris was killed by a Chinese sniper. The sniper got four of our patrol. He died instantly, a shot through the head."

"You saw him get killed?"

Petr avoided the captain's gaze and whispered his reply.

"Yes. I saw him and the others get shot and killed. The sniper couldn't miss. We were ordered to advance in the open. We knew the Chinese were up in the rocks. It was insane."

Elena sat in the corner and started to shake. Every word of Petr's created earthquakes of emotion within her. Suddenly, she erupted like an exploding volcano.

"Oh, pigshit! Lies and pigshit!" she screamed. "Boris wasn't 'killed' in combat; he was *murdered*! Murdered because he was one of us!"

Suskov's aristocratic face froze into a mask of shock. He said nothing. He just stared at the shaking, hysterical girl.

"Didn't you know, Captain Suskov, that Boris was a Solidarity activist? Oh, the KGB knew, or suspected him. Don't you know, Captain Suskov, that the gerontocracy has been sending Solidarity suspects to their deaths in this stupid, immoral war ever since they started it? Boris was *ordered* to his death, Captain. Ordered to die! His commander had his name on a death list. He knew that that sniper was up in the rocks ready to pick off Russian soldiers."

"Are—are you telling me, Elena, that my son's death was for nothing? Nothing?" Suskov raged. "Are you telling me that our government is purposely killing off its own soldiers?"

"That's *exactly* what I'm telling you. The government and Party are rotten to the core! You're too blind to see it because you're part of the damned, rotten system!" She shouted back, her face contorted, the cords of her neck exposed and knotted.

Suskov searched the eyes of the others for some sign of denial. Their expressions confirmed the truth of Elena's accusations.

"Good God! Has it come to this?" he exclaimed incredulously. "Has it finally come to this?" Tears of rage coursed down his cheeks as he slumped in his chair.

The private pulled his chair nearer to Suskov and timidly put his hand on his sleeve.

"Captain. Everything that Elena says is true. I wish that I could tell you that Boris's death was a noble sacrifice. The official letter will tell you that, but nobody believes these government lies. I don't think you do either."

Suskov stared at the wall. Elena was crying softly in the corner.

"Are you all Solidarity?" he asked, trying to control his voice.

They nodded in unison.

"And Boris was part of your—your 'cell' or whatever you call your group?" he added, his voice tinged with sarcasm.

"Just study group, Captain. Just call us a study group. You know all about 'study groups', don't you?" asked a sallow-faced student.

Suskov shot him a sharp glance and stood up abruptly, his face grim, his jaw muscles working.

"I want to thank you all for this information. Believe me, I will say nothing to the authorities. I've got secrets of my own to keep."

As Suskov turned to leave, a voice called out gently.

"Brother Vaclav. A word of prayer before you go?"

"Bro—brother?" Suskov looked into the eyes of the sallow-faced youth. "How did you . . ."

"Solidarity knows everything, Brother Vaclav. Elena. Pull the curtains and lock the door."

Shortly after, the group had formed a circle, their arms around each others' shoulders in the manner of the Russian Orthodox "Old Believers" of the nineteenth century. A prayer was offered for the departed spirit of Boris Suskov and for the growth and survival of Solidarity. The prayer was ended with a poem of Pushkin's, the lines of which were found in the Hymn of Solidarity:

> The heavy hanging chains will fall,
> The walls will crumble at a word,
> And Freedom greet you in the light
> And brothers give you back the Sword.

Renewed, Vaclav Suskov, underground Christian and now a Solidarity sympathizer, left the apartment building, his face set in an expression of implacable hatred toward the government that murdered his son—his mind spinning fantasies of revenge.

VIII.

Steve McMurrin nudged Nguyen Tranh with his elbow. Tranh nudged the huddled figure next to him and, like a row of dominoes, the ripple of movement spread down the line of fifteen more huddled bundles. McMurrin opened the door of the tar-paper shack a crack and peered out. The sky was dark. There was no moon. The outline of the primeval forest loomed beyond the gleaming piles of aluminum gasline pipes stacked on the flat railroad cars nearby.

Seventeen slave laborers, McMurrin and Nguyen Tranh in the lead, stalked from the shack to the cars some fifty feet away. McMurrin reached into the opening of a pipe and pulled out three large bundles wrapped in old copies of *Pravda*. Two of the bundles contained sticks of dynamite that the small band of conspirators had been stealing from the construction sites for many weeks. The other contained an assortment of improvised weapons—from stolen meat-cleavers from the camp kitchen to crude but effective knives fashioned from reindeer bones dug up in the course of their labors.

The dynamite sticks were stuffed inside their quilted jackets and the weapons were distributed. The eleven Vietnamese and six Americans slithered under the long string of railroad cars toward the small circle of men milling around a dying campfire half a mile down the track.

Each railroad tie was a painful, agonizing obstacle to McMurrin as he crawled the length of cars toward the fire, but the jarring crawl was necessary. The small camp where the campfire was located was the weak link in the security system along this stretch of pipeline. The guards were Yakuts, a Siberian minority tribe drafted by the Ministry of Energy to alleviate the chronic shortage of manpower that plagued the project in the Yakutskaya region of Central Siberia. The Yakuts kept to themselves and did not mingle with the other guards. Habitual drinkers, the Yakuts were attracted by the availability of free vodka as much as by the generous wage paid by the Ministry.

The Yakuts didn't hear McMurrin's group as they crept up quietly. In a flash, the seventeen prisoners were on them, cleavers and knives hacking and stabbing into the unsuspecting guards. The Yakuts, now dead things of meat and bone, were dragged into the bushes and stripped of their clothing and weapons. In a small trailer beyond the fire more weapons and clothes were found. It was more than McMurrin had bargained for: twelve AK-47 assault rifles, twenty-two bandoliers of ammunition, and nine pistols. The trailer was also stocked with enough food to provide a future banquet for the undernourished prisoners—but that would have to come later.

Somewhere, out in the dark birch and spruce forest a few miles from the trailer, a wolf was howling to its mate. The members of the group glanced with anxious looks at each other as they pulled on their articles of captured clothing.

"I prefer the wolves of the forest to the wolves back there," McMurrin drawled, jerking his thumb toward the tar-paper shack they had just left. "Does anybody want to go back?"

There was complete silence.

McMurrin surveyed the grim-faced men clad in their newly acquired pants and parkas. There was no turning back now, especially after the murder of the Yakuts. If captured, they would be summarily executed.

The seventeen escapees trudged across the spongy tundra, soft from the early May thaw, and headed for the unknown trials of the forest beyond.

"You've been in a quiet mood all night, Yuri," observed Raisa as she leaned her head on his chest.

Yuri shifted his body slightly, resting his head in the comforting arc between her breast and shoulder.

"I was just thinking of how much I'm going to miss you."

Raisa slid her knee on his naked belly and rubbed his chest gently. Although she fought to remain calm, his words lanced into her like a spear.

She had been ordered by Solidarity not to become emotionally involved with Yuri Spinnenko, but she was a woman, not a robot. Gregierenko and the others didn't understand. A woman couldn't get involved with a man like Yuri and *not* become emotionally involved. She might even be in love with Yuri. Certainly, her feelings toward him were different from those she felt toward Vasily. Yuri was so open—so vulnerable in his simplicity and honesty —that she wanted to protect him. Was this love, or was it guilt?—guilt that she was using him, ferreting out the dribbles of information that she could get from time to time about the security system of Lenin's Tomb and dutifully reporting to her Solidarity control agent.

She would often pray to God—yes, she still believed, she was sure—that the information she furnished to Solidarity would never be used to hurt Yuri—but she could never be sure.

"Can you tell me where you're going?" Raisa asked, resignation creeping into her voice.

"Why not? It will be publicized soon anyway. Just keep it to yourself until then, all right?"

Raisa nodded her head against his chest.

"In two weeks a special train will take the body of Comrade Lenin on tour of the entire country. We'll accompany the body as guards and honor it just as we would do here in Moscow. We'll be taking Lenin to the people, Raisa—from Moscow to Vladivostok, then back through Alma-Ata, the Ukraine, and back to Moscow."

Raisa sat up as if propelled by springs, the sheet falling from her pointed breasts.

"You're doing what?" she gasped. "You—you're taking Lenin's body out of the Tomb and carting it around the country—like—like a circus? Whose stupid idea was that?" Her voice was shrill with feminine anger.

"Raisa, just settle down." Yuri frowned, a puzzled expression on his face.

"No, damn it! It's a stupid idea!" Petulance flared from her like a flame spurting from a sharply struck match.

She glared at him with sullen, probing eyes. A solitary tear slid down her cheek. Her brain was filled with a myriad of frightening thoughts. When Solidarity found out about the tour of Lenin's body—and she would certainly report this to her control agent—would they sabotage the train? Would they capture Yuri? Would they execute him because of his Border Guard affiliation? Her thoughts flashed back to Vasily's directive: Find out all you can about the security system of the Tomb. Operation Samson involved the Tomb itself, not a train tour of Lenin's body. She forced a deep, convulsive breath.

"How long will you be gone?" she asked, her voice now hollow and metallic, devoid of emotion.

"About three months."

A wave of despair swept over her. Yuri Spinnenko was now too important a part of her life to be casually dismissed. What had started out as simply an "assignment" had turned into an affair. She felt completely at ease with Yuri, and he was a more than adequate lover. The only fault she could find with him—and she wasn't looking very hard—was that he was ideologically rigid. Yuri saw things in terms of black and white. Whenever she broached the subject of the social, political, and economic ills plaguing the Soviet Union, he would lapse into an impenetrable silence.

He kissed her reluctantly offered cheek.

"I'd like to think that your anger is—is because you'll miss me and not that the decision is wrong. I think it's a good idea. If—if the Soviet people could only visit Comrade Lenin, even for a moment, their faith in the ultimate triumph of communism would be restored." Yuri's voice was soft and remote as if divorced from himself.

Oh, pigshit! You can't really believe that, Raisa thought to herself as she studied the innocent naiveté in Yuri's face. His wide blue eyes blinked back at her in total honesty.

Raisa gave him a look of unconcealed exasperation and sighed wearily. He *did* believe it. Yuri Spinnenko: the model comrade, the true believer. If anybody had told her a month ago that Raisa Karezev, a key agent in the Solidarity movement, would fall for the likes of Yuri Spinnenko, she would have told them that they were insane.

"We'll have a little time together," she murmured. "Will you be able to see me very much before you go?" Raisa's eyes were filled with tears.

The ache in Yuri's chest became a general throbbing throughout the upper part of his body.

"I don't leave for two weeks, but I'll be involved in preparations." Suddenly he reached for his wallet on the nightstand.

"I've got a little surprise." He smiled as he pulled out two red and blue tickets.

Raisa brightened. "Are—are those . . ."

"Yes, they are." He kissed her gently on the nose. "And we're going Saturday afternoon."

"But the game's been sold out for months, Yuri. How in the world did you get them?"

"Connections, dear Raisa, connections. I'll pick you up at ten in the morning—this Saturday."

* * *

The annual game between the Red Army and the State Security Service—the KGB—was the highlight of the Moscow soccer season. The game had never failed to sell out months in advance and fill Moscow's Dynamo Stadium to capacity.

Outside of the game itself, the Red Army-KGB contest had another attraction: This was the one opportunity the average Muscovite had to shout, to curse, and to vilify the KGB to his heart's content in perfect safety and anonymity among the other one hundred thousand spectators. It was a source of amusement and satisfaction to the fans to observe the KGB personnel and their families sitting stiffly and grimly in the bleachers as the crowds roared and vented their hatred of the KGB every time the Red Army team scored. It had been a Moscow tradition since the games had started many years ago, and it was tolerated, although reluctantly, by the regime.

This mid-May Saturday the crowds were in a particularly ugly mood. Rumors had been rife that the "midnight visits" of the KGB had been reinstated. It was reported that entire families had been disappearing as if they had dropped off the face of the earth. It had been observed in Ivanova, some two hundred kilometers southeast of Moscow, that hundreds of open coal cars equipped with covering nets had been marshaled. They were to transport, it was rumored, captive Solidarity suspects to work on the huge network of natural-gas pipelines that were snaking their way from Siberia to Western Europe. In spite of elaborate security precautions, the word had gotten out: The KGB was finally resorting to the Stalinist and Chekist methods of the past in order to crush the Solidarity movement once and for all.

As the crowds filtered into the huge stadium there was a feeling of terrible expectancy in the air. The KGB men were thicker than usual in the crowds, and they were congregating in strategic places: by exits and restrooms, and at the end of bleacher rows. The families of the KGB personnel were conspicuously absent.

"Here's our section, Raisa: section ZZ and, let's see, row H, seats 26 and 27."

Raisa clutched Yuri's arm and panted, "That's almost to the rim of the stadium, Yuri. Let's stop. I've got to catch my breath." Minutes later they plopped onto the hard, concrete slabs which served as seats and spread a blanket over their knees. A slight cooling breeze was blowing off the Moscow river.

"It *is* on the rim, Yuri. How did you manage to get seats up here in the sky? The people on the field look like ants." Raisa chuckled, squeezing his leg.

"Be thankful that we've got seats at all, dear Raisa." Yuri stood, throwing his half of the blanket over Raisa's legs. "Look. You can see all the way to Moscow."

Raisa stood and peered over the edge of the stadium wall. Her attention was riveted on a long convoy of dark green vans that were crawling up the traffic-choked artery of Leningradsky Prospekt, the main highway from Dynamo Stadium to Moscow. The vans, over two hundred of them, took the off-ramps and parked in strategic spots near the outside exits ringing the stadium.

"I don't like the looks of this, Yuri." Raisa's voice was tinged with fear. "What are those vans for?"

Yuri's eyebrows twitched into peaks of incomprehension.

"Those are called Green Dragons. They're used to transport prisoners," Yuri responded grimly.

"But why so many?" Raisa rubbed her hands nervously, feeling the sweat greasing her palms. "They can haul the entire stadium crowd in the number of vans they have out there."

"Not quite," volunteered the heavyset man standing next to them, his binoculars glued to his eyes, "but the rumors are flying. The KGB will tolerate no nonsense at *this* game. Anybody overheard insulting State Security will be arrested."

"But they've always allowed that before!" blurted Yuri, his anger rising.

"Times are changing, lad," said the stranger prophetically. "Times are changing."

Fifteen minutes into the game the KGB team, as if guided by some prearranged signal, started to foul the Red

Army players consistently. The fouls were personal: an elbow in the kidney, a severe kick to the shin, a finger in the eye. The center forward of the Red Army team was carried off the field on a stretcher to the standing ovation of the entire stadium after being dealt a near-crippling blow from behind.

The Red Army struck back. Elbows, knees, and even fists started to gouge into the ranks of the KGB team. The Red Army-KGB contests had always been known as a grudge match—a microcosm of the larger struggle for prestige, power, and resources between the two giant organizations—but this game reflected a ferocity of feeling that was new. The crowds hooted their hatred of the KGB every time they fouled, and howled with delight when the Red Army scored.

Raisa scanned the knots of hard-looking men who were beginning to cluster in various locations below them. They were clearly agitated, some fondling what appeared to be weapons of some sort hidden in their jackets. Their tough-looking faces twitched with suspicion and hatred as they scowled at the hostile crowds. They cast intimidating glances at the spectators as the fans cheered on the Red Army team.

"Are those fellows regular KGB?" Raisa asked, squirming uncomfortably.

"I don't know. They're not the type you see around the Center. I wonder if they were brought in for crowd control."

"Most of them are Letts—brought in from the Baltic republics, Latvia and Estonia. The KGB has always used them as bullyboys. Even Lenin used Lettish sharpshooters to pick off demonstrators," offered the stranger sitting next to Yuri, his face screwed in disgust. "They'd cut their own mother's throat for a kopeck, those chort-eating bastards. I saw them being trucked in by the hundreds. I've got a feeling that all hell's going to cut loose, so I'm leaving."

There were many others who sensed the ensuing crisis and started to filter out of their seats and head for the exits. As the stranger moved down the row and started to turn toward the exit ramp a huge, blond, scar-faced Lett barred his way. Raisa strained her eyes as she watched the heated argument between them. The Lett reached into his jacket and pulled out a small club and jabbed it sharply into the stranger's stomach. He doubled over with pain, and was yanked up by the hair and shoved roughly back toward his seat. Others were treated in a similar manner.

"Yuri!" Raisa surveyed the frightened and dismayed spectators around her. "They're not letting people leave —what's happening?" The stranger stumbled back through the row, his face contorted in pain. He almost collapsed as he crumpled into his seat beside Yuri.

"The filthy prick!" he gasped, his face white from shock and anger. "That scum-sucking pig!" he gasped, holding his stomach. Within minutes there were shouting matches throughout the stadium as spectators tried to leave but were shoved back to their seats by the Lettish thugs.

A Red Army player, the right halfback, dribbled the ball toward the goal, his footwork a fantastic display of skill. Two KGB defensive players came pounding toward him and, in a series of clearly illegal body-blocks, sent him spinning to the ground clutching his testicles in agony. The referee refused to call a foul and penalize the KGB team.

The crowd rose as one person and screamed insults, cursing the KGB. Bottles rained down on the field, peppering the bleachers where the KGB-team reserves and coaches sat. Members of the Red Army team rushed to their fallen comrade. Heated words were exchanged and the fuse was lit.

During the argument both teams, now in an eyeball-to-eyeball shouting match, tried to refrain from physical violence, but the inevitable happened. A fist lanced out and a KGB player fell to the grass, his nose spurting blood. Soon the center of the field was filled with screaming, cursing players lashing out at each other in frenzied anger. A squad of uniformed militiamen rushed from the dugouts, truncheons in hand, and flailed into the Red Army team. The fans were now beyond control, and hundreds of those nearest the field leaped down on the turf and plowed into the KGB and the police. The enraged fans kicked, gouged, and beat the objects of their hatred until scores of bloody clumps littered the field. Suddenly, as if on cue, the Lettish thugs whipped out red armbands and slipped them on their left arms. Clubs and truncheons were yanked out of hundreds of jackets and the Letts waded into the howling crowds, mindlessly but methodically beating the spectators. There was complete pandemonium as people fell between the bleacher seats with cracked skulls and bloodied faces.

"I—I don't believe this is happening!" Raisa gasped, clutching Yuri's arm. "They're killing people, Yuri! They're killing people!" She was close to hysteria.

A huge, blond Lett bounded up the steps, snarling, a huge wooden club in his hand. His eyes were filled with a frenzied blood-lust. He clubbed a knot of fans two rows below Yuri until they fell between the rows, lifeless clumps of humanity.

"Stop it, you son of a whore! Stop it!" screamed Yuri, seething with rage.

The Lett spun in his tracks, his teeth bared in a wolflike snarl, and raced up the last few steps, his club raised. His vicious, porcine eyes glinted with fury as he swung toward Raisa. Yuri pushed her aside, but the wooden club grazed her scalp. She turned to Yuri screaming, her hands clutching her bleeding head.

Yuri's fist lashed out, catching the Lett on the side of the face. Enraged, he lunged at Yuri, but he sidestepped easily and kicked the Lett in the stomach. As the Lett doubled over, Yuri and the stranger grabbed him by the coat and pants and lifted him onto the top of the stadium rim. The Lett's eyes were orbs of terror as he suddenly saw the ground some two hundred feet below. He screamed for mercy, his hands clutching at the rough concrete exterior of the stadium, as Yuri and the spectator worked the Lett's convulsing body over the rim. With one mighty shove they jettisoned their burden and the KGB thug fell screaming to his death.

Yuri scooped up the red armband that had fallen from the Lett's sleeve, stuffed it in his pocket, and grabbed

Raisa's hand. They ran down the steps and, club in hand, Yuri felled several thugs. Raisa was pulled along, blindly following, holding her scarf to her wounded scalp.

The crowds were now fighting back. There were many Solidarity members and sympathizers in the masses of spectators—some had knives. After the initial shock of the KGB attack, groups of spectators started to retaliate in a semi-organized fashion. Many of the Letts were surrounded and knifed in the back. Their attackers ripped off their armbands and put them on, racing at other thugs and catching them by surprise and killing them. Hundreds of people, fans and KGB, were trampled to death in the melee.

"The way's clear to the exit, Raisa!" bellowed Yuri over the noise. "Hang on, Raisa—only a few more feet to the gate!" Yuri slipped on the armband and rushed to a uniformed KGB guard. Along the circular walkway at the base of the stadium, thousands of spectators were lined up, their hands held high above their heads as submachine-gun-toting guards held them at bay—the weapons' muzzles pointing menacingly at their midst.

The guard at the turnstile pulled his pistol and aimed it at Yuri. "Nobody leaves!" he yelled. "Everybody stays!"

"Look, my fiancée has been hurt," Yuri pleaded. "I've got to get her to a doctor." Raisa groaned dramatically, blood trickling through her fingers as she held her head. The guard shoved his pistol barrel into Yuri's stomach.

"My orders are that nobody is to leave the stadium."

Yuri reached for his wallet and pulled out his identification card.

"I am Sergeant Yuri Spinnenko of the Kremlin Guards. I demand to be released."

The gate guard was unmoved. A KGB sergeant came running up to the turnstile.

"What's going on here?" he barked.

"This bastard wants out, Sergeant. My orders are that everybody stays until screened."

Yuri changed his tactics, becoming more aggressive.

"Look, you idiots. Do you know who I am? Does the name Spinnenko mean anything to you numbskulls?"

A flicker of recall flashed across the sergeant's face.

"My uncle is General Spinnenko, Chief of the Border Guards, KGB. This woman your bullyboys clubbed is General Spinnenko's private secretary. He'll have your fucking heads for this. Now—let us out of here."

The sergeant was thoroughly cowed and apologized profusely.

"Let them out," he ordered.

Outside the stadium, the chaos was controlled. Long lines of people herded from the stadium—men, women, children, heads bloodied, limbs broken, some semiconscious—were shoved roughly into the waiting green prison vans. When they were filled, the vans roared from the parking lots, down the Leningradsky Prospekt to the Sadovaya Ring, took the exit, and sped toward the hastily constructed reception center at Ivanova.

Three hours later, Yuri and Raisa entered the ornate living room of his uncle's five-room apartment on the corner of Gorky and Georgievsky streets, an area where many Soviet officials lived. Raisa's head was swathed in a large bandage that covered the six stitches sewn in her scalp by the emergency-room doctor at the small clinic on Dasnovaya Street. In spite of the crowd of others who were seeking treatment, mostly casualties from the stadium fiasco, Yuri had got Raisa in immediately by flashing his Border Guards identification card.

Slumped in a large leather chair, a half-empty bottle of Stolichnya vodka beside him on the end table, was the squat figure of the general, his eyes fixed upon the flickering blue and white television screen before him.

The announcer's voice was a flat and dispassionate monotone as he continued his news coverage of the afternoon's disaster at Dynamo Stadium:

The Solidarity-instigated insurrection at Dynamo Stadium was resolutely crushed by the vigilant forces of the State Security Service. It was known in advance, through the astute gathering of intelligence, that the criminal Solidarity movement would use the annual game between the two sister services to initiate violence. The majority of the spectators, honest Soviet citizens, were outraged at this blatant attempt to scandalize and sabotage the government and cheered the efforts of State Security as they rounded up these Solidarity hooligans.

Pavel Spinnenko heard Yuri and Raisa enter the room. He turned around, and his beady peasant's eyes registered shock as he saw Raisa's bandaged head. He rose and grabbed her arm.

"Raisa! My dear Raisa! What happened to you?"

Raisa managed a thin smile. "I was one of those Solidarity hooligans punished by our stalwarts of State Security."

Spinnenko's chin dropped as he felt a surge of anger inside of him.

"You two were at the game?"

"Yes, uncle," replied Yuri. "That announcer . . ." he jabbed a finger in disgust toward the television set ". . . is full of pigshit! I don't know anything about Solidarity being involved, but the crowds were full of these Lettish thugs. They were as thick as flies in the crowds and wouldn't let anybody leave. They provoked the whole thing. We saw it, uncle. Those bastards created the crisis."

The general's lips curled into a snarl.

"Those bastards! Those stupid bastards! They've finally started it." He grabbed the phone and dialed a high-priority number in the Kremlin.

"Sergei? This is Pavel—Pavel Spinnenko. Have you heard the news?"

Yuri and Raisa could hear the excited voice of Sergei Gorsky, the Minister of Communications, coming loudly through the phone. The general listened quietly, his bullet-shaped head turning crimson. Finally, he exploded in a torrent of words, ending with ". . . Rakhmatov will plunge us into civil war! He has the intelligence of a wild radish!"

Pavel Spinnenko's hand was shaking as he slammed the receiver back in its cradle. The crimson in his face subsided as he exhaled a weary, resigned breath. He slumped back in his chair and rubbed his eyeballs.

"I—I don't know if it's the vodka or what I've just heard, but my head is splitting. Raisa, would you mind . . ."

"I'll rub if you'll tell me what's going on, Pavel." Raisa's fingers were already probing into the general's thick neck.

"What I'm about to tell you must *not* leave this room —understand?"

Yuri and Raisa nodded in unison.

"Gorsky was at a Politburo meeting last week—a special session—where they ironed out the details of the Solidarity crackdown. When they got into the planning stage, Gorsky was asked to leave. In this meeting they decided to create an incident at the game to show that the government meant business. It was designed to make an example of all who slander the KGB."

"But almost everybody, even the innocent, were rounded up, Uncle Pavel—how . . ."

"Oh, Yuri, don't be so damned naive! You were brought up to be a model comrade. Does this blind you to the things that are really going on in our country? Didn't your visit to the Politburo teach you anything? This country is in deep trouble, nephew. It's in deep shit! You'd better learn that fast because soon, very soon, you're going to have to choose sides."

Yuri was visibly shaken by his uncle's half-drunk barrage of invective. "What do you mean—choose sides?" he asked.

"Just—just forget what I've said and let me finish the rest of Gorsky's information . . . and don't interrupt, Yuri," slurred the general. "Those Letts were brought in to provoke the spectators. The people rounded up to be taken to Ivanova exceeded forty thousand."

"Ivanova—forty thousand—what in the hell?" blurted Yuri, his eyes wide with bewilderment.

"They've set up an interrogation center at Ivanova —tents, stockades—right by the coal cars that have been assembled there for the trips to Siberia."

Yuri's eyes blinked in disbelief.

"The KGB will make a feeble attempt to separate the innocent from the guilty, whatever 'guilty' means these days. I suspect that anybody who can show a government or Party card will be assumed innocent. The rest will be crammed into coal cars, have heavy nets thrown over them and tied down to the cars, and be taken to the pipeline project. That's what Krylenko really wants: bodies for the project."

"Won't—won't they be tried in the People's Courts?" asked Yuri, a dull ache now constricting his stomach.

The general stared at his nephew, not sure if the statement was said in jest or not. Embarrassed, Raisa lowered her eyes and concentrated on massaging the general's neck.

"Yuri—I—Yuri." Pavel Spinnenko sighed and shook his head slightly. "Yuri, right now . . ." The general's voice became soft and patronizing, the voice of a teacher trying to explain a complicated problem to a backward child. "Right now, some of the things that you've always assumed about our system have been, how can I say it, temporarily put in cold storage to meet this so-called 'emergency.' Some of our leading policymakers are totally out of touch with reality."

"But it's the *people* in the Politburo, not the system—not the teachings of Comrade Lenin. Right, uncle?" Yuri's voice was tremulous with anger and concern.

Pavel waved his hand wearily. "Under my right ear, dear Raisa. Just rub a little under my right ear."

"Yes, it's true, Yuri. The teachings of Comrade Lenin remain pure and undefiled. If *only* the leaders would remain true to the teachings of Comrade Lenin then we wouldn't be in this mess." The general's voice slurred mockingly. "Speaking of 'this mess,' I haven't finished my conversation with Gorsky. He told me that Rakhmatov has been appointed to replace Blinov."

"Rakhmatov!" Raisa almost screamed the name. "He'll ruin us! He's a primitive Chekist!"

"That's why he was chosen, my lovely Raisa. It will take a primitive Chekist to carry out the new policies. Rakhmatov's philosophy is 'It's better that a thousand innocent people be punished if we can catch one who is guilty.'

He's been given a blank check to execute the Solidarity crackdown."

The name of Rakhmatov sliced into Yuri like a sword. Even his innocent belief in the system couldn't excuse the fearsome reputation of the Minister of the Interior.

"Oh—two other items. Gorsky was full of gossip. The Red Army has been ordered to form several armies from the Central Asian minorities—Uzbeks, Turkmenians, Kazakhs, Tajiks, and others. We're opening up a new front in Sinkiang Province in China. Solidarity has already spread the rumor that this is the gerontocracy's way of cutting down the Asian population so we Great Russians won't be outnumbered. There are already rumors of 'minority death lists' being attached to operational orders."

"I've heard those rumors in China—about Solidarity death lists, uncle. There's nothing to it. Nothing! No Russian commander would send a comrade to his death like that."

"*You* didn't see it because you were in the Border Guards, and *I* command the Border Guards. *I* wouldn't do it, Yuri. I didn't have to, because the Border Guards doesn't take conscripts; but the army *did*."

Yuri's expression became grimly set, a combination of anger and humiliation.

"I've heard enough, Uncle Pavel. We're plowing up old ground. The system is perfect. *People* make mistakes but the teachings of Comrade Lenin ensure that the system is self-correcting. I'm sorry, uncle. Raisa. I have to leave. I promised a comrade that I would take his shift at the Tomb because of a favor he had done for me. I believe that this is the night I must repay him. Can you get a ride home, Raisa?"

Raisa nodded absently, her hands resting on the general's shoulders.

"I'll take her home," Pavel Spinnenko slurred deliberately, "and yes, Yuri, you do just that. You stand in front of our dear Comrade Lenin. Talk to him. Draw inspiration from our friend under the glass. Oh yes, Yuri: commune with our Great Father in the tomb. He has all the answers."

Silence: a silence of pain and anguish stilled the room

when the general had finished.

Suddenly, his face a mask of embarrassed anger, Yuri spun on his heel, slammed the door and ran down the apartment steps. He jogged toward the Tomb on Red Square.

IX.

"Ladies and gentlemen, we are now making our final approach to Moscow. We will be landing at Domodedovo Airport in approximately fifteen minutes. Please fasten your seat belts, put your seats in an upright position, and extinguish all smoking materials. Thank you for flying Swissair."

One minute Yossef was descending through murky clouds; the next, there was Moscow below him, stretching as far as the eye could see. The pattern of its lights drew spokes and concentric circles against the wet ground —like a great spiderweb spangled with dew. The eye of the web was the Kremlin, with Lenin's Tomb brilliantly lighted inside the eye. The similarity was uncanny, breathtaking; and it heightened his already sickening apprehension. He glanced at Yabin, but he was entombed in his own thoughts—staring out the window and stroking his cheek.

"Well, down there, Herr Schwender." Yabin grabbed Yossef's knee, his countenance changing dramatically. His teeth gleamed luminously under his dark mustache. "Our new home for awhile, eh?"

"Where are we staying tonight, Mister Mehaggian?" asked Yossef, using Yabin's assumed name—that of an

Armenian export executive from Cairo.

"At the Metropole for the first few nights, then the Swiss Trade Mission will find you an apartment."

"Near Raisa Karezev, I hope."

Yabin's mustache twitched a smile.

"Where will you be?"

Yabin's voice fell to a conspiratorial whisper.

"Don't worry. I'll be close—very close. Just settle into your work and blend with the staff at the Mission. A man named Alex Mullineaux will be your contact. You can't miss him. He weighs almost three hundred pounds and has almost white hair. He's a statistician at the Mission."

Yossef tugged nervously at a few strands of his newly grown beard. It was neatly trimmed and, when it had grown out, had become the color of mud. His naturally sandy-colored hair had been dyed to match.

The Swissair landing at Domodedovo was so smooth that Yossef didn't notice it until the tires squealed on the wet tarmac. As the plane taxied toward the passenger terminal he saw several airport service vans approaching the aircraft. In his anxiety he saw every van filled with armed KGB troops coming especially for him. He breathed deeply and flexed his muscles, forcing himself to relax, as the engines whined to a stop.

As Yossef and Yabin entered the bustling terminal, an attractive green-uniformed customs guard ushered them into a tastefully decorated waiting room. Every instinct of Yossef's screamed "escape" as he shuffled with the other passengers toward the long Formica counter. To his chagrin, the customs men did not greet him like totalitarian robots. They were pleasant and courteous, rifling through his luggage with care and skill.

Yossef's brown eyes, their color changed by his newly installed tinted contact lenses, registered a silent sigh of relief when the customs inspector stamped his passport, smiled, and waved him toward the waiting line of cabs outside the terminal.

"I hope that your stay in Moscow is pleasant, Mr. Schwender." The inspector smiled. Yossef gave a nervous bob of his head and started for the large glass doors which opened automatically as he approached the street. Yabin caught up with him and whispered, "Relax, Yossef. You're as anxious as a married man in a whorehouse. Don't worry. You're completely covered. Your position with the Swiss Trade Mission is perfectly legitimate and your cover story, right down to your birth certificate in the Berne City Hall, is authentic. You're Herman Schwender right down to your skin and don't you forget it. Just play that role and you're safe. Remember, too, that every cabbie is a KGB informer and the hotel room is bugged. Let's grab a taxi."

An hour later, Yossef fell into a deep, numbing sleep in his Metropole hotel room.

Vasily Gregierenko paced the floor of his Ankara apartment like a caged lion. His hands and head moved in tight little jerks as he spoke to the small assembly of key Solidarity leaders seated before him. Each person there was a district leader in the movement and exercised command and control over all of the personnel and resources in his area of jurisdiction. Every person in the room had gone to extraordinary lengths to sneak out of the Soviet Union, cross the fortified border, and make it to the Turkish capital for this Solidarity strategy meeting. The twenty-two representatives murmured among themselves as they discussed the pros and cons of Operation Samson. Suddenly an aide burst into the room and thrust a sheet of paper at the Solidarity leader. As he read it he felt a spasm of shock—a fleeting fear of despair.

"Vasily, what's wrong?" asked a district leader.

Gregierenko fought for composure, exhaled a nervous breath, and announced: "Brothers and sisters. Listen to this. In a week and a half, June 10 to be exact, the body of Lenin is going to be removed from the Tomb and taken on a tour of the Soviet Union. This tour will last approximately three months." There was a slight pause as he struggled to compose his thoughts. "The Politburo has decided to 'take Lenin to the people.' His railroad car will be a sort of mobile Tomb complete with Tomb Guards.

They're using his original sealed car, the one in the Lenin Museum, as his portable mausoleum."

His announcement caused a stunned silence in the small room.

"There goes Operation Samson—poof! Just like that." One of the group gasped in dismay.

Gregierenko paused again, trying to infuse his voice with just the right blend of urgency and anger.

"We mustn't let this throw us. Operation Samson *will* take place. We'll just have to rearrange our timetable." He felt an acid burning in his stomach and reached for his glass of iced mineral water.

"When you return, spread the word among your people; use every network. *Nothing* is to happen to that train. I'll have the head of *anybody* who attempts to sabotage it during its tour. We must get that damned Lenin back into his Tomb on Red Square."

"Vasily." The representative from one of the Siberian districts waved for recognition. "In the Yakutskaya region there are partisans operating in the forests. They're escaped prisoners from the pipeline project."

Gregierenko suddenly brightened. "Good! Good for them."

"Most of them are Vietnamese, with a few Americans."

"Americans?" Gregierenko frowned. "What are Americans doing up there?"

"These people are prisoners from the Vietnamese War. Some of them have been held since the late 1960s. The Vietnamese government sent them to the Soviet Union among thousands of their own people to pay off their war debts. These partisans have been wreaking havoc on the gas pipelines and on stretches of track on the Trans-Siberian Railroad. I can't be accountable for them."

"How many are there?"

"They began with a small band but they've been raiding the work camps and liberating other prisoners. Right now there are over three hundred, and they're growing every week. Their raids have been getting more audacious."

A gleam of inspiration flickered for a moment in Gregierenko's eyes. He drew himself up to his full five feet ten inches and spoke, his teeth bared, a taut smile on his face. His words had a galvanic effect on the people in the room.

"Georgi: make contact with this group. Form a permanent liaison. Try to smuggle them arms and explosives. Attempt to influence their strategy so it coordinates with ours. Convince them that they should call themselves the Solidarity Army of Liberation."

There was a babble of protest from some of the members.

"This is a premature phase of the armed struggle, Vasily. We're not prepared," counseled the representative from Kiev.

"We must take advantage of *any* opportunity!" Gregierenko shot back, revealing his irritation. "Here is the nucleus of a liberation army already in being—and functioning! Let's use it."

The Solidarity leader's arguments were persuasive. The district leaders voted to support the Siberian partisans.

"And Georgi." Gregierenko wagged an angular finger at the Siberian representative. "If those partisans blow up our 'Comrade Lenin'—if he passes through the Yakutskaya region—I'll have your bloody head on a platter."

Private Rolan Lonchakov stared dolefully out the dingy window of the troop train as it rolled through the Siberian taiga, his dark melancholy eyes half-lidded in boredom. The flat blue-green countryside of the Yakutskaya region had an almost hypnotic effect on him because of its terrible monotony.

Lonchakov, just out of basic infantry assault school like all of the others on this extra-long troop train, was being rushed to the North China Front for the Red Army's planned mid-June offensive—and to fill the desperate personnel gaps made by casualties and mounting desertions.

He shifted his AK-47 between his legs to get more comfortable, leaned his chin in the cup of his hand, and stared at the dense forest beyond. At each end of the railroad coach sat an armed political commissar whose duty it was to ensure the arrival of these reluctant recruits, members of the 439th Motorized Rifle Regiment, at the front.

The train began to slow to a crawl, its air brakes hissing in a series of sharp audible gasps. The KGB officer in charge of movement control burst into the engineer's cab.

"Why are you slowing down?" he scowled, his voice tinged with suspicion.

"I've just received word ove. the radio from the Transport Control Center at Kirensk. Bandits have dynamited a section of track between here and Lake Baikal. I have to back up to the cutoff and go by way of Ust-Kut," replied the engineer apologetically.

"Shit!" muttered the KGB officer. "That means we'll have to travel parallel to the pipeline. I've been ordered to avoid exposing the troops to the project if possible."

"If I don't go by way of Ust-Kut it may delay us for several days. It's hard to get a work crew up here in a hurry. The maintenance people at Kirensk sit on their asses half the time sipping tea. Kirensk told me that these bandits are escaped prisoners from the—"

"Yes, yes. I know all that," growled the officer impatiently.

"But they're attacking troop trains, too. Kirensk told me to tell the commander of the 439th that ammunition should be issued to the soldiers. They may have to leave the train and engage the guerrillas. We'll be passing through several ambush sites by going through the Ust-Kut hills."

"Piss up a rope!" The KGB officer pulled a papirosa from a pack that looked like he had slept on it, and lit it. "If it's not one fucking thing, it's another! All right. Back this son of a bitch up and go through Ust-Kut."

After three hours of backward motion the thirty-two-car gray-green troop train headed north toward the small prison-camp community of Ust-Kut on the Lena river. Not too far from the village of Ust-Kut was the prison-camp complex. Each soldier had been issued a full magazine of ammunition in case of ambush by bandits.

Lonchakov's boredom was replaced by a creeping fear.

He, like the other recruits, had never fired a shot in anger before and, like the others, had no desire to be in the army on his way to fight in China. But like most Soviet youths he was raised to obey the orders and authorities of the State.

The train slowed and crept past a parallel track. Beyond the track, to Lonchakov's left, were hundreds of workers: men, women, and children down to the age of ten, tearing at the spongy ground with picks and shovels. Huge triangular piles of pipe were stored nearby, ready to be buried in the newly dug trench.

The ragged, emaciated figures, miserable wretches of humanity, stopped and rested on their tools as the train crawled by. The young soldiers pressed their faces against the window glass and stared numbly at their fellow countrymen.

"I've never seen prisoners before—like that," exclaimed a young Lithuanian corporal. "It—it looks like they've got whole families out there. Damn! They look like they haven't eaten in weeks."

The troop train began to parallel another long train parked on the double track. The troops stared in shocked horror at the contents of the shallow coal cars. Thousands of people, clearly Russians, were standing, packed so tightly together that there was barely room to move. Heavy nets covered the packed masses and were tied to cleats on the sides of the railroad cars. It was obvious that some of them were dead but could not fall to the floor: they were propped up by the press of bodies. Some of the prisoners had managed to gnaw through the ropes and get their heads out through the nets. The smell of their urine and excrement filled the air like a noxious gas and penetrated the sealed windows of the troop train. Armed KGB guards were positioned on small platforms at the end of each car.

The soldiers cast pitying glances at their countrymen who were waiting to be taken to the prison camp of Ust-Kut nearby. The prisoners stared back in resigned helplessness at the thousands of young faces pressed against the glass. As the train hissed to a stop, Lonchakov took the opportunity to study the faces of the people in the prison car opposite him. He scanned the faces and suddenly his eyes locked into those of a woman, her head sticking out of a gnawed net. He blinked his eyes in disbelief and then frantically tried to open the window. It was sealed shut. In one angry movement he raised the butt of his assault rifle and smashed the glass and yelled out to the woman.

"Mama! Mama! It's me, Rolan! What—what's happened? Why are you here?"

The woman screamed a cry of recognition.

"Rolan! Rolan! Is that really you? It's Mama! Papa, Natya and Sergei are here with us. Natya is dead! She's standing next to me. Rolan! Rolan! Help us, please!" Her voice trailed off in a series of racking sobs.

Rolan saw the corpse face of his sister, only fifteen years old, jammed between his mother and another prisoner. Suddenly, the entire population of the prison train took up the plaintive cry for help.

"Help us, comrades! We are innocent of any wrongdoing! Many of us are dead. They haven't fed us for a week!"

Rolan's father shouted loudly over the tumult: "Rolan! Many of us were arrested at the Dynamo Stadium three weeks ago during a soccer game. We were taken to Ivanova and condemned without a trial and packed on this train. We haven't done anything! Rolan! We're all dying! Help us!"

A KGB guard climbed to his perch on the car, took careful aim, and shot Rolan's father through the head. His brain matter splattered over on Rolan in a bloody spray. In a burst of rage, Rolan jammed his loaded magazine into his assault rifle, took aim, and blasted the guard off the prison car.

A political commissar ran down the aisle of the troop train car, pistol in hand. He aimed it at Lonchakov and started to squeeze the trigger when a Ukrainian sergeant squeezed off a burst from his AK-47 and sent the commissar flying backward, his shattered chest a mass of blood.

The impact of this action rippled through the train like

a breeze through a field of wheat. It was so easy, so very easy, to kill your oppressors. Their terrible aura of authority could be ended by one burst of an AK-47 if one had the courage to do it.

Within seconds, hundreds of windows were smashed by the young recruits and KGB guards were shot like game animals. The soldiers poured off the train. Their officers and the political commissars were shot where they stood. Soon there was a pitched battle between the recruits and the camp guards, but the camp fell quickly into the hands of the rampaging soldiers.

The troops swarmed over the prison cars, cut the nets away, and took the survivors to the prison barracks beyond.

All communication between the remote Ust-Kut camp and the outside world had been cut off. After the fury of the soldiers had been vented on the KGB, a revolutionary council had been called by the Solidarity activists among them. The weapons and equipment cars of the troop train were broken into and every portable weapon—hundreds of shoulder-fired surface-to-air missiles, machine guns, grenade launchers, all of the weapons organic to a Motorized Rifle Regiment—were looted and distributed to the soldiers and liberated prisoners. There were hundreds of other weapons in the camp complex. These, too, helped form the growing arsenal of the rebels.

The following day, after a night of wild celebrating and feasting from the stores of foodstuff found in the camp, the dead were buried in the pipe trench and the camp systematically destroyed.

That evening, over three thousand soldiers and six thousand prisoners, some from the train, some from the camp, struggled off under their heavy loads of food and weapons and trudged northward. The mass of humanity was soon swallowed up by the tangled forest blurring the horizon.

Soon, very soon, they would make contact with McMurrin's growing band and swell the ranks of the newly created Solidarity Army of Liberation.

* * *

The Trans-Siberian Railroad is the longest in the world. It runs 5,778 miles from Moscow to Vladivostok on the Pacific, passes through eight time zones, and, if one takes an express, can finish the journey in seven days and sixteen and a half hours. The Express makes ninety-seven stops, crossing a land surface twice the size of Europe; traveling in the winter, a passenger would experience temperatures along the route as low as minus forty degrees Fahrenheit. The train would circumvent Lake Baikal, the deepest lake in the world, inhabited by fresh-water seals and transparent fish which melt in contact with the air. It would skirt the Sino-Soviet border near the war zone on the Amur River not far from where the Soviet offensive was bogged down on the North China front. It would then roll into Kharbovsk, which claims 270 cloudless days a year. Vladivostok, the Soviet Union's "window to the east," would be the last stop.

Yuri stood at attention with the other Kremlin Guards as the Politburo members, all twelve of them following behind the enclosed casket of Lenin carried by six young naval cadets from Kronstadt, approached the newly refurbished sealed car which had been brought down from the Lenin Museum in Leningrad. The undercarriage of the car had been strengthened and the wheels altered to fit the wide gauge of Soviet railroads. It looked absurdly out of place sandwiched between the gleaming red-and-cream-colored cars of the Trans-Siberian Express.

As the casket drew near the band struck up a mournful rendition of the "Internationale," the Communist anthem. Yuri snapped to attention and flipped his gleaming assault rifle into a salute as the casket was carried onto the car. Moments later, it was placed in a special receptacle on the floor. The cars flanking the Tomb car were for the guards and the other cars of the Express carried the many dignitaries who would accompany the body, the communications center, and the KGB security detachment. A shorter monitor train carrying explosives-ordnance disposal personnel and engineers and a flatcar carrying an observation helicopter would precede the Tomb train. Its mission was to fly ahead and scout possible ambush sites in partisan country or discover buried explosives along the tracks.

After the casket was safely on board and secured in its receptacle, Yuri and the Guard of Honor boarded the flanking cars and took their seats, sitting at attention. The train throbbed into life, gave a series of short, forward jerks, and began to glide out of Moscow's Far Eastern Station.

It was 10:00 A.M., June 10. Yuri was not due to return until September 3.

X.

By mid-July, Yuri was beginning to wonder if Raisa wasn't right: that "taking Lenin to the people" was a stupid idea. There was no doubt that the corpse of Lenin drew morbid crowds. At every city and village where they stopped, long lines of the curious trooped aboard the old sealed car and filed by the waxen image in the coffin, stupidly gawking at it like country bumpkins staring at a three-headed lady at a rural fair. In many areas the local Soviets organized a propaganda campaign among the population to encourage people to view the body. Their techniques were often similar to that of a barker at a rural fair. In the city of Omsk, Yuri remembered with distaste, surly and irreverent crowds shuffling by the casket, some cracking jokes, mothers trying to stifle crying babies or wipe running noses as they dragged their children by. The crowds in the rest of Russia did not share the reverent mood of the long, mournful lines in Moscow.

"Look, Sasha," commented one father holding a squirming four-year-old. "That's Lenin. His picture hangs in the city hall. He's the fellow who led the Revolution back in 1917."

"Is he dead, Daddy?" asked the youngster.

"No. He's just taking a nap, stupid," rejoined an older brother.

"Yes," interrupted the mother. "He's been dead for sixty-seven years."

"He looks like he's been dead a *hundred* and sixty-seven years," sulked the brother. "Let's get out of this place. It's creepy."

"Just wait until you get home, Mishka," scolded the mother. "I told you to keep your comments to yourself."

It was difficult for Yuri or the other guards to control themselves when such irreverent behavior took place, but they had to stand immobile, frozen, one at each end of the casket, staring at the face of Lenin while the crowds shuffled past.

Yuri had never really seen his own country before. His institutionalized life in the Kiev State Orphanage, the structured activities of the Little Oktobrists and Young Pioneers and other Communist youth organizations, precluded any contact with the harsh realities of Soviet life. Even his visit to the North China front was made over his homeland by aircraft and not through it. In spite of his professed idealism for egalitarianism, he was beginning to realize on this trip just what a privileged, secure, and even luxurious life he had been living all these years compared to the lives of the masses of his fellow citizens.

He was surprised and disturbed by the slums in many of the cities and towns he went through. Slums, he had been told all his life by Party propagandists, were to be found only in the decadent, capitalist societies of the West. The old *izbas,* the log-cabin structures so common in Russia four hundred years before, were still used everywhere. Life on the collective farms, idealized as happy and wholesome in Party propaganda, looked primitive and depressed from Yuri's train window. From his soft seat in the guards' car he could see hundreds of women and children toiling in stooped labor in the fields. The flat and depressing monotony of the countryside continued day after day until he wearied of it. After a month of traveling with Comrade Lenin, Yuri was bored almost beyond endurance.

It was in the small provincial city of Minusinsk that Yuri got hold of his first samizdat publication. It had been left in a seedy restaurant near the railroad depot. The restaurant was almost empty when he walked in out of the rainy night. He was wearing a pair of tan slacks and a flowered sports shirt; he took a seat in the far corner, and ordered tea and rolls. The waitress brought a pot of steaming tea and a platter of small, hard rolls and tried to engage Yuri in small chatter to relieve her ennui on the night shift. Yuri responded less than enthusiastically and she waddled back to the counter, muttering to herself. Yuri sipped his tea slowly, staring absently down the slick streets over his steaming cup.

His shoe rustled a paper on the floor. He looked down and, out of desultory curiosity, picked up a six-page newsletter, typed single-spaced on both sides. The first paragraph told him what it was: slanderous anti-State propaganda. He dropped it on the floor as if it were a writhing cobra. After a few more sips of tea, he looked around the restaurant furtively. He was totally alone, except for two old men near the front door playing chess. He could see for almost a block down the rain-slicked street for any potential customers.

He reached down and felt for the samizdat underground paper with the tips of his fingers, with a motion like kitchen tongs retrieving a hot potato from boiling water. He noticed that there was nothing on the paper to indicate that it was samizdat—no masthead screaming "Solidarity." To an observer it could look like any type of publication.

Yuri began to read as he nibbled on his tea-soaked roll. He had to admit—it read more engagingly than the sterile tabloids of the government and Party. Like most Soviet citizens, Yuri read official publications like *Pravda* and *Izvestia* between the lines in order to determine what the government really meant behind what was obviously said.

This particular issue of the samizdat was only three weeks old. Like most of the other more professionally produced samizdats, it was printed in Sweden or Finland and had been smuggled in sealed crates through the fully automated port of Archangel, the port newly designed and constructed by the Soviet Union to handle containerized cargo.

After ten minutes, Yuri was totally absorbed in the samizdat. It was devoted to the history of the Solidarity movement, its origins, its leading personalities, and its historical roots. He had always harbored a secret fascination for Solidarity and wondered how it had got started. Toward the top of the second page the caption almost leaped out at him:

The First Phase of the Solidarity Movement:
The Struggle Against Lenin

He dropped the paper to the floor and stared out the window, his mind reeling under the impact of the caption. No. There couldn't have been any struggle against Comrade Lenin while he was alive—by honest Soviet citizens. By White Russian civil insurrectionists and Tsarist capitalists, yes, but not by the ordinary people of the Soviet Union, and certainly not by Bolsheviks. The people back then saw and heard Comrade Lenin. They were actually there—close to the source of truth. If there had been a Solidarity "struggle" against Lenin back in those days, it must have been inspired by foreign agents to strangle the infant Communist state in its cradle.

Cautiously, Yuri reached down and picked up the samizdat again off the littered floor. To be fortified against the enemies of the State, one must understand their mentality. To know your enemy was only being a good Communist, he reasoned.

He began to read about a remarkable young American named Aleksei Dubrov, a convert to communism, a young favored revolutionary who actually lived with the Lenins and was exposed to his greatness as a member of his family. He was not much younger than Yuri himself, and had plunged into the making of a new world only to find that its chief architect was a power-hungry megalomaniac who had betrayed all of the ideals of the Russian Revolution.

The samizdat read like a novel, and Yuri was now totally engrossed. It dramatized the birth of little Georgi and the terrible ordeals of Natalya and her young son in the Kolyma camps and in the canal project on the Don. Yuri felt a rush of anger as he read how the guard had kicked the emaciated corpse of Natalya, trying to waken her, while little Georgi attacked him with his feet and fists.

The MOSSAD-originated story, extracted from the Makleff journal, narrated the odyssey of Georgi following his release from confinement and his subsequent reincarceration in the Vorturka camp in the Gulag. Certainly, the part about the massive Vorturka uprising was true. Even Khrushchev had excused the revolt (although he'd crushed it ruthlessly) as a legacy from the Stalinist past.

The last half of the last page dealt with the birth of Tanya's twins and their disappearance into the void of Soviet society. The babies, as yet unnamed, had been whisked away from Vorturka. One was smuggled out of the camp to an unnamed country and the other was placed in an orphanage somewhere in the Soviet Union.

Yuri calculated from the date of their birth to the present year. Those twins would be his age by now, he pondered. He wondered what their ultimate fate had been. Would the KGB have a file on the Dubrov twins? Certainly, they must have, somewhere—probably in the bowels of the Center. What kind of future would the twin living in Russia have with such a terrible anti-State legacy in his family?

Suddenly, the samizdat disappeared—snatched upward by a callused hand. He hadn't even heard them come in or approach his table, so involved was he in the Dubrov story.

Yuri looked up into the menacing, scowling faces of two uniformed militiamen.

* * *

"Solidarity forges documents like these all the time, my boy." The interrogator smiled, but his eyes were cold and appraising as he fingered Yuri's Kremlin Guards identification card. "You'd be surprised how many professionally printed but forged ID cards they have on display at regional headquarters in Krasnoyarsk. We could start a Solidarity museum up there, just specializing in forged documents."

The interrogator was a small wiry blond man about thirty-eight years old. His cold, bloodless lips looked like two strands of flesh-colored wire stretched across his face.

He had seen them all before, these Solidarity swine: students, professional people, even government bureaucrats and military men with beautifully crafted documents. This was a tremendous weakness in Soviet society, the interrogator often thought: in order for the State to control its citizens effectively, it required a document for practically every job and activity. Once the document was procured or produced, very few further questions were asked. Official documents were the lubricant that enabled Soviet society to function smoothly as a police state. Solidarity had discovered this weakness and exploited it by producing authentic-looking documents.

Yuri sat on the hard metal chair, his hands handcuffed behind his back. A single light bulb with a green shade dangled from the fly-specked ceiling and threw eerie shadows on the wall. He felt the fear creeping over him, the instinctive fear of the unknown.

"As a Soviet citizen I have the right to know what I'm being held for. It can't be for that stupid samizdat. It was just lying on the floor. I just glanced at it briefly."

"Liar!" The interrogator's calm demeanor changed abruptly. His right hand flicked out like a rattlesnake's tongue in a stinging slap across Yuri's face. "Even reading such a slanderous article like that one can get you ten years under Article 64, 'Slandering the State.' You were distributing this filth, weren't you? *Weren't you!*" He slapped Yuri again on the other cheek with the back of his hand.

It was now, in these first instants of fear and hysteria, that all the advantages were with the interrogator: Break him quickly before he can start to reassemble his shattered psyche.

Yuri reeled under the slaps, his mind paralyzed with rage and confusion. The benign face of Lenin gazed down at the agony of Yuri Spinnenko from its wooden frame on the slate-gray wall.

"I'll tell you for the tenth time: I am Sergeant Yuri Spinnenko of the Kremlin Guards. All you have to do is call the command car of the Lenin tour train. Ask for Major Koslavonov. He'll tell you who I am."

A second interrogator stalked quietly into the room. He was a gaunt man with a muddy complexion, hollow cheeks, and bad teeth. His eyes were the color of ice.

He lit a cigarette and inhaled gratefully with that very deep breath which marks the tobacco addict. Then he blew the smoke in Yuri's face and smiled with satisfaction as he relished Yuri's fear.

"We don't need to do that, Spinnenko—or whatever your name is." His voice was laced with alcohol. "You fit the description perfectly of one of the *brodyagi*, escaped prisoners, from the pipeline. You're a liaison agent between the bandits and urban Solidarity, aren't you? *Aren't you!*" He shoved the tip of a rubber truncheon hard into Yuri's solar plexis. The breath burst from Yuri's mouth like air exploding from a punctured balloon. His mouth gaped open in a prayer of pain as he gasped, tipped sideways, and fell off his chair to the cement floor. At this moment he wished that there was a God who would understand, who would assist him—but he, like millions of other members of the Party, had helped to banish Him from the land.

Rough hands yanked him upright and shoved him against the wall. The blond pulled a picture from his shirt pocket and thrust it into Yuri's face, spitting his words at him in a flat, menacing tone.

"This is you, isn't it? You're Ivan Navaroff, escaped in the Ust-Kut prison break several weeks ago. Your mission is to engage in anti-State propaganda and form a Solidarity terrorist cell here in Minusinsk."

Yuri stared at the photograph and shivered, disbelieving, wracked by fear, his breath coming in large anguished gulps. There was a resemblance—a slight one, but enough to cast suspicion on him—and, after all, he had been reading anti-State propaganda. Perhaps this punishment was just, he thought. He had committed a wrongful act. He had started to feel sympathy and respect for this traitorous Dubrov family. That, in itself, was deserving of the punishment he was now receiving.

The blond let a smile flicker an instant at the edges of his mouth, savoring the pain and tension in Yuri's face. It was intensely wearying to Yuri to stand against the wall with his hands behind his back, squinting against the glare of the light that grew more painful as the minutes crawled by. His feet began to protest and the joints of his knees throbbed. He struggled against the panic he was feeling, knowing now that if he gave way he would lapse into groveling terror; and that thought brought such intense shame and self-loathing that he breathed deeply and tried to stand straight.

An instant later a blow sent him sprawling to the floor. Yuri suppressed the oath just in time and struggled to get up, only to receive a sharp kick in the ribs. A hand grabbed his hair and jerked him up to meet a punch that snapped his head back against the wall. A second punch beneath the heart drove every bit of air from his lungs and left him paralyzed and gasping. He fell and rolled onto his side, knees drawn up, and struggled to breathe.

He was wrenched up again and struck by another blow from behind. The interrogator seemed to have mastered the technique of striking high on the spine, just below the shoulders, while kicking the victim's legs away so he would land headfirst. Half-conscious, head lolling from side to side, he was yanked to his feet and slapped hard.

"Please—please . . ." Yuri mumbled incoherently. "Must—must be presentable for—for Comrade Lenin. Guard mount tomorrow. Don't—don't bruise my face —please."

"Take him to the detention block. Give him time to think about his crime," barked the blond to the gaunt interrogator. The interrogation-room door squeaked open to admit the two militiamen who had arrested Yuri in the restaurant. They flanked him, huge Nagent revolvers hanging on their hips, and marched Yuri across an open courtyard that was bathed in the frigid mist of early morning. Dawn was breaking over the barbed-wire-topped brick wall of the Minusinsk Regional Detention Center. Yuri glanced at the sky. It was gray and bruised. A thin spatter of rain drifted across the cobbled courtyard as he looked again at the sky apprehensively. The terrible realization that this might be the last time he would ever see the sky in freedom filled him with a sense of sickening dread. The fear that coursed through him was so intense, so unexpected, that he thought he would vomit. He felt as if he were frozen, as if time had slowed, his body reacting only to autonomic control.

Yuri was shoved into a large holding cell containing about a hundred people. The walls were covered with Solidarity graffiti. The stench of urine, vomit, and dirty diapers was overpowering. In one corner of the cell were several young mothers with crying babies.

An unshaven young man, an army combat blouse draped casually around his shoulders, sauntered up to Yuri. His gentle green eyes looked evenly into his. Yuri, ashamed, averted his gaze.

"Are you here on an Article 64?" he asked.

"I'm here because I am guilty of reading anti-State propaganda," announced Yuri in a beaten voice.

"Ah, yes. An Article 64. You can get up to ten years in a strict regime camp for that," replied the prisoner scornfully.

Yuri was so ashamed and angry that he could not keep his hands from shaking. Fatigue was threatening to overwhelm him at any moment.

"What are—all of you people in here for?" Yuri asked tightly.

"Same thing. Article 64. 'Betrayal of the Motherland.' It's a garbage-pail charge. It covers anything that the police want it to: from reading samizdats to pissing on the sidewalks."

"What were you arrested for?"

"Me?" The young man broke into an infectious grin.

"I'm perhaps the only really guilty person here. I'm in on an Article 58, subsection 2: belonging to an anti-State organization and spreading slanderous anti-State propaganda."

"Solidarity?"

"Of course."

"I've never met anybody in Solidarity before." Yuri backed away slightly as if he might become contaminated by the prisoner. "I read this newsletter about Solidarity; the one about a family named Dubrov. That's why I'm here."

"Yes. The last issue. One of our best. It shows that our struggle is not new. I helped distribute them in my district," the prisoner boasted. "I've never seen such a strong reaction from the authorities. They ran amok in my district, confiscating every issue they could lay their hands on. Too bad you couldn't have hung on to that particular issue. It's going to be a collector's item after the revolution."

"The—revolution?" Yuri gave him an empty stare.

"Of course, my friend. The revolution that's coming. Not a new one, but a continuation of the original democratic revolution of the Russian people before Lenin betrayed it."

His words pounded into Yuri like a sledgehammer. He wanted to scream, "Let me out of here! I am the nephew of General Pavel Spinnenko of the KGB Border Guards! He'll have your fucking heads for this, you provincial idiots! Don't you know who I am?"

He turned and grabbed the bars of the cell so tightly that his knuckles turned white. He found that he could not catch his breath, and an ugly blackness was threatening to overwhelm him.

Suddenly, he was aware of the young man's hand on his shoulder.

"You are a troubled man, my friend. This is your first arrest, isn't it?"

Yuri nodded absently, feeling the energy drain from him.

"Look at these people." The prisoner gently, but firmly, turned Yuri around to face the others in the cell. "Ordinary Soviet citizens." He gestured toward them. "Heads of families, professional people. Their only real crime is a dedication to a dream; having an overpowering vision of a free and democratic Russia. See that fellow over there?" He pointed to a bearded man in a ragged tweed overcoat. "He used to be a secondary-school principal in Kierensk. One of the students didn't like him and accused him of passing out samizdats to the students. That's all it took. Now he is headed for the pipeline.

"See that woman over there?"

Yuri turned away, not wanting to look into the corner of the cell.

"The one over there changing her baby's diaper," the prisoner said through clenched teeth. "Look at them!"

Yuri bit at his lower lip and glanced into the corner.

"Her name is Valeria. Her husband was one of the brodyagi at Ust-Kut and a Solidarity activist. The militia tortured her for eight hours because they thought she knew where her husband was."

"They—they torture women?" Yuri asked in a deep, shaky voice.

"Good God, man! Where have you been? Of course they torture women, and children too if it suits their purposes. If you went through initial interrogation, you only received a sample of what they can do."

"What *can* they do?" Yuri asked fearfully.

"You have no idea what they can do to you in their torture chambers." The young man spit the words out. He described a few of their methods, and Yuri felt sick. "They are not human, any of them. They delight in inflicting pain, the most savage pain imaginable."

Yuri stared at his hands, watched them clench until the blood was squeezed away, and the roaring of the prisoner's words grew and grew in his ears. He looked up, and the blackness that threatened to engulf him again began to recede.

"The women?" Yuri said, striving to keep the desperation from his voice. His stomach knotted tighter until nausea caught at the back of his throat.

"It's much worse for a woman," the prisoner went on remorselessly. He paused to light a battered papirosa, and in the glow of the match Yuri could see the bleakness in his eyes. "There are so many more things they can do to a woman. Valeria and her child are going to the pipeline to take her husband's place; in fact, all of the women and children here are replacements for the husbands and fathers who have escaped. It's a new policy of the gerontocracy. The best people in this screwed-up country today are in prison."

Yuri blinked at him incredulously and did not want to believe him. He was clinging to his ideology as a dying man clings to his faith.

"I don't think you believe me, my friend. Ask them." He pushed Yuri gently toward the other prisoners.

Yuri took a couple of faltering steps toward them and hesitated. He turned back toward the steel bars separating him from the corridor. At the end of the hallway by the exit door two guards were playing a game with dice. In one minute, he could get them down here, mention his uncle's name, and be out. He was sure of it.

"Damn you down there! We demand to be released! We're all innocent, you pig-pricks!"

There was a world of feeling in Yuri's shout, of fear and rage, bitterness and humiliation—the savage, wounded pride of a stag at bay.

The guards ignored him. They were used to such outbursts.

Yuri looked back into the cell. The prisoners were watching him with an intensity he found frightening. He looked around him, fighting a feeling of naked exposure. He felt so alone.

"Go. Talk to them. They're your kind of people," demanded the young prisoner.

Yuri started toward them. No, he wasn't like them. These were ordinary people with no connections; with no uncles as KGB generals who could get them released. Ordinary citizens, not special citizens like Yuri Spinnenko.

For the rest of the morning Yuri mingled and conversed with his fellow inmates. They were honest, simple people —unsophisticated and straightforward provincials, not urbane and devious like many of the Muscovites and Leningraders he knew. These people represented the soul of the Motherland, and they were being wrongfully sentenced to slave labor.

Suddenly, there was a jangling of keys, the rattle of assault rifles being flipped to port arms, and the thud of heavy boots in the corridor. A troop of militiamen stood at the ready while the jailers opened the cell doors.

"Everybody outside! Into the courtyard! Move it! Move it!" shouted a militiaman, a truncheon held menacingly in his fist.

Some of the women began to weep uncontrollably as they shuffled down the cement corridor. The guard kicked at a three-year-old who was pulling away from his mother's tightly clenched hand. Yuri lunged for the guard but was struck in the back by a rifle butt. He got up, but the blow that followed was as sudden and unexpected as the first.

"Try that again and you're dead," hissed a guard's voice from behind.

Yuri yanked himself up defiantly. A word, right now, about his uncle Pavel would get him out of this. Just mention his name, he told himself again and again as he shuffled down the corridor.

But he didn't. He was feeling a bond, an identification now, with his fellow prisoners. He had heard rumors, just rumors, of slave-labor camps in his country, but had always dismissed it from his mind as simply anti-State propaganda. Now he was headed for one. He felt an inexorable determination to share the fate of these people, now *his* people. He felt a frightening, new, and powerful feeling—a controlled ferocity toward the people and policies that made this tragedy possible. He had been falsely arrested, beaten, humiliated and, as far as he knew, sentenced to the pipeline project with the others. Yes, he would share their fate at Ust-Kut or wherever he was sent. He would endure—and, when he had learned enough about these injustices, he would tell the authorities who he really was and get released. Then, heads would roll.

As he entered the courtyard, the wind rushed through the buildings surrounding the yard and sprayed great sheets of water from the puddles that had gathered on the cobblestones. He stood in a ragged line with the others, facing three open trucks. A loudspeaker spewed instructions, its iron voice bouncing across the courtyard. The truck engines racketed to life as the militiamen propped ladders up against the vehicles' bodies. Yuri shuffled forward, exulting in a strange feeling of belonging he had never known before. He knew within the core of his being that this was the first decision he had ever made without his Communist ideology as a frame of reference, his sounding board for determining what was right or wrong. He was embarking on an action that was inherently right. He knew it, and was experiencing a sensation of cleansing as he moved toward the open truck to share the unknown terrors before him.

He was about to mount the ladder when a familiar voice cut through the rain-soaked air.

"Spinnenko! Just *where* in the hell do you think you're going?"

Yuri turned abruptly, just as the sun broke through the leaden clouds in one final act of defiance, and looked into the puzzled but scowling face of Major Koslavonov.

XI.

The morning sun sent shafts of warm, probing ligh[t] through the large picture window of Yossef's bedroom[.] Dawn came early in Moscow in mid-July, and the sun hi[t] first the exclusive apartment complexes in the Lenin Hill[s] above the city.

Yossef got up, yawned loudly, and took a steaming ho[t] shower. After toweling dry, he made some piping-hot te[a] and heated some hard rolls.

After dressing he bounced down the stairs whistling t[o] himself and strolled casually to the bus stop. Over th[e] stunted hills to the east, the sun was edging above th[e] horizon in splendors of red and blue and the high cirru[s] glowed and shimmered in the growing light. In the excite[-] ment of his new surroundings, Yossef almost forgot wh[y] he'd been sent to Moscow in the first place.

This was Yossef's third week in the Soviet capital an[d] his life was settling into a predictable routine. He wa[s] actually enjoying his role, although he knew that it woul[d] change soon, and dramatically. His first impression of th[e] country, conditioned by the smiling and courteous treat[-] ment at the airport, had been rudely dispelled during th[e] first week. That kind of treatment, he discovered, wa[s] reserved for foreigners. The average Soviet citizen was th[e] victim of rude and insensitive treatment, not only b[y] government officials, but even by lowly clerks in depart[-] ment stores. It appeared that common citizens all vente[d] their fears and frustrations upon each other in a thousan[d] cruel little ways.

* * *

146

The Swiss Trade Mission was located in a modern three-story office building a block south of the Tretyakov Art Gallery in the Zamoskvorechie section of the city. It was reached by a pleasant trip by bus down Komsomol Prospekt and through Gorky Park. The park was an easy five-minute walk from his office.

In spite of the generally repressive atmosphere of the city, emphasized by the omnipresence of armed militiamen on every street, the members of the Swiss Trade Mission had extraordinary freedom and privileges. Yossef understood now why the MOSSAD had chosen the Trade Mission for his cover. The Swiss were the commercial middlemen between the Soviet Union and the West. The United States, Japan, and Western Europe had responded to the Soviet invasion of China with a total economic boycott, especially of industrial goods and equipment essential for the massive network of natural-gas pipelines being constructed in Siberia.

The Swiss, with their international connections and a labyrinth of commercial contacts and dummy corporations, were able to get the Soviet Union whatever it needed. Sweden, a partner in this endeavor, had built the completely automated port facilities at Archangel for the prepackaged, containerized roll-on-roll-off cargo coming into the USSR from all over the world. Because of the indispensable services of the Swiss Trade Mission, its members were granted a "most-favored person" status and could travel freely throughout western Russia.

Yossef's first contact with officialdom in Russia had been with the UPDK, the Soviet agency that supplied housing and maid service to privileged foreigners. A UPDK official was at his hotel room early on his first morning there, and Yossef was whisked away by a black Volga M-124 passenger car to his one-bedroom apartment in the Lenin Hills, only two blocks from Moscow State University. It was in an area where many of the *sovyetskiye detki,* a derisive term meaning "rich Soviet kids," lived in luxurious housing set apart for the children of the Communist Party elite.

It hadn't taken long for Yossef to discover that there was a gigantic disparity of wealth and privilege in Moscow.

The powerful, wealthy elite arrogated to themselves an institutionalized system for perpetuating a double standard in lifestyles—one for themselves and one for the rest of Soviet society. The Party and government took these advantages for granted with an arrogant disdain for the *narod*—the masses, the common people whom the elite treated with contempt.

In the Lenin Hills area, the sovyetskiye detki could be seen roaring down the Vernadsky Prospekt in their imported Western Mercedes or Ferarris, scattering the narod like chickens, speeding toward Zhukovia, the heart of the dacha country in the woodlands east of Moscow, where they would engage in weekend-long parties at their families' country villas.

In contrast, the narod lived mostly in massive prefab apartment blocks in the workers' sections of the city. The prefabs were deadening in their monotony, and pockmarked and graying with the instant aging that seemed to affect all Soviet architecture. The long queues of the narod with their string shopping bags seemed almost as gray and aged as their housing. Shopping for the average Soviet citizen was a nightmare, due to actual shortages—and now, with the crackdown on Solidarity, government-induced shortages designed to prove to the average Russian that what the government gives, it can also take away.

The nachalstvos shopped in special unmarked stores throughout the city where each family was entitled to the *kremlevsky payok,* the "Kremlin ration"—enough food, free, to feed a family of five luxuriously every month.

The elite, and especially the sovyetskiye detki, were also allowed to shop at the *beryozka,* luxury stores of imported goods where everything from Italian sports cars to American toothpaste could be purchased.

The stores, which catered to the wealthy and the powerful, were well-disguised: no sense of rubbing it in the faces of the *malenky chelovek,* "the little man"—another derisive expression used by the elite. And, indeed, Soviet society in 1991 was composed primarily of the malenky chelovek. The little man was everywhere, but had a tremendous sense of impotence before the apparatus of the elite. To survive meant that he had to go through the motions of publicly observing the rules, but privately exerting enormous efforts and ingenuity to bend or slip through the maze of regulations that controlled his life. He became a master at the art of lying low; of adopting the protective coloration of conformity in order to get by and not be discovered pursuing some special interest that would be crushed by the authorities if found out.

In the summer of 1991, the KGB was intruding into the lives of Soviet citizens everywhere. The uniformed militia were seen on every street and the *stukachi,* the secret KGB informers, riddled every unit of society.

What was happening in Yossef's Moscow was happening throughout the land. The elite were living like the Tsarist royalty at the trailing end of the Romanov dynasty in heartbreaking ignorance of the revolutionary pressures that were building. The gulf between the narod and the nachalstvos was, by this summer, unbridgeable. The minority republics were seething under a new policy which formed entire military units from among their populations and sent them into unequal combat with the Chinese. What the Party had been doing with Solidarity suspects, they were now doing with the Uzbeks, Tadzhiks, Kirghiz, and other minorities: whittling down their populations so the Great Russians wouldn't be overwhelmed demographically by their higher birth rates.

There were signs, many of them observable in the city, that the narod were retaliating in subtle—and not so subtle—ways. The little man could always escape into vodka and, indeed, public drunkenness was common. Vodka had always been the lubricant of Russian life. Vodka sales were up dramatically, and vodka was always available in government stores in great quantities.

It was felt by nearly everyone in the country that the regime was encouraging drunkenness so that the narod would forget their misery. This feeling was reinforced by the tremendous supply of tranquilizing drugs that were flooding the market at discount prices. Evidently the elite felt that if the masses were drunk or tranquilized they would be immune to the revolutionary blandishments of Solidarity.

There were signs, however, that the blandishments of Solidarity had tremendous appeal. The sheer volume of samizdats flooding Moscow, Leningrad, and western Russia was enormous. The themes of their messages were getting bolder. The newest samizdat, *Novy Rodina*—"The New Motherland"—was a blatant and successful attempt to portray Solidarity as a truly patriotic movement, truly Russian in values; and it portrayed the *vlasti,* the powers-that-be, the nachalstvos, as *nakitlebniki*—a common Russian expression meaning functionless parasites—living off the bread of others. This message had a gut-level appeal to the average Soviet citizen. He could endure a privileged elite, even a dictatorship like Stalin's, if it had a function. But in the Russia of 1991, it seemed that the only function of the elite was to seek privilege and power.

Things once sacred to the Soviet people were no longer sacred. The statue of Pavlik Morozov, a young Communist lad of fourteen who had turned his parents over to the secret police in 1932 for helping kulaks, was destroyed in Gorky Park. Though hated by the Soviet people for years, it had been untouchable—until the summer of 1991.

It was an article of faith in the Soviet Union that in spite of all the frustrations and hostility the average Russian felt for the regime, the sacred name, image, and reputation of Lenin was unassailable. Even schoolchildren were forbidden to draw pictures of him; he was too sacred. Lenin was a combination of George Washington, Santa Claus, and Jesus Christ. He was the most perfect human being who had ever walked upon the face of the earth. His portrait was everywhere, in every schoolroom and in every public building. In public parks and squares there was the ubiquitous and powerful statue of Lenin, usually in a wind-furled overcoat, confidently striving toward a better future, his eyes agleam, exhorting the proletariat to unite. The vibrant statues of Lenin were often a shocking contrast to the glum, shuttered faces of the Soviet street crowds who shuffled past their pedestals, their eyes often hollowed by fear and privation.

The last issue of the *Novy Rodina* was a bombshell. Its front page screamed:

> It is now Russia before the Revolution! 1991 is 1917! The widening gap between the elite and the masses is enormous. The concentrations of economic and political power are in fewer and fewer hands. The Communist Party of the Soviet Union is the new royalty and the Central Committee and the Politburo are the new Romanovs. There is now an unbridgeable gap between the leaders and the led. It's "them" at the top and "us" at the bottom, and they are perpetuating an alien, un-Russian philosophy.

This issue of the *Novy Rodina* spoke the unspeakable. It dared to attack the sacred name and reputation of Vladimir Lenin. Whole sections of the Makleff journal were included. The *Novy Rodina* promised a serialization of the true life and history of Lenin in future issues.

Coordinated with the samizdat campaign was a Solidarity effort toward the vilification and slander of Lenin. Two statues of Lenin, one in Sokolniki Park and one in Petrovsky Park near Dynamo Stadium, were vandalized by spray paint. A large official sign reading "Lenin Lived, Lenin Lives, Lenin Will Live" was changed: The word "Solidarity" replaced "Lenin."

The same thing was happening in Leningrad. A statue of Lenin in Karl Marx Park in the Polyustrovo district was vandalized, its arms broken off. Another Lenin statue was spray-painted outside the entrance to the Kirov Stadium.

Some of the samizdats were extremely clever in their analytical, almost clinical, treatment of the workings of the power structure in the Soviet Union. One issue dealt with the subject of guilt and how the system used guilt to control the masses.

The authorities, the samizdat explained, assumed that everybody was guilty of something. This created the unequal and intimidating confrontation between the narod and the organs of the elite. This floating, ever-present sense of guilt before officialdom contributed to the citizen's automatic submission to authority. The elite kept everybody on the defensive by suggesting or accusing them of guilt. The first reaction of a Soviet citizen was to try to correct his mistake. From childhood he had learned to feel guilty before authority and to try to explain himself. This psychological and official erosion of the spirit was reinforced by a vast army of petty bureaucrats and self-appointed busybodies who used the system's infinite labyrinth of regulations, rules, and documents to control, harass, humble, and hound the "little man."

Yossef had learned that the Moscow citizen, as well as every citizen in the rest of the country, was controlled through an elaborate system of rigid document control. The old Russian proverb from Tsarist times, "Without a document you are an insect, but with a document you are a human being," was all too true in 1991.

Another of Yossef's first contacts with Soviet official-dom had been at the Moscow City Hall, where he was issued his *propiska,* the basic control document which all Muscovites had to have. It was the residential permit to live in the city. Shortly after, he was issued a *spravika* with "Swiss National" stamped boldly on it. This was his basic work-document and had to be shown on demand to anybody who wanted to see it to prove that he wasn't a "social parasite" or draft-dodger.

Soviet society in 1991 was peopled by masses of mini-dictators in all strata of society, demanding to examine one's documents or correcting one for inappropriate behavior or unorthodox thinking. It seemed as if anybody with a shred of authority delighted in inflicting inconvenience and misery on his fellow citizens as his way of getting back at the system for the hardship and frustration that he himself was suffering.

Every evidence of a Solidarity victory was now a victory for the malenky chelovek. A defaced statue of Lenin; a clandestinely spray-painted wall slogan; an assassinated KGB informer—this was *his* victory. The sudden boldness of Solidarity actions in the very gut of the beast, Moscow, was a signal that the regime was not omnipotent —that it could be hurt.

* * *

Ever since the incident at Dynamo Stadium, there had been an unbearable tension between the Red Army and the KGB. It was felt throughout the entire nation. There had been reported cases of political commissars, KGB-appointed officers, being attacked by members of Red Army units. In staff meetings throughout Russia, Red Army commanders were demanding that the KGB assume a reduced role in the affairs of the military. The Politburo responded in its usual heavy-handed way by increasing KGB control, thus widening the chasm between the two services.

In mid-July, Solidarity issued a manifesto that was widely circulated via the samizdats. It was a statement of revolutionary goals—a Solidarity Manifesto.

We, the citizens of a new and democratic Russia, demand an end to the rule of, by, and for the State Security Service, the KGB.

Seventy-five years ago, Lenin and his Bolsheviks promised us a "Worker's Paradise," and the withering away of the State. We have seen, instead, the establishment of a Worker's Hell and the unbridled growth of the largest and most ruthless totalitarian system that the world has ever known.

We demand free political expression and the establishment of a free political party system. We demand that Marxism-Leninism be forced to compete with the other political and economic ideologies crying for recognition in our country. We demand an end to the State Security apparatus. A mature and democratic people cannot tolerate the cruel and unjust treatment meted out by the KGB.

A new and democratic Russia must be governed in accordance with the Helsinki Agreements. Civil and human rights must be protected. The old parliamentary Duma established by the democratic March 1917 Revolution must be the voice of the people.

Finally, we demand an end to the China War immediately. There have been endless debates on how to extricate ourselves from this morass. The answer is simple. Turn our troops around and march them westward—and home.

The manifesto ended with the words, "The hell with revolutionary slogans promising a better life for the future. *Today* is the future Lenin promised would be better. We want the future—today!"

The manifesto had a tremendous impact. It dared to state publicly what the narod were desiring secretly. The manifesto was the psychological and intellectual wedge which divided the "them" from the "us." Mentally, the individual in the Soviet Union who read the manifesto was making a choice. The manifesto now served the individual Russian as an ideological frame of reference, a Gibraltar of values and ideals which the "little man" could cling to and hope for.

Millions of choices were now being made throughout the country in the hearts and minds of its citizens. These decisions would remain silent, dormant, until some cataclysmic event galvanized them into action—an event which everyone in the Soviet Union knew would soon take place.

Major Koslovonov's explanation was logical but hardly comforting to Yuri. The militia authorities in Minusinsk *had* made a mistake; but even after they'd known that Yuri was not the escaped prisoner Ivan Navaroff, they were still willing to sentence him to the pipeline. After all, the regional KGB had slapped a quota on the regional authorities for the number of prisoners needed for the project, and the Minusinsk militia headquarters was behind. When Yuri had failed to show up for evening bed-check, his commander had begun a dogged search of the city. Koslovonov could only secure Yuri's release by threatening and using the name of General Pavel Spinnenko.

Yuri went about his duties woodenly, mechanically. His experience in the regional detention center had affected him deeply. It had confirmed many of the rumors which he had always heard but had dismissed from his mind.

And now his gnawing alienation was reinforced by scenes seen from his train window—scenes right out of the writings of Dostoyevsky and Solzhenitsyn, thousands of prisoners of both sexes and all ages tearing away at the earth to build sections of the Trans-Siberian pipeline. Several times, the Tomb train was shunted off to a siding while high-priority traffic screeched by, its wretched human cargo crammed into cars with heavy nets tightly secured over them. Here and there a human head was seen protruding through a gnawed section of netting.

The farther east Yuri traveled, the thinner the crowds that visited the body of Lenin. In the city of Chita in eastern Siberia, only a handful of people shuffled by the casket. One explanation was that there was a Solidarity-inspired disturbance and travel was restricted.

During his turn at Guard mount, Yuri would stand at Lenin's feet, head bowed, his white-gloved hands on his rifle, and gaze into the corpse's face. He would stare and ask questions. Did you, Vladimir Lenin, betray the original revolution as the Minusinsk samizdat accused you of doing? Did you personally witness and enjoy the torture and execution of the Kronstadt revolutionaries? Did you personally murder the young American comrade, Aleksei Dubrov, after witnessing his unspeakable tortures, and then have him buried in the Lubyanka? Are all of the things which I, and entire generations of young Soviets, have been taught from childhood about you untrue?

Yuri Spinnenko was thoroughly familiar with the face and hands of Lenin. He had stared at them enough during the course of his duties. He knew every pore and age spot by heart. The sealed car did not have the benefit of a constant temperature as did the Tomb on Red Square. A portable temperature-control unit was installed, but it malfunctioned repeatedly and was next to useless.

Yuri noticed changes, almost imperceptible at first, in Lenin's face. His left eyelid started to droop slightly and the corners of his mouth started to sag. Some of the age spots grew larger, the discolorations spreading and merging like blobs of oil. By the time the train was halfway through the Amurskaya oblast region the right ear had slipped down toward the neck more than half an inch. Lenin's face was changing daily, more rapidly now, as the tour continued.

The body was accompanied by three old men in their late seventies. The guards referred to them as "the Three Wise Men." They looked like they might have been among the original Bolsheviks who stormed the Winter Palace. On the personnel roster they were simply listed as "technicians". The Three Wise Men's actual job was the perpetual care of the body of Lenin. They had been assigned to the care of the corpse since the early 1930s.

In the small village of Kronitkya the train was shunted off into a siding and was sealed off by armed guards brought in from a nearby army camp. The regular guards and staff of the Tomb train were given a twelve-hour leave and told to stay away from the sealed car. The Three Wise Men stayed on board. Yuri and a fellow guard, a young Latvian with a thatch of reddish blond hair, hiked along the bank of a small stream, one of hundreds in the Amurskaya region which fed into the Amur River, and hunted for mushrooms.

The twelve hours went quickly, and by 8:00 P.M. Yuri was back in his seat staring at the virgin forests being engulfed by the rushing dusk as the Tomb train pulled out of the little village of Kronitkya.

The train pulled into the medium-sized city of Buriatskya at 9:00 A.M. the next morning. A Red Army band was on the station platform playing spirited marches as the train hissed to a stop. A longer-than-usual line of visitors for this early in the morning already curled around the old, red brick train station. A short propaganda speech was blasted through a portable loudspeaker by a local Party official as the doors of the sealed car were about to be opened.

Yuri assumed his position at the foot of the casket as the Three Wise Men strained at the casket lid, lifting it back, exposing the corpse under the glass that served as a protective covering.

Yuri almost lost his composure, and gasped as he saw the face and hands of Lenin. Inside the casket was a youthful Lenin—almost a radiant Lenin. The age spots had disappeared. The eyelids and mouth corners were no longer sagging. The ear was normal. Lenin's hair was fuller and more luxuriant. He had regained at least fifteen years of life, it appeared.

Yuri swallowed nervously and resumed his reverent stance as the first of the curious crowd trooped by.

"The best spot to place the charge is to the inside of the track, toward the bank, on the curve. When it blows, it'll blast the engine off the rails and take the whole train with it. It saves on explosives that way."

"Did they teach you that back at Belvoir?" asked the American POW sergeant in the tattered parka, taken from a murdered Yakut in the previous May's Ust-Kut escape.

Thirty-nine-year-old Richard Gagliardi from Providence, Rhode Island, ignored the sergeant's sarcastic remark and continued to emplace the charge. He had been a twenty-two-year-old second lieutenant when he was captured by North Vietnamese Regular forces while on a routine patrol near Bien Hoa in 1973. An MIA/POW for seventeen years, he'd made his escape from the Ust-Kut labor camp with McMurrin.

He tamped the dynamite sticks under the railroad ties, and then packed the dirt around them gently and carefully. He strung out the copper wires from the caps and covered them with dirt and leaves. The shine on the copper disturbed him, so he buried them as deeply as he could, at least four inches down into the soft earth.

Gagliardi's group had been operating independently and out of radio contact with the main body of the Solidarity Army of Liberation for five weeks. His band of twenty-four had never received the word that the Lenin Tomb train would be passing through his area of operations. His orders remained the same as those given by McMurrin before he'd left and headed east: If it moves on tracks, blow it up.

The monitor train crept slowly and cautiously around the bend of the mountain. A dozen guards peered down at the track and the shrub-filled terrain flanking it, assault rifles held at the ready. As the monitor thundered over the railroad ties, the vibrations caused the loose earth to give way, exposing a few inches of the shiny copper wires that ran from the dynamite charge, up the bank to where Gagliardi was hiding, his hand resting on an old-fashioned plunger-type detonator.

Gagliardi waited for the larger prize that he knew was following close behind. Small monitor trains often preceded the larger troop trains since the SAL had become active in Siberia.

As the last car of the monitor rumbled over the charge, an observant guard on the rear platform saw the glint of the shiny wire about two feet from the railroad tie. He squinted at the suspicious glimmer of light. He looked up and realized, to his horror, that the Tomb train was closer than the prescribed three hundred meters at this speed.

"Suspicious object. Stop your train!" he shouted into his portable transceiver. Almost immediately, the helicopter on the flatcar clattered into life and lifted off.

Gagliardi heard the squeal and hiss of air brakes as the train slowed.

"Shit!" he muttered. "The monitor spotted the charge. Oh well. We'll give 'em some busted tracks. At least we'll leave them a headache or two." He pushed the plunger.

The blast erupted in a shower of dirt, rocks, and twisted steel a hundred meters in front of the Tomb train's engine. The engineer reached up and yanked frantically on the emergency brake.

The train gave a series of violent shudders as the air-brake system locked the wheels on every car. Tables, chairs, and personal belongings shot forward as the train lurched to a stop.

Yuri was sitting in the forward section of the sealed car when the train began its shuddering stop. Lenin's coffin, bolted to its portable catafalque, popped out of the recessed receptacle on the floor and hurtled toward the forward wall. In a flash, Yuri responded, throwing himself between the hurtling coffin and the wall of the car. The forward edge of the heavy, metal casket slammed into Yuri's chest, breaking three ribs. Yuri's body had saved the casket from damage, but the blow had popped the lid off and jarred the body, exposing Lenin to Yuri's view.

A wave of pain and nausea assaulted him as he stifled the urge to scream, but he felt elated. He had saved Comrade Lenin.

He looked down into the waxen face of the corpse. The head was tilted at a grotesque angle. The neck, or where the neck was supposed to be attached to the torso, was a straight clean line—like the head of a doll. Protruding from the open neck on the torso was a section of a stainless-steel frame surrounded by what appeared to be chicken wire.

Yuri stared in horrified shock for a brief moment before rough hands tore him away from the open casket.

He gasped, grimaced tightly, and passed out from the pain.

THE JOURNAL OF ARIEL MAKLEFF

Moscow 1926–1953—Budapest 1956

April 1926

Rumors!

There are rumors all over Moscow that the embalmed body of Lenin which has been exhibited in the Mausoleum and enshrined as a near-icon, an object of worship by millions of faithful communists, is only a doll—a wax dummy.

To dispel these rumors, and to maintain its credibility, the Stalin government brought in a left-wing German physician (actually he was a tourist to Moscow at the time and not an expert) to examine Lenin's body.

He reported that he had observed Lenin's body under a 2000-candlepower light which revealed diffcrent shades of skin, and that there were spots on the skin, and the forehead looked like it had beads of perspiration on it. This was hardly a convincing report on the authenticity of the body: Corpses don't perspire.

I learned a year after Lenin's death that after the initial embalming, the body had deteriorated within six weeks. Two Russian professors were ordered by Stalin to "reprocess" the corpse. Papa was the medical officer in charge.

They began two months and eighteen days after Lenin's death. They were given a leaky old wooden structure to work in, in cold, wet weather. There was no air-conditioning system for a constant temperature control.

I discovered that in the course of the autopsy and the initial embalming most of the vessels necessary for embalmment had been destroyed. This, in itself, would have precluded the preservation of the body. The Russian "experts," however, claimed that they had invented a new process which would overcome this problem. They claimed that with this new embalming process they could actually bend Lenin's ear, that the cheeks would be soft and cool and that, when you lifted his arm or leg, it would fall back without stiffness. When the first embalming attempt was begun, bodily breakdown had progressed and mummification, especially of the face, head, and neck, had become apparent. An embalming procedure by intravascular injection was no longer feasible.

Papa described to me the next attempt to embalm poor Vladimir. It was a sick and grotesque procedure performed by quacks who promised the Soviet government a form of immortality for Lenin.

The body was immersed in water for several hours. It was removed, dried, and immersed again in a mixture of water and acetic acid and finally in peroxide of oxygen. Hundreds of deep incisions were made all over the body (but not in the hands or face). Finally, for its third treatment, the body was immersed in a solution of alcohol, glycerine, formalin, and potassium acetate. Supposedly, the bodily tissues would become more pliable after this treatment. Papa told me, however, that when Lenin's body was pulled out of the tank it had shriveled up in a hideous manner and the muscles had contracted. The "experts" pounded on his limbs with large rubber mallets until they were straightened. In the process, several of his bones were broken and had to be spliced together with splints.

1928

This process worked for about a year. By 1928, however, the body had so deteriorated that the government closed the Mausoleum for several months. Another team of "experts" were brought in from Vienna to "repair" poor Vladimir. The body was dissected and the parts soaked in a paraffin solution until impregnated. The parts were reassembled and an extensive reprocessing of the perforated body was again attempted.

In 1928, a secret committee within the Politburo was formed to reconstruct Lenin's body completely. By this time, it was apparent that the paraffin treatment was a complete failure so a secret agreement was made, and three expert practitioners of Mme. Tussaud's art of wax dummy-making were imported from Verona, Italy.

I learned from Papa, and others long since executed, that these artists created five dummies, all Lenin look-alikes. The original body was so far gone in 1928 that it was secretly cremated. Four of the "spare" bodies are kept in a room deep in the bowels of the Tomb on Red Square in case some catastrophic event befell the original. The body which is seen by millions of the faithful is counterfeit—a wax and plaster look-alike. The skull, however, is really Lenin's.

1930   In the early 1930s, shortly after the present Tomb was created, visitors to the Tomb noticed no protrusion where Lenin's feet should be. Later on, a protrusion was added. Did Lenin grow new feet? Also, Lenin's head displayed more hair than he'd had when he was thirty years old. Was death a cure for baldness?

Because of these observations and the questions which followed, the government again solicited the testimony of two "expert" witnesses. Doctors Vorobiev and Zharsky, old cronies of Yagoda's and loyal Party hacks, examined the body in 1934 and proclaimed that it was authentic and in good shape. They were awarded medals by the government for their "truthful" testimony.

Those who returned to see Lenin time and time again, as I did, noticed that his face had become younger-looking every time they returned. Death *had* cured his baldness, as his hairline seemed to be creeping forward every five or six months. The special Politburo committee would give the corpse a special bath every third month to preserve its fresh-looking appearance. It was an 8–12 hour process and the Tomb was always closed for this occasion.

In the early days, a visitor could file directly by the body and gaze, in the indirect lighting, at Lenin's head and hands. The flag of the Paris Commune covered the middle portion of the catafalque, covering Lenin's body.

During the Great Patriotic War, the body was removed to Kuybyshev. Another dummy was kept in Kazan, and still another in Tyumen in western Siberia. The other two were moved also but their location was not known to me.

The Soviet people were always under the impression that Lenin's corpse was kept in the Mausoleum, protecting the Motherland against the Nazi invaders. Even though the Tomb was closed because of wartime security measures, it was simply assumed that his protective spirit was in Moscow.

Those people who were initially involved with the autopsy, the embalming attempts, and the construction of the wax dummies, have all disappeared. They knew too much. The modern rulers of Soviet Russia know that their only legitimacy rests on the visible remains of Lenin, now elevated to the status of near-godhood. The cult of Lenin, now a State religion, is the one tangible reality that has given the regimes since Lenin's death any form of credibility.

I have always been aware that the Russian people need an ideology and a visible symbol of their value system, or they disintegrate. At one time they had the symbols of the Tsar and the Church. Now these are gone, replaced by the Party and the phony corpse of Lenin.

The Soviet leadership has always felt tremendously insecure about their system, as they know that it is based upon a betrayed revolution. They know that the true average Russian has an innate anarchy within him; that he is lawless in his soul; that he obeys power, not law. This is why the Party has gone to extraordinary lengths to perpetuate the mystique of Lenin as symbolized by the elaborate Guard ceremony at his Tomb.

I cannot read the minds of those who rule, and have ruled, the Soviet state, but I would imagine that the possibility of exposure of Lenin's body as a counterfeit, as a hoax of unimaginable proportions even by Communist standards, was and is a source of constant anxiety. I am one of the few remaining old Bolsheviks who know this secret, and I am sure that someday I will pay dearly for it. The country that can prove, irrefutably, that Lenin's body is false, can wreak havoc on the Soviet state.

1956,
Budapest

In 1956 I found my God and the courage to escape. As God would have it, I was attending a medical convention in Budapest toward the end of October 1956 when the

Hungarian Revolution broke out. For years I had been trying to generate the courage to escape and now the opportunity was dropped in my lap by the hand of Almighty God. I couldn't very well leave the desperate but gallant Hungarian people after their forces had saved me by taking over my hotel, so I stayed throughout the fighting and served as a doctor for the revolutionary army. When the Soviet army moved in with overwhelming force, I escaped and fled to Vienna.

The Communists, who do not believe in immortality, fabricated a wax dummy to establish *their* claim on eternity. To worship their idol, they deprived my old friend, Vladimir Lenin, of an honorable burial and denied him a final resting place.

It was the ultimate sacrilege and perpetrated the ultimate deceit on the Russian people.

END OF JOURNAL
MOSSAD EDITION

XII.

Yossef and Colonel Yabin drove down the narrow, tree lined dirt road to the edge of the water. It had been an hour's drive to Finland's lake country north of Helsinki. They drove along the edge of the water until they came to a large cabin tucked away in a stand of birch trees.

"Here it is, Yabin. This is the only cabin around with an aluminum boat-dock. What time is it?"

Yabin glanced at his watch. "Eleven forty-eight."

As they approached the cabin, a tall man in a tan windbreaker stepped out from behind a tree, a shotgun cradled in the crook of his arm. He held up his hand for them to stop.

"Yossef Ayalon?" the guard asked.

Yossef nodded.

"Brother Gregierenko is expecting you. You're right on time. And you must be Moshe Yabin."

Yabin nodded in the affirmative.

"Inside." The guard gave a jerk of his thumb. "They're all waiting."

"Yabin! My great benefactor," smiled the balding Gregierenko as he grabbed the MOSSAD colonel and kissed him on the cheek. "And Yossef. It's good to see you."

The inside of the cabin smelled of newly varnished logs and was spotlessly clean. Gregierenko had an almost compulsive need for neatness and order. The members of the Solidarity Revolutionary Council were seated around a large oak table.

* * *

After an hour and a half of discussions, Gregierenko stood and lifted his glass of mineral water in a toast.

"To Operation Samson and the liberation of Mother Russia."

The others responded with vodka.

"November 6 will be an ideal time, brothers. The Party will be celebrating the annual orgy of the cult of Lenin. We can expect at least six thousand of the elite at the Kremlin Hall of Congress for the sacrament of Lenin."

"You've lost me, Vasily." Yossef frowned. "What's happening on the sixth?"

"Every year," Gregierenko rapped his knuckles on the conference table, "the Party puts on this disgusting extravaganza commemorating the Bolshevik seizure of power. All of the Party and government big shots are gathered at the Hall of Congress for an all-star variety show portraying the storming of the Winter Palace, the cruiser *Aurora* firing on Saint Peter and Paul, and so forth. There are huge bands and choruses and lots of vodka. This year it's going to be even more spectacular because of the troubles. This is the seventy-fifth anniversary of Lenin's take-over. We'll give them something this year to remember, eh, Yossef?"

Yossef smiled weakly as Gregierenko slapped him good-naturedly on the knee.

"Yossef will arrange for your 'insertion' into Russia, Vasily," mentioned Yabin.

"That's been my one big concern, Moshe. What have you come up with?"

"Well, Lenin was sent by Germany into Russia in a sealed railroad car. Israel is sending Gregierenko by a sealed crate into the port of—"

"What?" Gregierenko broke in. "A crate? The Border Guards examine everything."

"That's true." Yabin twitched a sly smile. "Everywhere except Archangel. That's the Achilles heel of the border surveillance system."

Gregierenko concealed his anxiety with a cold smile.

"Explain—please."

"The port's fully automated. The cargo is prepared, inspected, and sealed at the point of origin. Border-guard plainclothesmen check the cargo at its source before it's loaded. The process after that is fully automatic. It's a series of conveyor belts, roll-on-roll-off cargo handling, and rail shipment, until it reaches its destination. Practically all of the pipeline equipment comes in this way—as well as tens of thousands of *Novy Rodinas*."

"Our samizdats?" Gregierenko brightened.

"Of course. Our 'Swiss' friend Yossef has been in a position to route the Archangel cargo under his jurisdiction to wherever he chooses."

"My fate is completely in your hands, Yossef." Gregierenko's eyes were chill and lusterless as they contemplated him. "I don't care how you do it. Just get me back into the Soviet Union for Operation Samson."

The Aeroflot airliner sideslipped, lost more altitude, and bucked in the turbulence as it approached Moscow.

Yuri could barely make out the spires of the Kremlin towers through the early morning mist rising from the Moscow river. He remembered his last approach to the Soviet capital back in January when he had come home as an honored, wounded veteran of the China War. The corners of his mouth twisted in a slightly sardonic smile as he remembered how excited he'd been about his anticipated assignment—to fulfill a boyhood dream to become a Kremlin Tomb Guard; and now, as he approached Domodedovo Airport, his disillusionment in the system and its primary symbol, Lenin, was almost complete. He couldn't help comparing his experiences with those of the American comrade, Aleksei Dubrov, who saw through Lenin's treachery and exposed him publicly. Fate had now thrust him into a similar position with his discovery that the most revered icon in the Communist empire, Lenin's body, was counterfeit: a doll! A wax dummy.

Yuri had awakened in an army hospital in Kharbovsk after the heavy casket had slammed into him, knocking him unconscious. He recalled the wizened faces of the Three Wise Men peering down at him as he lay fighting for each agonizing breath. His ribs were tightly taped and each attempt to breathe was excruciatingly painful.

The three old Bolsheviks had questioned him unceasingly, asking what he had seen. Yuri had feigned ignorance and answered them with questions of his own.

"What did you expect me to see under the circumstances? I had to save Comrade Lenin. What would you see if a five-hundred-pound metal casket hit you in the chest? I saw nothing but light and stars. The shock and the pain were so intense that I could see nothing," he lied.

Satisfied, the Three Wise Men had shuffled out of the hospital room.

"Never—never, Sergeant Spinnenko, tell anybody what happened today or your life will be forfeit," slurred one of them in a final warning before he closed the door.

"Yuri! Dear Yuri!" cried Raisa Karezev as she ran through the airport lobby and flung herself into Yuri's arms. Yuri winced as her supple body merged with his and she coiled her arms around his chest and kissed him repeatedly.

"Oh! Oh dear. I've hurt you. I—I forgot about your ribs. Yuri, I'm so sorry!"

Yuri grinned broadly. "That's the kind of pain I can well endure. Let's have some more of it." He grabbed Raisa and kissed her fully on the lips. Gently, she curled her arms around his waist.

Pavel Spinnenko slapped his nephew on the shoulder. "I'll settle for a firm handshake." He laughed. "It's good to have you home, Yuri. How much leave time do you have?"

"I have a thirty-day medical furlough. No duties for awhile. What am I going to do with myself for thirty days? I'll be bored out of my mind."

The general shot Raisa a sly smile. "Well, it just so happens that I'm giving Raisa a three-week leave of absence—a new assignment as escort to a national hero. After all, you did save Comrade Lenin."

"How did you know that?" Yuri's voice dropped a register to a hoarse whisper.

"The word gets out. Your commanding officer wrote you up for the Order of Lenin. These things travel fast."

"Well, I don't deserve it," Yuri mumbled sullenly, a muted hint of defeat in his voice.

"Don't be silly." Raisa clutched his arm as they walked toward the baggage counter. "This is one of our country's greatest honors."

Yuri sighed wearily. "Yes, I suppose it is," came his unenthusiastic response. "Let's get my baggage and get on home. I'm tired."

The general shot Raisa a confused glance and shrugged his massive shoulders.

The three of them rode silently toward the general's luxurious apartment in a chauffeur-driven Border Guards staff car. They drove down Red Square and past the Tomb. Yuri glanced at it briefly and turned away. Anger and disgust welled up inside of him as he thought of the enormous betrayal being inflicted upon the Soviet people. The whole Communist system, he thought, was as hollow and phony as the wax dummy that the government was carting around the country. Lenin's probably in Vladivostok right now, he pondered, and the crowds are probably shuffling by, marveling at how lifelike and youthful he looks.

"When are you resuming your duties, Yuri?" Raisa asked.

"Oh, uh—what did you say, Raisa?"

"I said—when do you go back on Guard mount?"

Yuri felt like screaming, "Never! I'm through with that counterfeit son of a bitch!"

He shrugged, striving to appear nonchalant.

"Oh, in . . . in about a month, I guess. I should be healed by then."

The car glided to a stop in front of the general's apartment.

"Yuri." Raisa's voice was soft and seductive. "I want to take you out to my family's dacha for a few weeks. It's about fifty kilometers from Moscow. Are you willing?"

Yuri permitted himself the trace of a smile.

"I'd like nothing better, Raisa. Peace, quiet, and . . ." he gave her a suggestive wink.

Raisa glanced back nervously at the general, who was several feet behind them as they walked toward the front entrance.

"Sssshhh! You lustful beast," she teased. "There will be none of *that* until your ribs heal. You're going to confine your activities to short hikes along the river and hunting mushrooms."

Yuri stopped in the doorway of the entrance and kissed Raisa gently on the cheek. His eyes were glazed with a film of tears.

"Raisa. Dear Raisa." He kissed her again. "You're the only real thing that's ever happened to me. In this whole upside-down and make-believe world, you're the only genuine thing that's ever been a part of my life. I love you for that."

Raisa threw her arms around him with a sudden passion and held him tightly. Then, suddenly, she was flooded with guilt as she realized that she must report Yuri's unexpected return to her Solidarity control agent.

The next day was a Saturday. Raisa stopped by for Yuri at Pavel Spinnenko's apartment. He met her at the entrance with a small suitcase and slid into the front seat of her cream-colored Zhiguli, a Soviet-made Fiat. She wheeled into the street and onto the Sadovoye Ring Road. There was hardly any traffic. Few Muscovites had private cars these days and, if they did, they couldn't obtain the strictly rationed gasoline for pleasure trips.

Within minutes she peeled off the Ring Road and onto the Rusakoyskaya Boulevard and headed east toward her family dacha in Zhukovia.

"You never told me that your family had a dacha out here," Yuri said as the smell of sweet green grass filled his nostrils. Raisa smiled slightly as she kept her eyes on the many potholes that cratered the road.

"That's because you've never asked me. My family has had it since 1955. It was a gift to my grandfather by the Khrushchev regime for his pioneering work in mathematics. It came with his Lenin Prize."

"Lenin Prize?" Yuri gave her a skeptical look. "That's a big one."

"For pure mathematics research. My father followed in his footsteps and has carried on his work."

* * *

Zhukovia was the heart of Moscow's dacha country. It was really the nerve center of Moscow because so many important people lived there, especially in the scientific community. It was a lovely, tranquil, and timeless place sitting on a bluff overlooking the sluggish Moscow River. It was the unhurried and unspoiled Russia of the past.

Raisa's Zhiguli squealed to a stop in front of a rambling, old, vine-covered country house. It was a large dacha, more a permanent dwelling than a country hideaway. It had a huge wide porch that surrounded the entire house. From the rear of the dacha one could overlook the Moscow river.

A pleasant-looking woman in her middle fifties emerged from the front door. Yuri could see the resemblance to Raisa immediately and guessed correctly that it was her mother. A tall man with bushy graying hair followed her, a leather-covered pipe lodged in the corner of his mouth.

"Mama! Papa!" Raisa hugged her parents enthusiastically. "It's good to be home. I've got three weeks with nothing to do except take care of Yuri Spinnenko. Yuri." Raisa reached out and grabbed his hand. "I want you to meet my parents."

"So you're Raisa's young man, eh? The Tomb Guard, right?" He held out his hand and shook Yuri's. "It's an honor to know you, Sergeant."

They trooped into the large living room, a room with the faded elegance of a bygone era. It was a lived-in home, and the memories of children and family activities stared down from the walls and from the mantelpiece over the huge fireplace in the form of dozens of photographs.

That evening, the Karezev table groaned under a variety of traditional Russian foods. Her parents were joined by four younger brothers and a sister. By Soviet standards, the Karezev family was inordinately large.

After eating, the family went out and sat on the large rear porch overlooking the river. It was so quiet and peaceful in the Zhukovia countryside. The crickets provided the background music for Raisa's playing of traditional Russian folk songs on the balalaika. Soon, the entire family was singing the songs of Mother Russia: the plaintive melodies of peasants struggling to wrest a living from the land and of soldiers going off to war.

One by one the family members bid Yuri and Raisa goodnight until they were left alone on the large striped couch. The moon was nearly full and hung in mid-sky, a silver beacon strong enough to light the water. Somewhere along the river some wild thing was rustling the reeds.

Yuri stroked Raisa's cheek absently and stared at the water.

"It must have been wonderful to have been raised in an ordinary family like yours," he said thoughtfully.

"It was," Raisa responded. "I have much more than I deserve. I've been insulated from the trials which have afflicted most of our countrymen, Yuri. My grandfather's and father's status in the academic world has assured us of all this." She waved her hand toward the dacha.

"You have a large family. Was it planned this way?"

"Yes." Raisa added quickly, "My parents are much more Russian than Communist. They treasure their children more than their degrees, their status, or anything. My grandparents instilled in them that children, if you can raise them properly, are one's real wealth."

"Tell me, Raisa—do you want a large family?"

Raisa twitched an embarrassed smile.

"Yes."

"How many?"

"At least four."

"If you had to live as an ordinary citizen in a working-man's flat, and queue up for groceries every day, would you still want four?"

Yuri's question stabbed into Raisa like a hot blade. It was a direct affront to the fantasy-life which she had created of an idyllic family based on privilege.

"I would not choose to have any children under the present regime," she said with finality.

Her statement acted as a trigger that caused Yuri to flood her with his experiences during the tour and his incarceration at Minusinsk. He told Raisa, in graphic detail, of the thousands of prisoners he'd seen working on the pipeline. He clenched his fists in a spasm of involuntary rage at the memory.

Raisa listened with a growing amazement which quickly turned to a grim anger.

"What you experienced at Minusinsk is what hundreds of thousands of our people experience every day, Yuri." She spoke flatly and without emotion.

"Is—is it right for us to live so well, Raisa, when so many of our people live so wretchedly?"

She shot him a nervous glance. "You're starting to sound like a Solidarity sympathizer. I would whisper remarks like that, Yuri."

"It was *because* of Solidarity that I was thrown into detention at Minusinsk."

"You didn't mention that. How was Solidarity to blame?"

Yuri told her about the samizdat at the railroad depot and the heroic but tragic life of the Dubrov family.

"I can't get this Dubrov family out of my mind. Aleksei Dubrov actually lived with Lenin and saw how he betrayed the Revolution. He suffered unspeakable tortures and finally death for his honesty and courage. His wife and child suffered likewise. I—I wonder if I could suffer for the truth like that."

Raisa snuggled against his shoulder as he draped an arm around her.

"So? What do you propose to do about it, Yuri?"

"Resign my position as Tomb Guard. Perhaps even leave the Border Guards."

"What reason would you give to your superiors?"

Yuri swallowed hard, forcing the words out.

"On the grounds that my job is a sham. That I'm not guarding Comrade Lenin or Comrade Anybody; just a cleverly made wax dummy."

Raisa gasped and twisted toward him, her face turning white in the moonlight.

"What do you mean, Yuri?"

Yuri told her about the deterioration of the body and the role of the Three Wise Men. He explained what the impact of the casket did to the head of Lenin, exposing the body as a fabrication. Suddenly, the implications of Operation Samson made a terrible sense to Raisa. She shuddered, breathed deeply, and squeezed Yuri's knee sympathetically.

"Those experiences are worse than the war. When are you going to tell them?"

"Soon. Perhaps in a week; anyway, before Lenin comes home. I can't stand the thought of going back inside the Tomb."

Yuri's face suddenly became contorted in anger.

"When I think of the emotions I've wasted on that bastard! I've devoted so much of my life and energies to guard and honor a wax doll! I've wasted a good twenty-five years of my life to perpetuate a gigantic hoax. I've—I've lived like a soldier since I was a child. My 'parents' were military men in the Kiev State Orphanage. I was raised to be a model Communist; an example. I always put this before my own personal desires. Whenever I had an impulse to do something for myself I'd always ask: 'What would Comrade Lenin want me to do?' Whenever I had secret yearnings for real brothers and sisters, a real family like yours, I'd kill those feelings and would tell myself how lucky I was to have the State as my parents, and my fellow 'model comrades' as my brothers. I never had a life of my own because I felt that I always had to set the example of the model comrade."

"Did they mistreat you in the orphanage?"

"Oh no. They gave us everything we needed. In fact, we were pampered. But I can never, ever remember anybody ever telling me that—that they loved me." Tears started to form in the corners of Yuri's eyes. "They just didn't tell you things like that there.

"We had a commanding officer at the orphanage, a Major Kirov. I used to imagine that he and his wife were my real parents. As a little fellow I would often look across the small parade ground we had there at his house and imagine that I was curled up on a large, soft couch with his wife's arms around me, telling me a story. I would see a little brother and sister playing on a furry rug in front of a fireplace, playing with some toys. My 'father,' Major Kirov, would pick me up after I kissed my mother and brother and sister goodnight and take me upstairs, put me in bed and tuck me in, and then tell me bedtime stories, you know, real bedtime stories about fairies in the forest, not Comrade Lenin stories. I'd sit on the cold steps of the administration building and stare at Kirov's house for hours, just fantasizing. After being with your family tonight, Raisa, I realized what I've missed all these years, and what's really important."

"And what *is* really important, Yuri?" she asked, choking on her words, as a solitary tear coursed down her cheek.

"A loving wife. A family. Children. The freedom to raise those little ones as you wish. Those are the values which are enduring. They will last. The only thing which keeps the values of Lenin alive are people like me: soldiers with guns in their hands."

"What about your uncle? Hasn't he been like a father to you?"

Yuri exhaled a weary breath. "He's tried, I guess, in his own blustering way. I think he was given the assignment by the Party to adopt me, even though he is my mother's brother. I've never felt that Uncle Pavel was a father. I wish he had a wife."

"I've guessed that you and your uncle have had your differences. I still remember the night of the Dynamo Stadium incident."

A strange, vacant look flooded Yuri's face.

"That's typical of our relationship. Now that I think about it, Uncle Pavel would often attempt to get me into conversation about the problems in our country. My reaction was usually a rigid ideological one, you know, the Party line. He'd just look at me, sigh in exasperation, and turn away. I feel that he wanted to share a lot of his doubts and frustrations with me, but I wanted to avoid it. For all I know, he may have felt that I'd report him. This system makes us all paranoid."

Raisa snuggled closer to him, kissing him on the cheek.

"But, of course, you wouldn't."

"No. Especially now. I'm actually looking forward to telling him about Minusinsk. Maybe he can do something about that place."

"We'd better go to bed, Yuri. You look awfully tired.

We'll finish talking about this later. We have lots of time."

Raisa kissed him tenderly on the corner of the mouth and led him by the hand to his bedroom.

Vasily Gregierenko exploded in a torrent of words when he received the message from Raisa's control agent. He turned to the members of the Solidarity Revolutionary Council seated around the table. He fought to control his emotions, drew a shaky breath, and began.

"It appears that Yuri Spinnenko wants to quit his job as Tomb Guard. He's become a Solidarity sympathizer."

He paused long enough for them to absorb the impact of his statement.

"There goes Operation Samson," wailed Shermatov, a council member from Alma-Ata. "Without Spinnenko it's finished."

"What can we do, Vasily?" asked another.

Gregierenko paced the cabin floor like a caged lion, pounding his fist repeatedly into the palm of his hand.

"He's got to play his part at least until the first week in October. He's got to be on duty until Yossef takes over," he muttered, a gleam of desperation in his eyes.

"How?" asked the council member from Murmansk.

"Raisa Karezev is the key." Gregierenko slammed his fists on the table. "It's all up to Raisa!"

Raisa didn't see the middle-aged woman in the blue flowered dress slip into the passenger seat of her Zhiguli parked in front of Zhukovia's communal store. She was too absorbed in arranging the several bags of groceries in the rear trunk. Raisa sucked in her breath involuntarily when she saw her.

"Ludmila! What are you doing here? This is dangerous," she whispered fearfully.

"I know. I know," replied the control agent. "But this is so important that I told them at the Center that I was sick so I could come out here to see you. You haven't been too accessible since you've been wet-nursing Yuri Spinnenko, you know."

Raisa flushed slightly as she shifted into first gear.

"Let's go out by the river and park. There aren't too

many people out there," she said.

Thirty minutes later, the control agent had relayed Gregierenko's instructions to Raisa.

"If this means that Yuri will be hurt in any way, I won't go for it, Ludmila. I don't give a damn if they bring back Stalin, I won't put Yuri's life in danger."

"On the contrary, Raisa. If *anybody* survives Operation Samson, it will be Yuri Spinnenko."

Raisa heaved a sigh of relief.

"Tell Vasily that it won't be easy, but I'll use every trick I can think of to get him back in the Tomb. He'll be back by the first part of September. I think I can promise that."

The *Liepaja*'s multiple gas turbines throbbed into life as the last of the wounded Soviet soldiers were brought on board. Captain Third Class Vaclav Suskov stood on the bridge, looking out over the dreary flatness of the warehouses and docks of Haiphong Harbor. Below, the resentful eyes of the Vietnamese dock workers could be felt as they stared at the Soviet naval officers standing in their starched white uniforms in the hot, late-August sun. Vietnam had almost ceased to be their country anymore. It was practically a Soviet colony—totally dependent on the "Mother Country" for military and industrial sustenance. Like Cuba, Ethiopia, Angola, and other Soviet client states, Vietnam now paid off its debts by sending its young men into the grinding maw of the China War to make up for Soviet losses.

The *Liepaja* backed away from the wharf, the small tugs gently nosing her sleek hull toward the mouth of the harbor. Turning around, the tugs broke away, and the guided-missile cruiser headed for the open sea.

Admiral Vagorshnik had fulfilled Suskov's request and replaced some of his key officers and enlisted men with Solidarity activists. Vagorshnik knew who they were. The Baltic Fleet was riddled with Solidarity members and the admiral, as well as other high-ranking officers of the fleet, took great care to keep their identities secret.

The *Liepaja* now had an active Solidarity cell with Suskov as the titular head, but his executive officer,

Lieutenent Smedlev, was the real leader, the activist on the ship.

As the cruiser passed the breakwater, Suskov muttered a sarcastic final goodbye to Vietnam. Part of the breakwater was composed of old scuttled ships, to keep the pounding South China sea from Haiphong's docks. Sitting on the bottom of the shallow seabed, its rusting superstructure contrasting sharply with the blue-green water, was the *Osipenko*: the old liberty ship which had brought Suskov's son, Boris, to the China War—and his execution. Suskov felt the familiar chill in his intestines as the *Liepaja* slid by the breakwater.

The executive officer understood his commander's feelings and slapped a patronizing hand on his shoulder. Suskov winced slightly. He wasn't used to subordinates slapping him on the shoulder but, after all, Smedlev *was* his superior in the Solidarity organization.

The cruiser started to roll slightly as she reacted to the swells of the open sea. The smell of Vietnam was gone, the putrid stench of the jungle giving way to the freshness of the ocean.

The revenge fantasies which Suskov had been nurturing since he learned of Boris's death would come true as soon as the *Liepaja* entered home waters around the first week in November.

When the *Liepaja* entered the Gulf of Finland toward the end of October, a skeleton crew of Solidarity activists would assume operational control and sail toward the city of Lenin—Leningrad.

The cruiser was to be one of the major actors in a conspiracy against the government.

Code-named: OPERATION SAMSON.

XIII.

Yuri stood in front of the full-length mirror inside the Spasskaya Tower guardroom and carefully checked his pea-green Tomb Guard uniform. As usual, everything was in order. He gave a slight tug to his leather garrison belt and rubbed his sleeve over his gleaming brass belt buckle.

It would be at least fifteen more minutes before he would begin his slow, rhythmic goose-step from the Kremlin tower out to Red Square and to the Tomb. He studied his face in the mirror. It must remain expressionless: free from any look of disdain or disgust. He was doing this for Raisa and not for "Comrade" Lenin.

It was almost two weeks before that Raisa had told him she had discovered from "confidential" sources that he was right: the "Lenin" in the Tomb train *was* a wax dummy. The regime did not want to take a chance with the real body. The real Lenin had been left in the locked Tomb on Red Square.

She assured Yuri that the body he had been guarding with such reverence in the Tomb *was* the real body of Lenin. It always had been. Certainly, she argued, he could see why the Krylenko government had gone to such extremes in safeguarding the *real* Lenin.

He was surprised at the vigor of Raisa's arguments. She was extremely persuasive. He had always considered her to be a "radish" Communist: red on the outside and white on the inside, showing her public, dogmatic exterior and revealing her private interior only to close friends and family. But her views on the honoring of Lenin were apparently sincere and deep-rooted.

To please her he had agreed to go back on duty by September 7. Now he was ready to march the one hundred and fifty-three meters from Spasskaya Tower to the Tomb for the Changing of the Guard. In thirty minutes he would be standing at the feet of Lenin—the real Lenin, he hoped.

The Kremlin bells in the belfry of the tower struck the hour: ten o'clock. The Spasskaya Tower door opened and Yuri and a fellow Guard emerged like figures propelled from a cuckoo clock. They began their slow goose-stepping march down the cobblestoned walkway leading to the Tomb. Off to their right was the usual horde of the reverent who viewed the Changing of the Guard as a near-religious ritual. All was quiet except for the thud of their hobnailed boots on the flat stones and the whirring and clicking of tourists' cameras.

They marched parallel to the Kremlin wall with their free arms swinging in wide, rhythmic arcs and their bayonetted rifles balanced upright in the butts of their extended palms. At the mausoleum, they made a series of sharp, quickly executed turns and smoothly replaced the old sentinels. Yuri then marched into the Tomb and placed himself at the feet of the body of Lenin.

Yossef shuffled forward in the long line which had been queueing since six in the morning. The Tomb had been open to the public ever since the Tomb train returned from its much-heralded "triumphal" tour of the country on the first of September. He had received word through the Solidarity network that this was to be Yuri's first day back on Guard mount.

The line waiting to enter the Tomb led across Red Square, ran down a gentle slope beside the Historical Museum, turned a corner through iron gates, passed the eternal flame of the Unknown Soldier, and ended in the gardens beneath the fortress walls of the Kremlin.

Yossef felt a tingling sensation in his scalp and a slight burning behind his brown-tinted contact lenses as he came to a well-guarded police barricade at the foot of the hill. Two policemen and a plainclothesman straightened out the line and paired the spectators off into twos.

Yossef shuffled forward a few more feet. The long line grew quieter now—more reverent as the Tomb became visible. At another militia barrier, women's handbags and people's packages were collected to be returned later. No bundles of any kind were allowed in the holy of holies. The people in the line were talking in respectfully quiet voices now as they walked in short half-steps toward the mausoleum. The column marched across the cobblestones straight toward Saint Basil's Cathedral, then, in the middle of Red Square, made a sharp ninety-degree pivot toward the Tomb.

The uniforms of the Moscow police gave way at the pivot to the blue shoulderboards and collar tabs of KGB uniforms. Instinctively, people stopped talking. A person or two who had suspicious bulges in their clothing were yanked out of line and inspected.

A slight trickle of perspiration coursed through the wiry hairs of Yossef's beard and under his collar as he saw the entrance to the mausoleum. It looked so much more formidable and threatening than the plywood model in the South African tablelands. He felt as if he were about to enter a dungeon cell for a life sentence as he stumbled toward the mausoleum steps.

There were more guards near the steps. More checks. People had to remove their hats to have them inspected. Yossef's breathing became labored as he trudged up the steps and passed between two immobile honor-guard sentinels, gleaming, bayonetted rifles held in a rigid salute as he entered the Tomb. Immediately, a KGB officer directed the column to the left and it moved more rapidly now, the cool black marble interior settling over the hushed crowd like a gigantic shroud.

Left, then right. Two flights of stairs now and into the main crypt room. At every turn there was an armed uniformed guard watching the column of visitors with an intense scrutiny. Suddenly, Yossef was filled with an almost overpowering array of emotions: of dread, of anxiety, of excitement at seeing a twin brother for the first time, and—of guilt.

This Tomb where he was now encapsuled was the

centerpiece of a nation's religion. He was being sent by a hostile, foreign power to destroy its most sacred relic. No matter what Lenin was, or had been, he was central to the hopes and expectations of millions. He, Yossef, felt like a barbarian entering the Vatican with the intent of destroying and plundering.

Yuri was feeling a general uneasiness settling over him. It wasn't Lenin; he had almost resolved his conflict with him, at least temporarily. This feeling was different. He felt an actual presence in the crypt room where he was posted. It was more than an abstract sensation. It was related to something or someone who was inside the Tomb. He knew it, and the feeling grew stronger, filling him with an overpowering sense of dread and excitement. He felt an almost overwhelming urge to drop his rifle and run along the line of spectators looking for the source of his discomfort. He wiggled his toes inside his gleaming combat boots—the only movement he was allowed—to relieve the mounting pressure.

Yossef was now well into the main crypt room. The perspiration had now become multiple rivulets which had found pathways through his beard, onto his chest, and under his arms, soaking his undershirt. To his horror he realized that the security had been increased. There were at least thirteen armed Guards in the room. Two were at the head and foot of the brightly lit coffin. Because of the Solidarity threat, security had tripled within the Tomb.

The crypt room was constructed so that visitors entered, immediately turned right and walked up half a flight of steps along the wall; turned left, and then walked along another wall on a balcony overlooking the coffin; turned left again and descended another half a flight of stairs. At this point, the visitors filed by the coffin and then exited the room.

Yossef could see the murderer of his grandfather now. The semicircular route he was taking permitted a view of Lenin from both sides and from the feet. Everything in the Tomb seemed to be in almost satanic hues of red and black. Lenin looked remarkably small lying there in a black suit and black and red tie. Only his hands and face were visible. They looked waxy, showing a yellowing and a slight darkening.

The Guard with his back to him was Yuri. It had to be! His broad shoulders and torso were the same as his. As he shuffled slowly by his brother he tried to appear nonchalant, but he could hardly control his emotions. He noticed Yuri's white-gloved hands resting on his rifle. He was rigidly fixed in the same position that Yossef had practiced for hours in the Drakensberg canyon. He thought he detected a slight tremor in Yuri's hands as he began to pass him.

The tension and anxiety were unbearable. Yuri wondered if he was losing his mind. He was physically ill. His intestines cramped and his head throbbed with an unearthly pain.

Yossef paused briefly by the coffin and gazed into the dead face of Lenin. What an arrogant-looking little son-of-a-bitch, he thought; little men were often the cruelest tyrants of all. Then he shifted his gaze to his brother standing at the end of the coffin.

Yossef recoiled slightly. It was himself! His eyes swept over Yuri's pea-green uniform. His build—his face. He was as identical as a twin could be.

Yuri couldn't stand it any longer. He committed the unpardonable act for a Tomb Guard. He shifted his eyes and locked them into the staring eyes of his brother.

The sun was warm as Yossef stood with the other spectators waiting for the changing of the Guard. He paced nervously along the rope which separated the crowds from the walkway. A uniformed KGB trooper shot him a suspicious glance. Yossef breathed deeply and began to calm down. He had to get a better look at his brother in the light.

The mausoleum door swung open and the two Guards appeared. One was Yuri. Yossef swallowed. His mouth was dry and parched. He watched the new Guards replace the old in a series of well-executed moves. It was done so expertly that he wondered if he could duplicate the intricate procedures when the time came. He'd have to practice some more, he was sure of it.

Yuri saw the bearded man among the spectators as he was being relieved by the new Guard. His feelings of dread and anxiety intensified. Who *was* he? What ghost from his vague and murky past had risen to torment him? He must confront the stranger when he had completed his duty. He should be able to change into his civilian clothes and be out on the Square in twenty minutes.

Yuri began his slow, rhythmic march back to Spasskaya Tower with his fellow Guard. He was on the outside, toward the rope. If he were careful he could get a good look at his tormentor; but he must be careful.

Yossef inched up to the rope barrier as Yuri approached. He stared at Yuri's face, focusing his thoughts on his brother. Somewhere he read that identical twins could feel each other's emotions and conflicts even though they had been separated for years. Could he communicate with his brother through some form of mental telepathy? He had to try.

Hello, brother Yuri. He concentrated his thoughts on the approaching Guard. You have a brother. A twin brother. It's me, the bearded one standing in front of you. My name is Yossef. We'll meet, and soon.

Yuri was almost close enough to touch. He appeared not to be affected by Yossef's telepathic bombardment as he thudded closer in his slow cadence.

This is stupid, thought Yossef as Yuri approached. He doesn't even know I exist.

Don't go away! Please! Stay where you are!

Yuri wanted to scream the words to the bearded stranger staring at him from across the rope. Yuri was able to discern his features now. He cautiously shifted his eyes to the stranger.

Yossef flashed him a quick smile—a smile of recognition.

I've seen him before! I know that man from somewhere in my past! He's an important part of me—somewhere —the part that's lost. Please—please stay where you are until I can get back to you!

Yuri drew nearly abreast of Yossef and again their eyes connected briefly. Great beads of sweat had formed on Yuri's forehead. He was so engrossed with this intruder that he almost lost the mental cadence he was counting.

Yuri was now abreast of Yossef. With a little effort, he could reach out and touch his sleeve.

"Hello, brother," Yossef said softly in Hebrew.

The words lanced into Yuri like the thrust of a spear. He didn't know what they meant, or what language they were in, but they were personal—from a significant person in his life. He knew it and felt it in the very core of his being

The large wooden doors of the Spasskaya Tower guardroom swallowed them up. Yuri raced for his locker to change. Regulations forbade the Tomb Guards from wearing their duty uniforms on the street.

Yossef waited nervously. What would he say to his brother? He hadn't thought of that. In fact, this whole thing was an exercise in futility and stupidity. He could blow the potential success of Operation Samson sky-high

Suddenly he felt a massive hand on his shoulder. He looked around and saw the stern, disapproving face of Yabin.

"No, Yossef. This is not the time. Be patient, my young friend. It will happen. It will happen. Just—be patient."

Yuri tore from the Spasskaya Tower exit and raced toward the crowd of spectators. The stranger was gone. Frantically, he looked around. He wasn't in the crowd.

He looked toward the parking area and saw the stranger entering a large black Zil limousine. He yelled for the car to stop, but it pulled away.

* * *

As Yabin pulled into the traffic lane on Red Square, Yossef glanced sorrowfully into the side mirror. He saw his brother running and waving at the Zil as it picked up speed and roared away toward Saint Basil's Cathedral.

XIV.

"Raisa, it was somebody I knew at one time. I recognized that man. I felt his presence even before I saw him. He even talked to me. It was in another language. It was something like *'shalom achi'* and the last word was kind of guttural."

Raisa's deep green eyes probed into his, a faint smile playing across her lips. She extended a hand and lovingly caressed his cheeks, playfully skimming the skin of his ears with her long fingernails.

"I've never seen you so agitated. Were you on any kind of medication yesterday?"

"No, damn it!" Yuri twisted away from her. He lurched to his feet from the couch in Raisa's Moscow apartment and stalked to the window. "I'm fine, I'm healed, and I'm thinking straight."

Yuri sat back down beside her, his expression hardening.

"Raisa, remember the Dubrov family I told you about —the one in that samizdat in Minusinsk?"

Raisa nodded, a slight frown wrinkling her brow.

"Do you think that man was a Dubrov?" Her tone was faintly mocking. Yuri ignored her comment.

"A case like that would have been documented by the old CHEKA or the NKVD, wouldn't it?"

"Of course," she replied. "They kept files on every little thing. Nothing was ever overlooked."

"You mean they would still have a file on Aleksei Dubrov's life—back to 1921?" Yuri brightened.

"Yes, I'm sure. The KGB throws nothing away. Everything is kept in the cellars of the old Lubyanka at the Center. There's a big project going on right now of microfilming the old records and forming them into a library."

"Raisa, I'm going to ask you for a big favor. I wouldn't ask it of you if it wasn't very important to me." He leaned closer and draped a conspiratorial arm over her shoulder.

She just stared at him, waiting for his request.

"Do you have access to those old files?"

Raisa nodded.

"Could you make a copy of the Dubrov file and get it to me so I can read it?"

A slight, almost imperceptible shiver ran through her body.

"That samizdat really got to you, didn't it?"

"I just want to know more about these people," he said defensively. "Will you do it?"

Raisa smiled and pinched his cheek. "You're going to get me the firing squad, you know that, don't you?"

Yuri's face registered shock.

"No, Raisa! If there's any real danger . . ."

She laughed a deep throaty laugh. "Yes, I can do it. It's not that big a problem. I take classified documents home with me quite often to study and edit for Pavel. I'm sure that some moldy old records in the morgue won't be that important. I know somebody I can trust to make a single copy of everything in the file for you. She owes me a few favors."

The chief clerk of the microfilm project was a Solidarity member named Olga Yurevna. She was a career civil servant with the KGB but had lost her conviction of the infallibility of the State and Party when she became privy to the policy-making transcripts of the Politburo. She became convinced that the aging leadership was totally out of touch with reality and that only a nationalist, non-Communist movement like Solidarity could save the country from disaster. At that vulnerable point in her ideological transformation, Raisa had recruited her for the movement.

Olga had been making two microfilm copies of everything: one for the KGB, and one for Solidarity. After the past two years of microfilming, the Solidarity collection was almost as extensive as the Center's.

"Here's two copies, Raisa. I've got to have one back in a week."

"To be sure. Does this one go to the photo department or to you?" Raisa held up the best copy.

"Reroute it to photo processing. It's a clear copy. That's one of the thickest files in the old CHEKA section. I didn't get a chance to read it, but it looks interesting. Are these Dubrovs anybody you knew?"

"I just do as I'm told." She patted Olga on the sleeve. "Thank you."

"Do you have it?" Yuri's eyes were wide with expectation when he arrived to pick Raisa up.

"I've got it in a safe place at the office. I'll have to—"

"Raisa, I wanted it tonight!" Yuri's anger flared like a struck match as he grabbed her hand.

"Well, I just can't walk out with documents anytime I feel like it. Damn it, Yuri! You've been impossible ever since this . . . this Dubrov obsession," she said testily, disengaging her hand.

"It seems like *other* people have the same obsession." Yuri flung a new *Novy Rodina* down on the couch.

Raisa scanned the samizdat and scowled.

"This whole issue is about the Dubrovs. What's Solidarity trying to do—replace Lenin with Aleksei Dubrov?" Her voice dripped with sarcasm.

"I saw some graffiti spray-painted on a wall, driving here. It said 'Aleksei Dubrov Lives'—so, maybe Solidarity *is* trying to replace Lenin—and what's wrong with that?" Yuri said, watching for her reaction.

Raisa drew a deep, controlled breath. "You know what this means now. It means that the security people will realize that this Dubrov thing is important and will move the file to a secure vault."

"But you *did* have it copied?" Yuri's eyes bordered on panic.

"Yes, but I've got to wait until your uncle gives me some documents to take home; then I can slip the Dubrov copy in. I can't take it out by itself."

Raisa slipped on her coat and punched her arm angrily through the sleeve.

"Come on, Yuri. Let's go and forget about those damned Dubrovs for the evening."

The Arbat was more crowded than usual for a Tuesday evening. The student throng was clearly in an agitated mood, even an ugly mood. The impact of the latest *Novy Rodina* had created a feistiness that bordered on open rebellion. After every issue of the *Novy Rodina* there was an increase in student activism. Alienation from the cult of Lenin was growing and becoming bolder. Several students in the crowd were wearing anti-Lenin pins.

The Arbat was a place where samizdat poetry was read aloud. A young poet with long hair, a pale complexion, and one leg hobbled up to the platform and braced himself on the piano.

"Greetings, brothers and sisters. My name is Pyotr. That's all you have to know about me. I was going to recite a poem honoring my leg—the one I left in China—but perhaps I should recite one to the new plastic leg the government promised me six months ago.

"This poem, however, is dedicated to the most efficient of our government's ministries, the Censorship Department, and to those tireless, dedicated bureaucrats—our censors."

There was a scattering of applause as the one-legged veteran pulled a wrinkled sheet of paper out of his shirt pocket.

> Amen
> I have killed a truth. Killed it unborn

> To hell with it.
> We bury
> Bury truth. Come see
> We bury

There was no applause. Just a deafening silence as the long-haired poet hobbled down from the stage.

Another poet scrambled up to the piano. He too was a veteran of the China conflict. He wore a single military medal on his jacket, upside down—a symbol that his country was in distress.

There was no introduction or title to his poem. There didn't have to be. The subject was fresh in the minds of the young in Moscow.

> Where are your graves
> or maybe just mounds
> Georgi and Tanya Dubrov?
> Where can we put a monument?
> There are no graves

> You cannot be frozen into statues
> like some docile teacher's pets
> you blaze
> from the pedestals of the world stage
> Georgi and Tanya Dubrov

Yuri suddenly stood and walked briskly to the exit, his handkerchief held to his eyes.

Raisa followed him outside and slipped her arm reassuringly through his.

Wordlessly, they walked the three and a half miles through the Belygorod back to Raisa's apartment.

Raisa left her apartment the next morning to catch the 7:00 A.M. metro to the Center. She walked rapidly along the street, swinging her briefcase, and headed for the subway entrance.

The man with the mud-colored beard and brown eyes

peered at her cautiously over the top of his newspaper as she started to descend to the lower level of the metro's Blue Line.

Yossef took a deep, approving breath, tucked his newspaper into his raincoat pocket, wheeled around and followed her down to the train level. He dropped the ten-kopeck token in the turnstile, took the popped-up ticket and joined the throng waiting for the Moscow Center train.

Yossef felt a slight twinge of excitement as Raisa sat on a bench, her long legs crossed invitingly. Her movement wasn't lost on the other males in the waiting crowd. A Red Army officer walked slowly by her and glanced down at her cleavage. Raisa stared ahead, oblivious of the stares —lost in her own thoughts of Yuri and the Dubrov problem.

A bell rang and a blue light flashed above the passengers. The light of the train could be seen approaching down the dark tunnel to the left. The expectant crowd shuffled toward the bright yellow line and waited obediently for the subway train to hiss to a stop. Yossef always marveled at how obedient and passive Moscow crowds were. There was never any shoving or impatience even in the longest and most frustrating of queues.

He maneuvered himself in back of Raisa. His heart was now pounding wildly as he felt the press of bodies in back of him which pushed him forward, crushing his hips against Raisa's buttocks. A sudden stirring filled his loins, and the fear that she would detect his hardness crashed over him like an ocean wave. She didn't respond. The average Muscovite, especially the subway commuter, took the press of others' bodies as an occupational hazard.

Raisa took a seat by the window. Yossef timidly sat next to her even though there were other seats available. The smell of her perfume filled his nostrils, deepening his stirrings. He breathed deeply, then, fearful that she might read his intentions, took out a handkerchief and blew his nose with studied care.

She stared out the window as the Blue Line train

clacked over the tracks toward central Moscow. She noticed her fellow passenger's face in the window. He kept stealing sideways glances at her. She knew him from somewhere, she was sure of it. Where had she seen that face before? Did he work at the Center? Impossible, she thought. Beards weren't approved of; a sign of bourgeois decadence.

Raisa impulsively reached in her string shopping bag and took out a hard roll. She broke it in half and turned to the bearded stranger.

"Care for half a roll?" she asked with a smile that made Yossef catch his breath.

Yossef's heart seemed to leap into his throat as Raisa's beautiful green eyes trapped his. He fought to regain his composure.

"Thank you," he said in his well-rehearsed, accented Russian.

"You're not Soviet, are you?" Raisa's eyes were now boring into his and scanning his face. Mentally she was stripping off his beard, trying to discern his features.

"No. No, I'm not," Yossef replied. "I'm Swiss. I'm with the Swiss Trade Mission. My name is Herman Schwender. And yours?"

Raisa shook his hand vigorously. "Raisa Karezev." She smiled, a few crumbs from the roll dribbling from her full lips.

The warmth and strength of Raisa's hand now set Yossef's heart beating so hard that he thought it would tear from his chest. He wanted to hold her hand longer, but released his grip.

A bell rang and, almost as one body, the passengers arose. The train glided to a stop and Yossef and Raisa left and headed toward the turnstile.

"Thank you for the roll, Miss Karezev. I hope to see you again."

Raisa smiled her most dazzling smile and headed for the escalator.

Suddenly, Yossef felt drained of all of his energy. He flopped on a nearby bench, marveling at his encounter with Raisa Karezev.

"Did she recognize you?"

"No, Yabin. I was very discreet. That lady is going to be worth it all." Yossef sighed a satisfied sigh. "For the first time I'm actually looking forward to this little venture. When do I become Yuri?"

Yabin ignored his question.

"Do you think you could fool Raisa in bed, Yossef?"

"What do you mean, Yabin?"

"Could you make love like Yuri?"

"How in the hell should I know? I've never seen him screw."

"You're going to see him now. Are you ready for this, Yossef?" Yabin smiled a wicked smile as he inserted a cartridge of Super-8 film into a portable projector. He then removed a large picture from the wall in order to use the apartment wall as a screen.

Yabin dimmed the lights and flipped on the switch of the projector. It whined into motion and the sound of a small speaker was heard.

"What is this, Yabin?" Yossef demanded. His face was wrinkled in an effort to visualize what the MOSSAD colonel was up to.

"Solidarity had a movie camera installed in the apartment adjoining Raisa Karezev's bedroom. These shots were taken through a two-way mirror. They also bugged her place. Luckily, Yuri is a daytime lover, so they caught all the action."

The scene on the white wall flickered in a grainy gray, focused, and showed Yuri and Raisa naked on her bed. Yossef shot forward in his chair, his eyes drinking in Raisa's naked beauty.

"This is obscene!" Yossef emitted a low, sensual groan. "We shouldn't be watching this." His vision was glued to the wall.

Yossef strained to hear Yuri's voice. He had heard other tapes of his brother talking but never in the act of making love. Now he was hearing and viewing Yuri's sex techniques.

After a few preliminary gestures of foreplay, Yuri mounted Raisa. It seemed like seconds—actually it was a minute and a half—and then Yuri rolled off. Raisa just lay there, her pelvis still undulating slightly, a look of frustration on her face.

"That's it?" Yossef asked incredulously. "That's what the Americans call 'wham-bam-thank-you-Ma'am.'"

"It's the Russian way, m'boy," chortled Yabin. "Russian men have traditionally had a chauvinistic attitude toward sex. It's their role to be satisfied and to hell with their ladies. The women don't know any better. Raisa probably thinks she had a pretty good lay."

"Good lay, hell!" Yossef bit out the words. "Look at her ass. It's still gyrating and that stupid brother of mine is almost asleep. There was no foreplay, no afterplay —nothing. Is he totally ignorant of what it takes to please a woman?"

Yabin gave him a lazy smile. "They have an old folk saying in Russia. It goes back to the time of Peter the Great when he brought in thousands of foreigners, especially Frenchmen, to advise him on modernizing his country. It goes something like this: A Frenchman will hurry you into bed and when he gets you there, he takes his time; but a Russian will take his time getting you to bed, and then hurries up."

"And Soviet women just accept this? I thought they were liberated."

"Old traditions die hard. This is a closed society, Yossef. These poor females have never had any foreigners to compare their men to." Yabin looked suggestively at Yossef in a long, sideways glance.

"Well, I know of one tradition that's going to die a sudden, thundering death when I take Raisa to bed. She's going to get some quality loving for a change. I hope she can handle it. I'm in a different league than these Russian he-goats. All of my experiences at embassy parties, or after them, will be at Raisa's disposal. What a lucky lady!"

"Remember, Yossef." Yabin smiled a warning. "You have to duplicate your brother in every way."

An expression halfway between a leer and a smirk played over Yossef's face.

"Well, between now and the time I take over, Yuri Spinnenko will receive one hell of an education on sexual

techniques—and Raisa Karezev will be the first to notice."

Raisa could feel a slight autumn nip in the air as she left
her flat and headed for her car in the basement parking
area of her apartment complex.

It was September 20, a Saturday and, as usual for
Moscow weekends, the pedestrian traffic was heavy but
the vehicular traffic was slight. As she pulled into the
street and headed for Yuri's apartment, hers was about the
only private automobile on the road.

Yuri opened the door almost as soon as Raisa knocked.
A look of hopeful expectancy was on his face.

"Did you bring it?"

She edged in by him and sat on the couch, crossing her
legs suggestively. "How bad do you want it?" she teased, a
bemused smile on her face.

He sat beside her, kissed her quickly, and tugged at her
handbag.

"In here?"

Raisa sighed resignedly and pulled out the large buff-
colored folder.

"You're about as romantic as an expectant father." She
plopped the folder in his lap and crossed her arms across
her chest.

"And who knows what this will give birth to." Yuri
chuckled nervously at his own joke. "Oh, Raisa. Would
you mind if we got together later this afternoon? I'd like to
read this by myself."

"Well!" Raisa rose suddenly. "I wouldn't want to dis-
turb your reverie. I may come back and I may not," she
pouted.

Yuri paid no attention. He was busy flipping through
the pages of the file.

"Oh, by the way, I've got another tidbit of information
for you—if you're interested, that is."

"What's that?"

"The comment of the stranger; the one at the Tomb."

"Yes, yes!" Yuri was suddenly attentive.

"It's Hebrew. *Shalom achi* means 'Hello, brother.' I

talked to one of the linguists at the Center. It's the personal form of 'brother' and means a blood relation, you know, a real family brother, not the way we use 'comrade.' Are you sure that he was talking to you?"

"Of course I'm sure he was talking to me!" Yuri barked the words at her. "He was looking right at me. Now, if you'll excuse me." He was almost pushing her out the door.

Raisa stood in the corridor, fuming, as she heard Yuri bolt the door behind her. She spun on her heel and flounced down the hallway toward the street.

Raisa received Yuri's frantic phone call at two in the afternoon.

"Raisa! I've got to talk to you!" His voice edged on hysteria. "Please! Please come over as soon as you can."

She stifled a yawn, her dark brown bangs falling into her eyes. She brushed them out of the way and tried to focus her thoughts.

"Yu—Yuri. You woke me out of a sound sleep. I was taking a nap, since my day is ruined anyway. You weren't very good company this morning." She waited for his apology, but it didn't come.

"Raisa, please. *Please!* Come over right away." Yuri's voice was choked with emotion.

"All right, all right!" There was a trace of anger in her reply. "Give me thirty minutes, will you?"

Raisa reread the passage from the Dubrov file, a look of puzzled amazement on her face.

The Dubrov twins, sons of Georgi and Tanya Dubrov, ringleaders of the Vorturka uprising, were separated in 1960. It was discovered later that the one called Yossef was smuggled out of the country to Israel. The one named Yuri was sent to the Foundling Home in Sverdlosk where he was kept until he was two. He was given the last name of Kiktev and a background legend (Appendix C).

At age two Yuri "Kiktev" was assigned to the Kiev State Orphanage where he remained until he was fourteen. At that age he was assigned to Pavel Spinnenko, then a major in the Border Guards Directorate. In 1975 Pavel Spinnenko was ordered by the First Directorate to formally adopt Yuri Spinnenko. The legend of uncle was assigned to Spinnenko as brother of the boy's mother.

Raisa scanned the rest of the page in mounting shock. She was too stunned to react; then, in a sudden movement, she buried her face in Yuri's shirt and sobbed loudly.

"Yuri! Oh, Yuri! I was so rotten to you this morning. Will you ever forgive me?"

He lifted her chin and gazed steadily at her. There was a strange determined set to his jaw that frightened Raisa.

"Of course, Raisa. How were you to know any of this?"

"You—you are a Dubrov." The realization of this fact now struck Raisa like a thunderbolt. "Your grandfather is—is the one that was murdered by Lenin and you grandmother was Lenin's niece! You're a Dubrov!" she repeated, backing slightly away as if he might be contaminated.

"Yes." A distant but satisfied smile was fixed on Yuri's lips. "I know who I am and where I come from. Now I know what I must do. Aren't those the three biggest questions of life, Raisa? I mean, I never *really* knew where I came from or where I was going—until now. Isn't it remarkable how some moldy old documents can change your life?"

Yuri threw back his head and laughed a strange, almost maniacal laugh.

"All the pigshit they filled me up with for the last thirty years has been flushed down the toilet with *these*!" He shook the Dubrov file under her nose. "The *truth*, Raisa, the truth! Thirty years of lies dispelled by one short paragraph. Don't you realize what this means, Raisa? I'm free! I'm finally free! My name is Yuri Dubrov and I have a brother named Yossef. It was him at the crypt. It was Yossef near the walkway. I knew I recognized him behind that beard because I recognized myself! Don't you see it, Raisa? The Hebrew greeting. It all fits!"

Raisa continued to stare fixedly at the strange, frightening look on Yuri's face.

"And what will you do now?" Her voice was hoarse with emotion.

His words were issued like a pronunciamento; a definite statement that permitted no further questions:

"There really isn't any choice, is there, dear Raisa. I'm a Dubrov. I must carry on the work of my parents and grandparents."

XV.

The wooden packing crate on the wharf of Bergen Harbor looked like the hundreds of others stacked on pallets waiting to be loaded onto the long conveyor belt. Heavy steel bands crisscrossed the crate, and a special epoxy sealer had been sprayed all over it to keep the moisture out, giving it the appearance of old varnish.

Inside, Vasily Gregierenko rested in a cushion of foam, an oxygen bottle fastened securely to the interior wall. Small packets of concentrated food were stacked nearby and several plastic envelopes of water with attached drinking tubes dangled from the ceiling. Surrounding his small compartment, separated by another wooden wall, were hundreds of valve fittings for the booster pumps in the Soviet pipeline projects.

Suddenly, Gregierenko felt his foam-and-wooden cocoon lurch, as a forklift stabbed into the pallet, lifted it high, and carried it to the conveyor belt. A Soviet Border Guardsman in plain clothes, permanently assigned to the Norwegian port, had given the crate a casual inspection, signed off the shipping and inspection papers attached to the crate, and signaled for the cargo to be loaded.

The pallet was gently placed on the belt that entered the yawning dockside opening of the huge roll-on-roll-off container ship. The belt full, the automated loading procedure took over as crate number 115116 moved in a series of short jerks toward the craft. Automatic cargo-handling devices separated the uniformly sized crates and piled them in the hold. Gregierenko held his breath during the loading process, hoping the machines would respect the "This Side Up" markings stenciled on the sides.

Two hours later, the cargo doors swung shut and the container vessel was nudged into the channel by three tugs. Past the breakwater, the ship headed north for Archangel. Inside his sealed foam womb, Vasily Gregierenko took a sleeping pill and dozed off into oblivion.

The members of the Solidarity Revolutionary Council had been infiltrating the city during the past week. They had been able to establish their temporary headquarters in an ideal, though not the most likely location: the State Mortuary Shipping Office on Petrovska Street facing the vast Moscow freight yards. From here, the already embalmed bodies of non-Muscovites who had died in the city while visiting or dwelling there temporarily were shipped back to their homes in the far reaches of the Soviet Union. The personnel in charge of the Petrovska Street operation were all Solidarity. The shipment of hundreds of caskets to various parts of the country each month served as an ideal conduit for the smuggling of weapons, explosives, and samizdats to Solidarity cells throughout Russia. Every region of the nation had a State Mortuary Office, and for the past several years Solidarity had been clandestinely installing their people in this obscure, but strategic, government agency.

Yossef and Yabin walked between the long, double row of rectangular shipping crates, each enclosing an empty casket. They were preceded by a effeminate-looking shipping clerk, his shirt pocket crammed with pens and pencils and a clipboard swinging in his hand.

Zhores Platonov, a squat little tree stump of a man with a permanent limp, motioned them into a musty-smelling storeroom.

"In here," he whispered dramatically.

Inside, sitting on a variety of odd-sized boxes, were the seven members of the Moscow Solidarity leadership cell. A nervous rustle rippled through the group before Platonov spoke.

"Brothers. We're moving up our timetable for the first phase of Operation Samson. Yossef, you'll be taking your brother's place right away—perhaps in a day or two."

Yossef sat in silence, his hands dangling listlessly between his legs.

"Why?" he finally asked.

"Because your brother knows who he is, and now knows who you are. Raisa Karezev copied the original CHEKA file of the Dubrov case and gave it to him to read. It was stupid of her. It's all there. Everything about your family. He told Raisa that he now has to carry on the work of his parents and grandparents. He became very emotional. Raisa couldn't reason with him."

"Then why don't you let Yuri be the inside man? He *is* the ideal person for it, isn't he? And now that he's converted to the cause it would relieve me of the responsibility." Yossef felt a surge of hope.

"We've already discussed that possibility, Yossef," Platonov replied. "Sorry. You're still our man. In Yuri's frame of mind he's too unpredictable; in fact, we're going to have to nab Yuri the night after next before he does something rash."

A look of resignation swept over Yossef. "And when do I go on duty?" he asked, speaking softly to disguise a slight tremor in his voice.

"Not for a week: September 30. And here comes the best part, Yossef. Raisa will be taking you out to her dacha in Zhukovia for several days while her family is on vacation. You'll have nothing to do but romp with Raisa. It'll give you a chance to know her," Yabin concluded.

"Where will you keep Yuri?" asked Yossef.

"Right here," said Platonov. "We have a room—a little prison, actually, all set up downstairs. Nobody ever comes here unless they have business, and even then, they can't wait to get out of here. This isn't a place where people come and browse.

"In another few days we'll have another guest," Platonov continued. "Vasily Gregierenko will be arriving at the automated freight annex about a mile from here. His crate will be routed to the distribution center for pipeline equipment, so we've got to extricate him from his little home and bring him here before he winds up in Siberia. I suspect he'll be more dead than alive, so he'll have to spend some time here recovering."

"Let's be on our way." Yabin rose and clapped a meaty hand on Yossef's shoulder. "Come, my boy. I've got to brief you on some of the twists and turns of Yuri's mind so you can be authentic for your lady friend. You've got to play the part of one who is writhing in moral agony over his newly discovered identity. But you also have to function as an honor guard for the bastard who murdered your grandfather. We've got a lot of rehearsing to do."

Yossef gave the Council a weak smile and a little wave of his hand and shuffled dejectedly after Yabin, his keeper.

A few drops of rain told Yuri that it was time to head for a bus stop and get back to his apartment. Ever since he had learned that he was a Dubrov, he had been walking the expanses of Sokolniki Park trying to figure out just what he was to do. His dramatic declaration to Raisa was followed by confusion and indecision. He was not a born conspirator; in fact, he was one of the most naive of men raised in a system in which everything said by an authority symbol was regarded as the absolute truth. Even though his faith in the system had come dramatically crashing down, he couldn't shift his mental and ideological gear overnight to be a Solidarity activist. And Solidarity, he knew, was the key to his future. Somehow, he had to make contact with the movement and become part of it. But how? Yuri Spinnenko, a Lenin Tomb Guard, model comrade, and now a holder of the Order of Lenin, just couldn't walk up on the stage of the Arbat and declare his disaffection and his desire to join Solidarity.

And Raisa wasn't any help. In spite of her professions of

sympathy she was a careerist. As long as she could play with her beloved computers at the Center she would serve the regime loyally.

A sudden clap of thunder and a burst of rain from the night sky sent Yuri scurrying under the eaves of a closed concession stand. He noticed a swarthy man sharing his shelter. He must be an Armenian or a Georgian, he thought.

"Rough weather, eh?" remarked the stranger, his smile revealing a row of stainless-steel caps on his front teeth.

"Yes. I hope I can make it to the bus stop without getting soaked," answered Yuri. "The last one to Tanganskaya Square leaves at eleven."

"You live near there?" asked the swarthy man.

"Yes. I have an apartment on Nizhegorodskaya Street."

"Nice neighborhood. You must be in the foreign ministry, or a scientist."

Yuri shuffled his feet, embarrassed at the man's probing. It was clear to the stranger that Yuri was a member of the privileged elite.

As Yuri opened his mouth to respond, the stranger held a small tube up to his face. At first he thought it was a nasal inhaler. Suddenly, the man flipped the tube around and squirted a spray of foul-smelling liquid in Yuri's face.

Yuri's first reaction was a mixture of annoyance and amusement. His mind was trying to say, He mistakenly reversed his nasal spray and got it all over me, the idiot.

His thought became arrested in midstream: the fog of a sudden, narcoleptic sleep hit him like a rush of anesthesia. He was mumbling something as he collapsed in the stranger's arms.

Two other men darted around the corner of the stand and lifted Yuri. Furtively, they stole to a waiting sedan and placed him gently in the trunk.

The three-man Solidarity kidnapping team then sped their captive to the State Mortuary warehouse on Petrovska Street.

Yossef removed the brown-tinted contact lenses and flushed them down the toilet. Then, methodically, almost ritualistically, he snipped off the longer portions of his beard until only a stubble remained.

"Close enough?" he asked.

Yabin and the barber nodded, and Yossef slipped into the kitchen chair. The barber, a member of the Moscow Solidarity organization, lathered the stubble and shaved off the remainder of his beard. He then snipped and clipped his hair until finished.

"Take a look in the mirror," said the barber proudly.

Yossef stared at his reflection while Yabin held up a recent photograph of Yuri.

The comparison created a spasm of anxiety. Yes. He could fool Raisa Karezev, Uncle Pavel, and his Tomb Guard comrades. He felt the slow but inexorable surge of fear expanding in his chest again.

He then took a tube of cream and rubbed a dab of it vigorously into a patch of discolored flesh on his left forearm. What appeared to be a raspberry-colored birthmark started to fade. Yossef washed the area with soap and warm water and rinsed it off. The tattoo, needled into his arm during his South African training, appeared.

"Here are some of Yuri's clothes. Put them on," commanded Yabin. "Some Solidarity people visited his apartment last night. And here are his wallet, keys, and military identity disc."

"What now?" Yossef asked after changing clothes.

"Now, we take you to within a block of Yuri's apartment. Go there and familiarize yourself with everything. Look through all of his personal belongings."

"Can I call Raisa?"

"Do whatever you want, Yossef," Yabin replied softly, almost sadly. "You do whatever Yuri Dubrov would do."

Yossef had been asleep for almost two hours when he heard the metallic sound of a key softly probing the lock. He was almost paralyzed with fright as his heart pounded frantically. Was it the KGB? Had they found out about him so soon? Was it General Spinnenko? He looked at his watch: 3:30 in the afternoon. It was mid-week, a Wednesday. Who would be visiting Yuri's apartment at this time?

A rush of perfume preceded the intruder and Yossef knew that it was Raisa. He feigned sleep as he heard her put a heavy bag on the kitchen table.

"Yuri?" The tone of her voice was tinged with surprise. He heard her walk over to the couch and felt her body sink onto the cushion next to him. Her warm hands were then on his shoulders, gently kneading and massaging.

"Yuri, what are you doing here? I thought you were in the Lenin Library?"

Yossef rolled over and focused his eyes on Raisa's face, his mind scrambling for an answer.

"I was too tired, too depressed," was his weak reply.

Raisa lay down beside him, her pelvis fitting to his as she stroked his freshly cut hair.

"Poor baby," she purred, nuzzling his cheek with her cold nose. "You've been through so much lately. Most men would crumble under the kind of pressure you've been under."

Yossef thought his loins would explode as he fought to control a mounting erection. He tried thinking other thoughts: terrible, gloomy thoughts of entering the Tomb and guarding Lenin. The fear generated by these thoughts reduced his stirrings.

"What are you doing here?" he asked sleepily. "I thought you were at work."

"You know my time is flexible. I heard that a shipment of oranges came in to State Store Six, you know, the one on Kalskaya Street, so I beat the queue. I know how you love oranges so I thought I'd leave them here and surprise you. You did give me a key, you know." She smiled that dazzling smile again.

Yossef sat up, his unbuttoned shirt exposing his hairy chest, and wrapped his arms tenderly around her.

"Raisa, Raisa, dearest and sweetest Raisa," he cooed in her ear. "If it wasn't for you I'd be in a straightjacket in a psychiatric ward. I owe you so much."

An overwhelming flood of affection washed over Raisa as she felt Yossef's strong arms surround her tenderly, caringly, his hands gently exploring her back. She melted against him, her mouth sliding over his cheek and fastening on his.

Her passionate kiss filled Yossef with an almost uncontrollable desire, and he could feel his heartbeat in a dozen parts of his body. His penis was fully erect and filled with an intense throbbing that almost made him nauseous.

"Raisa." He backed away, his arms slipping to her waist. He had to control himself. This was not the time or the place to make love to her.

"We're going to have four fantastic days at your parents' dacha. There's so much I want to tell you. We'll have time—for everything." He kissed her softly on the corner of the mouth.

Raisa looked deeply into Yossef's eyes and smiled a puzzled little smile. There seemed to be a new sense of depth, of caring, to Yuri. Perhaps the discovery of his true identity had tempered and matured him, she thought. Her fear of his doing something rash or self-destructive was somewhat diminished.

"And we'll have no more talk about you carrying on the Dubrov tradition?" she scolded in a teasing manner.

"No more. I promise," Yossef assured her. "I've pretty well sorted out my feelings and set some priorities. I want to share them with you when we get out to Zhukovia."

"Am—am I part of your priorities?" she asked, her eyes dancing mischievously.

"You, dear Raisa, are at the very top of the list."

Yuri's eyes burned with a sensual intensity she'd never seen before. It excited and frightened her.

"I—I'm off Thursday and Friday. I'd like to pick you up at nine-thirty tomorrow morning."

"I can't wait." Yossef kissed her wrist and the back of her hand, and gave her knuckles a little nibble.

A series of involuntary shudders coursed through her body. Her eyes were pleading with him to take her into the bedroom and make love, but there was something forbidding in his demeanor: something which said "wait."

Raisa rose and headed for the door. Yossef followed, thankful that the bagginess of his pants helped conceal his erection.

Raisa turned quickly and planted a full, wet kiss on Yossef's mouth. He responded, now holding her closely, his hardness fast against her. His hand slid to her buttocks as he cupped a cheek in his hand.

"Oh Yuri, Yuri!" she panted, her tongue probing his ear. "You've been through so much. I want to comfort you so badly. You need me so much."

Yossef slipped his hands up to her face, his eyes now hooded in self-control.

"Yes, sweet Raisa. I do need you." He kissed her on the forehead as one would kiss an impatient child. "Tomorrow you will find out just how much I need you. Your dacha will bring out the very best in me, I promise." He winked suggestively, amazed at his own self-control.

Raisa left and walked slowly down the corridor, her loins aching and inflamed with desire.

The first sensation Yuri felt upon awakening was the terrific pounding in his head: the pounding and throbbing of a dozen jackhammers.

A slim shaft of light from a narrow transom stabbed into the room, giving him the chance to view his surroundings.

Now he remembered: the stranger in the park! The tube! The spray! He was in a KGB cell. This must be in the Lubyanka. No. The Lubyanka wasn't a prison anymore. They'd remodeled it in May, according to Raisa. Then it must be Lefortovo Prison on the outskirts of the city. They know that *he* knows that he's a Dubrov. His mind flashed back to the detention center at Minusinsk. Could he handle that kind of treatment again? No. This time, he feared, he would lash out at his tormentors, hoping that they would kill him. But they might not kill him. They might just wound him and subject him to continual torture as he lay helpless.

The bed he was lying on was soft enough. He arched his back and carefully bounced on the springs. It was a single bed, not a narrow cot. The smell of the fresh sheets and the soft blanket was incongruous with KGB treatment. As his eyes adjusted to the semidarkness he could make out a small bathroom and a chest of drawers to his left. Hanging on a wire stretched across a corner of the room were several changes of clothes, *his* clothes, that had hung in his apartment closet.

Cautiously, Yuri slid off the bed and tiptoed to the door and tried the doorknob. It was locked. He fumbled for a light switch. He found it near the door and flipped it up. A small reading light went on over his bed. To the left, against the wall, was a small bookcase full of books and magazines.

"You out there!" Yuri pounded on the door with his fist. "I want to talk to somebody."

"You're finally awake, eh, Yuri?" a soft voice called from behind the door.

"Yes. I'm awake, damn it. Who are you? What is this place? Why am I being held here?"

"Are you hungry?"

The thought of food caused Yuri's stomach to constrict. He glanced at his watch. Two-thirty. In the morning or afternoon? He had no sense of time in his little prison. How long did I sleep? he wondered.

The knob turned and he heard a bolt slip back.

"All right, Spinnenko," commanded the voice. "Stand back. We don't want any heroics. There are three of us out here." Yuri shrank back to the head of the bed. An overhead light was switched on from the hallway.

Zhores Platonov's squat frame filled the doorway as he limped in with a large tray. Two armed guards with AK-47s remained outside. Yuri stared at the heaps of food: borscht soup, mauve and curdled with dollops of cream, black bread rolled into pellets, and *kuban* pies. This definitely was not a KGB prison menu.

"Who are you people?" Yuri's tone was softer and less demanding.

"We are your brothers, Yuri Dubrov. You're here for your own good and you will not be harmed if you behave."

"You're not with State Security, are you?" Yuri already knew the answer to that question by now.

"No," replied Platonov.

"Can you tell me who you are and why you kidnapped me?"

"To be sure. We're Solidarity and we're keeping you out of circulation for a while again, for your own good."

"I'll be missed."

"No, you won't," Platonov assured him.

"Are you involved with my brother, Yossef?"

Platonov smiled and nodded. "Yes. Yossef is a very important part of us. You'll be meeting him very soon. Now, you enjoy your food. Knock when you finish."

"Let me ask you one more thing. You brought me here because—because the KGB will arrest me now that the Dubrov story is out. I'm a living reminder of that family and now that they've become public martyrs the KGB will try to find me, won't they?"

Platonov grinned, his stainless-steel teeth gleaming, pleased that Yuri had provided his own answers.

"You're very perceptive, lad. We don't want to lose any more Dubrovs. We need you both for the revolution."

The revolution! Yuri remembered the discussion he'd had with the young prisoner at Minusinsk. To complete the original Revolution of March 1917; the truly democratic revolution begun by the Russian people before it was betrayed by Lenin and his Bolsheviks some nine months later.

The door closed and the bolt slid back into place. A feeling of peace and satisfaction spread over Yuri as he sat down to his sumptuous meal. Perhaps he would be allowed to carry on the Dubrov tradition after all.

Yossef wasn't prepared for the charming tranquility of Raisa's Zhukovia dacha. Solidarity should have given him a briefing on this place, he thought as he mounted the steps behind Raisa, watching her hips swaying slightly before him.

"Just take your suitcase to the bedroom," she said.

What bedroom? Yossef moaned to himself. Solidarity should have been on top of this. His mind groped for an appropriate response.

"Raisa, come here." He held her and kissed her neck. "Would you lead me to it?" Something like a flame licked through his eyes, which excited her.

"To be sure." She smiled coyly. She took his hand and led him down the corridor to a back bedroom with a window that overlooked the river.

"Ah, it's good to be back here. I feel like I've never left."

Raisa looked at him, a strange, almost puzzled little smile playing across her lips. She sat down on the bed and absently fluffed her hair.

"I hope you'll be as comfortable as you were last time. Mama changed some of the furniture around. She moved the bed over here so one can see the river lying down," she said deliberately.

"Oh yes, I've noticed," Yossef lied casually.

"Let me know when you're ready and we'll think of something to do." Raisa smiled, a slight, almost imperceptible frown knitting her brow.

An hour later, Raisa and Yossef were hiking along a small trail above the river. It was a beautiful early-autumn day. The sky was cloudless and the leaves of the silver birches shimmered in the bright sunlight. They stopped in a grassy clearing and Raisa spread a blanket, opened up a small basket, and took out a bottle of Georgian white wine and two glasses and poured for Yossef and herself. A jet chalked a white line against the cobalt sky and the sun was throwing shoals of light on the blue-gray river.

They touched glasses with a slight tinkle and sipped their wine lazily. Without a word, they lay on their backs, hands held lightly. The sun was casting leopard-spots of warmth on their bodies. There was an aphrodisiac quality to the open air, the sun, and the birch woods.

"Ah, this is the good life, Raisa. I wish it could go on forever. I'm glad that Uncle Pavel was willing to let you off."

Raisa squinted against the sun as she raised her knee. Her dress fell to the middle of her thigh, revealing her long, tanned legs. Yossef swallowed in appreciation and put his hand on her exposed knee, stroking her leg to the lower calf, gently and sensually.

"When I was a little girl I used to come out to this spot," Raisa said absently, her eyes focused on a distant memory. "This little place was my fantasy-land. Here I could be a famous ballerina, a great writer, or anything I wanted to be."

Yossef probed Raisa for details about her childhood, her secret fears and hopes. He wanted to know everything about her. She rambled on for two hours. She was being skillfully and carefully interrogated, but didn't realize it. All she knew was that, for the first time, Yuri wanted entrance into her private life and thoughts, and she was willing to share as much of her inner self as she dared.

"You are a remarkable woman, Raisa. Besides your beauty, you have a soul that is as big as the world."

"My soul?" She flushed slightly in embarrassment. "I thought that you were only interested in my body." She tried to be flippant.

"Your lovely body is part of the rest of you. The beauty of your soul radiates from your eyes—the windows of your soul. You are a very good person and that goodness will last long after your beautiful body has started to sag and fade."

"How graphic! And what about your soul, Yuri? What are you going to do, now that you know you're a Dubrov?"

Yossef knew that she would ask that question and was well prepared with what he hoped would be a satisfactory answer.

"I've thought about that a lot," he began, still rubbing her leg. "I've walked the city parks for hours asking myself just what an ordinary person like me can do. You know what profound answer I came up with? Nothing! Absolutely nothing. If I did something stupid, like getting involved with Solidarity, I'd put everybody I love in jeopardy. You and Uncle Pavel might lose everything —even your lives. I can't risk that."

"So? What *will* you do?" He felt her eyes boring into him, measuring his reactions.

"Just more of the same, I guess." Yossef's eyes reflected resignation. "Stay with the Guards until my tour is over, then I think I'll resign and go to the University. But believe me, Raisa, I will *not* do anything stupid. The system is just too enormous and powerful for one person to deal with."

Raisa felt a mixture of relief and disappointment. Yuri had chosen the path of millions of her countrymen —passive indifference and accommodation.

"Let's get back, Yuri. I'm getting sunburned," she said, a tinge of sadness in her voice.

After a leisurely walk back to the dacha, Raisa and Yossef had a light snack of hard black bread and cold lamb cuts washed down with the rest of the Georgian white wine.

"Where did you say your parents went on vacation?"

"Oh, I thought I told you, Yuri. To Yalta, to a scientific conference. Papa is to read some papers on mathematical analysis."

"Yes. I think I remember. I'm sorry. My mind has been on other things."

Raisa slid over next to him and kissed his cheek. "Poor baby. I know, I know. You've been through so much."

Her hot breath on his cheek and neck caused a sudden current of excitement to surge through him. His lips turned to meet hers, and soon Yossef's hands and mouth were probing, exploring, caressing in a way that set off earthquakes of desire in Raisa.

"Yuri! Oh, Yuri! Let's go into the bedroom. I want to comfort you! To please you!" she moaned.

In minutes, they were on the bed and Yossef's hands were skillfully unbuttoning her blouse. Eagerly, she shrugged it off; underneath, there were soft but firm breasts barely restrained by wisps of silk.

In another minute both lay naked on the bed. The sunlight filtering through the curtains had taken on the radiance of early afternoon and coated her skin with gold.

Raisa purred with delight as Yossef's hands rubbed and fondled every part of her body. His caresses and probings were accompanied by whispers of love as he skillfully worked her up to a peak of excitement.

Suddenly, Raisa was on her knees and began to rub Yossef's chest and manipulate his hardness. She preened like a cat, arching her back so that her breasts shivered seductively. They played and toyed with each other until they were laughing. He leaned over and playfully bit her on the inner thigh. Giggling, she pursued him across the wide bed until he was trapped on the edge; then she swarmed over him, all legs, arms, and teeth until he was laughing so hard he could hardly stand it. She persevered, with more giggles, and then mounted him and slipped his hardness into her. She put her hands on his shoulders and rocked and rocked until his thrusts matched hers in desperate need. Their lovemaking seemed to last forever, until both exploded into exhaustion.

Yossef rolled onto his back, his body a welter of perspiration. Rarely had he been subjected to an emotional assault like this afternoon's.

He had barely had time to catch his breath when Raisa's strong arms pulled him over on top of her. They began to make love again, more slowly and with deeper pleasure than before.

Finished, he propped the pillows against the headboard and smiled as she shook her head, stretched languorously, and then burrowed against him.

"Good," she murmured sleepily. "So good." She was deliciously exhausted.

And then, the tears came as her body shivered with sniffles, and then sobs.

"Raisa. What's wrong?"

"I've never been so happy; so fulfilled. I've never known such a feeling of contentment. It's like—like somebody pulled the plug in the bathtub and drained all the dirty water. All the tensions of the past few months have disappeared, at least for now."

"Are you saying that all I did was pull your plug?" Yossef laughed.

Raisa held him so tightly that her long fingernails dug into his back.

"I'm saying that you're the most important person in my life. If anything ever happened to you, I couldn't go on living.

"I love you that much, Yuri. I love you so very much."

Vaclav Suskov shaded * * * his eyes against the hot West African sun as the last of the Soviet wounded were carried off the *Liepaja*. The low white buildings of Luanda, Angola's capital city on the South Atlantic, gleamed like a collection of bleached bones.

Smedlev, his exec, had arranged some strategic personnel changes among the ship's crew. New sailors, all Solidarity activists, had replaced others. The personnel-management officer at the Soviet South Atlantic Fleet headquarters based at Luanda had seen to that.

It was a skeleton crew that now manned the *Liepaja*. The size of the crew had been cut almost in half. Every crew member had to do double duty to maintain the vessel's functions, but every member was with Solidarity and every member had committed himself to die, if necessary, to carry out the *Liepaja*'s role in Operation Samson.

XVI.

The twelve members of the Poliburo sat stiffly around the T-shaped table waiting for Rakhmatov to give his presentation. Premier Krylenko had aged markedly in the past few months. The strains of the unwinnable China War and the turmoil within the country had taken their toll on the Soviet leader.

As each Politburo member reported on his area of responsibility, the trend was apparent: The Soviet empire was in a state of decline, if not disintegration. There were now massive revolts in the provinces and the satellites.

Farmers on the collective farms had been burning crops and slaughtering their livestock, thus ensuring further food shortages in the cities. The minority republics were seething with unrest as reports of heavy casualties among their young men on the China fronts came home. The Solidarity Army of Liberation was on the rampage in central Siberia, its ranks swollen by deserting troops from the Red Army. And in the Soviet Expeditionary Force to China, entire units had refused to advance against the enemy. For the first time in Soviet history there had been riots against the draft. Students and young workers clashed with militiamen and KGB goon squads in Moscow, Leningrad, and Kiev. Solidarity, as usual, was blamed for the disturbances.

Rakhmatov stood with the aid of a cane, looking every one of his seventy-four years. His hair, what was left of it, was grayish-yellow and greasy, popping out from his skull in disorderly little spirals that invariably sprinkled a glaze of dandruff on the shoulders of his dark suit. Before speaking, he took a gulp of iced mineral water and surveyed the frightened and dismayed men around him.

"Every counterrevolution needs its heroes and its martyrs," Rakhmatov began with a rasping drawl. "The White counterrevolution had its Kolchaks and its Wrangels. Solidarity has Vasily Gregierenko, but as everybody knows, he is a physical and moral coward and has preferred to run the counterrevolution by remote control from abroad.

"And so, Solidarity has created its own martyrs from the bones of our history. It has resurrected a family who were anti-State subversives from the beginning."

"This Dubrov family!" slurred Krylenko, scowling in disgust.

"Yes, Comrade Premier. This all-but-forgotten nest of traitors has been 'rediscovered' by Solidarity, and their exploits have been dramatized in their *Novy Rodina*. During the past month, Solidarity has been viciously attacking and vilifying the sacred image and name of Lenin. We have had to post guards around statues of Lenin in many parts of the country now because they have been singled out for vandalizing. State Security has had to spread its manpower very thin to guard and protect public utilities and installations. We've had to assume these functions since we can't rely on the Red Army to . . ."

Marshal Anatoli Deriabin, the Minister of Defense, slapped both of his hands on the table and half rose out of his seat, his eyebrows twitching in anger. He shook a warning finger at the KGB director.

"Let me remind you, Comrade Director, that the mission of the Red Army is to protect the country from *external* enemies. It is not our function to guard bridges and statues in the Motherland. Our manpower shortages are so bad that we are now using units of Vietnamese, Cambodians, and Laotians, not to mention Cubans and Ethiopians. This scheme to draft men from our client states to pay off their debts to us might be good economics, but it's a disastrous military policy. It's created horrendous racial and morale problems at the front."

"Enough! Enough! Comrades." Krylenko held up his hands for quiet. "It's bad enough to have the country in an uproar. I've done some investigation of my own on this Dubrov family. Some of our findings might surprise you." He pressed a buzzer on the table and a tall, gaunt-looking woman stalked in.

"Lydia. Report your findings," said the Premier.

The Premier's aide droned through the old CHEKA Dubrov file, the same one that Raisa had copied for Yuri.

"As was common CHEKA practice, the burial plot of every executed prisoner was dutifully recorded on burial maps. Then as now with our own State Security, the deceased wore an aluminum identity disc with a name and a number, similar to that of the military. The discs were buried with the prisoner, hung around the neck. Comrade Krylenko ordered the bodies of the Dubrovs exhumed, positively identified, and then destroyed. Here are my findings from the exhumation efforts."

She paused dramatically as she flipped through her papers and slipped out another sheet.

"Georgi and Tanya Dubrov, leaders in the Vorturka uprising of 1960, are two of the individuals now being near-deified by Solidarity. In the burial plot outside of the camp complex we excavated the soil where their plots were located. The bodies had already been exhumed a month before by individuals who claimed they were State Security people. We sent a team to a little village named Valuyki on the Don, not too far from Kharkov. The mother of Georgi Dubrov, Natalya, died near there and was buried in the village church cemetery. The church still had an active congregation then. We found a small wooden cross, freshly painted, with her name on it. When the team dug, it found, again—nothing. We interrogated some of the local villagers and they said a government team had been there in June—the same time as the Vorturka exhumation."

"Solidarity!" thundered Rakhmatov, paling under the effort to rein in his temper.

Lydia concealed her annoyance at his outburst with a cold smile and continued.

"The most disturbing part of all this pertains to Aleksei Dubrov. He was executed in the Lubyanka and, according to Comrade Lenin's wishes, was buried in the lateral corridor between cells 34 and 36. It was later covered by a cement floor.

"As you all know," the aide continued, pushing her glasses down on the bridge of her nose and staring over the tops at the assembled Politburo, "the final phase of the Lubyanka's remodeling took place last summer. A work order was submitted by an 'Arkadi Golosov,' a nonexistent person from the maintenance department of State Security, to repair a buckled floor. The cement floor between cells 34 and 36 was torn up and the remains of Aleksei Dubrov were removed. Again, the people involved in this cannot be found anywhere. We tore up the new floor and could tell from the fresh fill that someone was buried there. Pieces of cloth, similar to the prison garb worn by the early CHEKA prisoners, were found."

"And there it is, comrades," interjected Krylenko. "This should give you a frightening picture of the scope of Solidarity's activities. They are operating right in the Center itself, perhaps even in the Politburo." His lips drew together to form a white streak and his dark eyes narrowed, scanning the twelve members. Sergei Gorsky felt Krylenko's eyes fall upon him, linger for a moment, and move on.

Rakhmatov sputtered a protest.

"Comrade Premier! An investigation like this is under my jurisdiction. I had planned to do the very same thing."

Krylenko waved aside his protest with a near-obscene gesture of his hand.

"Well, I couldn't wait for you, Comrade Director," he slurred sarcastically. "I knew that Solidarity would make such a move when their articles on the Dubrovs came out in their samizdats. You should have seen it coming, Rakhmatov. Now, Solidarity has *its* martyrs. Our people need visible evidences of legitimacy. While we have only *one* Lenin in the Tomb, they have four Dubrovs and—"

"Six," interrupted the aide.

Krylenko's bushy eyebrows lurched upward.

"Six?" he blurted incredulously.

"Tanya Dubrov had twin boys in 1960. The information on the children has been removed from the Lubyanka file and the Document and Evidence Repository. There is no additional information on these children."

"You mean there are *living* Dubrovs in the country?" Krylenko's face suddenly became flushed and his Adam's apple bobbed convulsively.

"Most likely, Comrade Premier. They would be thirty-one years old by now."

Krylenko slumped in his chair, rubbing his eyes and the bridge of his nose.

"Six Dubrovs!" he exclaimed into the shocked silence "Four martyred dead and two living symbols of the Solidarity movement. I fear these Dubrovs more than al of the Solidarity members put together."

He shot to his feet, his fists clenched and shaking, his face and neck knotted cords of anger.

"Find those damned bodies and those twins! I don' care if you have to turn this whole country upside down Find those damned Dubrovs! All of them!"

* * *

Yossef thought he detected a certain reserve, a certain aloofness, in Raisa this morning. It was Saturday and the two days that they had spent in Zhukovia had been among the happiest of his life. Yes. Raisa Karezev, he determined, was the kind of woman one could spend the rest of one's life with.

Since waking, however, she was quieter, not so spontaneous as she had been yesterday. She acted as if she were wrestling with an immense personal problem. There was something disturbed, or disturbing, in her eyes.

"Some tea, Yuri?"

"Yes. That would be nice. A hot drink always starts my day off right," Yossef exclaimed a shade too heartily to compensate for his uneasiness.

She handed him a steaming cup, a guarded expression on her face, and watched as he slowly sipped the hot liquid. His back was to her as he stared at a couple of frolicking kittens on the front porch.

Raisa took a deep breath and made her decision to say it.

"Shalom achi, Yossef." She covered the cutting edge of her statement with a frosting of sweetness.

The words hit Yossef like the impact of a truck between the shoulder blades. He spun around so fast that his tea spilled on the rug. He stared at Raisa for a moment, his lips forming a denial, but the words were trapped in his throat.

"Shalom, Yossef Dubrov—Yuri's twin brother." Her voice was now coldly metallic.

Yossef kept staring, fumbling for an answer. Finally he blurted, "What kind of a game are you playing now, Raisa?" He went to embrace her but she spun away from him, her face contorted in rage.

"Too many things, Yossef. Too many little things which tripped you up. Oh, you thought you were so clever! It started as soon as you got here. I took you to a different bedroom than the one you stayed in before, and yet you said it was the same one. I thought I'd test you. I told you that Mama rearranged the furniture!" Now her cheeks flamed a sudden red. "She never touched that room! Your face, where your beard was, is a little too white compared with your neck and forehead. You were the bearded man on the subway and at the Tomb. Weren't you! You were checking me out—looking me over. It all fits, Yossef Dubrov. I'm not stupid. And—and then there's the way you made love to me. That was *not* Yuri Spinnenko. *No way* was that Yuri!"

Yossef kept denying Raisa's accusations but her insistent barrage of invective wore him down. He sighed, gave an elaborate shrug of his shoulders, and threw up his hands.

"All right, Raisa. The ball's in your corner. What do you do now?" he said sardonically. "Turn me in to the KGB?"

"The ball's where? What do you mean?" she frowned.

"An American expression. It means that it's your move now. I suggest we approach this whole thing like adults. Let's not get emotional and mess things up. Solidarity and Operation Samson depend on both of us keeping our wits about us."

"Keeping our wits? Acting like adults?" Raisa exploded. "You sound like Vasily Gregierenko. I'm sick and tired of the men in Solidarity using me—like a piece of equipment! First Gregierenko, then Yuri, and now you. You've all used me!" Her voice was shrill and tremulous. "Whenever any of you want something or need to unload your burdens, there's always Raisa Karezev, the 'big sister' of Solidarity. Isn't that why you're here? To 'test' me? To see if you can fool me and pass yourself off as Yuri? It is, damn it! I've been used by everybody!" she stormed. "Nobody gives a damn about me or my feelings. I'm only the 'inside girl.' I can risk my ass stealing things from the Center, or memorizing whole lists of names and addresses of security agents so we can assassinate them, but that's all I'm really good for. Do you know how many deaths I'm responsible for? Hundreds! But I'm not supposed to feel anything about those people. I'm just a piece of equipment plugged into the wall. When the revolution comes, I can be unplugged and discarded."

Yossef reached over and seized her hand and pulled her

down on the couch. Tears of anger were streaming down her cheeks. He tried to put his hand on her shoulder but she wrenched away.

"All right, Raisa. I am Yossef. My last name is Ayalon. I *am* Yuri's brother and I was raised in a kibbutz in Shareem, in Israel."

Yossef caught his breath and continued, his voice rising in tone and increasing in tempo.

"You're not the only one who's been used, Raisa. I found out last winter that I had been groomed for Operation Samson, or something like it, since I was a baby. My entire life was shaped and molded by the MOSSAD, the Israeli Secret—"

"I know what it is," Raisa interrupted sarcastically.

"Even my adoptive parents, who I always thought were my real aunt and uncle, were phony—part of the make-believe life I lived, all created by the MOSSAD. I lived this lie for thirty years until last winter when a journal was left to me by an old friend."

Yossef spent the rest of the morning telling her about his life, the Ariel Makleff journal, and his reluctant participation in Operation Samson. He was aware that he kept repeating himself at times but he couldn't help it. He had to make her understand. Their dialogue was punctuated by arguments which would escalate into shouting matches. Unlike Yuri and most Russian men, Yossef did not sulk into a stony silence when confronted. He countered every accusation of Raisa's with justifications of his own.

"And didn't you feel at all guilty taking your brother's girlfriend to bed? Have you no shame?" Raisa asked in self-righteous indignation. "Isn't that as low as you can get: making love to a woman, pretending to be her real lover?"

Yossef dismissed her accusation with a flippant wave of his hand. "No! Why should I feel guilty? I'm risking my life for your people—for your liberation movement. *I'm* the one taking the real risks," he noted with a certain pride in his voice. "And don't worry about your precious Yuri. He'll be safe. I'll probably be the one to get killed in this half-brained operation."

A conflict of emotions overwhelmed Raisa. Now she saw Yossef as a separate identity, not just as a carbon copy of his brother. The thought of his possible death filled her with an impending dread.

"And where is Yuri?" she asked, her eyes having lost none of their chill.

"Safe and comfortable," Yossef said acidly. "He can sit on his ass and ride out Operation Samson until it's over. If we all lose, Yuri survives. The rest of us will lose it all."

Raisa's chin began to quiver and there was a nervous tic to her Adam's apple.

"What a fool I've made of myself. I—I really let myself go the day before yesterday. I did, and said, things I never meant to do or even thought I was capable of doing." Her cheeks were red with embarrassment as she remembered their lovemaking the day before.

"You said you sensed I was deceiving you the first day. Why were you so free and uninhibited if you thought I might be me?" Yossef asked, a malicious twinkle in his eye.

Raisa averted her gaze and stammered out her reply.

"Because I—I wasn't—wasn't sure. You were so vulnerable. I thought you might be acting that way because —because you were upset about the Dubrov thing. Damn you Dubrovs!" she flared. "Working in Solidarity is risky enough without all of this emotional turmoil!" She jumped off the couch and paced the room. "I can't handle it anymore!" she shrieked, her own voice unrecognizable, her heart pounding wildly. "I just can't handle the three of you! If I were a man I'd volunteer for the China front and get you all out of my life!"

Yossef leaped up and followed her around the room, trying to get a word in edgewise as she ranted on, wildly gesticulating with her hands.

"Raisa. When you told me that you loved me and couldn't go on without me, were you talking to Yuri, or Yossef?"

"Why—why, that's stupid!" she sputtered. "I'd never make love to a stranger, let alone say things like that!"

"Well, if you thought I might be Yossef, or even had a

slight suspicion, why didn't you stop me when we went to bed?"

She shifted nervously and glared at him as he continued his relentless questioning, a smirk now twitching at his lips.

"Could it have been, dear Raisa . . ." he slurred the words mockingly, "that you were enjoying yourself too much to want to know just who . . ."

The slap caught Yossef squarely on the left cheek. Before he could recover, a second slap followed on the right. He threw up his hands to protect his face but Raisa was on him, shouting, scratching, cursing and crying as they fell to the floor. Her fingernails dug viciously into his neck, drawing blood.

"What do you think I am, a whore?" she screamed. "I'm a human being! I'm not to be made fun of and used. Damn you, you pig-prick! Damn you to hell!"

Yossef grabbed her arms and pinned them tightly behind her back. She tried to knee him in the groin but he pinned her legs with one of his. She used her head as a battering ram, smashing against his eye. Her eyes were wild with rage as she tried to bite him. Bubbles of saliva formed at the corners of her mouth after she spit in his face.

"I hate you," she hissed venomously. "I hate all of you."

He held her tighter, afraid to let go. He could feel the blood from his gouged neck streaming down his back.

They lay tightly entwined without moving for what seemed an eternity.

"Let me up," she demanded, her eyes glimmering with malice.

"And get my throat cut? Not a chance, lady. You're dangerous."

"I said—let me up!" She tried to wrench herself free but Yossef squeezed her so tightly that she gasped for air.

"Look. I'm sorry for all this. I've been a bastard, and you're right, Raisa; I'm no better than the rest of them that have used you. I shouldn't be in your country mixed up in its problems—or with you."

Yossef suddenly released her and, roughly shoving her

away, leaped to his feet.

"If you attack me again, I'll break your arm," he threatened as Raisa staggered to her feet with the aid of a footstool.

Yossef collapsed on the couch as Raisa slumped in the living room chair. The sound of their heavy and irregular breathing filled the quiet dacha and mingled with the ticking of an ancient onyx Hermes clock on the mantelpiece.

After what seemed to be hours—it was only twenty minutes—Raisa broke the silence in a calm and controlled voice.

"I'm sorry."

"I am too. For everything," rejoined Yossef.

Yossef cringed slightly as Raisa rose from her chair and went into the kitchen. She returned with a cold rag and sat beside Yossef, dabbing at his scratches.

"We must put Solidarity before our personal feelings. The survival of our countries depends upon us, you know that, don't you?" Her voice was flat and without emotion.

Yossef breathed deeply, rubbing his bruised cheek, seeming to shrink under the impact of her words.

Raisa laid her head on her arm, resting across the top of the couch. She squeezed her eyes shut as if she were trying to eliminate a painful memory.

"I haven't lost my temper like that since I was a child. I must have looked a horror. I'm so ashamed."

"And I haven't been that scared since I fought a PLO Regular hand to hand in Lebanon back in 1982. I was a lieutenant in the army then. I took his knife away and let him go. He still came at me. I leveled my Uzi at him and shot at his feet and he tried to stare me down. I didn't want to kill him. Finally he left—just sauntered away, cursing my family back ten generations.

"I was wrong in taking advantage of you," Yossef continued, shifting his eyes with shame. "This whole business has made me callous and insensitive. Knowing that I might die in that damned crypt with that phony Lenin has dulled my conscience. If things were different, I would never have treated you the way I did."

Raisa's hand crept over the top of the couch and made

contact with his. Their fingers gently curled around each other's.

"And how would you treat me if—if we were just regular people and not 'super-conspirators' planning to overthrow the most powerful nation on the planet?"

The enormity of their task was made even more forbidding by Raisa's question. Suddenly, Yossef began to chuckle, then laugh uproariously.

Raisa stiffened, a quizzical expression on her face. "And what do you find so funny about that?"

"Your question made me think of a joke a friend of mine in the American Embassy in Berne told me. It describes our predicament perfectly."

"An American joke? How does it go?"

"Well, I can't remember all of it, but you've got to picture it in your mind. It's about these two ants crawling up an elephant's leg with rape on their minds."

Her face screwed up in a puzzled frown, then brightened, and she threw her head back in a gale of laughter.

"Of course! I can see it now. The enormity, maybe the impossibility of our mission. What a clever way to describe it."

It warmed Yossef to hear her laugh. He reached over and placed his hand on her waist, expecting it to be slapped away. Instead, her eyes were warm and inviting.

"Are we all done fighting, little ant?" She grinned sheepishly.

"Yes, little ant," chortled Yossef. "Let's continue our journey up the elephant's leg."

Raisa crushed her body against his until their lips found each other's. They kissed softly and tenderly.

"Friends and co-conspirators from now on, and no more playing around?" Yossef smiled.

"Friends and conspirators yes. I can't make any guarantees on that last part." She pinched a roll of skin on his stomach playfully.

"Whatever happens between us in the future, Raisa, just remember—I'm Yossef, not Yuri."

Nine days after crate number 115116 left the Bergen wharf, it arrived at the State Mortuary Service warehouse.

Platonov and Yabin hovered nervously nearby as the Solidarity Council members attacked the crate with hammers and crowbars. In spite of the incessant noise, there was no sound from inside the temporary home of the Solidarity leader.

"Dear God! Please. Don't let him be dead," wailed Platonov over and over. The outer casing was dismantled and hundreds of valve fittings spilled on the floor.

The second inner box was torn into and inside, shrunk in a fetal position, was the unconscious Gregierenko.

The Council members lifted him out and placed him on a nearby cot. A doctor placed a stethoscope on his chest while a nurse checked his pulse.

"He's alive." The doctor smiled.

"Pulse is slow, but regular," added the nurse.

"Get him washed up and get the food and crap out of the crate. Vasily was supposed to use the little portable toilet but I guess he forgot, or was too lazy," said Platonov.

An hour later, Vasily Gregierenko started to stir. His eyes were glazed and dulled, but his speech was coherent.

"Did I—did I make it?" he gasped in short, uneven breaths, unable to focus on Yabin's face directly above him.

"You did indeed, my friend," said Yabin, brushing a few strands of his hair back on his balding head.

The doctor punched a needleful of adrenaline into Gregierenko's arm and in minutes he was sitting up, his eyes clear and his speech articulate.

"Are Yuri and Yossef Dubrov where they're supposed to be?" he asked in a stronger, commanding voice.

"Yes, Vasily," replied Platonov. "Yuri is in a secure room downstairs and Yossef is with Raisa at her dacha in Zhukovia for a few days."

What looked like jealousy flickered for a moment in Gregierenko's eyes.

"Well, our little swallow is getting her share of attention," he grunted. "Do we have everything on hand for Samson?"

"Yes. The remains of all four Dubrovs are downstairs

along with the photographs and documents you requested," continued Platonov.

"CHEKA identity discs? Certificates of death? Everything must be absolutely authentic. The Russian people would never forgive us if we deceived them. The credibility of Solidarity would go *poof!*—just like that."

"I've double-checked everything," Yabin assured him. "Your exhumation teams did a remarkable job right under the noses of the KGB. We've dug up old newspaper clippings, photographs, even family pictures from America. Your research people could put together a family album."

Gregierenko grinned and shook a finger at the MOSSAD colonel. "Ah! You've anticipated our next issue of *Novy Rodina.* That's exactly what it's going to be: a photographic essay of the Dubrovs—the true martyrs of the struggle against Leninism."

"But not Yuri and Yossef's pictures, I hope," warned Yabin.

"Oh no. In fact, we were able to get all of the incriminating evidence about the boys out of the files and the repository. When does Yossef enter the Tomb?" Gregierenko asked.

"September 30. The 10:00 A.M. shift," said Yabin. "The day after tomorrow."

XVII.

Yossef looked over his Tomb Guard uniform carefully in front of the full-length mirror in the Spasskaya Tower guardroom. He gave a slight tug to his tunic and rubbed his sleeve over the gleaming brass buckle of his garrison belt. He looked around, fighting a feeling of naked exposure, drew a deep breath, and calmed himself.

9:45: It would be another fifteen minutes before he would make his first goose-stepping march to the Tomb. Raisa had said she would be there this morning to watch. That should help, he thought; but so far it had been easy. His mind was clear now, icy and calm.

MOSSAD and Solidarity had trained him superbly. He recognized every detail of the Spasskaya Tower guardroom and recognized his fellow guards from the photographs he had been shown. Intimate details of their lives, and of the usual locker-room banter they engaged in, had been thoroughly ingrained in Yossef by Yabin and Platonov.

A red light flashed. Time for Yossef and his fellow guard to stand in front of the exit door. That damnable surge of fear slashed through his chest again.

He waited, his gleaming assault rifle resting comfortably on his shoulder, the butt snugged securely in his white-gloved, extended hand. He glanced briefly to each side and bit his lower lip.

The sound of the buzzer almost caught him by surprise, though he had been trained to anticipate it. The door swung open and Yossef could see the Tomb looming one hundred and fifty-three meters away at the end of the runway.

He took a deep but concealed breath and began the slow cadence, his goose-steps sounding hollow and metallic on the ancient cobblestones.

The Changing of the Guard ceremony took almost fifteen minutes, and Yossef executed his moves flawlessly. Before he realized it, he was standing at the foot of the likeness of his grandfather's murderer, staring reverently into his waxen face.

Raisa was a wreath of smiles as Yossef emerged from the Spasskaya Tower street exit. She grabbed his arm and momentarily laid her head on his shoulder as they walked toward her Zhiguli parked nearby.

"I was so worried that you'd do some little thing wrong that would give you away. I said a little prayer as you marched out the door."

"It was easier than I thought. There really isn't much to the stupid job. An idiot could do it after you get the routine down."

"Did it bother you? Standing in front of the man who murdered your grandfather?"

"How can anybody get mad at a wax dummy? I kept staring at his face, telling myself that he's only wax and acrylic. Only the skull is his. No, I'm not bothered like Yuri is."

"Speaking of Yuri," Raisa's voice was soft and distant, "when can you visit him?"

"Thursday. Yabin wanted me to go through the six-day Guard mount. He felt that if I met Yuri during Guard mount I might get upset and make a mistake. He might be right, too. It's going to be an emotional circus meeting my twin brother for the first time."

"Oh, Yossef, I'll be so glad when this is over—when our lives can get back to normal."

"The normality of the grave, or the firing squad? Do you really think that there's a life for us after Operation Samson, Raisa?" he asked, resignation creeping into his voice.

She shot him a worried glance. "Yes, don't you?"

"Hell no!" he said with finality.

She turned toward him quickly, keeping her hands on the wheel as they drove through the city streets. "Then why are you doing this if you feel it won't succeed? Is this your way of committing suicide?"

Yossef grimaced, a fatalistic expression on his face.

"Have you ever heard of the *Masada* mentality? We Israelis are famous for it."

Raisa shook her head.

"Masada was an ancient fortress in Israel held by about 960 defenders between 66 and 73 A.D. It was a hilltop fortress; actually it was on a vast tableland in the middle of the desert. They held off the Roman Tenth Legion for many months until it was apparent that they'd be overwhelmed. Just before the Romans stormed the Masada the defenders drew lots to see who would kill the others. Of course, each father was to kill his wife and kids, then the men would kill each other—all by the sword—until one was left. Then he fell on his own sword. As a cadet officer, I hiked up to Masada with my batallion and took an oath to defend Israel as my ancestors did almost two thousand years ago. I am programmed to die for my country." Yossef gave a mirthless laugh. "That's really funny. My ancestors are American and Russian. I don't have a Jewish bone in my body."

"Then are you doing this for Mother Russia? Is that what you're saying, Yossef?" She gave him a sympathetic smile.

"Or Mother America," Yossef replied. "It's funny. All three countries would benefit if we succeed. Oh, how absurd the whole thing is, Raisa. The fate of two—maybe three—countries depending on one little counterfeit Jew guarding a counterfeit god in his abysmal crypt. What a stupid way to end one's life." Yossef's voice was full of defeat.

"Do you think that you are the whole of Operation Samson?"

"Aren't I?" Yossef answered tightly.

"No, Yossef. Operation Samson involves thousands of people operating thousands of miles apart. It includes some very important people in government and the military. What you are, Yossef, is the 'trigger.' When you and your people take over the Tomb on November 6, you're going to start a chain reaction of falling dominoes which will reach from Leningrad to Vladivostok. I've been authorized to tell you that much."

"What an interesting way to put it," Yossef replied sarcastically. "Knowing that I'm the first domino makes me feel better about my annihilation."

Yossef continued to stare out the window, a curious lassitude having settled over him.

"You'll make out all right though, Raisa. You'll win no matter what," he muttered with uncharacteristic bitterness.

"Well, how do you figure that?" She looked at him with a measuring glance.

"If I die, and I'm sure I will, you have a spare to fall back on—a carbon copy of Yossef Ayalon."

Raisa spun over to the curb and slammed the brakes on so hard that Yossef almost went through the windshield.

"Damn you! Damn you, Yossef! After all we've been through in the short time we've been together, can't you get it through your thick skull that I care? I care for you deeply." Her words exploded in his ear.

"Can't you tell by now that I see you as completely different than Yuri? You're not a carbon copy—you're you, and—and I love you for your courage and dedication. Yuri is not doing what you're doing. You're risking your life for my country and for the welfare of my people. Don't you think I realize that? What you're doing is the noblest kind of courage, Yossef. I love you for that, believe me."

"I wish you loved me for more than my nobility." He tried to smile, but failed miserably.

"I do, Yossef, I do." She glanced to either side to see if there were any pedestrians coming. There were none. She pulled his face to hers and gave him a long, sensual kiss.

"I think we'd better stop at my apartment and finish our discussion," she whispered seductively. "I think you need some more convincing."

* * *

For the past four days Raisa had sensed the unusual tension at the Center. People went about their duties with a sense of intense involvement. Gone was the carefree banter that usually characterized the interaction between Center personnel. The reason, Raisa discovered this Thursday, was that Dimitri Zakharov, the director of the Special Investigations department of the KGB, was auditing all of the documents, activity logs, and actions of each department for the past six months. The Registry and Archives Department in the basement of the old Lubyanka was especially scrutinized by Zakharov's security auditors.

The name of Zakharov was known, feared, and hated by everybody at the Center. Whenever he and his teams descended on a department, they left a wake of emotional wreckage in the form of official reprimands, ruined careers, and even prison sentences. His investigators poked and probed everywhere. From time to time selected employees were brought to the interrogation room and emerged shaken, bruised, or in handcuffs.

Raisa strode purposefully down the corridor of the Supply Directorate section of the Center, her arms loaded with office supplies.

Two men walked up silently from behind and flanked her, each one grabbing her by an elbow. Her supplies clattered to the floor.

"What—what is this?" she sputtered fearfully.

"Routine questioning, Raisa Karezev. Your goods will be picked up and delivered. Come quietly. No fuss, eh?"

Strong hands held her elbows and half-lifted her as they marched her down the empty corridor. They took a left turn down a lateral and right again into a narrow, tunnel-like hallway. They stopped before what looked like a cell door and pressed a buzzer. Another buzzer from inside was followed by an audible click as one of her abductors opened the door.

The room was cloaked in semidarkness as she entered. It had the stench of a condemned man's cell.

The lights were turned up gradually, and Raisa's attention became riveted on a huddled form in the corner. She strained to make out the features of the bruised and bloodied face and realized, to her horror, that it was Olga Yurevna.

"Raisa, Raisa! I—I had to tell them!" she gushed through broken, bloodied teeth. "I couldn't stand it any longer! They know about the Dubrov file!"

Raisa swallowed nervously and breathed deeply, trying to compose herself. She had anticipated arrest over and over again in her mind, rehearsing what she would do if it happened. Could she withstand torture? she wondered. She didn't know. How could she explain her wanting the Dubrov file?

The lights were slowly, almost dramatically, turned up, and there, sitting behind a metal desk, was Dimitri Zakharov.

She had never seen anybody so loathsome before. He had an embryo's body and a ballooned forehead with facial skin stretched taut over a visible skull, his scalp depositing live flakes on pathetic shoulders. A nervous twitch clutched his lips, revealing stubs of chlorine teeth.

He rose and half hobbled over to her, and with a leer—although he may have intended it as a smile —fondled her blouse, ashes from his trembling cigarette leaving a trail on the floor.

Raisa stared into the bloodshot eyes which were too big for his head. She realized that she was looking at a man who kept his insanity under very careful control. She knew now how a small bird felt as the snake approached. There was horror—a premonition of what was to come and, worst of all, the knowledge that there was absolutely no way to avoid one's fate.

"So this is Raisa Karezev, our little Solidarity agent in residence." Zakharov lisped softly, watching her reaction, his protruding eyes staring fixedly.

She gaped at him, swallowing, a lump of fear caught in her throat.

"Surely, Comrade Zakharov, you are mistaken. I have been a loyal member of the Center's work force for almost five years," she said, striving to keep the desperation from her voice.

"Of course. Of course you have, Raisa." He grimaced a taut, teeth-baring smile. His voice was friendly enough, but his expression was threatening and his eyes were hooded. Zakharov was deadly as a cobra and twice as unstable.

"Tell us why you took the Dubrov file!" he shrilled, his slight hand stinging Raisa across the face.

At that moment Raisa thought she might vomit. She breathed slowly through her nose, at the same time tightening her diaphragm, to control her gag reflex.

She continued to sputter her denials in spite of Zakharov's continual slapping.

The gaunt, skeletal figure of another KGB man, half-hidden in a corner, unfolded from its seat, giving her a ghastly smile. The grayish light in the room heightened his gauntness by carving great hollows beneath his eyes and in his cheeks, so that for a brief moment his face was a leering skull. He stared at her, still smiling, then flicked away his cigarette, watching it spiral down to her feet, where it disappeared in a miniature explosion of sparks.

"Do you know what we do with pretty little girls accused of treason?" he sneered grotesquely. "How would you like to be hung from wires? Or have electrical shocks to your nipples? Or be given enemas and douches with sulphuric acid? We have people we will turn you over to if you don't talk here, Raisa Karezev. And they won't stop after you've confessed all, because these people like the job they do. Traitorous little Solidarity girls are a treat for them—a reward—like candy. They can do what they want and nobody will ever stop them. Do you know that we use women to torture other women because they know how to hurt you best. You'll pray for death, Raisa Karezev, do anything, on the promise to kill you and end the pain."

Raisa tried to speak, but her protest stuttered into babbling incoherence.

"Your supervisor is General Spinnenko, is it not, Raisa?" Zakharov's manner was studiously polite and icily formal.

Raisa nodded dumbly. There was no recognition in her eyes, only the starkest staring terror.

"I see that my associate has upset you, Raisa." Zakharov's eyes hooded themselves. "You and your friend need some time to meditate—to reflect on your crimes." He jerked his head abruptly toward a small black door behind his desk.

The KGB men spun Olga and Raisa around and shoved them roughly through the door Zakharov opened. Olga struggled, shrieking a mindless plea.

Raisa sank down on her haunches like a caged animal in the small cell, enduring the recurring waves of fear that washed over her with an intensity she had never known before.

The interior was pitch black. There was no sound. They designed it this way, she told herself over and over again until it became a chant. They designed it this way to make you concentrate on your own terror.

Olga was sobbing uncontrollably in the corner, wrapped in a cocoon of her own terror. Raisa vomited in her corner of the cell and gagged and tried to vomit again; her stomach was empty, but the retching went on and on. When the spasm subsided, she lay back on the cold cement floor and breathed through her nose.

Pavel Spinnenko picked up the phone and heard Zakharov's voice on the other end. The first flow of his policeman's adrenaline told him that something was very wrong.

"You have my secretary in a holding cell? On what charge, Comrade Zakharov?" the general snapped, blood suffusing his face. The word *treason* sounded like a thunderclap through the telephone receiver.

"Have you reported this to anybody else, Comrade Zakharov?" the general asked, his tone now deferential.

"No, General Spinnenko. We wanted to give you the opportunity to confront her yourself. Perhaps the shock of seeing you will convince her that confession is better than, ah, what would naturally follow if she didn't tell us here."

"I'll be right down. Keep the little bitch locked up until I get there," Spinnenko thundered.

"Shit!" he swore in astonishment, his bald bullet-shaped head turning red. He made two phone calls and then bolted out the door.

Raisa heard the door creak open before she saw the slim shaft of gray light. The KGB men dragged their prisoners out into the interrogation room, where they were yanked upright.

Zakharov smiled a sinister smile and said, "Your boss is coming to visit us, Raisa. I'm sure you'll have a lot to say to him."

The door opened and the squat figure of Pavel Spinnenko stormed in. An aide followed and stood off to one side. The general's smoldering eyes burned into Raisa.

"You piece of pig-flesh!" he barked. "You Solidarity whore!" he spat.

Raisa recoiled in shock. She knew that Pavel Spinnenko was a man of dark and unpredictable moods at times, capable of temper tantrums so violent that he could, literally, smash the furniture in his office.

"Pavel, Pavel," Raisa pleaded, "it's all a mistake! I can explain everything!"

"Special Investigations never makes mistakes," hissed Zakharov as he stubbed out his cigarette with a vicious twisting motion.

Another Border Guard aide slipped in almost unnoticed and stood on the other side of the general.

"Is this room bugged, Comrade Zakharov?" A strange expression passed over the general's face.

"No, General. It's completely secure. You may do whatever you want with these women and no one will hear," Zakharov finished with a smirk.

It happened so fast that the women didn't have time to scream. The general and his two aides whipped small automatic pistols from inside their blouses and fired pointblank at Zakharov and the three KGB men. Their silencers made the shots sound like the muffled pop of air rifles.

The wounded Zakharov fell to the floor and stared up grotesquely at the general as he approached, aimed directly at the ballooned forehead, and blew his brains out.

An aide stepped into the corridor and brought in four heavy canvas bags from a large metal cart parked outside. The bodies were stuffed inside and thrown back on the cart. These were "burn bags"; bags designed to hold secret and top-secret documents collected each day at the Center and sent to the crematorium, a vast furnace that consumed tons of classified materials every week.

The other aide wiped the blood off the floor and tossed the crimson rag into a bag before tying it.

"You know what to do?"

The aides nodded, saluted, and wheeled the document-destruction cart down the corridor.

The two women stared at the general in uncomprehending disbelief. Raisa's lips moved, but no sound came out.

"You've probably got a question or two." Spinnenko bestowed an ironic smile on her.

"I've—I've got a hundred," Raisa finally managed to say.

"Well, save them until later. There's a washroom down the hall. Get cleaned up and come back here. We'll be leaving the Center by the Maly Theater Alley exit. Do you know where that is?"

Raisa and Olga nodded dumbly and staggered off toward the restroom.

An hour later Raisa and Pavel Spinnenko were rocketing along the river road in his Zil staff car toward the Zhukovia countryside. They had delivered Olga to a dentist who could be trusted to fix her teeth and keep his mouth shut.

Raisa didn't know how to begin. She was still in a state of shock. Surely, she reasoned, the general didn't kill Zakharov and his men out of loyalty or affection for her.

"Why, Pavel? Why did you kill them and rescue us?"

"Because we need you, Raisa. If you confessed everything you know, and are, Operation Samson wouldn't get off the ground," he said as he slowed down his Zil.

"Operation Samson! How did you know about that?" She stared at Spinnenko, her voice trailing away in astonishment.

"Raisa," the general chuckled patronizingly, "I knew you were involved with Solidarity last winter. It was I, dear Raisa, who arranged for your assignment to edit and program the Center's personnel register. I knew that, with your keen memory, you would report these clandestine *stukachi* and active agents to Solidarity. You might say that I was assassinating my enemies through you and the Solidarity apparatus."

Raisa regained her composure and shook her head, managing the trace of a smile.

"I can't believe it. All these months working for you, sneaking around doing things I thought I had initiated, and all the time you were using me."

"Yes. I was using you," Spinnenko agreed.

"Well, that's number four now," she muttered under her breath.

"What? What's that?" he asked.

"Oh, nothing. Just a private little joke," she murmured with a wry smile.

"Raisa, do you realize that this is perhaps the fifth time I've saved you from the firing squad?"

"How?" Raisa cast him a dubious glance.

The general listed the mistakes and the security violations she had committed during the past few months.

"Oh! Oh, my God!" Her face fell into her hands as the realization hit her.

"You know," the general laughed, "I often felt like one of those circus clowns who follow the elephants around with a broom and a pan. You've seen them when they parade out at Gorky Park. I had to rush to and fro sweeping up after you before Special Investigations swept *you* up."

"Thank you," Raisa whispered softly, her head now resting on the back of her seat.

"And then there's the theft of the Dubrov file." The crimson started on Spinnenko's neck and spread to the top of his bald head. "*That* was the stupidest thing you've done yet."

"But Yuri wanted it so badly I couldn't refuse him."

"And if Krylenko ever found out that Yuri, a Tomb Guard, was related to his grandfather Aleksei, it would have meant the boy's death. You can't imagine what I had to go through to remove all of the files and evidence linking Yuri with the Dubrovs."

"I'm sorry. I'm so sorry, Pavel," Raisa sobbed.

* * *

The general wheeled his Zil into a grassy clearing in the countryside. They got out and walked into the woods. Insects droned lazily in the warm autumn air and a light breeze rustled the trees. A distant cicada thrummed; a small stream gurgled nearby, and the water chuckled over the moss-covered stones.

"I have a hard time showing it, Raisa, but I love Yuri as much as any man could love a son. My own son was killed during the invasion of Czechoslovakia in 1968—one of the few Soviet soldiers to be killed in that operation. No, I can't say that honestly. According to a fellow soldier, he invited his own death, so ashamed was he of our crushing of the Czech people. My wife died shortly after from cancer, complicated by grief."

"Pavel—I had no idea. I'm so sorry."

They sat down beside the brook and the general absently swished the water with a long twig.

"When I was given the assignment to adopt Yuri, I hoped he would fill the void. He did, in many ways; but he was motivated to do all of the 'accepted' things by a system which I gave up on long ago."

"Do you know what happened in Minusinsk?" Raisa asked.

"Yes. Yuri didn't tell me. I learned from other sources. The way he stood up to those bastards really made me proud of him."

Spinnenko stood and extended his hand, pulling Raisa to her feet.

"We're lucky that my people got to the 'morgue' and removed all references to Yuri. State Security is turning the country upside down looking for the Dubrovs."

"Again, I'm sorry for putting Yuri's life in danger. I'm so ashamed."

"We've covered our tracks well, Raisa." He patted her arm. "Zakharov and his people will simply be another Solidarity kidnapping. In the document-destruction furnace even the bones are reduced to ash. The Lubyanka prison used to dispose of bodies there, back in the old days of the NKVD."

"What—what do we do now, Pavel?"

"Just more of the same. We play our roles until Operation Samson. We'll receive specific instructions just before then."

"Pavel, how do you fit into all this? I mean, you have so much to lose."

"Ha!" The general laughed sarcastically. "I have absolutely *nothing* to lose. The Politburo is planning a massive purge—a blood purge—of all government agencies and the military the month after next. Krylenko and Rakhmatov have become as paranoid as Stalin was back in the early thirties. Vasily Gregierenko's intelligence people let some of us know what's going to happen. The expected numbers will run into the many thousands. The potential victims have been contacting each other for the past six months. We all feel that Solidarity is our only hope, not only for saving our own skins but for saving the country. I am one of those to be purged and sent to the Gulag, perhaps shot.

"But this is not 1936, dear Raisa. This time the victims will not march passively to their fate."

"Nervous?" asked Raisa.

"Yes," Yossef replied as he bounced in the rear of the State Mortuary Service van. "I'm scared out of my wits."

The van pulled into the mortuary warehouse garage, and two attendants immediately pulled the door down.

Yabin met them at the loading ramp and smiled broadly, his full mustache twitching slightly.

"So this is Raisa Karezev!" he gushed. "You're just as beautiful as everybody has described you," he continued, as he took her hand and kissed it in a courtly, Old World manner.

Raisa reddened. Flustered, she mumbled an embarrassed greeting.

"Raisa's not used to such decadent bourgeois niceties, Yabin. You're going to spoil our Russian women if you keep that up." Gregierenko laughed as he stepped from behind some crates.

"Vasily!" Raisa cried as she ran up to him. She threw her arms around the Solidarity leader, kissing him on the cheek.

"Hello, little swallow," he beamed. "How are you faring

with all of this attention from the Dubrov boys?" He winked.

Raisa reddened again, catching Gregierenko's meaning. She favored him with a ghost of a smile, but her embarrassment was now manifest and intense.

"Come! Let's not keep Yuri waiting," Platonov intervened. "The poor lad's been on tenterhooks ever since he learned that Yossef was coming."

Yuri sat on the edge of his bed straining to hear some activity in the hallway. Suddenly there was the sound of many footsteps, and above the noise he could hear the raucous laughter of Yabin.

He stood, swallowed nervously, and smoothed out a crease in his pants and brushed back his hair in a quick, nervous gesture. The door opened and Raisa burst in, kissing him fully—but lightly—on the lips.

Yuri's eyes widened in shock as he stared at her, mouth agape. "Raisa? Raisa?" he gasped in disbelief. "You're —you're with them? With Solidarity?"

"For almost two years, Yuri."

Yuri shook his head slowly in disbelief. "Now I think I've seen it all. Raisa! My little radish Communist, a Solidarity activist!" He clapped his hands to his head in mock despair.

"Where's Yossef?" he asked, his wide blue eyes now full of surprise and anxiety.

Yossef stepped from behind Yabin and entered the room and stood before him.

"Here I am, Yuri," he said, struggling in his excitement for the correct words. "Here I am, your brother."

Yuri stared, his mouth moving but no sound coming out. He extended his hand awkwardly but said nothing.

Yossef shook it vigorously, grabbing his elbow with the other hand, his own anxiety dissipating.

"I know how you feel, brother Yuri." He smiled warmly. "I felt the same way when I first saw you in the crypt."

Yuri threw his arms impulsively around Yossef and hugged him tightly. Yossef responded and they stayed locked for a long moment.

"Incredible! Just incredible!" Yuri managed to say,

holding Yossef by the shoulders. "We look so much alike. This is wonderful, just wonderful." He said it over and over again: "Wonderful."

The others stole from the room and left the brothers alone.

Two hours later, the door creaked open and Yuri stuck his head out into the corridor.

"Hey! You left the door unlocked. Are you starting to trust me now?"

"We've always trusted you, Yuri!" Platonov yelled back good-naturedly. "We just didn't want you wandering off before you met Yossef."

Yossef emerged, grinning broadly. "Sorry we took so long. We were catching up on the last thirty-one years." They both laughed and threw an arm around the other's shoulder.

"Now that you've met each other I think it's time you met the rest of your family," Yabin said. "Let's go back into your room."

The next hour was spent looking at old photographs of their parents and grandparents. Some were newspaper articles from *Pravda* about the trial of Aleksei Dubrov.

Platonov slipped two large photographs of their grandfather out of a large manila envelope.

"I think you will find these interesting. Here's a picture of Aleksei in his American navy uniform. It was taken in New York City in 1916 just after he enlisted."

The boyish, idealistic gaze of the young sailor stared out at his grandsons from the old photograph. The resemblances to Yuri and Yossef were obvious.

"And this one was taken five years later when he was an ensign in the new Soviet navy! It was taken just before the rebellion at Kronstadt."

It was the same expression, but a different uniform—a different cause.

"Where did you get these?" marveled Raisa, her eyes moist. "They're priceless."

"If I tell you," Gregierenko broke in, "Yuri has to promise me that he won't collapse in a dead faint."

"Don't worry, Comrade Gregierenko—oh, pardon me: it's 'brother' now, isn't it? Don't worry. After today, nothing would surprise me."

"One of my inside people lifted them from the Archives and Registry Directorate," Gregierenko said. "Everything and anything pertaining to the Dubrovs was collected and stored there. All originals. No copies. He got it all."

"So? Where's the surprise?" Yuri asked.

"Our inside man is General Pavel Spinnenko."

Yuri slumped in his chair, a stricken look on his face.

"Uncle Pavel?" His tone was disbelieving. "No. Not Uncle Pavel! That *can't* be true."

"Raisa. Tell him," commanded the Solidarity leader.

Raisa related the story of the murder of Zakharov and the three KGB men, and the conversation she'd had with the general near Zhukovia.

"Pavel and thousands of others are to be swept up in a purge planned for December, two months from now," said Gregierenko. "Knowing this, we fed the information to your uncle and Sergei Gorsky, the Minister of Communications and Politburo member. In spite of Pavel's appearance and bluster, he is one of the most intelligent and perceptive leaders in the government. He's a decent man, too. His Border Guards are fiercely loyal to him personally. That's why he's dangerous to the gerontocracy. Your uncle, Gorsky, Admiral Vagorshnik of the Baltic Fleet, and Anatoli Deriabin of the—"

"*Marshal* Deriabin, the Minister of Defense?" Yuri gasped.

"The very same, Yuri. They're all living on borrowed time. We have information that those to be purged will be invited to a special conference at the Kremlin's Assembly Hall in the Old Senate Building and then be pounced on by a special KGB tactical force. The leaders will be swept up first, and their subordinates can get picked off at leisure later on. Rakhmatov has planned mini-purges in all of the republics, too. It will be nationwide and even affect Soviet personnel serving overseas."

"Uncle Pavel!" Yuri kept saying over and over. "I—I can't believe it. He's one of us. All of these important people in Solidarity. I would never have believed it."

Yossef tossed a brotherly arm over Yuri's shoulder. "I wish that you had time to prepare for this like I did. I don't want you to have a heart attack, and lose my only living relative."

"We have some more photographs. I'm sure that these, more than the others you've seen, will convince you of the righteousness of our cause."

Gregierenko spread several dozen large photographs of professional quality on the bed. The twins stared with fascination and awe.

These were the original wedding pictures of their grandparents and parents. One showed a beaming Lenin with a paternal arm around a radiant Natalya, resplendent in her wedding dress. Even the usually dour Krupskaya was smiling, standing by her niece.

Another photograph, the one that caused a spasm of intense anger to lance through Yuri, showed a smiling Lenin with his left arm draped around his young grandfather. His right hand was clutching a glass of vodka raised in a toast. Aleksei was smiling happily, looking very martial in his blue and white ensign's uniform.

"Our mother was so beautiful," murmured Yossef as he gazed lovingly at a college graduation picture of Tanya Dubrov.

A faded, waterstained picture showed a happy Georgi and Tanya on their wedding day posing under an arch of flowers.

"Would you like to meet your parents and grandparents?" Platonov asked.

"We sent out exhumation teams to Vorturka, some little village on the Don . . ."

"Valuyki," added Gregierenko.

"Yes, Valuyki," Platonov continued, "and to the cellar of the Lubyanka."

"You mean you got into the Lubyanka and dug through the concrete floor and retrieved Aleksei's body? How?" Yossef asked.

"It's a long and involved story, Yossef. I won't bore you with the details. We have the remains of your people down the hall in the casket-room warehouse. Would you like to pay your respects?" asked Platonov.

* * *

Minutes later, Yossef and Yuri were standing before four plain wooden coffins.

"Are you sure you can handle this?" Yabin asked.

"Yes," Yuri replied. "I want to see my parents and grandparents even though they're just skeletons."

"He speaks for me too," added Yossef.

"Well, that's all they are—skeletons. But they *are* the actual remains. They're intact and in pretty good shape after so many years."

The wooden lids were lifted off one by one, and more lights were turned on. Inside, the grinning skulls rested on complete skeletons, the bones brownish-yellow with age. The name of each person was painted inside the coffin, above the skull. A chain with an identity disc still encircled the neck vertebrae.

Yossef and Yuri slowly, reverently, walked around the coffins without speaking, a watery glimmer in their eyes. Yossef stopped before the petite skeleton of his mother and fingered her KGB identity disc.

TANYA DUBROV—#1897870
VORTURKA

"The little lady who gave us life, Yuri." Yossef choked on his words. "In a howling blizzard almost thirty-two years ago, and then fought those bastards tooth and nail. What a woman she must have been."

Yuri's eyes smoldered through hot tears.

"In the name of everything that's sacred to me, I promise that if we survive Operation Samson—if we win—that these Dubrovs will replace that bastard Lenin in his Tomb."

XVIII.

Moscow had developed a schizophrenic character during the first week of November. In direct contrast to the frightened and shuttered faces of the Moscow crowds who plodded the streets under the thousands of red banners gaily festooning the city were the happy, ebullient throngs of foreign Communists who flooded the city to fawn over Krylenko's Bolshevik universe and show support for his faltering empire.

As Yossef drove through the city, he was reminded of one section of the Makleff journal—Petrograd, January 1918—and his description of the Socialist birds who migrated to Russia to see the dawning of Lenin's new world.

November 6, 1992, would be the seventy-fifth anniversary of Lenin's betrayal of the democratic revolution. These hordes of gaggling, foreign pseudo-revolutionaries from the comfortable bourgeois democracies would remember this, the Diamond Jubilee of Lenin's takeover: Operation Samson would guarantee that, Yossef smirked to himself. Some of these birds had been making their migratory pilgrimages since the 1920s and, like faithful Moslems journeying to Mecca to visit the Ka'aba, the Communist faithful would visit the sacred Tomb of Lenin as an annual ritual.

How did Makleff put it? Yossef asked himself: Men invent their own revolutionary lands. They invest others with qualities that they miss in their own universe. These sickening parasites who annually propped up the tottering tyranny of Krylenko were the "festering lilies which smelled far worse than weeds."

An ironic smile twisted at Yossef's lips as he drove Raisa's Zhugilis down Prospekt Mira and observed a fawning group of Nicaraguan and Cuban Communist Party officials being shepherded by an Intourist guide. It's possible, just possible, he chuckled to himself, that these foreign comrades might have arrived just in time to witness the final setting of the Leninist sun.

Raisa flashed her Border Guards staff card as she drove through the militia checkpoint entering Pushkin Square from Novoslobodskaya Street. She drew a deep anxious breath as she slipped her staff car into second gear and drove into the brightly bannered square. Off to her right, behind coils of barbed wire, were the frightened, haunted eyes of a hundred or more men, women, and children who had been indiscriminately rounded up to be interrogated. Some would be released, but many would be sent to the temporary holding camp at Ivanova.

Raisa parked in front of her building and walked up the two flights of stairs to the apartment. She popped two aspirin into her mouth and took a swig of iced mineral water.

She flopped on her bed, her brown curly bangs damp on her forehead. Tomorrow, November 5, Yossef would be entering the Tomb for the last time. At approximately 10:45, the Tomb and the crypt room would be sprinkled with Solidarity commandos along the line of spectators, small Czech Skorpion machine pistols strapped to their inner thighs. A long slit along the seam of their inner pants leg, held together by a Velcro strip, would conceal their weapons. In the bowels of the mausoleum, in the storerooms and maintenance rooms, explosives, arms, ammunition, gas masks, and food and water had been surreptitiously stored away over a month's time by two maintenance workers who were Solidarity activists. In a little over a day and a half, Yossef would be gone forever, killed by a hail of bullets from the KGB tactical force which would storm the Tomb; or he might be a hero. A national hero: the Solidarity Dubrov who took over the Tomb to avenge his grandfather's murder.

Her heart pumped wildly as she thought of the possible success or failure of Operation Samson. If it failed, things would be simple, she told herself. She would flee the Soviet Union with Yuri and start a new life in the West. Yossef would be dead.

But if it succeeded, then Yossef Dubrov would be the man of the hour in a new democratic Russia: the Russian-American from Israel who had risked everything to wreak his vengeance upon Lenin and complete the work of his parents and grandparents. What a life she'd have with Yossef! His place would be assured forever in the new Solidarity universe.

And she knew that she loved him—deeply, sensually, more than she had ever loved anybody in her life. She had found new depths of passion with Yossef. Each experience *was* a rediscovery, a redefinition of her own sexuality. Yossef was everything that she had ever wanted in a man—and by the end of the month he would be a dead martyr or, if he emerged triumphant from the Tomb, a hero.

But Yuri was Russian. In his mind, in his upbringing, in his very soul he was Russian. Whatever Yuri was not, still he epitomized the very essence of the Motherland.

Raisa turned her face to her pillow and drifted off into a fitful sleep.

A chilly but clear dawn spread over Moscow as a dull red sun crept above the Lenin Hills, bathing the city in a golden glow. Red Square was a blaze of color with banners and flags that fluttered everywhere in preparation for the mammoth military parade to be staged tomorrow. Yossef had said his goodbyes: an emotional hug from Yuri, who begged Yabin and Gregierenko to let him take Yossef's place; a firm handshake and kiss on the cheek from the Solidarity leader. The surprise came from the usually unflappable Yabin. The MOSSAD colonel threw his arms around him and cried openly, dredging up memories of when he'd changed Yossef's diapers just before delivering him to the Ayalon family so many years before. "Yossef," he had sobbed. "You're as close to me as my own son. God knows I'd take your place if it were possible."

He'd said his goodbye to Raisa last night. He had spent the night with her in her apartment; but their attempt at lovemaking, usually a wildly exciting experience, fell flat. They talked cautiously of commitment—skirting the subject of marriage—if Operation Samson were successful. They avoided talk of failure. After meeting Yuri and the remains of his family, he was consumed by a fierce determination to play out his preordained role. If he were not successful, he would add his bones to the Dubrov heap. That was the life-script written for him long ago, and he would follow it to the letter.

Yossef trudged across Red Square toward Spasskaya Tower, a little needle of apprehension pricking at the base of his skull. It was nine o'clock and the Kremlin bells pealed tunefully, bouncing their echoes off the expanses of stone, concrete, and macadam of the square. Yossef's path paralleled that of the serpentine line of spectators waiting to get into the Tomb. Spaced at regular intervals in a portion of the line were the Solidarity commandos who would take over the Tomb. There were twenty-two in all. They were organized so that when the first commando was about to exit, each of the others would be in close proximity to a guard. Luckily, a chill wind gusted across the Square, justifying the heavy overcoats that concealed their weapons. Each member of the takeover team had been issued a forged pass and button by the Moscow Solidarity cell, designating them as Party officials from the Soviet provinces.

Yossef stood in front of the wooden door of the guardroom, impeccably uniformed, his gleaming assault rifle fully loaded on his shoulder. The fellow guard who would goose-step the 153 meters with him was Lance Corporal Leonid Togulev, a loudmouthed lout from Minsk. Good, thought Yossef: I'm glad he's my partner today. He's one person I'll enjoy blasting if he reaches for the alarm button just under Lenin's head on the catafalque.

The buzzer sounded with the first peal of the bells. The door swung open and the two guards thudded their way to the Tomb, past the clicking cameras of the foreign faithful. In twenty minutes, Yossef was at the foot of the dummy, his white-gloved hands resting gently on his AK-47.

Zhores Platonov was the first of the militants to approach the Tomb. It was now, right now, he thought, that Operation Samson can be blown sky-high. If the maintenance man in the Tomb's basement did not disconnect the circuit wires to the metal detector embedded in the marble door frame, then it was all over. As he shuffled through, he braced himself, expecting the alarm to go off. All was quiet as he stepped through the door.

The first thing that Platonov noticed as he entered the mausoleum was the position of the guards. As he moved with the reverent line, mostly Bulgarian, Cuban, and American Communist Party officials, he counted the Tomb Guards: thirteen in the main crypt room and seven posted elsewhere, not counting the one at Lenin's head. Good, he muttered to himself: things hadn't changed since his last dry run. When he reached the exit there would be a Solidarity commando within reach of each one of the guards. He filed by the phony corpse and glanced up at Yossef. He was as immobile as the dummy.

As he approached the exit, his hand grasped the police whistle in his overcoat pocket. Hiding it in his handkerchief, he raised it to his mouth. The other hand held his spray tube.

Platonov's whistle shrieked, filling the black marble interior with an unearthly, echoing sound. Each commando whirled around, spraying the guard closest to him full in the face. They ripped open their Velcro strips and aimed their deadly Skorpions at the stunned spectators. The outside sentinels flanking the exit and entrance doors acted on reflex and burst in; they were met by a hail of submachine-gun fire. They lurched backward and sprawled, dead, on the outside steps, to the horror of the waiting spectators.

As soon as the whistle blew, Lance Corporal Togulev lunged for the alarm button on the catafalque. Yossef's weapon was already poised. It stuttered briefly and Togulev spun backward, a lifeless heap on the polished marble floor.

"Everybody freeze! Hands up! Up!" Platonov screamed out his orders, glaring at the hostages with a cold, merciless stare. Solidarity commandos rushed for the heavy black marble doors and locked them.

Platonov found the switch exactly where Yuri said it would be: recessed into the wall and hidden by a small swinging panel of thin reddish marble that matched the stone around it. He pushed the button; there was the distant sound of a pneumatic system and the whine of a large motor as a heavy steel door slid across the entrance of the long maintenance tunnel leading from the Kremlin into the mausoleum. The Tomb was now hermetically sealed off.

From underneath his overcoat, a militant whipped out what looked like a large blob of putty and squeezed it onto the glass directly over Lenin's face. He placed other blobs of plastic explosive at the foot and middle of the body. Wires were hastily strung from the explosives to a detonating device in an isolated corner of the Tomb.

"Up against the wall, all of you!" barked Platonov, brandishing his Skorpion for maximum effect. Suddenly, the impact of what had happened registered upon the hostages. The incredulous eyes of fifty-six horrified people stared into the steady barrels of the submachine guns as they shuffled backward until they came up against the reddish marble wall.

As the effects of the knockout spray began to wear off, some of the guards started to stir, their glazed and unbelieving eyes trying to focus on the scene around them. Instinctively they reached for their rifles. They were gone, scooped up in the first moments of the attack. One guard, more alert than the others, noticed the blobs of explosive plastered on Lenin. Impulsively he bolted for the casket, shrieking something about saving Comrade Lenin. Yossef swung his rifle in a wide arc and smashed his skull.

"Spinnenko!" yelled a guard. "You're with them?" His eyes were wide with disbelief.

"My name is Yossef Dubrov," he answered loudly and

evenly. "In the name of Solidarity and a new democratic Russia we have taken over Lenin's Tomb. Any attempt to resist will result in death. Any attempt by the government to storm the Tomb will result in an explosion," he tapped a blob of explosive, "which will obliterate the precious remains of our friend here, not to mention all of us." The dead air in the mausoleum seemed to quiver under the impact of his deadly message.

The tension in the tomb was electric now as the hostages realized the magnitude of their plight. Nobody moved. They stood rigid with fear, expressionless. The commandos searched them and took their wallets to check their identification.

"An interesting assortment of comrades," snorted Platonov with disgust. "The Secretary-Treasurer of the American Communist Party, the Deputy Director of the Bulgarian Security Service, and the Minister of Marine and Fisheries from Cuba. Some small and middle fry too."

The guard-station phone rang inside the Tomb, jangling everybody's nerves. Yossef picked it up and said nothing, waiting for the caller to identify himself.

"This is Major Koslovonov, Commandant of the Guards. Who is this?"

"This is the Kremlin detachment of the Solidarity Army of Liberation—Field Marshal Yossef Dubrov speaking," he chortled. "Lenin's mausoleum is ours. We have twenty-one of your guards and fifty-six hostages: Bulgarians, Cubans, and Americans. The national icon, Lenin, is with us, and we have the old boy encased in plastic explosive. Any attempt to storm the Tomb will be met by one hell of a blast. We've got two drums of Nippolite downstairs. If you try to hold your parade tomorrow, we can blow this whole structure to rubble. I would caution Krylenko and the Politburo to stay off the reviewing platform on top. That could be dangerous." He chuckled. "Get one thing straight, Major, and pass it on to Krylenko: we're all willing to die and take Lenin, the mausoleum, and the hostages with us." Yossef hung up the phone.

* * *

Koslovonov pushed a series of buttons on the console in front of him, sounding a general alert. Sirens and klaxons went off, and within minutes, security detachments poured out of the Alarm Tower, the Tsar's Tower, and the Senate Tower exits on the Kremlin wall.

Inside the courtyard, soldiers and attendants were running and scrambling to get to emergency stations, roughly shoving tourists and foreign Communists out of the way. KGB tactical troops cordoned off all government buildings within the Kremlin complex and the piercing sound of a siren, perched on top of the Nikolskaya Tower, wailed a warning all over the Square. The Kremlin gates were slammed shut; an armored column roared into Red Square and formed a semicircle of tanks and armored cars around Lenin's Tomb.

Premier Krylenko could barely hear the wail of the siren through the heavy, bulletproof windows in his office in the Upper Arsenal Building. Rakhmatov burst in without knocking, a vein on his forehead pulsating so wildly that it looked like it might burst.

"Solidarity! Solidarity!" he panted breathlessly. "They've taken over Lenin's Tomb!"

Before the Premier had time to react to the minister's hysteria, the high-priority phone jangled on his ornate mahogany desk. He dragged the phone to his ear as if it were a leaden weight.

"It's a direct call to you, Comrade Premier," said the KGB security operator. "I routed it directly to your office. It's Vasily Gregierenko—Gregierenko of Solidarity!"

Krylenko listened carefully, taking notes, his face drawn and ashen. He mumbled a few words, almost incoherently. Suddenly his body stiffened as if jolted by a current of electricity. He slowly replaced the receiver, in the state of shock of one whose whole world was tumbling about his ears.

"That was Vasily Gregierenko." His helpless eyes stared at Rakhmatov. "He said that we're to cancel all of the celebrations. Solidarity will issue an ultimatum soon. We are to do as he says if we want Lenin's remains preserved.

If not, he'll blow the Tomb to powder.

"The leader of the group which took over the Tomb is named—named Yossef Dubrov. His twin brother Yuri is somewhere in the city. He's the leader of the Solidarity Army of Liberation in the Moscow area."

"We've received clearance from Tallin Naval Security to proceed to Kronstadt, Captain Suskov," smiled Smedlev triumphantly. "We're ordered to the turret-repair division at the Kronstadt naval gun factory. They fell for our story of needing a turret overhaul."

"Excellent! Excellent," exclaimed Suskov. "When we get to Leningrad, are you quite sure that our brothers can open the Bolshoy Prospekt drawbridge?"

"All I can go by are the promises of the Leningrad cell, Captain. When we pass Vol'nyy Island, we head up the Little Neva River. The Bolshoy and Peter and Paul bridges will be opened for us. We can slip into the open berth next to the *Aurora* off Museum Point," answered the executive officer.

"Have you heard anything on the radio yet from Moscow?"

"Yes, sir. We received word that the Kremlin has been sealed off by State Security and Red Square is off limits to the public. There have been troop movements all over the city. We monitored the KGB frequency, but so far the government hasn't announced any takeover of Lenin's Tomb."

"We should be getting word from Gregierenko's people at any time."

The *Liepaja*'s hull knifed through the calmer waters of the Gulf of Finland as it slid by the Estonian headlands, the southern lip of the Gulf's mouth that separated it from the Baltic Sea. The phone rang on the bridge and Smedlev answered. His sea-beaten face crinkled into a smile.

"They did it! Operation Samson is on! That was Solidarity—Moscow. They've taken over the Tomb and given Krylenko an ultimatum to cancel all of the celebrations for tomorrow—the parade, everything!"

Suskov twisted his face into a wry smile.

"What a pity. They are going to re-enact the actual

takeover of the Winter Palace tomorrow in Leningrad. They have the old *Aurora* already loaded with blanks to fire on Peter and Paul. Maybe we can add a little excitement if we can just get through those damned bridges. I'd hate to disappoint all of the foreign comrades who came to see the fireworks."

XIX.

"All Gregierenko wants to do is discredit us by making us cancel the celebrations. Our choice is clear, comrades. We can either make this concession and save Lenin, and ourselves, or we can use force and lose it all. If Lenin goes, what credible symbol of the State are we left with?"

Sergei Gorsky's words stabbed into each Politburo member like a hot blade. A cloud of despair seemed to hover over the assembled members seated around the green-covered T-shaped table.

"We can wait them out!" thundered Rakhmatov. "After a week or two in the mausoleum they'll start to crack under the strain. It's easier to negotiate with terrorists when they feel a sense of isolation and hopelessness."

Krylenko listened to the various factions that had already developed within the twelve-man body since the Tomb had been taken over that morning. Within an hour of the general alert, the Politburo had been convened in emergency session. They finally agreed that afternoon that they would cancel all celebrations to be held in the capital. That's all that Solidarity had demanded—so far.

Premier Krylenko seemed to pull his head down into his jacket like a wizened old sea turtle withdrawing into its shell. He set his glasses on the table and rubbed the bridge of his nose in fatigue and strain, agonizing over the next statement he was about to make—a truth that had been a carefully guarded secret restricted to a trusted few for over sixty years.

"There is another dimension to this problem which we must deal with; one which only I myself and two others among us know about."

A rustle of apprehension rippled through the assembled Politburo.

Krylenko pulled his massive bulk upright and braced his hands on the table. He looked like he might collapse and fall at any moment.

"Comrades," he began slowly. "The body of Lenin —the body of Lenin . . ." Each word seemed to weigh a ton. ". . . is a skillfully made wax dummy. The only original part of Comrade Lenin is his skull. The body had deteriorated shortly after his death and a wax and plaster counterfeit was made. Afterward a new dummy of wax and acrylic was made. What Solidarity has captured is a phony Lenin. The present dummy, and the one before it, has deceived countless millions who viewed it as the actual remains of Comrade Lenin. Can you see the problem if this leaks to the outside world?"

Silence. A terrible silence filled the Upper Arsenal meeting room. Rakhmatov slumped in his chair and stared at the tabletop. Each tick of the clock seemed like a miniature explosion.

Gorsky shook his head numbly from side to side in shocked astonishment.

"All these years! After all these years! We've accused religion of being the opiate of the masses and for over sixty years the State and the Party have perpetrated one of the greatest frauds in the history of mankind."

Again Sergei Gorsky had said what the others were thinking but dared not say.

"What if the Solidarity terrorists start to examine the body and discover it's false?" queried Romanovich, the Party theoretician.

"They wouldn't *dare* tamper with the sacred body of Lenin!" Rakhmatov burst out impulsively. His words seemed absurdly inappropriate under the present circumstances.

"The only course of action open to us is to give the appearance of being willing to do anything to save Lenin," offered Bovsky, the Party Treasurer. "Anything less would send the wrong signal to the Soviet people. We must demonstrate that Lenin's body is so sacred that we'll make *any* concession." The members shot him nervous glances. "Within reason, of course," he added hastily.

Rakhmatov stood, his florid face full of frustration and rage.

"No! Give the chort-eating bastards nothing! Storm the Tomb. Let Solidarity blow it to rubble. Then the evidence of sixty-odd years of deception is totally destroyed."

There was a collective gasp from the seated Politburo.

"All right, comrades. What other choice do we *really* have? I was never informed about this—this dummy business, and I'm in charge of Tomb security. We may destroy our national icon, but this gigantic hoax is gone —forever."

"But his body is the glue which holds our system together. The people always had Lenin when they had nothing else. Without Lenin—without the mausoleum . . ." wailed Romanovich.

"Other governments survive! Other systems continue without their founders locked in tombs for people to gawk at," countered the KGB director.

Gorsky stood, shaking with anger, and pointed an accusing finger at Rakhmatov.

"Yes! Yes, Comrade Director. But *they* have credibility with their people! Their laws and policies are consistent! Today's truth is *not* tomorrow's heresy in other countries. We have systematically destroyed all of the anchors which have moored the Soviet people until only one is left, and now Comrade Krylenko tells us that even *this* anchor is phony. Never, never in the history of our planet has a government perpetrated such a gigantic deception, and for so long. I warn you, comrades: when Lenin goes—we go! Marxism-Leninism goes! Communism will be replaced by an ideology which can deal with today's problems."

"Treason! Treason, Gorsky! I always knew that your sympathies were with Solidarity! By your words and actions you have just condemned yourself to the Black Wall of the Lubyanka!" Rakhmatov shouted hysterically, the vein in his forehead pulsating uncontrollably.

Krylenko's voice sliced through the volcanic arguments erupting in the Upper Arsenal meeting room.

"Comrades! Let's keep our heads and have no more accusations. We all want the government to survive. I've given this problem some thought and I believe that Comrade Gorsky is right. We have made some inexcusable mistakes. Some we have inherited from the past and can do nothing about. We must accept the possibility of compromising with Solidarity if they make further demands. Lenin *is* the one visible symbol of consistency and credibility left. We must make it appear that we will do everything to save him."

The twelve old men slumped into another gloomy silence. The regime had never faced a crisis of this magnitude before. This time, the enemy had struck at the very soul of the system and threatened to destroy it. The cult of Lenin was a secular religion. The Kremlin leaders had historically resorted to a continual, almost mystical incantation of Lenin's name as a source of legitimacy for whatever policies they pursued. The tortuous twists and turns of state policy could be justified in any way by citing Lenin as scripture. The total legitimacy of the Party and State was derived from one man—Lenin. It was the Leninist creed on which rested the infallibility of the Communist Party and its leaders. Without the visible remains of Lenin to perpetuate the illusion of immortality, the legitimacy of the State would crumble with the first blast of the Solidarity commandos.

"So, we negotiate and compromise?" Gorsky brightened.

Krylenko stood and laid his hands on Gorsky's shoulders like a priest bestowing a blessing.

"Yes. And you can handle the negotiations, Gorsky. Solidarity will trust you more than any one of us. You have a reputation for honesty and for speaking your mind."

The Politburo members filed out of the meeting room but Rakhmatov remained.

"Comrade Director." The Premier locked the door behind him. "We have the Novocherkassk rebellion to deal with."

When the trouble at Novocherkassk had begun the week before, it came as no surprise. Thirty years earlier the great industrial city had erupted in worker riots when wages were slashed at the giant NEVZ locomotive works. The rampaging workers took over the entire city for three days in June of 1962. More frightening was the fact that units of the Red Army stood by and did nothing. Some of the soldiers even gave their weapons to the rioters.

The KGB response was massive. The city was completely sealed off and three divisions of KGB tactical troops were brought in to mop up the workers. Thousands of the guilty and innocent alike were shipped off to the Gulag. It was an extremely bloody affair and hundreds of KGB troops were killed and wounded.

The question of quelling internal rebellions of the magnitude of Novocherkassk had been discussed in the Politburo. The Director of the KGB demanded the right to use low-yield nuclear weapons—about half the size of the Hiroshima payload—if the KGB were to suffer too many casualties in repressing another Novocherkassk.

The Red Army was aghast at the Director's proposal and argued vigorously to keep all nuclear weapons within the military and to use them only against external enemies. The debate ended in 1963 with the agreement that all nuclear weapons were to be under the operational control of the military and were never to be used to crush internal rebellion.

That was before Solidarity.

The mausoleum was cold. The black and dull-red marble seemed to soak the frigid air from outside and conduct it to the interior of the tomb.

The hostages were sitting on the cold floor, slumped against the wall. At first they'd experienced a huge hammering of panic that paralyzed the mind, then a sense of imminent death, a conviction that they had only seconds to live, then the slow dissipation of shock and gradual return to consciousness. And suddenly the full impact of reality, a suffocating sensation of deadly menace permeating the air of the Tomb like a heathen incense.

The body of Lance Corporal Togulev was dragged downstairs, leaving a wide trail of smeared blood. It was left to dry on the marble floor, a visible reminder of the resolve of the commandos to kill everybody, themselves included, if necessary.

The guard's phone jangled. Platonov picked it up.

"It's Vasily!" he shouted excitedly. "He's on the line!" The commando leader listened, his head bobbing up and down, and then hung up.

"What did he say?" asked Yossef.

"Good news, brothers. The government has agreed to cancel all celebrations in Moscow and seems willing to negotiate on other things."

"I wouldn't trust those bastards," muttered a militant. "I hope that Vasily is watching out for tricks."

"He's no fool. He cut his call short so it can't be traced. Part of the deal with Krylenko so far is to keep the line open so he can call us at any time."

"One other thing," Platonov continued. "It seems as if we have a well-known terrorist manager among us. He used to be a professional assassin himself. It's Constantin Lapusnyik, the Deputy Director of the Bulgarian Security Service. He's a real son of a bitch. Watch him."

Yossef picked out the Bulgarian from the rest of the hostages. He had a tan face and cunning eyes, now little slits of rage, and a mouthful of unevenly spaced yellowish teeth. Yossef immediately disliked him.

Platonov muttered under his breath, "I've heard of Lapusnyik before. He was involved in the assassination attempt on the Pope back in 1982."

"The assassin was a Turk," countered Kurdirka, Platonov's demolition expert.

"True. But Lapusnyik was involved in planning out of Sofia."

Platonov sauntered over to the Bulgarian.

"Get up, Lapusnyik," he ordered.

The Bulgarian casually arose; the smirking expression on his face was actually a mask of fright.

Platonov stuck his Skorpion under the man's nose so he could smell the oil on it.

"Constantin Lapusnyik. One-time assassin and now unleasher of terrorists all over the world. Involvement with the attempt on the Pope's life about ten years ago. Right?"

The Bulgarian said nothing, but just stared impassively. Platonov flicked the safety of the Skorpion right under his chin and grinned when he flinched. Platonov grabbed a handful of Lapusnyik's hair and shoved him back down against the wall.

"Any trouble and you're the first to die, Bulgarian."

The air in the Tomb was now heavy and oppressive. There was no air coming through the ventilation ducts. The system had been turned off by the maintenance men so the government could not circulate toxic gases through it. Like a leaden shroud a feeling of isolation and oppression had started to descend over both the captors and captives. The subdued light of the crypt added to the gloom. The waxen figure of Lenin seemed to shine with an evil glow as shimmers of light reflected off of the protective glass of its case.

"It's going to be a long night." Yossef sighed resignedly. "We'd better settle down for a long vigil because this place is going to drive some of us over the edge before the week is through. We should have included a psychiatrist among us, or at least we should have stashed a TV set downstairs."

"We'll make it, Yossef," Platonov replied, patting his Skorpion. "We can always amuse ourselves by shooting a hostage or two to show Krylenko we mean business." He glared at the Bulgarian when he said it.

The *Liepaja* churned toward the bright lights of Leningrad, which were little sparkles in the distance as a chill wind swept up from the city's harbor. Vaclav Suskov stood on the open bridge, his binoculars trained on a bright glow, brighter than the others on the city's skyline.

"That's Kirov Stadium at the end of Krestovskiy Island. We turn into the Little Neva between Vol'nyy and Dekabistov Islands," he informed Smedlev. The cruiser threaded the straits between the two islands and headed up the Little Neva. The docks along the river were crowded with foreign vessels of all types, from the dull gray warships of Communist Bloc and client-state nations to the brightly lighted passenger liners of the West, all bringing tourists and the faithful to the festival of Lenin.

Suskov could see the Bolshoy Prospekt bridge now. It was broken and the two halves tilted skyward. The *Liepaja* slid through, its antennas just missing a girder. The Peter and Paul Bridge was still closed, but the cruiser plowed ahead.

"Better slow down and prepare to reverse speed, Captain," cautioned Smedlev.

"If the Peter and Paul Bridge doesn't open, we're going through anyway. I don't give a damn if it takes our superstructure off. We're going through." Suskov grimaced as the Bolshoy Bridge locked shut behind them.

As if prompted by his threat, the bridge yawned open and the *Liepaja* sailed through into the wide expanse of water where the Little Neva, Great Neva, and Neva rivers met. They could see the bright lights of the Peter and Paul Fortress this side of the Kirov Bridge and the outline of the old Winter Palace on the southern shore, next to the admiralty building. Anchored off Museum Point was the old Tsarist cruiser *Aurora*, a national shrine held in almost as much reverence as Lenin's Tomb. Strings of multicolored lights blazed from the ropes and wires of its masts, giving it a carnival effect.

The helmsman warped the vessel to within a few meters of the old cruiser and dropped anchor. The Solidarity skeleton crew padded silently to battle stations. The *Liepaja*'s eight six-barrel 30-millimeter Gatling guns were manned and trained on the landward approaches to the cruiser. The forward 152-millimeter triple-gun turrets swung southward and trained on the Winter Palace. Several members of the crew hung large strips of canvas over the name *Liepaja* on the bow and stern, renaming the ship the *Aleksei Dubrov*.

* * *

Petty Officer First Class Oleg Bandera held the hatch open for Suskov as he descended into the missile-control room from the stern. Bandera, a small, intense Ukrainian of twenty-nine, had nursed an overpowering, almost irrational hatred of everything Soviet since he had learned that his father and older brother had been given life sentences in the Gulag. His family had been active in the Ukrainian nationalist movement since the 1960s. Two years before, the Ukrainian movement, like many of the other nationalist liberation movements within the Soviet empire, had forged strong links with Solidarity.

A wizard in electronics and physics, Bandera was the nuclear-missile section chief in the crew. Suskov bolted the hatchway while Bandera opened the circuit panels, cutting some wires and reconnecting others. He reset and recalibrated several control systems.

"A simple job, Captain." He grinned. "The missile can't be launched, but if we press these two buttons . . ." he tapped two red circles ". . . after turning the two fire keys, we detonate the device. Twenty megatons should level the city of Lenin and a twenty-five-mile radius quite nicely."

Smedlev and the other crew members continued their duties on deck, unaware that Suskov and Bandera had been secretly developing their own version of Operation Samson below the stern missile deck.

XX.

"I wish you could just flash your Border Guards ID card and walk to the head of the line," Raisa whispered, stamping her booted feet on the cold pavement.

"Ssshhh! You'll get us mobbed and strung up from a lamppost," Yuri replied, rubbing his newly grown stubble of beard. "I don't think these people would appreciate me flashing a KGB ID card around in order to get special privileges."

Raisa and Yuri shuffled forward, looking like the hundreds of other workers and their families in the long queue that stretched from State Store 42 on Proletarsky Prospekt, a mile past the rows of concrete-slab apartments, numbing in their Orwellian monotony.

Since the takeover of the Tomb, there had been sudden and severe food shortages throughout Moscow. The city's inhabitants now shopped by rumor, and rumor had it that State Store 42 had received a fresh shipment of meat and produce from the Crimea.

Solidarity had released Yuri from his comfortable confinement on November 5 and introduced him into the clandestine world of the revolutionary movement. Wherever he went he was followed and watched by Gregierenko's men and was usually accompanied by Raisa. General Spinnenko had found ways to cover for her absence from the Center. Not that he really had to, for he himself had been conspicuously absent from his office, making frequent staff visits to Border Guard units throughout western Russia.

264

"This damned line is moving about a foot an hour," muttered Yuri in frustration. "If I wasn't so damned hungry I'd forget it. They'll probably tell us they're all sold out when we finally get up to the counter anyway."

"This is what most of our people go through every day, Yuri," Raisa said softly, clutching his arm.

A truck full of militiamen seemed to materialize out of nowhere and squealed to a stop across the street. The troops jumped out, assault rifles slung over their shoulders, and posted themselves along the winding queue. This had become standard operating procedure since the Dynamo Stadium incident. Whenever there was a concentration of people, the militia would stand by to intimidate or to forestall trouble. There were already small-scale disturbances in the capital—near-riots in some cases —and this part of the city, known as the Southernport district, had the highest potential for revolutionary violence.

A huge militiaman with a pockmarked face stood a few meters from Yuri and Raisa. He banged his black mittens together with a smack and stamped his boots on the cold street. His beady black eyes darted to Raisa, eyeing her with a lustful stare. Yuri felt a surge of anger in him and shot the soldier a menacing look.

A militia officer appeared, a silver whistle in his mouth, and shrilled it in the cold morning air. The militia troopers unslung their weapons and held them at port arms. The pockmarked soldier leered at Raisa, anticipating his commander's orders.

"All right! Everybody turn this way and form into two rows. This is a routine search," barked the officer.

"We'll lose our place in line," complained a short, bandy-legged worker with a sun-creased face.

"Well, fuck your line!" snapped the officer. "Just do as you're told."

"Well, fuck you too!" the little man bristled. "I've been standing here for three hours just on the *rumor* that I can get food for my family. I'm not getting out of line for Krylenko himself!"

The militia officer lunged for the belligerent fellow and

dragged him out onto the pavement by the hair, clubbing him with his pistol as the worker tried to protect himself.

"All right, you little chort-eating scum-sucker. We'll search you the *hard* way!"

Two militiamen pounced on the little man and held his writhing body hard against the cold pavement as they ripped off his clothes until he was stark naked. Even his shoes and socks were removed.

"Cavity search," the officer laughed.

The militiamen forced the little fellow to his knees while one stuck his fingers down his throat, forcing him to vomit. The other wet his finger and jammed it up the victim's rectum so hard that he screamed in pain.

"I think he's got a machine gun up there," laughed the soldier as he twisted his finger around the man's insides.

"Does anybody else want to be searched 'the hard way'? Any volunteers?" the militia officer screamed at the crowd.

Everybody in the line averted his eyes from the assaulted worker in embarrassed shame and anger.

"All right! Search all of them, and be thorough!" the officer commanded.

The pockmarked soldier made straight for Raisa, a smirk twitching his lips. He took off his mittens and stuffed them into his greatcoat pockets. Eagerly, he unbuttoned Raisa's heavy coat and plunged his hands under her arms as she raised them reluctantly. His hands probed her upper body awkwardly and crudely until he found her breasts. His meaty, sweaty hands kneaded them under cover of her coat. Raisa closed her eyes and prayed that Yuri wouldn't notice.

The pattern of search was repeated all along the queue. The soldiers had chosen the youngest and prettiest women for their initial examination.

The militiaman now became carried away with his lust. He patted down Raisa's hips and thighs and then squatted on the balls of his feet and stuck his fingers into the tops of her boots. Then he slid his hands up the inside of her legs, toward her vagina. Tears of helpless rage coursed down Raisa's cheeks as the soldier's frantic probings found the warm moist mound between her legs.

"Just a routine cavity search, dear lady." The militiaman chuckled hoarsely. "You might have a hand grenade hidden in your pussy."

Yuri's boot lashed out and caught the soldier square in the Adam's apple. He thudded to the street clutching his throat in agony, a trickle of blood oozing from his mouth. Other militiamen sprinted toward their fallen comrade, rifles ready for firing. The two soldiers in the back of the truck aimed their heavy machine gun over the tailgate at the crowd.

Everything seemed to happen at once. Twin explosions vomited from the open truck and lines of submachine-gun fire stitched into the ranks of militiamen. Almost as one person, the queue surged against the surviving soldiers and tore into them with fists, feet, and captured weapons. Raisa scooped up a fallen AK-47 and crunched it into the skull of the wounded pockmarked militiaman again and again until it was an unrecognizable bloody pulp.

A team of Solidarity militants rushed into the fray and dispatched the rest of the soldiers with their tiny Skorpions.

"Now you've done it, Dubrov! The fat's in the fire. We were hoping you wouldn't get yourself into trouble. Now it looks like you've just started the revolution!" said the team leader.

The workers broke into the store and looted the contents. A gas station down the street was taken over and Molotov cocktails were manufactured by the hundreds. Soon, fires were raging all over the Southernport area, from the Simonov Monastery to the Moscow river docks. The workers had disappeared into the rabbit warrens of apartment complexes with their captured weapons.

By mid-afternoon, the Southernport district had erupted into a full-scale rebellion. The militia arsenal on Volgogradsky Street was stormed and the weapons taken to supply the rebel ranks. Riots spread like a raging brush fire to other parts of southern Moscow. Huge fires now billowed their acrid smoke into the clear November air as government and Party buildings were put to the torch.

"We can't stay here, Dubrov," yelled the team leader as he raced through a burning street, dodging the falling, flaming boards. Yuri and Raisa followed, each clutching a weapon.

"Do you know how to use that rifle for anything besides crushing skulls?" Yuri grinned.

"Of course." Raisa panted with indignation as she jogged beside Yuri. "Every Soviet woman has had marksmanship training if she was in the Pioneers. Don't worry about me, Yuri. I can handle myself."

They reached a hastily constructed barricade of overturned automobiles, furniture, and anything else the rebels could lay their hands on. Other barricades had been erected in strategic areas throughout the Southernport sector.

A KGB tactical-force convoy crashed through the barricade at the corner of Simonov and Kretskaya streets and rolled relentlessly between the gray rows of concrete apartments. Hundreds of Molotov cocktails rained down on the line of armored and wheeled vehicles, turning the narrow street into a tunnel of fire. The hatch of the lead armored personnel carrier was flung open and two KGB soldiers scrambled out. Raisa pulled her AK-47 up to her shoulder and, almost casually, squeezed off a burst which sent the KGB men scrambling off the APC.

Small-arms fire raked the stalled convoy as the KGB troopers streamed, many in flames, from the inferno. Within minutes, the slaughter was over. Three hundred and forty-two soldiers were killed. The wounded were quickly dispatched by the rampaging rebels.

Yuri turned a grimy, stubbled face to Raisa who was crouched behind an overturned chest of drawers.

"This is it, Raisa. We're in it now. There's no turning back," he said somewhat condescendingly.

"Look, 'Brother Dubrov'!" she snapped sarcastically, still squinting down the barrel of her weapon at the smoldering bodies of the KGB men. "I've been waiting for this for over two years. I know damned well there's no turning back."

A new, more menacing sound could barely be heard over the crackling fires of the burning vehicles. It became more distinct now as thousands of rebel faces turned skyward—toward the northeast.

"Shit!" Yuri burst out. "Now we're in for it."

The rotors of a dozen M-18 Red Army assault helicopters chopped through the cold air as they flew directly toward the Southernport sector of the city.

The camera crews positioned themselves where they could catch the full sweep of the action in the square before the Winter Palace. To many of the Communist faithful from the Leningrad Party organization, the "storming of the Winter Palace" was an annual affair; a chance to don old uniforms and relive, at least for a night, the "heroic" assault staged in much the same manner as it had been conducted some seventy-five years ago.

The actors stood, rank upon rank, clutching their old Tsarist rifles as huge floodlights lit the square. The bulky old Maxim machine guns, dragged out of half a dozen museums for the occasion, trained their black barrels on the entrance to the Palace, their feed-belts loaded with blanks.

A thunderous roar from the old *Aurora* signaled the attack. A collective war cry from thousands of Bolshevik throats rent the chill night air as they surged forward to the clatter of the old Maxims.

The spectators lining the square, most of them brought up from Moscow because of the cancellations of the city's celebrations, watched wondrously as the make-believe revolutionaries charged across the plaza to the clicking and whirring of their cameras.

Suddenly, there was a series of new thunders from the vicinity of Museum Point. This wasn't in the script, but the movie cameras kept grinding away as the assault force was now running up the wide stone steps of the Palace.

The square and the steps erupted in gigantic sheets of flame and debris that seemed to envelop the cast of thousands. The broken and charred bodies of the make-believe assault force were hurled and scattered in every direction. The 152-millimeter shells of the *Aleksei Dubrov* now fell among the packed throngs of spectators, tearing huge, bloody, gaping holes in their ranks.

* * *

At Kirov Stadium, another extravaganza was taking place at the same time to accommodate the crowds brought up from Moscow. There were film-shots of Lenin on a series of huge movie screens placed around the stadium. There were operatic solos, thundering choruses with gigantic military bands, and great shafts of light shining on a magnificent white statue of Lenin in the center of the stadium.

The whiteness of Lenin's statue projected a sense of purity, a resurrection, a religious moment intended to inspire and revive the faith among those who had grown hard, cynical, or forgetful. The celebration at Kirov Stadium this evening was a kind of Communist sacrament.

The *Aleksei Dubrov* swung a turret of its triple guns to the northwest and systematically lobbed shell after shell into the packed bleachers of the stadium.

The regional KGB barracks and detention center flanking Vosstaniya Square, four kilometers to the northwest of the Monastery of Alexander Nevsky, was the next to feel the anger of the cruiser. Multiple volleys fell among the complex of structures. The red-brick and stone gingerbread Victorian buildings collapsed on hundreds of KGB soldiers who were either asleep or watching the festivities on television.

The *Aleksei Dubrov* swung its multiple turrets and, almost casually, bombarded preselected targets in Leningrad. Its computerized sighting system guaranteed complete accuracy. The Leningrad Communist Party headquarters near the Smolny Institute received several salvos, completely demolishing the building and all of its records. The huge Smolenko Hotel, packed with thousands of the Party faithful from the Eastern Bloc, received several direct hits.

The first shots of the *Aleksei Dubrov* were the signal for the Leningrad Solidarity cells to spring into action. Teams of saboteurs attacked the city's power stations, and assault teams stormed the lightly defended city militia stations. Most of the local militia and KGB troopers were on emergency duty in the center of the city.

Frantic calls for assistance were made by the KGB and militia commanders to the various Red Army units in the Leningrad military district. A similar plea was made to the Kronstadt naval base for detachments of naval infantry to reinforce the hard-pressed KGB tactical forces.

There was an ominous lack of commitment from the units contacted.

"I don't like it," Yossef mumbled, his forehead beading in a cold sweat. "We haven't heard from Gregierenko in over twenty hours, and every time we try to call we get cut off."

The gloomy Tomb and the monotonous prison routine now had all the appearance of permanence. That the captors and captives had not seen daylight for over forty-eight hours now preyed on their nerves; and living in constant semidarkness created a sense of endlessness in which it became difficult to distinguish night from day.

The hostages were no longer paralyzed with fright. They seemed to have mastered their initial shock and rage and were now in a kind of semitrance. But this soon gave way too, and they now simply glowered at their captors in helpless fury. Stolen little whispers among them suggested that a conspiracy of some sort was in the making.

"How can I get up to the reviewing platform?" Platonov asked Yossef while his eyes stared at the hostages with a look that exuded menace. "Behind the crypt room there's a ladder which leads to a steel hatch. It looks like the hatch on a submarine. It locks with a wheel from the inside."

"I'm going up and take a look around."

"Zhores! That's insane! There are probably hundreds of troops ringing the Tomb and posted on top. They'll pick you off as soon as you stick your head out."

Platonov ignored Yossef's warning. "Somebody get me that battery-powered portable bullhorn we stashed downstairs." One of the commandos bounded to the maintenance storeroom and retrieved it.

The commando leader crept up the tubular steel ladder, the loudspeaker dangling from his neck by a canvas strap. He stopped at the locked wheel and listened intently. Slowly and cautiously he turned it, trying to make as little noise as possible. The hatch cracked open and tiny slivers of sunlight slid into the darkness. Platonov's eyes swept the reviewing platform. Three guards were casually leaning on the wall of dark red porphyry and black granite smoking cigarettes. He couldn't see over the smaller waist-high wall—the one that the Politburo would be standing behind right now if the parade hadn't been canceled.

He flung back the metal cover with a loud clang. The guards unslung their rifles from their shoulders in fluid motions and pointed them toward the open hatch. Platonov stuck the flared end of the bullhorn slightly out of the opening. "I want all of your people off the Tomb in sixty seconds or we blow up Vladimir Lenin. I'm counting right now. One, two, three . . ."

"All personnel off the Tomb!" barked Major Koslovonov over his own bullhorn, his voice tinged with near panic.

"You're crazy, Zhores! Don't go out there!" Yossef yelled from the bottom of the ladder.

"I know what I'm doing, damn it. Bring the Bulgarian out here. Loop a length of rope around his neck and tie his hands behind his back. Be ready to bring him on top when I say so."

Platonov heaved himself out of the hatchway, half expecting a bullet to plow into his skull. He scuttled like a wounded crab on all fours to the waist-high wall and peered over it. An awesome display of power confronted him. The cannons and machine guns of eighteen tanks and armored personnel carriers were trained on the mausoleum. Two helicopters clattered overhead and at least two hundred KGB tactical troops ringed the tomb.

Platonov heaved a fatalistic sigh and wrenched himself upward. He was standing exactly where Krylenko himself would have been standing now. Hundreds of guns swung on the Solidarity leader.

"Lower your weapons!" yelled Koslovonov. "No shooting! No shooting!"

Platonov gazed at the skyline beyond Red Square. The billowing smoke from many fires smudged the horizon. The static of gunfire and the wailing of fire engines could be heard all over the city. He put the bullhorn to his lips.

"Your government has cut us off from our people. It was agreed that the telephone line would stay open."

"I don't know anything about that," the Kremlin Guards' commander snapped back. "The government has been negotiating with your leader for the past two days. We are acting in good faith, I assure you."

"Do you call your being here with a small army an act of good faith?" Platonov replied sarcastically.

"We are here to protect *you* from the wrath of the Soviet people," Koslovonov said indignantly.

"Oh, pigshit!" Platonov snorted. "Bring up the Bulgarian," he shouted.

Lapusnyik, half-climbing and half-hauled, came up the ladder. A commando frog-walked him over to Platonov. The Bulgarian's smirk was gone, replaced instead with frightened eyes, now huge circles of fear. Platonov grabbed him by the hair and yanked him upright.

"Up on the wall, Bulgarian."

Uncomprehending, Lapusnyik clambered onto the low wall while the Solidarity commando leader tied the end of his neck-rope to a cleat. Platonov's shrill voice echoed throughout the Square.

"This prick of a pig is Constantin Lapusnyik, a nachalstvo in the Bulgarian gestapo. One hostage will be executed every ten hours if Solidarity demands are not met—and that includes keeping the phone lines open. We have seventy-seven hostages in all. We'll kill them all until we're down to Lenin. Then he goes, we go, and the Tomb goes."

Platonov yanked a Makarev nine-millimeter automatic pistol from his waistband and jabbed it against the Bulgarian's skull.

"In the name of decent people everywhere, I sentence this piece of shit to death."

To the assembled soldiers in the Square, it looked as if Lapusnyik's head had exploded in a spray of reddish orange. His body convulsed, then seemed to spring from the wall as if propelled by a catapult. It fell five feet and was jerked to a stop by the rope around his neck.

The Bulgarian dangled grotesquely against the red wall

of the mausoleum, his blood turning the white grout between the granite slabs a dark red.

"Comrade Director!" panted the aide. "There's a cruiser in the Neva shooting up Leningrad. It's creating havoc!"

Rakhmatov's chin fell on his chest.

"A—a Soviet cruiser?"

"Yes, Comrade Director. And saboteurs and hooligans are attacking power stations and militia units. Hundreds, maybe thousands have been killed by the shelling and—"

"It's the Solidarity uprising, damn their rotten souls to hell! The people, Popov. What are the people up there doing?"

The aide swallowed nervously.

"They're just waiting. Just watching the fires. It seems like everybody up there is waiting for something to happen."

"Why hasn't the navy or the air force blown the damned cruiser out of the water?"

"It's anchored right next to the *Aurora*. The local military units are acting strange. They won't even respond to our requests for help. The navy says that it's an internal security matter and the air force doesn't want the responsibility of destroying a national shrine."

"These damned national shrines are destroying *us,* Popov!" Rakhmatov sank into his overstuffed chair and rubbed his eyes in despair.

As dawn slid over western Russia on November 8, the billowing flames from Leningrad's center could be seen for miles. Thousands of Leningraders crowded down to the riverfront to gawk at the *Aleksei Dubrov* as if it were an alien spaceship. It was inconceivable that a vessel of that size could slip into the inner city, past all the security checks, and casually pound parts of the city to rubble, unless the military approved. It seemed to the city's population that there was a massive paralysis of will on the part of the government to deal with the cruiser and the Solidarity uprising.

By mid-morning, the crowds in the Zoological Park and

on the grounds of the old Peter and Paul Fortress reached a hundred thousand. The huge canvas on the bow, with *Aleksei Dubrov* painted on it, was clearly visible. From its stern flew the newly designed Solidarity ensign. One would have to look carefully to distinguish it from the Soviet flag. It was still the blood-red banner, but instead of the yellow hammer and sickle in the upper left-hand corner there was a new symbol: a sword thrusting upward through a circle of fallen, broken chains.

The phone on the bridge of the *Aleksei Dubrov* buzzed twice before Smedlev snapped it out of its cradle.

"Captain Suskov!" he exploded. "Just where in the hell have you been? We need you topside. Nobody's been able to find you since the shelling. Where were you?"

"Never mind, Smedlev." Suskov's voice sounded strangely distant over the phone from the missile room. "I want you to patch my phone into the external speaker system. I have a message for Krylenko."

"Captain. Just what do you think you're doing? Solidarity hasn't approved of—"

"The *hell* with Solidarity! I'm waging my own war now. Bandera has rigged the warhead down here to blow. We're taking out the city of Lenin if Krylenko doesn't meet *my* demands. *My* demands, Smedlev! In the name of my son, Boris, and the hundreds of thousands of other young soldiers killed in China, I'm holding the city of Lenin hostage with twenty megatons. That's twenty million tons of TNT, Smedlev."

"Captain, you're—you're insane!" his executive officer gasped. "You can't murder seven million people."

"I don't want the people, just the city." Suskov's voice was now tinged with madness. "I want the city completely evacuated in seventy-two hours."

Suskov's metallic voice boomed across the water to the throngs along the river.

"People of Leningrad. The Krylenko dictatorship has immersed the Motherland in an insane, immoral war of aggression against the Chinese people for several years. My own son was sent to his death in this stupid conflict because he was a Solidarity activist.

"My vessel, which we have renamed the *Aleksei Dubrov* after the first martyr to Lenin's tyranny . . ." a cautious burst of applause rippled through the crowds ". . . has fired the first shots of the Russian Revolution of 1992!" This time the applause was a thunderous ovation accompanied by loud cheers.

"We, the officers and men of the *Aleksei Dubrov*, demand an end to the war. We demand that Krylenko bring home the soldiers, sailors, and airmen." Suskov's voice was rising in tempo. "We want no more young Russian boys executed because they have chosen to resist tyranny!"

The tens of thousands of Leningraders were now cheering themselves hoarse at Suskov's demands.

"We have given the regime and the foreign parasites just a taste of our sting. Under the stern of this vessel, there is a missile with a twenty-megaton warhead. My dear Leningraders, that is twenty *million* tons of TNT. It will level the city and everything around it in a twenty-five-mile radius. If the Politburo does not meet our demands, we will detonate. We will destroy the city of Lenin. Everything will go!"

Suskov's voice now verged on hysteria.

"My dear Leningraders, I do not want to destroy *you*. It is the accursed city of Lenin I want. I want all of you out of the city—beyond the zone of destruction—in three days. If there is any attempt by the government to destroy this vessel or take us by assault, we will detonate.

"Remember, Krylenko: three days! Three days to end the China War and bring our boys home. You've murdered my son! You will not murder any more Russian boys. End the war and meet the demands of Solidarity. Start the evacuation now!"

There was a stunned silence across the river. For a moment nobody moved; and then, a few drifted away. Soon, some were running. In an hour the entire crowd along the riverfront had disappeared.

* * *

Unlike the massive KGB reaction of 1962, the government did not pour thousands of tactical troops into the Novocherkassk cauldron. It would have been too costly. When the workers rampaged and took over the city the KGB personnel were ordered out, but the Tenth Guards Regiment of the Red Army was ordered to remain. Not that it made any difference: a good number of the soldiers had already joined the rebels. The rest of the unit were confined to their barracks.

Novocherkassk had been a hotbed of Ukrainian nationalism for years. Located at the far end of the eastern Ukraine on the lower Volga, it had been wracked with disturbances since Lenin's reign and was now riddled with Solidarity cells. Novocherkassk was definitely not one of Krylenko's favorite cities, and Rakhmatov would turn fairly livid at the very mention of the dissident city.

It came as no surprise to the Politburo or the Central Committee when Rakhmatov announced that the rebels would be wiped off the face of the earth. Krylenko gave the KGB director complete authority to use any means necessary to deal with internal rebellion, since the Red Army was proving more and more unwilling and unreliable in dealing with domestic disturbances.

On the evening of November 4, a few days after the workers had taken over the center of the city, a special tactical unit of the KGB overpowered the sentries at the Rostov military aerodrome's nuclear-weapons repository and stole a ten-kiloton air-droppable bomb. It was a small and simple device compared to earlier weapons. It could be handled by two men easily, delivered to its target by a medium fighter-bomber, and dropped to airburst at any altitude.

The agreement made in 1963 between the KGB and the military was to be dramatically and tragically terminated.

The morning of November 9 dawned clear and cold in the eastern Ukraine. The usual smoky-gray of the city's atmosphere was gone because the great factory furnaces were unattended. Food was scarce, since all incoming transportation had been prevented from entering the city by the government.

By eight in the morning Novocherkassk's central square was packed with throngs of workers and their families waiting to receive news of the outside world from the militant leaders and to obtain emergency food rations. The Solidarity revolutionary leadership had been resorting to mass rallies like this morning's to keep the militant spirit from flagging.

At 8:47, a single Tupolev TU-22 medium bomber swooshed low over the city, climbed straight up into the sun, and turned in a tight arc.

The dense pack of humanity in the city's center paid little attention to the jet. State Security had been regularly monitoring the dissident city with reconnaissance flights since the rebellion. After two more passes, the TU-22 zoomed up to ten thousand feet and started to make its target run.

What looked like an oblong canister tumbled from the belly of the aircraft. At five thousand feet, a white parachute blossomed from the gun metal gray device.

The assembled masses noticed it now. Their reactions were mild. Leaflet canisters had been dropped before, showering them with appeals to abandon their struggle or be destroyed.

At one thousand feet, a white-hot artificial sun flashed in the sky. In that instant, the incandescent heat seared the life from over 120,000 bodies in a flash of pain.

A sixth of the population of Novocherkassk was calcined to black ash.

XXI.

"They're not firing on us, Yuri! What's happening? Why aren't they shooting?" Raisa shouted over the babble of noise around her.

"I—I don't know. Look! Two of them are heading toward the Krutitskoye Church!"

Yuri and Raisa watched in astonished disbelief as the assault helicopters hovered for a moment, lined up their rocket pods with their ground targets, and let their ordnance go with a deafening roar. A KGB barricade near the old church was blown to bits. The other M-18s systematically destroyed the vise of military force which the KGB had deployed around southern Moscow.

"They're with us!" Yuri's triumphant yell was unheard over the cheers of thousands. "The military's coming over! Gregierenko said this would happen."

The command helicopter dipped, then hovered over the street intersection where Yuri and Raisa were standing. The rotor blades slowed to a recognizable blur that whipped the street dust into a localized whirlwind. After landing, a Red Army major leaped to the pavement and trotted over to a knot of rebels. After a moment of animated conversation, he strode over to Yuri.

"Yuri Dubrov?" he asked.

On reflex, Yuri gave him a sharp salute.

"I'm Major Bychov, Sixth Guards Air Assault Battalion. Marshal Dcriabin ordered me to find you and take you both back with me." .

"Sir, you just shot up several State Security units. I don't want to ask a stupid question, but does this mean that the Red Army is coming over?" asked Yuri.

The major gave a slight chuckle. "Some of us have had our marching orders for over a week. We just had to be sure that you and your brother could do your part. This whole country is coming over, son. All it took was for Krylenko to do something *really* stupid. Novocherkassk did that. It's the KGB against all of us now. Nobody will ever forget Novocherkassk."

"Novocherkassk? In the Ukraine? What happened there?" Raisa's face was a mask of puzzlement.

"You haven't heard?" asked the major.

She shook her head.

"Novocherkassk rebelled. The people took over the city. Rahkmatov retaliated by dropping a nuclear weapon on the city's center during a mass rally. One hundred and twenty thousand people were burnt to a crisp—killed instantly. Thousands more are wounded and radiated."

Yuri and Raisa stared at the major, their mouths agape.

"Come," he said abruptly. "Into the helicopter. I'm taking you to Gregierenko."

"The rebellion is no longer confined to Moscow and Leningrad, comrades. The word about Novocherkassk is out all over the country. This is a revolution! State Security can't contain it anymore. We need the military," wailed Romanovich.

Krylenko rose from the T-shaped table in the Politburo meeting room, his face ashen and drawn. He seemed to have shrunk, physically, from the strains of the last ten terrible days. He scanned the vacant seats.

"Deriabin and Gorsky are gone. They cannot be found. Gorsky never did initiate negotiations with Solidarity, so the responsibility fell upon Bovsky. The military now controls the communications system and Solidarity is using it to coordinate the revolution all over the country. The satellite system is broadcasting our troubles to the world!"

"It's Gorsky!" thundered Rakhmatov. "I knew we never should have appointed him as the Minister of Communications when Spassinov died."

"Leningrad, Comrade Director. What do you intend to

do about the maniac in the cruiser up there? There's panic in the street. Chaos! People are starting to pour out of the city."

Rakhmatov shot to his feet, his gnarled finger jabbing the air.

"He's bluffing! It's already past his deadline and nothing's happened. This Suskov's bluffing and I'm going to call it. I'm going to discredit Solidarity so badly that it will collapse like a punctured balloon. A defeat of this magnitude will destroy it."

"How?" asked Krylenko.

"By forcing the population to stay in the city. Suskov won't kill seven million people. I'll count on that."

Krylenko sighed wearily. He was relieved to pass on the burden of oppression to the director of State Security. He seemed to be the only member of the government capable of action anymore.

"What about our negotiations with the rebels inside the Tomb?" asked Romanovich. "Have we conveyed the impression to the people that we're willing to go to any length to save Lenin?"

"We've been broadcasting bulletins every hour. We have created the illusion that Lenin is so dear to us that we will make extraordinary sacrifices, short of handing over the government to Solidarity," came Bovsky's cynical reply.

"That's exactly what they want us to do, comrades!" bellowed Rahkmatov. "Solidarity doesn't want concessions anymore—it wants capitulation! They want to sweep away the tide of history and consign Marxism-Leninism to the ash heap!" He was shaking uncontrollably now, the vein on his forehead pulsating markedly.

"They will *never* take over! If I have to repeat Novocherkassk a hundred times, Solidarity will never destroy communism in the Soviet Union. I'll show them at Leningrad. The City of Lenin will be the Stalingrad of this struggle!"

The highways leading to Leningrad were choked with the convoys of the KGB tactical units from all over western Russia. The major cities had been stripped of their State Security personnel to close the ring around Leningrad. It was at Leningrad that Solidarity would be defeated. The city of Lenin is where the Krylenko regime would concentrate its power. For the moment, Lenin's Tomb could wait. If Solidarity blew it up, then who could prove that Lenin's body was a counterfeit?

By November 14, news of the Solidarity uprising and the Novocherkassk slaughter had spread throughout the entire North China theater of operations. Chinese psychological-warfare loudspeakers lost no time in broadcasting their versions of the events to Soviet troops.

Corporal Yanov Baiduk of the 128th Motorized Rifle Regiment huddled in the long serpentine trench with hundreds of his comrades. It was nine in the morning, a time when the mist over the millet fields was being dissipated by the early rays of the sun. The desolate hills in front of him, the same hills that his unit had had to assault five times only to be thrown back with heavy casualties, now rang with the early-morning news broadcast. It was from the Chinese loudspeaker that Baiduk first learned of the Novocherkassk holocaust. Grim details of the bomb's effects were elaborated upon by the Chinese announcer.

The 128th was a unit composed primarily of Ukrainians and Crimean Tartars from the Novocherkassk Oblast. It was one of the minority units that the Krylenko regime had hurriedly created in order to decimate with suicidal attacks. Baiduk's platoon alone had suffered 43 percent casualties since their arrival in China.

"Yanov," whispered his trench-mate, "the Tartars said that over 120,000 people in your city were killed. Is that possible?"

Baiduk thought of the huge central square in Novocherkassk. As a youngster he had marched with thousands of others in May Day parades there.

"Yes, Alek. It's possible. The Tartars said that the bomb was dropped during a rally of some sort. The Square can easily hold that many."

"Your family, Yanov. Do you think that . . ."

"My family's flat is only three blocks from the center of the city. I fear the worst."

Three KGB political officers instead of the usual one had been assigned to the 128th. The 128th was considered politically unreliable—a high-risk unit. They were nervously pacing in front of the command bunker smoking cigarettes, as the Chinese loudspeaker blared the news. Finally, it stopped.

"Tartar lies! All filthy lies!" yelled one of the officers as he paced along the lip of the trench, haranguing the men. "State Security would never use nuclear weapons on our own people."

Vivid images of the devastation of his home city ravaged Yanov's mind. He could visualize the charred heaps of bodies in the central square. He imagined the horribly seared bodies of his parents and little Tanya, his eleven-year-old sister, screaming and writhing in agony from their burns. He squeezed his eyes tightly shut to blot out the vision, but it wouldn't go away. The hated voice of the haranguing political officer kept pounding in his ears until he couldn't stand it any longer.

Yanov leaped to the edge of the trench with a shriek and leveled his rifle at the KGB man. For a moment they just stared at each other, then the officer reached for his pistol. Baiduk's rifle stuttered, then swung toward the command bunker. Another burst and the other two KGB officers spun to the ground.

The commanding officer raced out of his bunker and stared at the carnage. Baiduk stalked toward him, his rifle poised for firing. His commander shrank back and did nothing as he walked by him and then turned to his comrades in the trench.

"I'm going home! I'm going back to what's left of my city. If I have to walk all the way, I'm going back to Novocherkassk. The enemy is there!" He jabbed a finger to the west. "In the Kremlin, not in front of us."

Another soldier leaped to the lip of the trench and followed, dragging his rifle in the dust. Soon another got up and left; then, whole groups were stumbling westward after Baiduk.

In less than twenty minutes, the entire regiment, or what was left of it, had left their trenches and were walking away from the China War.

The impact was electric. By mid-day, word of the 128th's desertion had spread throughout the entire North China front. Political officers of other units suddenly became targets and were murdered by their troops. The 429th Motorized Infantry Battalion left their positions en masse, led by their commanding officer.

As dawn broke over the Soviet lines the next morning, the sun slanted down on miles of empty trenches and bunkers. The Soviet North China Expeditionary Force was going home.

The Chinese did not attack or pursue them.

Squadron Commander Major Stefan Yetsenko banked his MIG-28 sharply to the left to get a better view of the scene below. Fleecy billows of cumulus clouds obstructed his vision. The white of the clouds seemed to merge with the newly fallen snow, the season's first.

His orders were explicit enough: A Soviet unit had deserted. Use your squadron of nine aircraft to force them back into the trenches. Strafe, napalm, or rocket in front of them. Kill some if you have to, but force them back.

As Yetsenko burst out of the sky, he wasn't prepared for the awesome sight below. The plains of North China looked like a huge field of white covered by tens of thousands of mud-colored rodents groping their way westward. He swooped low, making several passes over the deserting soldiers. Only a few fatigued and haunted eyes glanced skyward. The men were too tired to care anymore. Most of them knew that it was only a matter of time before their own aircraft would be ordered to destroy them. If the Krylenko regime could obliterate a Soviet city with a nuclear weapon, what would prevent them from destroying a deserting army with conventional weapons?

"I can't do it! I won't do it!" crackled the radio in Yetsenko's cockpit. "My brother's probably down there among them."

Another pilot broke in. "Major, the whole damned

Expeditionary Force is down there. This is like World War One and the Revolution. Can't you see that? They just got up and walked away. The war has collapsed. It's over, Major."

Yetsenko swallowed, knowing that his next statement would be an act of treason.

"Then are you in favor of—of flying support for them? It means our ass if we do. We'll be one of them. We'll be considered deserters."

"Affirmative!" an enthusiastic voice crackled over the radio. "Affirmative!" the others agreed.

The nine fighters came in low in a tight formation only a few hundred feet from the ground, thundering over the ragged hordes. They waggled their wings, an age-old sign of support and friendship among airmen.

Yetsenko could almost hear the roar of cheers over his engines. He saw thousands of hats and helmets fly into the air as the relieved and jubilant soldiers shouted themselves hoarse.

Steve McMurrin had heard of the collapse of the North China front but wasn't taking any chances. Unless he had absolute confirmation, he would consider any Soviet military unit to be the enemy.

The SAL commander slithered across the slick pine needles to the edge of the forested ridge overlooking the main track of the Baikal–Amur railroad line just inside the Soviet border. He focused the adjusting knob on his binoculars and peered down into the broad valley.

"Well I'll be dipped in shee-it!" he marveled in his New Mexico drawl. Members of his staff wriggled forward and peered below. The scene which confronted them was proof enough. The Soviet Expeditionary Force had crossed into their own country and was heading home.

A half-dozen long troop trains were strung along the double tracks in the valley, end to end. There were soldiers everywhere—inside, hanging from the outside, and clustered on top of the cars. Flanking the railroad, the highway was choked with vehicles of all types filled with men and equipment. And there were those who walked:

Thousands, tens of thousands, plodded wearily westward. Periodically, large transport planes would land in open fields, swallow up a few hundred men, and fly into the sunset. Overhead, helicopters and fighter aircraft flew cover as supply planes dropped food and water at selected points along the way. The mass desertion now had a semblance of order and organization. It had the look of an army reinvading its homeland.

The hammer-and-sickle battle flags had disappeared, replaced by the sword-and-broken-chain ensign of Solidarity.

McMurrin nudged Nguyen Tranh with his elbow.

"Didja ever think it would come to this when we knifed those Yakuts with reindeer bones last May, old buddy? We're going to Moscow, Nguyen! I wanna be in Red Square, or whatever Solidarity's gonna call it, when the shit hits the fan. C'mon. Let's find out who's leading that pack down there and join 'em."

Vasily Gregierenko looked over the final copy of the *Novy Rodina.* It was professionally done, since it was printed in the newly liberated facilities of *Novy Mir,* a well-known news magazine.

The *Novy Rodina* in Gregierenko's hands told the rest of the Dubrov story and included pictures of Yossef and Yuri. The full story of Lenin's death, embalming, and entombment was the feature article. The final chapters of the Makleff journal were also included. After this issue hit the streets, followed up by nationwide broadcasts, the entire nation would know that the body of Lenin was a counterfeit and always had been.

"You realize that this will seal the fate of Yossef and those in the Tomb," announced an anxious Yabin. "When this hits, Krylenko and Rakhmatov will have nothing to lose. They'll make their assault and kill everybody."

Yuri nervously paced the floor. "Why in the *hell* doesn't General Deriabin commit the armed forces? Why doesn't he just make a broadcast calling for the military to support the revolution? Only a few units are actually helping us."

"Ah, Yuri." Gregierenko's hand fell patronizingly on his shoulder. "It's just not that easy to defect. You, of all people, should know that. Marshal Deriabin has devoted his life to serving his country and the Party. He's taken an oath to defend the Motherland. In spite of what he knows to be right, it's difficult for him to go public with his feelings right now. Be patient with him. He'll do the right thing. We have to have faith in him."

"And while he's writhing in moral agony over this, my brother's going to be slaughtered. No, damn it! When this issue hits the streets, I'm going to hit that tactical force surrounding the Tomb. I can round up enough people to do it *my* way. There's enough of us."

"Rifles and paving stones against tanks, Yuri? The KGB has Red Square completely sealed off. The entire downtown section is fortified. State Security left the outer perimeter and the suburbs to us, but they control the Square, the Kremlin, and the Center," said Gregierenko.

Raisa was crumpled on the floor in the corner of the room, utterly exhausted. She rubbed her upper eyelids, trying to control her pounding headache. Fear washed over her as she thought of Yuri trying to storm the KGB force in Red Square to rescue Yossef. She had been dreading the choice she would have to make between the twins after the revolution. Now she was confronted with having *no* choice to make if they both were killed. A life without either one of them was unthinkable.

She glanced up at Vasily with tired red eyes. Would she have to settle for the Solidarity leader? Never, she told herself. Not after experiencing the tender love of Yuri and Yossef. A wave of desire rippled through her loins as she thought of her lovemaking with Yossef. It was followed by another feeling—a wave of guilt as she thought of Yuri and what they had been through in the past few days.

Would the future history books of a new, democratic Russia admit that one Yuri Dubrov had ignited the revolution because his girlfriend was molested by a militiaman? There was no doubt that the Southernport area had burst into flames because of Yuri's action in the grocery queue.

For hours they had fought at the barricades as revolutionaries, and Yuri was magnificent. Wherever he went he mobilized people into effective and cohesive fighting units. The name of Dubrov was magic to the street rebels, and surely, the name of Yuri Dubrov would be enshrined in the new nation's history as one of the founding fathers.

But it was Yossef, the foreigner, the Israeli who consciously and premeditatively imprisoned himself in that hideous Tomb in order to save his own country and liberate mine, Raisa thought: she loved him as much for that as—for other things. If the revolution succeeded, and both of the twins survived, would Yossef want to go back to Israel or stay in the new Russia and become part of its history? When she made her choice—and it was inevitable—would it destroy the newfound and beautiful relationship the brothers had developed?

Raisa heaved a weary sigh, leaned her head against her rifle, and dozed off to sleep.

The deadline announced by Suskov had been extended several times, thanks to the efforts of Smedlev and other Solidarity crewmen who assured him that the China front was on the verge of collapse and that the war was as good as over.

Suskov and Bandera remained, however, in their self-imprisonment, paranoid and suspicious of everybody. They might have extended their deadline, but they weren't coming out. Not yet.

By November 16 the KGB was forging a ring of steel around Leningrad. Many who had fled were forced back over the bridges and into the city. Tanks and machine-gun emplacements were positioned in strategic locations, preventing escape.

Suskov and Bandera listened to the special KGB frequency on the missile-room radio as orders were given to units to deploy around Leningrad. Another government radio station, controlled by State Security, was making false announcements about a new Soviet offensive in North China.

Suskov seethed with a silent rage as he listened. Smedlev and the others had lied! The China War was still going on and the KGB had sealed off the city. He and Bandera had been betrayed!

The phone on the bridge buzzed. Smedlev snapped it up.

"Smedlev? Suskov. Patch me into the external speaker system and the government radio net. Do it now!"

"Captain—what—why—we agreed to . . ."

"Silence!" Suskov roared over the phone. "You betrayed me. You've all betrayed me!" His voice tremored with anger. "The war is still going on. They launched a new assault. Now Krylenko has twenty-four hours. Twenty-four hours, Smedlev! I'm starting the countdown right now!"

"Captain, I heard the broadcast. It's a KGB trick, I assure you."

"Now, Smedlev, now. Patch me in, or so help me God I'll blow us all off the face of the map this instant!"

The executive officer sighed in defeat and gave the order. In five minutes, the metallic voice of Suskov boomed over the water and crackled over the airwaves.

The pandemonium in Leningrad was unlike anything that anybody could remember since the siege of Leningrad during the Great Patriotic War. People, whole families, poured into the streets and took whatever transportation they could to reach the exit roads and bridges.

The KGB massacre of the city's inhabitants began at the Okhten Bridge over the Neva, one of the main exits to the south. Machine guns swept the structure from the opposite bank, killing hundreds. The mass of humanity kept coming, scrambling over the piles of dead into the machine-gun fire. Some were trying to work their way over the girders, only to be picked off by KGB snipers. Many jumped into the river and swam for shore. KGB soldiers lined the banks and casually shot their countrymen as they struggled in the water. A section of the Neva, from the Liteyniy bridge near the Summer Palace to below the Monastery of Alexander Nevsky, was choked with the bullet-riddled bodies of thousands of Leningraders.

"Captain Suskov!" Smedlev yelled into the phone. "The KGB is slaughtering the people! Can't you see what they've made you do? You've panicked the city into fleeing, and State Security is shooting them down like dogs. The people are blaming us, Captain. Solidarity is being discredited. You've got to call off the countdown."

Even Bandera was convinced by now. He pleaded with Suskov to end the panic. The cruiser captain just sat and brooded, his handsome face clouded with indecision.

Bandera lunged for the two firing keys and yanked them out of the circuit panel. To his surprise, Suskov did not fight for them. He just sat, lost in his own thoughts.

Gently, as one would talk to a troubled child, Bandera coaxed the captain up the ladder. Suskov's expression was strangely passive. His mind had lapsed into a paralyzed indifference.

"Come on, Captain. Let's go out on deck, into the fresh air and sunshine. We'll both feel better."

Tears of fury coursed down Pavel Spinnenko's broad peasant face as his helicopter clattered up the length of the Neva. The river was red with the blood of thousands. The shooting was still going on. The KGB was now firing over the river onto the Tavricheskiy Palace grounds, where huge throngs had congregated in confusion and fear.

General Spinnenko shouted into the microphone he held in a sweating hand.

"Border Guards One. Border Guards One. Get me Marshal Deriabin's headquarters." Soon, the tobacco-wracked voice of the Minister of Defense crackled over Spinnenko's headphones.

"Marshal Deriabin! State Security is destroying the population of Leningrad! There—there are bodies everywhere. The Neva's red with the blood—literally red, Marshal, with the blood of our fellow Russians. From up here, it's a scene right out of hell! Krylenko and Rakhmatov have gone mad! Marshal, declare the armed forces for the revolution. Go on radio and TV, I beg you! Gorsky has everything in readiness. Marshal Deriabin, I beg you in the name of God, declare for the revolution!"

In his command trailer at Novgorod, the Minister of Defense sat slumped in his chair, a half-smoked cigarette dribbling ashes on the carpet. He had never done anything in the name of God before. It was always done in the name of the Party and the State—the same organizations which were now killing thousands of his countrymen. He sat apathetically before the radio console as Spinnenko's pleas poured from the speaker.

Deriabin's world was collapsing. The military effort in China had crumbled. Soviet soldiers were now streaming home from Afghanistan and Eastern Europe. He knew that if he didn't act now and order the armed forces to support Solidarity, another would do it for him. If he didn't declare for the revolution, he would have no future in the new Russia that would emerge from the ashes of the one now being destroyed.

But it was one thing to commit a few units to help the Moscow rebels. It was another thing to go public and commit the entire military to a nationwide revolution. He had taken an oath to the Marxist-Leninist system. One does not sweep away sixty-four years of conditioning in one day. He'd have to think about Spinnenko's request. He'd declare for the revolution when the time was right.

He switched off the radio, cutting off Pavel Spinnenko's pleas in midsentence, and reached for the bottle of Armenian brandy on the lamp table.

XXII.

It was November 21, and a curious silence had settled over Moscow. The sky was heavy and leaden and threatened the season's first snow.

It was expected by many in the Solidarity organization that the streets would be full of angry Muscovites after the city's population had been exposed to the latest *Novy Rodina,* but the streets were empty except for those manning the rebel barricades.

Leningrad, too, was quiet. Smedlev had called off the countdown and the panicked population had returned to their homes. The dead remained where they were, floating in the Neva or heaped on the bridges. Fortunately, the chill temperature of late November prevented the thousands of corpses from putrefying too rapidly.

Inside the mausoleum, the tension had reached pressure-cooker intensity. All communication had been cut off. Major Koslovonov's tactical force still surrounded the tomb. On the outside wall, nine more bodies hung beside the Bulgarian's.

Vasily Gregierenko was perplexed. He had been sure that the Moscow crowds would rush into the streets after the discovery that Lenin was a phony. He had been certain that Rakhmatov would launch a final assault on the Tomb to destroy the evidence. But these things hadn't happened.

It was the military, Gregierenko conjectured. Both sides were afraid to commit themselves to a definite course of action until some authority figure declared the armed forces for or against the revolution. That was the Soviet way—the result of over seventy years of conditioning. Unless somebody in authority, Deriabin preferably, committed the military, the forward momentum of the Solidarity revolution would grind to a halt.

Pavel Spinnenko sat huddled in his uniform greatcoat in the rear seat of his Zil staff car. He stubbed out his papirosa in the ashtray, opened the door, and stepped into the chilly night. Assembled in the tree-ringed clearing on the edge of the northwestern city of Novgorod were eighty-eight Border Guard commandos, their camouflage-painted faces barely visible in the dull light of the half-moon. The steam from their breath rose like a white vapor as the general gave them their final orders. But the general's words were really a pep talk; they knew their mission by heart.

A salute, a wave of Spinnenko's hand, and the small commando group disappeared into the woods.

It was a desperate gamble, but the general was sure of success. Although nominally under the control of the KGB, the Border Guards by 1992 were associated in the public mind with the military. It was the Border Guards who'd absorbed most of the initial combat in China. Through a series of shrewd political moves, Spinnenko had elevated the Guards to full military status and now reported directly to the Minister of Defense in all but a few police matters. In deference to the Guards' combat role, the Politburo had made Pavel Spinnenko a Deputy Minister of Defense.

In three hours it was all over. It was a bloodless operation. The commandos could have casually walked into Marshal Deriabin's command complex and taken over, since here, as well as in other areas of the military, all discipline had broken down. Overwhelmed by the determined show of force by the fierce-looking commandos, Deriabin's headquarters staff meekly raised their hands in surrender, many in apparent relief.

A hurried radio message was flashed. Ten minutes later, Spinnenko's black Zil roared into the Novgorod command center. The general burst into Deriabin's trailer and found the Minister of Defense snoring soundly on the couch in a drunken stupor. Three bottles of Armenian brandy littered the floor.

Spinnenko sighed, a tired little smile tugging at the corners of his lips, and sat before the large radio console. A technician made some necessary adjustments and nodded to the general.

"Before I begin, Sergeant, did you make a final check with Sergei Gorsky, the Minister of Communications?"

"Just as you ordered, sir," responded the commando-technician. "He assured me that your broadcast will be received by every army unit down to batallion level through the national command network. Equivalent commands in the navy and air force will also receive your message. The advance elements of the Solidarity Army of Liberation are . . ."

"This American McMurrin's group?"

"Sir. The entire North China Expeditionary Force now goes by that name. The American group is only part of it. They've established an advance base at Penza."

"That's only 250 kilometers from here!" exclaimed Spinnenko in surprise.

"Yes, sir. They're flying in men by the thousands. The entire Air Transport Command is being utilized in bringing them west."

A warm glow of satisfaction spread through the general. He hadn't counted on a force as large or important as the SAL being within striking distance of the capital.

The long hand on the clock over the radio console inched toward the six. A red warning light flashed. Spinnenko gulped half a glass of mineral water and loosened his collar. At 4:30 A.M. a green light went on.

Soon, the general's husky voice was filling the airwaves throughout the Soviet Union.

"Vasily, I can't find Yuri! He's gone!" Raisa panted as she burst dramatically into the Solidarity command center on Rutiniskaya street.

"Damn!" Gregierenko banged both fists on the small table in front of him, scattering sheets of paper all over the floor. "He's been pacing around like a nervous lion ever since the last *Novy Rodina* came out. When he heard his uncle's voice on the radio he stalked out of the building without saying a word. Now—I'm afraid he's heading for Red Square. We've got to stop him."

"He won't get very far. The KGB has barricades surrounding the Square. Yuri might be desperate, but he's not suicidal. Has anything happened since Pavel appealed to the military?"

Gregierenko's face brightened into a broad grin.

"Yes, little swallow. Unit after unit has declared for the revolution. The Baltic Fleet is officially with us now. Here is a list of the cities where the military have taken over and are with us."

Raisa stared at the computer printout in amazement. Seventy-four large metropolitan areas in every one of the country's military districts had committed themselves for Solidarity.

"Surely, Krylenko and Rakhmatov must see the handwriting on the wall," offered Yabin. "I wonder what they're doing right now?"

"Probably planning to execute Operation Barabinsk," Gregierenko answered.

"Barabinsk?" Yabin frowned.

"Their contingency escape plan. Very secret." Gregierenko laughed. "But we've known about it for weeks. I'd like to see the looks on their faces when they discover that all of their escape routes have been cut off."

The KGB forces surrounding Leningrad were totally unprepared for the ferocity of the assault. Spinnenko's Border Guards launched a surprise attack against their rear while the Kronstadt-based naval infantry slipped across the Neva in inflatable boats and completed the annihilation. On November 22, the siege had been lifted and the jubilant population poured into the inner city as the Border Guard-Naval Infantry forces rolled down Kirovsky Prospekt. The city's air-defense command formed an aerial protective umbrella over the city in case Rakhmatov attempted to repeat Novocherkassk.

Vaclav Suskov stood on the bridge, a prickle of apprehension needling the base of his skull as the hordes of Leningraders poured onto the deck of the *Aleksei Dubrov*. The sailors were swept off their feet and embraced by the grateful visitors.

Lieutenant Smedlev joined Suskov. He knew what the captain was feeling: guilt and anxiety.

"Captain." He clapped his hand on his shoulder. "General Pavel Spinnenko was able to take over the military because of what State Security did here, and *you*, more than anybody or anything else, created the situation which showed up the KGB for what it really is. If it weren't for you, we might still be waiting for the armed forces to swing over."

"Do—do you really believe that?" Suskov asked timidly.

"Yes sir, I do," Smedlev answered patronizingly. "The inhumanity of the KGB far overshadowed your threats. The revolution will succeed because of your actions."

Suskov breathed a shaky, but relieved, breath and stood a little taller.

Yuri knew that a direct attack on the mausoleum would be impossible. He peered around the corner of the Moscow Art Theater and spied the formidable State Security barricade at the point where Gorky Street entered Red Square. Pressure from the Solidarity revolutionaries, now reinforced by defecting military units, had pushed the KGB from the Inner Boulevard Ring to a triangular-shaped defensive position—from the Kremlin to the Maly Theater, and from there to the Rossiya Hotel. The Moscow River served as the base of the triangle and as its defensive moat. The three bridges leading from the Zamoskvorechivo sector to the triangle were covered by heavy machine guns.

"Yuri! Yuri!" He turned when he heard Raisa's voice. A machine gun stitched a dead-straight line of little concrete explosions on the wall above him.

"Raisa! Get back!" he shouted fearfully, inching his way along the building until he was out of range.

Raisa hugged him tightly and kissed him fully on the mouth. Yabin and Gregierenko were nearby, huddled over a radio transmitter. The Solidarity leader was barking out orders to the several rebel units which were closing in on the Square.

"Vasily. What's the situation?" asked Yuri.

"The city is ours except for the inner core. That's KGB. It's just a matter of time. We've been monitoring the Kremlin Command Center. They're sending contradictory orders to Koslovonov. He was ordered to attack two hours ago. The order was rescinded, but now he's been ordered to storm the Tomb. I don't think Krylenko knows what he wants to do."

At that moment, a swarm of jet fighters swooped down over the city. They were Russian, but the red star on their wings was gone—replaced by the Solidarity ensign. The skies over Moscow belonged to the revolution.

The rumble of tanks was heard. The roar of their throbbing diesels filled the inner city. Raisa and Yuri stared at the steel formation rolling five abreast down Gorky Street. The armored column extended at least a mile and a half down the boulevard. Soldiers of all descriptions clustered on the turrets and hung from the chassis. Sitting on the forward slope of the lead tank was a tall, lanky, freckled American accompanied by several Vietnamese. Steve McMurrin had arrived in Moscow to savor the end of the Leninist regime.

When the news of the Gorky Street armored column swept through the city, the population poured into the streets. Statues of Lenin were pulled off their pedestals and pounded to pieces with sledgehammers. The posters and pictures which adorned every building were tossed into the street and torched. The Lenin Museum was looted, its contents piled at a street intersection and turned into a gigantic bonfire. After seventy years of serving as the state deity, Lenin was rapidly becoming a nonperson—a familiar enough process in the Soviet Union.

Major Koslovonov listened grimly to the new orders being transmitted by the Kremlin Command Center: Attack and destroy the Tomb even if it means obliterating

Comrade Lenin. Tears filled his eyes as they fixed on the hammer-and-sickle national ensign fluttering from the standard atop Spasskaya Tower. It was all over and he knew it. His little force and the State Security troops defending the Inner Ring were all that was left of the Krylenko regime. Even now, Dzerzhinsky Square was being attacked. An SAL tank had shot the statue of old Feliks right off its base. The Center was empty of all KGB personnel and fires were raging all over the buildings. The Registry and Archives section was completely gutted, destroying decades of painstaking secret police work.

Koslovonov gazed wearily at the mausoleum. The ten bodies hanging there had putrefied and bloated grotesquely, a constant reminder of the fanatic dedication of the rebels inside.

The Kremlin Guards commander did not want to destroy the Tomb and the body of Lenin. He had dedicated years of service to protecting the mausoleum. He just couldn't blast it to rubble so quickly and so casually. He must call the command center again and get absolute confirmation.

Before he could make up his mind, five M-18 assault helicopters clattered over the Square, hovered briefly, and bracketed Koslovonov's little army with rockets and machine-gun fire.

The M-18s then flew along the KGB's perimeter and systematically destroyed their defensive barricades.

The flood of tanks, soldiers, and armed civilians crashed into Red Square like a tidal wave bursting through the dikes of a levee. Sporadic but ineffective gunfire blazed down on the rampaging masses from the battlements in the Kremlin walls, but the Krylenko soldiers were quickly gunned down by SAL tank gunners. Shortly after, the first of Solidarity's tanks burst through the Spasskaya Tower gate and into the Kremlin courtyard.

The mausoleum was not quite soundproof. The muffled sound of gunfire could be barely heard inside. Platonov's face was creased with weary desperation as he glanced nervously at Yossef. Yossef was lost in his own thoughts;

he cradled his rifle in the crook of his arm and stared at the black marble doors facing Spasskaya Tower. He stroked his two-week-old growth of beard and yearned for a cigarette. After the seizure of the Tomb on November 6 he'd confiscated every cigarette he could find on the hostages and indulged in an orgy of smoking. He'd puffed the last one to a glowing stub three days before.

It would just be a matter of time, perhaps minutes, he thought, before those black marble doors were blown open and the tactical force stormed in. Well, he'd take as many as he could of the sons of bitches with him, he grimly decided, before he'd push the detonating plunger and blow the tomb to rubble.

His last thoughts would be of Raisa. Yes, he loved her and, if things had turned out differently, he would have married her. Yuri would just have had to accept it, that's all.

"What's taking them so long? Why don't they blow the doors?" Yossef asked, beads of cold sweat trickling down his neck.

"Don't know. Don't know," countered a tired, irritable Platonov. "Yossef," he snapped, "forget about killing them with your rifle. Get over here. Behind Lenin. Let as many come in as possible before you detonate. You'll kill more. You'll go faster too."

Yossef moved and crouched behind the casket. The dead, counterfeit face of Lenin seemed to leer at him as he peered over the protective glass toward the doors. Perhaps you'll have the last laugh after all, you little prick, Yossef thought as he waited for the KGB onslaught.

Twenty minutes slid by. Nothing. No explosion. Silence. The muffled rumble of guns was stilled.

"Damn them! Where are they?" Yossef panted hoarsely, the sweat stinging his eyes.

The slight tapping noise came from the metal hatch. It followed a definite pattern. It was a signal.

The militants looked at each other with a variety of expressions: fear, confusion, hope.

Yossef raced up the ladder to the circular wheel. "It's

Solidarity!" he shouted triumphantly. "They've reached the Tomb! That's Yuri's signal!"

"No, Yossef, no! It could be a trap! Don't open it!" screamed Platonov.

"Zhores. Keep your hand on the plunger. If they break in, blow us to hell, but I can't stand another minute in this accursed place. I'm taking my chances!"

With one hand Yossef aimed his rifle toward the hatch while he slowly turned the lock wheel with the other. It was an awkward and laborious process—he had to hold on to the ladder with his knees—but he was determined to blast the first hostile face he saw.

The tapping stopped as the wheel started to turn and the lock clicked open. Yossef breathed deeply and shoved against the heavy cover, half expecting hand grenades to be tossed through the opening.

As it cracked open and the chill sunlight probed in, several pairs of fingers eagerly inserted themselves under the hatch and flung it back.

Yossef stared upward into the jubilant faces of Yuri and Yabin.

Yossef wasn't prepared for the awesome spectacle. He stumbled, blinking in the bright sunshine, across the reviewing platform. Red Square—soon to be renamed Solidarity Square—was a sea of hundreds of thousands of faces. As the twins approached the wall, a thunderous ovation greeted them. Armored and military vehicles of all types filled the square. Soldiers wearing a variety of uniforms, Chinese prisoners of war, ex-convicts from the Gulag and the pipeline, Vietnamese and Americans, stood on tank turrets, waving Solidarity banners.

It was a global media event; Sergei Gorsky had seen to that. Dozens of television cameras were trained on the Tomb. The name LENIN had already been obliterated from the red granite structure. Another name would soon replace it. Already, the satellite hookup was beaming this, the continuation of the democratic March 1917 Revolution, into hundreds of millions of homes around the globe.

It started as a faint cry from the vicinity of the GUM

department store and soon became a rhythmic chant. The chant was repeated by the thousands in the square.

DU-BROV, DU-BROV, DU-BROV, DU-BROV, DU-BROV.

Yuri and Yossef clasped their hands and raised them in a victory salute. The crowds were now wild with jubilation. Out of the corner of his eye, Yossef could see Gregierenko mounting the stairs and walking toward the platform with Raisa by his side.

He wanted to let go of his brother's upraised hand and run to her, smother her with kisses, and tell her how much he loved her; but Yuri clasped his hand a little tighter as if he could read his intentions.

A new chant roared from the sea of revolutionaries.

"We want Lenin! We want Lenin! We want Lenin!"

"Throw us the phony chort-eating pig-prick!" yelled a bearded ex-convict from the pipeline, still dressed in his prison garb.

The twins gave each other uneasy glances and then descended into the mausoleum. Yuri stood before the protective glass and raised his rifle. He started to swing downward but stopped in midair.

"Yossef, I—I can't do it. I promise you that I can do everything else but—but not this."

"I understand." Yossef gave him a sympathetic smile.

Yossef blinked numbly into the dummy's face. It *was* only a dummy, wasn't it? That's what the Makleff journal said it was. Wasn't that what Yuri had seen on the Tomb train?

Yossef closed his eyes and remembered in vivid detail the fantasy he'd had in January on the slopes of Mount Ramon. Now, his fantasy was about to come true. It was incredible, he thought: An hour ago he was ready to blow himself up in defeat. Two weeks ago he'd entered the tomb with a fierce determination to follow his family into oblivion. Now, hundreds of thousands were chanting his name. And his own country, a thousand miles away, had been saved: When the Arab nations learned of Solidarity's victories, they withdrew their armies in anger and humiliation.

Yossef raised his rifle above his head, prayed aloud in

Hebrew, and smashed the butt into the crystal glass, shattering it completely. Yuri recoiled as if a bomb had exploded in his face.

No pungent odor escaped like a hissing green gas; only the faint aroma of musty fabric.

Cautiously, as if handling something dread and diseased, Yuri felt the face. It was cold and hard. He scraped the cheek with his fingernail. Nothing peeled off. What did he expect, he wondered: wax underneath his nail like wax from a candle? What if the body *was* real? he asked himself. Feelings of guilt flooded him as he lifted the lower hinged covering. The body was complete. There were legs and feet, in spite of rumors that only the torso existed.

Yossef took the body by the shoulders as Yuri grabbed the feet, and together they lifted it out of the casket. It wasn't as heavy as a body should be, but it was heavy enough. They hauled it out the door and up the side steps to the platform. Yossef unceremoniously rolled the dummy over with his foot so that it was face down. In one deft movement he plunged his bayonet between the shoulder blades and twisted viciously. Then, as Yuri watched in horrified fascination, he stuck his finger into the hole his weapon had made.

"Ouch! Damn it to hell!" Yossef withdrew his slightly bleeding finger and sucked it. "Real corpses don't have wire or whatever the hell is in there. He's hollow, dear brother."

"Why, you scummy little bastard!" Yuri shouted as he thrust his bayonet into the dummy's buttocks. Together, they lifted it on their bayonets and walked to the reviewing-platform wall. Suddenly, the vast crowds were hushed as they gaped at the national icon held aloft on the points of the Dubrov twins' bayonets. Ripples of apprehension coursed through the Square as the thousands of silent Russians, uncomprehending, stared at the grotesque scene.

"Well? Do you want him, or don't you?" bellowed Yossef. His voice boomed across the Square almost to the GUM department store.

The bearded ex-pipeline prisoner at the base of the

Tomb screamed, "I want him! Throw the little shit over here!" Others took up the cry and soon thousands were clamoring for Lenin.

The twins cocked their arms, and, with a mighty heave, threw the dummy down to the crowd. As it left the points of their bayonets, it sailed in a wide arc and landed in the prisoner's arms. He laughed and danced obscenely with it. Then it was passed—hand over hand—over the heads of the crowd. Some posed with it while others took pictures. One man simulated sex with the phony Lenin.

"Burn him!" someone suggested.

In minutes, the body was propped up against a concrete lamppost. Boards, papers, and other combustibles were stacked around the dummy. The makeshift pyre was soaked with gasoline and someone in the crowd tossed a match onto it.

"Get the cameras over here! Quickly!" shouted Gorsky. "I want the world to see this!"

The wonder of satellite communication made it possible for over three-fourths of the planet's population to watch the end of an era, and the beginning of a new one. A quarter of a billion television screens around the world showed the flames engulfing the body of what everybody outside of Russia thought to be the actual remains of Vladimir Lenin.

The flames licked the trousers, then the black suit coat, and soon the red tie flared up. To the horrified amazement of a world audience, the wax and acrylic skin ignited dramatically. The face began to melt and sag like a scene from a cheap horror movie. The glass eyes fell out of their sockets and rolled around on the cobblestones. The rest of the body flared in a series of miniature splattering explosions. The clothes burned off rapidly now, exposing the waxy, melting skin underneath. Bluish-yellow flames sputtered from the sagging acrylic and fell off in little black puffballs.

Soon, only a chromium skeletal frame surrounded by something like chicken wire remained. Teetering grotesquely on top of the frame was the actual skull of Lenin. It fell to the cobblestones with a clatter, rolled around, and lodged beneath a tank tread. The tank's engine roared into life and lurched forward, then backward, grinding the skull to fragments.

Yossef and Yuri watched the spectacle with a sense of morbid pleasure. Operation Samson had succeeded beyond their wildest imaginings, and the revenge of their parents and grandparents was almost complete.

Raisa nudged her body in between theirs and slipped her arms in theirs. Yossef and Yuri shot each other nervous glances, then turned away and resumed watching the smoldering remains of the Lenin dummy.

Gregierenko paced back and forth on the reviewing stand waiting for some news of the Kremlin battle. The shooting was still going on, and he was ordered by the Revolutionary Council to stay put until the fighting stopped. Most of the Kremlin Guard had melted away when the frighteningly huge crowds burst into Red Square and stampeded toward the Kremlin gates. There had been only a few fanatical diehards, but the Solidarity revolutionaries believed that they had mopped up all of them.

A Solidarity officer rushed up to Gregierenko and whispered excitedly in his ear.

"Yuri! Yossef! Come with me. You too, Raisa. Yabin, you also. I want you all to see this."

Without any explanation, the Solidarity leader led them through the Spasskaya Tower gate, across the broad expanse of macadam, past the Supreme Soviet, and toward the Upper Arsenal Building. It was the same route, Yuri thought to himself, that he had taken when he reported to Krylenko and Blinov last March.

In front of the Cathedral of the Archangel, a Border Guards Command helicopter had just landed: its rotors still spun slightly. The familiar figure of Pavel Spinnenko strode over to meet them. The general threw his arms around Yuri, engulfing him in a crushing bear hug.

"Pavel. Come with us," said Gregierenko. "I want you to burn this scene into your memory."

They entered the Upper Arsenal Building and cautiously climbed the stairs, which were scattered with spent cartridges. This was where the last battle to save the Krylenko regime had taken place. Bodies of Kremlin Guards littered the hallways. Yuri shuddered slightly. If it hadn't been for Minusinsk and Solidarity, his body would have been one of those scattered through the Kremlin.

Yuri recognized the door to Krylenko's office—the same one he'd had to wait outside for his appointment. Propped up against the wall, his body riddled with bullets, was one of the guards who had escorted him to this building last March.

Krylenko's office was empty. Piles of documents still smoldered in the fireplace.

"In here," Gregierenko commanded as he opened the door to the Politburo meeting room.

The first thing that Yuri noticed upon entering was the bloodied head of Igor Krylenko slumped on top of the green T-shaped table. His hand was extended in front of him, still clutching the small automatic pistol he had used to blow his brains out.

Rakhmatov's head was thrown back, a teeth-baring grimace clutching his lips. His brain matter was spattered on the wall behind him. His pistol had fallen on the Oriental carpet.

The remaining members of the Politburo were seated to each side of the Premier and the Director of State Security . . . each dead by his own hand.

XXIII.

The twins were awakened by a sound totally unfamiliar in Moscow. Yossef pulled his pillow over his head, but Yuri sprang to the double casement window in their Kremlin apartment and flung open both louvers.

"Listen, Yossef. Isn't that beautiful?"

Yossef mumbled in his semi-sleep and turned over, his tongue caught in the morning dryness of his mouth.

"Bells," he muttered. "So what."

"They're church bells, brother!" Yuri playfully tossed a pillow at him. "Get up! This is history." He ran over to the bed and pulled off Yossef's blanket. "Church bells haven't rung in this city since the early 1920s."

"Uh—uh, why not?" Yossef yawned loudly and stumbled to the window, shivering as the cold air hit his face.

"Because Lenin's League of Militant Atheists turned all of the churches into antireligious museums or warehouses and tied the bell clappers up. He vowed that no church bell would ever ring in a Communist Moscow.

"Just listen, Yossef. That's what we've been missing, for over seventy years."

It started in the old Saint Katrina's Church, long a warehouse for office supplies. Two young revolutionaries had climbed the church's tower looking for a suspected sniper. They noticed three old rusted bells with rags tied around their clappers and frayed pull-ropes coiled around one of the supporting beams. Hurriedly, they untied the rags and uncoiled the ropes. Cautiously, one of the youths gave one of the ropes a slight tug, afraid that it might break. It held, and the coat of rust that had held the bell immobile for seventy years broke free. The bell jarred slightly, and a pure and beautiful tone bounced out over the neighborhood.

In a frenzy of excitement, they started to pull on all three of the ropes. More rust broke free and the peal of the old bells filled the air.

The impact of the bells on the city's population was immediate. In less than an hour, the bell clappers of over a dozen old churches had been cut free, and the old bells were put to work—ringing out the news that a new era was about to be born.

By eight-thirty, when the bells woke up the twins, every Moscow church was having its bells rung constantly and loudly, from the deep mournful sounds of the Ivan the Dread bell to the high-pitched carillons of Saint Basil's.

After a cup of bitter Ethiopian coffee and two cigarettes, Yossef was now fully awake. A warm glow spread through his chest as he watched the rays of the early-morning sun glimmer off the two inches of newly fallen snow.

It was November 25, the day that the Solidarity Revolutionary Council had chosen to declare a new government from the top of the mausoleum in Solidarity Square.

Yossef cupped a match against the slight breeze blowing in through the open window and lit his third papirosa. He took a deep, meditative drag and drank in the ringing of the bells. Yes. The ringing of the old bells seemed to be a most appropriate way to usher in a new government.

The morning was indescribably beautiful from up here, Yossef thought. The newly fallen snow was a light, white shroud that rested gently on the buildings surrounding the Square. Yossef, freshly shaven, took his place next to Yuri behind the reviewing wall. They stood directly to Gregierenko's left. Raisa stood to his right.

There were the usual patriotic songs and the huge military bands blaring out traditional marches. After a few appropriate remarks by the Revolutionary Council, Vasily Gregierenko stepped up to the battery of microphones. Over a dozen television cameras were focused on the new Russian leader.

Yossef leaned back slightly and glanced to his right, behind Yuri and Gregierenko, and tried to catch Raisa's eye. She was staring straight ahead, studiously avoiding any eye contact with either of the twins. When would he be able to see her alone? he wondered. Since emerging from the Tomb, every minute of his time had been monopolized by either Solidarity or an adoring Russian public. And tomorrow at this time, he'd be standing at the same place, listening to Gregierenko's funeral oration for the Dubrovs after Solidarity had placed their remains in the Tomb in a mammoth ceremony.

Vasily Gregierenko was at his best as he addressed the huge throngs on this, the first independence day of a new, democratic but still socialist Russia. He ended his fiery speech with the words, "This government will no longer act for and in behalf of the KGB, but for and in behalf of the personal and political freedoms of the Russian people."

A tidal wave of cheers and applause echoed and re-echoed throughout the Square and beyond. Raisa impulsively threw her arms around Gregierenko's neck and kissed him on the cheek.

The first shot whipcracked across the Square and was clearly heard above the tumult of the crowds in the clear chilly air. It took two more shots in rapid succession before the people on the platform realized that they were being fired upon.

At the sound of the first report, Raisa's arms locked and tightened around the Solidarity leader's neck as she pulled him down on the frigid floor.

"Spasskaya Tower!" screamed a soldier on the steps of the mausoleum. "There's a sniper up in the clock in Spasskaya Tower!" he repeated, pointing to wisps of blue smoke drifting from the face of the clock.

A squad of soldiers rushed up the tower stairs to where

the Kremlin chimes were located. There was a brief battle with a KGB fanatic, a lone Kremlin Guard, who had hidden behind the clock mechanism and awaited his chance.

"We've got him! We've got him!" shouted a triumphant voice from the tower. The bullet-riddled sniper was hurled to the pavement.

Slowly, still fearful, the dignitaries got up. Yossef and Yuri lurched to their feet and helped others. Yossef stumbled over to Raisa and held out his hand.

"Come, Raisa. It's all over. They got the son of a bitch."

Raisa stared back at him, a strange and distant, almost confused, look in her eyes, which were becoming large and luminous. Yuri walked over, a puzzled look on his face when he saw her still lying on the platform.

"Raisa?" His voice was tremulous with concern.

When she tried to speak, bright red bubbles of blood started to froth at the corners of her lips.

"Good—good God! She's been shot!" wailed Gregierenko. An army doctor rushed to her side and cut away her jacket to probe her body. He pushed against her abdomen and she moaned loudly, forcing another rush of blood from her mouth and nostrils.

The doctor found the wound: a large, perfectly shaped hole under her right armpit. The path of the large-caliber bullet had angled downward until it had disintegrated in her lungs. There was no exit hole.

Two medics worked on Raisa as the doctor shuffled in defeat to the Solidarity leader, now crying unashamedly and pounding on the top of the reviewing wall.

"That bullet was meant for me!" he cried. "When she threw her arms around me and—and kissed me . . ." Gregierenko was sobbing uncontrollably ". . . She took the bullet that was meant for me and pulled me down out of the way." He clenched his fists so tightly that the blood was squeezed out of them. He took a deep breath and exhaled. He looked up at the doctor, filled with apprehension.

"Doctor—what—what are her chances?"

The doctor shook his head in a gesture of terrible finality.

"She's been shot with a 7.62 millimeter Dragonov sniper's rifle. It's a vicious weapon. I've seen wounds just like hers in Afghanistan."

The doctor rested his hand gently on Gregierenko's shoulder.

"The bullet literally explodes inside the victim like a hand grenade. Raisa Karezev is drowning in her own blood. She won't last more than a few minutes. The medics have given her shots to ease the pain."

Yossef and Yuri knew that Raisa was dying. They had both seen death wounds before. They knelt on each side of her, numb with shock and grief; her eyes darted from one to the other. Every time she tried to speak, more blood streamed from the corners of her mouth.

Slowly and painfully, she reached up with both of her hands and hooked them around the backs of their necks to pull their heads down to her breast.

Raisa shuddered slightly and stiffened, as if jolted by an electric shock. Then her hands fell from the brothers and thumped on the cold marble.

The five gun carriages towed by artillery tractors rumbled turtle-like over the cobblestones down the wide expanse of Gorky Street toward the Square. Solidarity banners covered the coffins, each secured on its carriage: the four sealed zinc caskets of the Dubrovs and the coffin of Raisa Karezev. Yuri, Yossef, Yabin, Gregierenko, Pavel Spinnenko, and Zhores Platonov marched in front of the slow-moving procession, black armbands on their sleeves. A military band was playing a mournful funeral dirge as they entered the Square.

The carriages bumped to a halt in front of the mausoleum. A new name had replaced Lenin's: SOLIDARITY. Everybody knew that it stood for the Dubrovs and now, too, for the first martyr of the new democratic government, murdered when it was only minutes old.

The pallbearers made five separate trips from the gun carriages, up the stairs, through the black marble doors, and into the crypt room. Raisa's coffin was flanked by those of the Dubrovs. Aleksei's rested on the same small catafalque that the counterfeit Lenin had lain on for so many years.

The twins, still numb from grief, took their positions at opposite ends of the line of caskets, their white-gloved hands resting reverently on their rifles as the lid of Raisa's coffin was lifted off.

Yossef wanted to wrench his head away, but he couldn't. His beautiful Raisa looked so peaceful lying there. A slight turn to the corner of her mouth made it appear that she was about to break out into one of her heart-stopping smiles.

The Guard mount lasted only two hours, long enough for the foreign and Russian dignitaries to file by and pay their last respects before the Tomb was sealed.

A light snow was now falling from the heavy, gray clouds as the Solidarity leaders took their positions on the platform. Yossef felt the numbness of the past twenty-four hours beginning to wear off. Since Raisa's death he had acted like an automaton, his emotions shoved temporarily into a deep freeze.

The great sea of humanity in front of him made him feel even more isolated and alone. This was not his country. These were not his people, in spite of their adoration for him. Now, more than anything, he longed to return to Uncle Viktor and Aunt Sophie and the warm, dry solitude of Shareem.

The voice of Vasily Gregierenko droned on, punctuated with sobs, as he spoke of Raisa to the crowds. Most of his words were lost to Yossef as he concentrated on his breathing in order to keep his emotions in check. He musn't break down. Not now. He glanced down into the crowd. There was Yabin standing by the lamppost where they'd burned Lenin. Yossef slipped away from the crowded platform and joined him. He looked up at the Tomb. His eyes connected with Yuri's and a look of understanding passed between them.

Yossef touched his hand to his forehead and Yuri returned the salute, his eyes glazed with tears.

As Yossef turned to leave, he saw a small, jagged fragment of bone—all that was left of Vladimir Lenin. He picked it up and clenched it tightly in his fist. At least he would leave Russia with some souvenir of Operation Samson.

They walked to the rear of the Kremlin, toward the Lyusinovskaya Street Bridge over the Moscow river. The snow was falling harder now, descending rapidly in heavy wet pellets.

The bridge was empty. It seemed as if the entire population of Moscow was in the Square. All was quiet except for the snapping of the crisp new national banners in the breeze.

Absently, Yossef toyed with the fragment of Lenin's skull, flipping it up and down with his thumb. With one, final flip, he tossed it into the river. It floated briefly, bubbled, and sank beneath the wind-whipped waves.

Yossef and Yabin could hear the music now from the Square above the gusting of the wind. The words carried over the water—a verse from the new national anthem.

> The heavy hanging chains will fall
> the walls will crumble at a word
> and Freedom greet you in the light
> and brothers give you back the sword.

Yossef thrust his hands into his greatcoat pockets and lowered his head to meet the buffeting wind. Yabin clapped a protective arm around his shoulder as they trudged across the bridge, toward the airport, and home.

SOLDIER
OF FORTUNE
MAGAZINE PRESENTS:

BESTSELLING BOOKS FROM TOR